MW00959091

Where Violets Bloom

A STALKER ROMANCE

DAISY JANE

Copyright © 2022 by Daisy Jane

All rights reserved.

No part of this book may be reproduced in any form or by any electronic or mechanical means, including information storage and retrieval systems, without written permission from the author, except for the use of brief quotations in a book review.

Cover design:

Photo from Stetsik

Editorial services:

Geeky Girl Author Services

❀ Created with Vellum

Foreward

ALL EXTREMES OF FEELING ARE ALLIED WITH
MADNESS.

-VIRGINIA WOOLF

Warning: this book contains themes possibly distressing
or upsetting to some. Before reading, please visit the
reading guide on my website for all content warnings.

Please be advised: additional content warnings will NOT
be listed at the beginning of each chapter. Read accord-
ingly to have the safest, most fulfilling reading
experience.

Prologue

ONE YEAR AGO

DONOVAN

"I'm already fucking obsessed."

The tips of my fingers work, peeling the edge of the label, pulling it back from the amber bottle. My eyes stay on the screen, where a tall man pulls a black ski mask over his face. On the sidewalk. In broad fucking daylight.

God, movies are so fucking stupid.

I lift the beer to my lips, pausing before I take the last swig. Briefly, I survey my surroundings. Clumps of people huddled together on quilts, some with extra blankets draped over their legs. Couples, girlfriends, there are even some people that brought kids with them. Young, old, married, or single–they all stare at the screen, wide-eyed and slack-jawed, their own stupid fears holding them captive to the film.

I finish the beer and tear off the rest of the label.

The man in this movie represents their greatest fear.

Being followed. Being watched. But they're as fucking stupid as the movie. Because it wouldn't happen that way. It doesn't happen that way. They're afraid of the wrong thing.

It's never the man in the black mask that you don't see coming. Hell, he's wearing a fucking *black mask in the middle of summer, standing on the sidewalk with only his eyes showing.* That's not a man headed to read to kids at a fucking library. You'd see him and know he is clearly up to no good.

They're scared of someone obvious, someone they can anticipate and identify as blatantly bad or evil. But, again, as we've already established, *they're fucking stupid.*

The real fears are undetectable.

True monsters blend seamlessly with the masses, folding themselves into culture and environment so well that when you bump into him at a movie at the park, you don't even remember the color of his eyes.

He's nobody.

Just a guy wearing a plain t-shirt, sipping on a beer, with evidence of sun on his skin and a forgettable smile fading from his lips.

He's the one these people are *actually* afraid of; only they don't know it. By the time they realize that the real dangers are in plain sight and that all the ideas of bad guys that movies filled their soft brains with were wrong... It's too late.

The man with the easy smile and the forgettable clothes is already just a pace behind you, his palm itching and his throat tight with strain. His urges are frothy and wild at the surface, no longer containable.

By the time you realize that he isn't wearing a ridiculous fucking ski mask and an outfit matching the color of the night sky, it's too late. He's in your apartment, his broad hand pressed to your face, the smell of his afternoon coffee burning up your nose.

They never see it coming. Because stupid fucking movies have them thinking they *will*.

I drop the torn label and empty bottle into the trash. Pulling my baseball cap down over my eyes–okay, that's the *only* thing movies sometimes get right - *the hat* – I make my way to the sidewalk leading out of the park.

On Saturdays, they play movies on the big screen. They start and end at eleven–all day.

I walk behind a couple. She lets her head rest against his arm as they walk, linked at the fingers, away from the park. Her hair is brown, and it grabs my attention because it's plain brown–all one color. No highlights, nothing exciting. Her clothes are plain, too. Blue jeans and a t-shirt, some sneakers. Nothing about her is special or memorable, and he's no different.

They're perfect.

My feet move more quickly as my chin dips to my chest in preparation. When I'm close enough behind them to know they use fabric softener or, at the very least, scented detergent, I close the remaining sliver of safety between us.

Theirs, not mine.

When I'm right at their heels–the toe of my sneakers brushing the heels of his unfortunate New Balance 608's–I do something I never do.

I *don't* attack them.

I *don't* reach out.

I *don't* take their elbows with a grip so tight that I start our exchange with '*don't scream.*'

My pace falters as a voice distracts me. A hushed "yes, sir" spoken in a tone so feminine and gentle that my skin grows bumpy in reaction.

"You think they care if you show up here? They don't. They don't give a shit about you so tell me why people who don't fucking care about you are more important than your father? Hmm?"

The pseudo-dominance of his tone makes my upper lip twitch. But assholes are a dime a dozen; that's not what stops me.

"It's for work, dad," says the perfect voice belonging to what has to be the perfect fucking girl. "I had to come for work. It was a mandatory potluck."

Her voice is light, the type of weightlessness that comes with perpetual defense. This girl with the work potluck is used to defending herself to her dad, accustomed to being talked to this way. The way a beaten dog cowers to the sight of a boot, the girl with the soft voice is used to explaining herself. So much so that her tone remains even keel, even as the man drags her past me, holding her by the elbow.

Her shoulder bumps mine, and my eyes are already on her when she tosses me an apologetic glance. "Sorry," she mouths quickly before being jerked forward by her father.

Then I do something else I've never done.

I follow them with no intention of robbing them, then disappearing into the shadows.

I follow them so I can follow *her*.

Because that one flash of her green eyes and that sweet tone that makes my skin hot and my dick hard... I'm already fucking obsessed.

Chapter One

VIOLET

I have to smile.

I've managed to lay low this week, but now that our monthly achievements assembly is here, I know I'm going to have to face him.

The principal.

Funny thing is, when I was in high school, being around the principal made me nervous because I didn't want to get in trouble. Not that I did anything I'd be in trouble for but still... His presence looming in the back of the classroom when he did pop-ins made it impossible for me to focus. Now when I see the principal–the *very same* man that roamed the halls when I was in school–I *still* get nervous.

The way my belly feels when I see him these days isn't quite the same, though. These days, a sea of *please don't look at me* and *where is the nearest exit* swirls around in my gut. I get nauseous at the sight of him, and when I'm at the whiteboard with my back to the students, and I hear the door open, the back of my neck grows clammy, in case it's him.

Mr. Wheeler stands outside the double doors, their periwinkle blue paint blending nicely with his school polo of the same color. He acknowledges students with a nod, slapping the occasional shoulder blade, and gives a dip of his head to the female teachers.

I keep my eyes on the quickly dwindling line of students as they feed through the open doors past him. I'm grateful that somewhere inside of him he realizes that students are off-limits. At least as far as I know.

I'd rather it be me than any of these poor young girls. They're here to wear high ponytails (that are only acceptable at this age, thank you very much), go to school dances where no one dances, and swap yearbooks. They don't need to add dodging the hands of a fifty-something pervert with a bad toupee and an even worse power trip to the list.

I'm not the most beautiful teacher on campus, not by a long shot. Kristi Reed, the PE teacher, and varsity girl's volleyball coach, has legs that start at her eyeballs, I swear. And Diana Cortez, the AP Spanish teacher–she's a dead ringer for a young Salma Hayek. Voluptuous with skin like burnt caramel, tan and smooth.

But he chose me, and I know why. Because it's the same reason my dad chooses me to hate.

Because I'm weak.

When I need backbone, I turn to putty. When it's time to use my voice, it goes missing. When I should push his hand off me and take a stance, I cower and pray for him to quit.

I guess I've always been weak. I've always been prey. Because I don't have a single memory of being strong, putting my hands on my hips and puffing my chest out in sheer defiance. Me? Violet Carlisle? Brave? Not even once.

It's one of those things where I don't know if *they* made me this way–my mom, dad, and sister, or if I really was just born weak. I guess it doesn't matter. Because that's what I am, no matter when I became it; I'm weak. But in my experience… The fight never seems worth the inevitable injury and pain.

"Miss Carlisle," Mr. Wheeler greets me from still ten feet back, the first of my students not even to the doors yet. He raises a hand to the completely cloud-covered sun, making a show of it's non-existent brightness before sliding his sunglasses up the bridge of his nose.

The only way that man would care about the sun being in his eyes would be if it were blocking him from perving on me. And as it's behind him, I know it isn't.

The sunglasses are part of his disguise. Part of the way he keeps his supreme creepiness annoyingly secret. A way to hide how his gaze crawls over my skin like fire ants, leaving him satisfied, and me feeling like I want to tear my skin off.

It's not like I want people to see how he is with me–attention is not my friend. But if anyone saw or noticed, he'd be forced to stop, at least for a while.

And I could use a break.

"Why aren't you in your school spirit shirt?" he asks, his tone all light and easy like his eyes aren't glued to my tits through those stupid drugstore sunglasses.

On Fridays we wear our spirit shirts. Willowdale Wildcats. With the appalling and utterly confusing school colors of periwinkle blue and eggplant purple. You'd think we'd be a dolphin or maybe even a walrus, to keep with alliteration.

But no. We are the blue and purple wildcats. Our school logo looks like something off a cereal box in the nineties.

I do what I can to avoid wearing that shirt, even on Fridays. This time, however, I don't have to lie.

"Washing machine was busy," I replied through a controlled, small smile. I *have* to smile. I have to be nice. He's my boss.

"Okay, go ahead," I say through cupped hands to the student first in line. They begin moving inside, which brings me closer to him with each inevitable step.

I can taste my breakfast in the back of my throat.

"Is that right?" he asks, his voice dipping to a private tone that makes the hairs on the back of my neck stand up. The insides of my cheeks tingle and saliva pools beneath my tongue. The sound of his voice nearly makes me sick at this point.

"Yes."

"Well, we'll have to get you a spare so that you don't stick out like a sore thumb." He smiles, and his years of coffee drinking are all I see.

Glancing behind me, I see that my class isn't the last one in, *thank god*. He tips his glasses up as I breach the threshold of the cafeteria (and gymnasium).

I was *almost* inside.

Inside is the equivalent of base when you're playing tag. *Safety.* He can't disrobe me with his eyes in front of the rest of the school. He can't bring his lips far too close to my ear. He can't rest his hand on my back or my knee or... my breast.

"Come by my office after the bell rings; I think I have an extra one in there that will fit you." The shades drop back down onto his nose as he smiles with satisfaction. My lips tingle as the contents of my stomach threaten to eject themselves.

Stepping past him, I focus on my exhale as my eyes struggle to adjust to the change in light intensity. It's much darker inside, so I have to blink a few times to get my bearings. But when I do, he's there. His beady, wide-set eyes rake over me in a way that makes me want to cry. The door seals closed behind us, and he walks behind me all the way to the stage.

The students stop in a clump while deciding who will sit next to who, and it gives Mr. Wheeler just enough time to let his palm graze my ass before taking the stage stairs.

Instead of lining the walls with the rest of the teachers, I take a seat on the ground, cross-legged, and try to think of all the ways to get to my car after the bell without him noticing.

Chapter Two

DONOVAN

He knows me better than anyone else, yet he's even in the dark about the worst part of me.

"You good, man?"

He drives his arms up, locking the weight-loaded bar out above him. I count the plates and look back down at him. His lips are curled around his teeth as he groans out an exhale, lowering the weight to his chest.

"Good," he grits out. "Warming up."

I nod and take a seat on the bench adjacent to him. Some old rap song vibrates through the walls, and the lights are still dim since it's only ten past four in the morning. I like my iron paradise in the morning, dark and chill. It makes lifting a religious experience. Something that requires focus, devotion, discipline. When it's still and calm in this place, and you can push past your limits, you can do anything. I know this to be true firsthand.

He reracks and sits up, the strain of the lift slowly draining from his face. "Chest day. You fuckin' ready?"

With a closed fist, I thump my chest twice. "Fuck yeah, I am."

He catches his breath, and I take a long pull from my gallon jug of water. No one else is here.

"Bran isn't here yet?" I ask of our friend, the gym's owner.

Malibu's eyebrows drift to his hairline as he grins. "He texted me to open up. His plate is full this morning."

Now it's my turn to lift a brow. "His plate, huh?"

Malibu shrugs, pushing a hand through his heavily sun-bleached hair. "Plate, mouth, same thing, right?"

"Eating is eating." We laugh then lift.

At the side of the bar, I adjust the weight plates until I'm ready for my first set. Malibu tugs at his white tank top, using the hem to wipe sweat from his eyebrows. I smirk at him. The man cannot keep his shirt on, and it *always* starts with a harmless sweat wipe.

"Shit, you already tryin' to strip for me?" I tease, taking the last drink of my pre-workout.

"You know me."

No matter what part of the body we are working out, Malibu has to look at himself in the mirror with no shirt. I don't know who loves Malibu more; women or *Malibu*.

It might be a tie.

After getting comfortable on the bench, I do the first set easy, twelve reps to my chest and up again. When I sit up, Malibu stands before me; his shirt hangs from his balled-up fist. Well, that didn't take long.

In between sets, I use the privacy to my advantage. "Think I can use your truck later?"

He takes a drink of his water, the mostly-full jug making his fatigued arm shake a little. "Do I want to know what for?"

I shrug. "You tell me."

He stares at me for a minute, and I stare back. His blue eyes are always grayer in the morning before the adrenaline of the pump has kicked in. His gaze narrows to a point, prodding me for information.

I fold my arms across my chest. "Have I ever brought any heat on you?"

His lips twitch, but his eyes remain skeptical. He trusts me; I know for an indisputable fact that he does. Still, I also know he'd like me to quit my extracurricular activities.

Whenever that lecturing gaze of his–complete with flat eyebrows and a tight jaw–hits me, I always have to hold back a little chuckle. Because even though Malibu is one of my best friends and he knows me better than anyone else, *he's* even in the dark about the worst part of me.

He doesn't think he is, though. He thinks my little hobby is my big, dirty, dark secret.

"It's not like that," I say, and it does make me happy that it's the truth. I always like telling him the truth. It doesn't always happen–for his own safety–but still, I make a valiant effort.

"No? So… if I give you my truck tonight, I'm not going to read in the paper tomorrow that some poor fucker in Lakeside took a hand to the throat while some tall, strong fuck yanked his wallet?"

I can't help the grin that spreads across my lips.

He steps closer to me, lowering his water jug to the floor. With his hands at his hips, the effort from his last set glistening over his bare chest, he tips his head forward a bit. "One of these times, someone's gonna catch you."

Lying back against the bench, I position my hands on the bar. "I'm not worried."

He snorts, a cross between annoyed and incredulous. "I would be."

I complete my set before sitting back up to respond to him. Panting and a bit out of breath, I say, "you're not the only good-looking fuck in the group, you know." I wiggle my eyebrows as he rolls his eyes. "And besides, I'm Officer Drake. The Willowdale Police force community favorite."

His playful eye roll turns into a pensive frown. "You aren't the community's favorite; *I am*. Even the Chief says so."

"Keep thinkin' that, Mally boy, keep thinkin' that."

We finish our workout, and in true dick-measuring form, we both make a point to PR our bench press.

Chapter Three

VIOLET

Taking my time is my fatal mistake.

I didn't sleep well last night so avoiding the snooze on my alarm this morning was really hard. But the sooner I get up and get ready, the sooner I am out of this house.

After a quick shower–quick because everyone in the house has already taken their leisurely morning showers leaving me with exactly *three and half minutes* of hot water–I get dressed in my favorite black pencil skirt and ivory-colored blouse. My marigold cardigan pairs well with this combo, so I toe into some black suede flats before going to my closet.

Being a teacher for the last five years has made my wardrobe pretty... boring. I don't buy clothes if I can't wear them to work, so most of what I own has a long hem and a high neck. We're talking *Under His Eye* status. But once meeting with Principal Wheeler as a grown woman–no longer just a school girl–I realized it was probably for the best that I dressed like an Amish nun with an aversion to sunlight.

The cardigan, though, isn't in my closet.

Believing I know the location of my favorite sweater–since sweaters do not grow legs and walk–I finish getting ready before gathering my nerves to go down the hall.

What twenty-five-year-old woman needs to gather her nerves before talking to their younger sister? She may be an adult at nineteen years old, but she has the emotional maturity of someone who'd apply to be on that MTV show, *Sweet Sixteen.*

Though we aren't the typical sisters–best friends who trade secrets and braid each other's hair–I wish we were closer to some *Full House* symbiosis than what we actually are: enemies.

I guess we aren't *mutual* enemies.

I have nothing against Rose.

Rose... the *golden* child. My parents' favorite.

Her extracurriculars were always where the extra money went. And while I was starting college and she was starting eighth grade, my parents decided her undeniable and god-given talent for the piano deserved the money they'd stashed away for my school.

Rather than four years at my university, they paid for one year of expensive private piano lessons, a fancy grand piano, gowns for recitals–all for the *prodigy* to get bored and decide she'd rather do something less time-consuming. I think her exact words were, *"it sucks, and I want to go out with my friends."*

The money they'd saved was gone, so I started to save; I worked to make sure I stayed out of debt while I got my degree. I did pretty well, too, considering I worked non-stop and had no "remember when" college memories to cherish happily. Instead, my memory of college was this: *If I wasn't in class, I was at work.* College bookstore during the days, tending bar and waitressing tables at night.

And the last five years that I'd been living with my parents while working as a third-grade teacher? I'd been saving - *again* - as hardcore as I did in college. On the outside looking in, I would appear to have the work ethic and drive of Elon Musk.

From the inside, however, there was a very different plot that no one else could see.

I needed to save money so I could *get out.*

I ate ramen noodles in my bedroom every night for years; I reused school supplies that students often teased me about, I didn't get Starbucks or buy new paperbacks.

Sacrifices to save were worth it, though, because I was saving to buy a home and get away from here.

And six months ago, I was ready.

I had the down payment. I qualified for the loan. I found the cookie-cutter house with the charming white cabinets and the built-in fireplace. Everything was perfect. I was ready to make my offer, so I did.

And it got accepted.

But just two days after that, I had an accident.

And the most perfect, beautiful, amazing nest egg that I'd saved? I needed it. For hospital bills and then physical ther-apy. I withdrew my offer only a week later.

Rose has never liked that I didn't move out.

Despite the fact that I don't harbor any anger towards Rose simply because they chose her instead of me to *actually* love, still, she hates me. Loathes me. And since I didn't give up the bigger of the bedrooms–the only non-master in the house to have its own en suite bathroom–she hates me even more now.

Truthfully, I'm always a little surprised they don't just move me out of that room when I'm at work one day. But that would require actual work–not just words–so dad hasn't done that.

With my palm to my belly, I inhale slowly, reminding myself that a college freshman is no one to be afraid of. At work, I'm in a sea of nine-year-olds who are just learning what attitude is and have no problem using it. Rose is nothing.

I knock, and my heart gallops as I wait.

"What?" she hisses in an irritated, too-loud tone.

"It's Violet." I swallow and edge closer to the closed door.

"It's Violet," she sing-songs in a way that would deflate *anyone* just a little. "No shit. What?"

"I was wondering if you had my marigold sweater?" I press my palm to the door and move my lips to the seam of the doorframe. "You know, my cardigan?"

A beat passes, my heart races, the door jerks open, and I stumble forward inside. Before I can step back, Rose's bony hands are on my shoulders, shoving me backward.

"Get the fuck off me, Violet!" she shouts unnecessarily because freaking *obviously* I didn't want to do that. *I didn't think your rude ass was going to open the door.*

When she shoves me back, I hit the doorframe. My skull burns when it connects, and instinctively I reach back to feel the fast-growing knot stashed under the mass of my blonde hair.

Her fair skin illuminates with her rage. "You fucking baby," she says, rolling her eyes. She turns back to the mirror and continues applying her wing-tip liner. I rub my head, and swallow my desire to stab her in the eye with that freaking pencil.

Even when she's a bitch, starting shit with Rose is pointless. There is no one here on my side, and like I said, I don't hate her. I know how the sausage was made.

My eyes go to her bed where my cardigan sleeves are laced through a leather jacket, the long tail of it dangling out. She was wearing it. Or planning on it. And with a cropped leather jacket? What vibe is she trying to give off? Slutty librarian? My lips twitch with a smirk I have to hold back.

"Oh, there it is," I say calmly, reaching for it slowly like I'm making a move for a live wire.

Taking my time is my fatal mistake.

She whips around after eyeing me in the reflection and swoops the cardigan up. "I'm wearing it today. And just say yellow. You sound like such a fucking pretentious loser saying marigold."

My ear drums are filled with the rapid throbs of my pulse.

"Can I have my sweater back, Rose?" I say, forcing some strength into my tone.

She smiles in a way that makes my stomach hurt and my skin grow clammy. "I'm wearing it today, Violet." Then she puts her hands on me, walks me to the hall and slams the door in my face. Then, through the door, she yells, "you wouldn't have to deal with me borrowing your shit if you'd just fucking MOVE OUT ALREADY!"

I don't say anything back because there's no point. I'm sure my dad believes me cowering to Rose is some pack-leader bullshit and it probably gives him some weird hard-on for her even more but whatever. I know you can't argue if the outcome is predetermined. And in this house, it always is.

If I can come back from having no college fund, I can come back from my beautiful nest egg being swallowed by an *accident.*

In the meantime, I'll rebuild. And take extra care to prevent future... "accidents."

Chapter Four

VIOLET

Bologna for life.

As soon as I back out of the driveway, I'm calling Sasha, my friend.

"What's up?" she answers, a flurry of noises in the background.

Sasha and I work at the same school, but she lives next door to it, making her commute all of one minute. She's probably still getting ready. She may just be getting out of the shower, in fact. "You're not coming in? Why are you calling so close to the first bell?"

I huff out a frustrated sigh, willing the aggravation of Rose and this morning to leave my body. "Rose wouldn't give me back my cardigan. Can you bring me one? The rest of mine were dirty; tomorrow is laundry day."

"Your mama should've named her ass Thorn, not Rose,"

my friend says, but I can hear the metal clink of hangers kissing. "Yeah, I got one. What colors are you wearing?"

"Black and white."

She snorts. "Why'd I even ask?" Then I hear her turn her water on as I flick my right blinker on. "What sweater did she take?"

"My favorite cardigan. The yellow one."

"Oh," Sasha says. Even though her style is far more exciting than mine with loud-printed tunics and fun leggings, wild earrings, and a streak of glitter across her eyelids–she respects that I like the classics. We're opposites, Sash and I. But we work.

"Wait, your *marigold* cardigan?" the word sizzles on her tongue.

I purse my lips in satisfaction that at least one person knows the sweater is marigold and not just yellow. "Yes, the marigold cardigan."

"Little witch," Sasha says.

"You mispronounced that I think." She snorts and I snicker, because that's what best friends are for.

"See you soon. Can you bring it to my classroom? Pretty please?"

She sighs as if I'm asking for a kidney. Though, I think she would give me a kidney. "Fine," she adds dramatically. Her classroom is just next door. "But you owe me."

"I owe you," I agree. "But I can't buy you anything or take you anywhere, and I'm not bi so I'm not really sure what I can offer you. A hug, maybe?" I tap my chin in thought as a low, thoughtful hum vibrates on my lips. "A bite of my fried bologna sandwich?"

She gags, and I laugh.

What started out of frugality ended up being my weird favorite–fried bologna, sweet pickles, and tabasco on wheat bread–so good. Kind of my thing now. But I only eat it at school for lunch because my dad hates the smell of bologna. *Bologna for life.*

"You know, what I want is for you to like, find a roommate or something. Get out of that back-handed manipulative toxic situation you're living in. There are freaking pitbull dogs who have it better than you, Vi."

My smile slides away. That always happens when I think about my actual life for more than a few seconds. "I don't want a roommate. I don't like the idea of someone I don't really know being in my space."

I pull into a parking spot and throw my tincan commuter car into park. "Great, Wheeler is here already."

"Because he knows you will be," she replies, and I hate that it's true. I hate that some stupid spider sense in Mr. Wheeler has locked onto my inability to stand up to people. Predators smell their prey; Mr. Wheeler knows how pathetic I am. He knows I won't ever stand up to him.

But I need this job. Job = money, money = my own place, my own place = new life.

"I know," I say, sighing again. My lungs feel tired today and it's not even eight in the morning. "I probably only need another year and then I can at least get an apartment. One more year of saving and I should have enough for everything I need."

She pauses, and I shift the phone to my other hand as I reach across the cab for my purse and bag. I pull them across the console, wrapped around my shoulder.

"You need a damn GoFundMe so you can get the hell out of there."

I laugh. "Yeah, yeah. I'm working on it," I say, ending the conversation around this topic. She isn't wrong–I need out.

If Sasha even knew how bad I actually needed out, she may actually start a crowd-sourcing account for me. She knows the most of it, the worst of it.

I hide it from everyone else, though, because I don't want this to be my life. I don't want *assaulted by her father* to be tethered to my story in any way.

I just need to get out.

"See you in a few. Don't forget the cardigan."

I hide in my classroom with the lights off and the door locked, trying to give off the illusion that no one is inside. In a student's desk tucked into a corner, I sit down and pull out my spiral notebook from my bag.

Flipping the pages until I meet my last stopping point, I click the top of my pen and begin to write. Thank god for this notebook and Sasha.

Chapter Five

DONOVAN

Resistance is futile.

Okay, so Malibu wasn't exactly wrong in suspecting I'd use his truck for less-than respectable activities. Except I wasn't doing what he thought I was doing.

Mally and I have been best friends since high school. We're partners when we're on shift together. I trust him. Therefore, he knows about my... hobbies.

Or should I say, *hobby?* He knows I *scare* people.

That's all I'd call it. I never hurt anyone–I've never even accidentally made someone trip. I wouldn't call it assault or robbery because when they pace around the corner once they know it's safe, they find their money on the ground. Their wallet. Their purse. Everything completely intact.

Because I didn't take anything, I *gave* them something. I mean, they're probably all too dumb to see it that way.

But I gave them a *chance.*

A chance to wake up and realize how good they have it. A chance to see that their perfect shining bubbles can be punctured at any fucking second. I'm giving them an opportunity to *wake up and fucking live.*

You're welcome.

Mally trusts and believes me when I tell him no one gets hurt. That's the only way he's even a small amount *"okay"* with my hobby.

He was around when my parents were killed. He knows–even when he doesn't want to admit it–that I am slightly, uh, how do I say this? Fucking peeved. Off my rocker. Perpetually irritated. Dark and damp. However you want to word it, I'm that, and he knows it.

He also knows how good I am at strangling that side of myself for the majority of my existence. At work, I'm a good guy. In the gym, I'm a helpful bro. With women, I'm an alpha catch. I'm a very good guy all the fucking time. How?

I have a little personal "banking" system.

Every day I'm a very good guy, I earn myself some time–thirty minutes, a stroll down the pier, an afternoon on a jogging trail–to be a *very* bad man. The man that seems to be at my core.

I used to fight my bad side. Tell myself it was late-form grief or even depression. Told myself I could medicate my way out of it. But with medication, I only had more clarity. So I stayed sober and forced myself to fight.

Clearly, I lost.

Well, I didn't really lose; I just stopped fighting; resistance is futile.

But I set parameters to my urges, limits to my needs.

No one gets hurt, no one recognizes me, I don't do it in my town.

21

The first time I did it, I told Mally. Spilled my fucking guts to him after in a rush of adrenaline. Told him every-thing. Over the phone, no less. One cop telling another one he assaulted a civilian just for fun, breathlessly laughing with the sick intention to do it again.

Not so bright on my part.

But it was freeing to have him know. To feel like at least one person existed that truly knew me–ugly, monstrous side and all–and loved me anyway.

Best friend or not, Malibu does not know about my other hobby.

Stalking Violet Carlisle for the last *year*.

I could tell him. I could explain how it happened, make him see how I got to be this way. He would understand. I know he would. Because I have a logical explanation, I do.

I know it sounds like I'm crazy–and I know crazy people start sentences that way. Of course, they do. But that's not me.

That night in the park, a year ago, where her dad was yanking her by the arm and talking to her like a fucking bag of trash... her eyes. Those emerald eyes.

Violet with the emerald eyes.

She's a rainbow of beauty, with full pink lips, sparkling green eyes, flowing goldenrod hair, thick black lashes, and fair skin sprinkled with freckles. Fuck. She's a fucking knockout. And that's just her face.

Don't even get me started on that fuckin' body.

I'm a gentleman, believe it or not. I know how to treat a woman. I am a good fucking listener and a really good communicator. That gets you very far with women, fellas. Trust me.

But her body is so fucking sinfully, deliciously cock-hardeningly hot that all I want to do is plunge my dick between those sweet, luscious lips and hold my thumb on her neck so I can feel my cock slip down her throat.

The most supple, full, palm-achingly perfect tits you've ever seen. Got hard that day in the park just seeing the profile of one. And like I said, I'm no virgin coming in my pants when I touch a thigh.

I've had experiences.

But nothing sets a live wire off in my chest and puts steel in my cock like Violet Carlisle. She's the first to get me this way. No one else ever has.

So... what do you do when you feel something between your ribs that makes your brain trip and your stomach twist? Do you just stop and let it get further and further away from you? Watch it disappear?

Fuck that.

No fucking way.

I make choices in my life now. I'm in control. And when I felt those green eyes fracture my heart... I had to know her.

So I followed her.

It really did start harmlessly.

I followed them to their house, googled their address, found their white pages listing, found her name on the *"also lives here"* on the listing, then googled her, found her Facebook and every other social media account linked to her, or anyone bearing her name.

Pretty easy, really. Not at all *it puts the lotion on it's skin.* Nope.

I found out she works as a teacher at the elementary school, and fuck if I didn't like that. It's cute as hell thinking she's good with kids. I've always wanted a girl who wanted kids of her own. My mom was a good mom.

I followed her to school the next weekday. I waited down the street until she left her classroom.

She seemed uncomfortable around a certain man with what appeared to be a *bad* fucking rug. I didn't like that. Right away, I got a bad feeling. The way she shirked toward the parking lot traffic away from him... if a woman would rather get hit by a car than stand next to you, *you are not a good guy.*

I ended up making sure she got home safely.

I did that a few times.

Then I found myself sliding open the back door after her whole house was empty for the day. Stumbling upon her room, I explored and found her underwear drawer. Smelling her bras; getting hard with my nose pressed inside the cup– I know, it's pathetic. And I sometimes can't even believe I'm this guy. But after I saw her, I just wanted her so much.

I needed more. So I followed her more. And yet, the more I saw her, the more I needed to see her.

I kept telling myself I'd stop following her and find a way to introduce myself. But I just... I never could.

So I kept following her, and that brings us to me borrowing Malibu's truck last week.

I wasn't shaking anyone up with a new getaway vehicle. I was just getting a ladder from the hardware store. A ladder wouldn't fit in my Tesla SUV.

I told Malibu I'd be trimming trees–I didn't want him worrying when I had his pickup. Also, it'd make him less likely to say yes if he had a whiff of real suspicion, so that morning at the gym, I played it off. Made it seem like I was definitely up to no good; that way he'd think I wasn't. I knew how his mind worked. He wouldn't believe anything so obvious.

I got the ladder. I trimmed exactly two trees so that if he came by my house with Bran, the story would check out.

I really just didn't want him to worry. I wanted him to know that I was doing what I said I'd do. Like clockwork, Bran and Mally rolled through on their way to Bran's gym, Paradise. They saw the trees and me loading them into Mally's truck.

It played out perfectly.

Because today I am borrowing his truck again, to trim more trees. And this time, I know Mally, he won't be driving by.

And what am I actually doing today?

This morning, I put on my electrical company uniform, which I stole off a uniform truck a couple months ago. Tugged a hat down over my eyes, slapped an electrical company magnet on the side of Malibu's truck, slipped a fake plate over his, and took my newly purchased ladder to Violet Carlisle's house.

Watching her for a year has been… *life changing.*

But I've developed a tolerance. My hunger is rampant, knows no bounds. I need more of her. I need a taste, I need something. *Anyfuckingthing.*

And that's how I got to be in Violet's bedroom, having just installed a fish-eye lens camera through the stucco and drywall. After letting myself into her bedroom through the window to clean and cover up the camera with spray-painted netting, I decided to spend an extra minute in her room, just breathing the air that she fucking breathes.

It's lighter. It fucking smells better. God, it's so good here. In her space. My cock gets hard just knowing she's been here.

There's that notebook she always carries. The one that

gets pressed to her tits when she's walking to her classroom, the one that she scribbles in over her steering wheel before going inside her house at night. The one she reads from at the park sometimes.

I snatch it up, my head whirring with bad feelings, but I stuff it inside my uniform before I can think twice.

That brings us to now. That one minute I was going to take inside her room has now turned into a *greedy five*. In addition to snatching her notebook, I also used her chapstick, my cock leaking as the tube of wax that touched her lips passed over mine.

Fuck.

I'm so *all in* on this fucking girl.

I need to quit this shit and just meet her already.

As that thought–the one I have a million times a day minimum but seem to always manage to ignore–flits through, there's a noise, and *holy shit*.

Fuck. *No way.*

I thought that noise was the fucking washing machine or, I don't know, the fucking bathroom next door. It's well after nine in the morning; there's no way Violet would be home.

She has school.

But the squeal of water being shut off is familiar, as are the remaining drops of stubborn water that trickle from the head long after the valve is off. The *tink, tink, tink*, the gentle thud, thud, and then the drain does a throaty little growl, absorbing the last of it.

It's the shower.

And Violet or not, someone is in there. Rose, her younger sister? Whatever other flower or garden item is stashed in there, I don't fucking know... But I don't have time to get out the window safely, so instead, I take a sniper-like breath and slide into the farthest side of her closet.

I have never seen her open this side of the closet, despite the fact I have watched her in her bedroom many times. She usually only opens the other side.

My life's kind of banking on that right now.

A soft humming permeates the slatted closet doors, and my balls tingle as my breath catches. I haven't seen her yet so I don't know for sure but it doesn't matter–I know, *it's fucking Violet.*

Chapter Six

DONOVAN

The Heavens part.

I took her fucking notebook. Fuck. *Fucking fuck.*

I know why my impulse took over. I needed more of her. She carries that thing everywhere, and for a fucking year I've ached to know what it holds. Her secrets? Does my girl have fears? Dreams? They're in there, I know it.

And I *need* to fucking know.

I swear this is the last thing. I'll read her notebook, and then I'll stop stalking her. I'll go full "normal person" and just... *meet her.* Okay, maybe not *full* "normal person." Maybe I'll devise a situation where we meet under the *perfect* circumstances, crafted just right. I could use all the favor when it comes to her.

I know it sounds crazy but I swear, one day she will be mine. And I'll tell her all of this because that's how we'll be together as a couple. Transparent. Clear. Our truest selves.

I hope she forgives me. That is if we make it there.

I pat the notebook under my shirt and take another steadying breath just as the bathroom door clicks open. Steam rushes out in a rolling white cloud that drifts dreamily through the slats in the closet door. Temporarily, my slits of clarity are taken, and my heart really goes fucking nuts. Like, Uma Thurman taking the adrenaline to the neck in *Pulp Fiction* type of nuts.

Is today the random time she chooses to open this side of the closet? What the fuck will I do then?

I'll grab her. I have to.

If she opens the closet door and sees me–complete in my fucking phony electrical company uniform–I'll have no choice. I'll have to fucking snatch her before she screams or tries to run. Then I'll explain to her once I get her somewhere... safe.

The steam melts away, and my heart immediately freezes when my vision connects with her.

A faded old beach towel is pooled at her feet.

My eyes travel up the lines of her body. I've never seen her in so much as a bathing suit in the last year I've been... ahem, *watching* her.

Those legs of hers that look slender in her black slacks, skinny jeans, and pencil skirts–even better without any of that shit. Smooth and bare; there's evidence that she isn't lazy in the way her calves and thighs bear tight muscle beneath her sleek porcelain skin.

Before I can silently pray to any and all possible Gods in existence that my sweet Violet lotions before she dresses, she props a delicate foot on the edge of her bed. The tell-tale click of a lotion bottle opening makes my cock twitch, and I silently close the gap between the tip of my nose and the slats, inching as close to her as possible.

My eyelashes graze the wood of the door as I peel my eyes wide, screaming at them not to blink. White cream leaves her palms as she drags her hands up one leg. I clamp my teeth over my bottom lip to prevent the fucking groan clogging my throat from escaping.

Rubbing and smoothing, my eyes alternate between watching the cream melting into her velvety skin, and watching her perfect tits sway with the motion.

Her nipples.

God they're even more perfect than anything I could have imagined. Hard, tiny little pink pert toys–utopia for my mouth. On cue, saliva pools under my tongue. Those little nubs blend effortlessly into a circle of peanut butter-colored areolas.

I fucking love peanut butter.

I've jerked off to these tits–smothered by blouses and tank tops–many fucking times. But seeing them stark naked, just a few feet from my hungry mouth–my cock is at full attention.

If she walked out of this room right now, I'd still need a few *cold* minutes in the closet before I could walk out.

Unless...

She makes her way across the room, raising an arm over her head to free the clip from her honeyed hair. She tugs it, wiggling her neck a little, waves of golden hair cascading down her back, blocking her bare shoulder blades from me. My eyes make it to the ends of her perfect hair and then down to find the split of her ass. Her cute little globes jiggle as she digs through a dresser drawer on the opposite side of her bedroom.

She huffs out a frustrated sigh before yanking open another dresser drawer. She tosses all her blonde hair to one side, exposing the back of her neck to me. *I could have my lips on the slope of that neck right now.* I'm just a few paces away.

But *no.*

That's not how this goes.

I'm strong enough to know this is the *wrong thing to do right now.* I'm pathetic enough to use the noisiness of Violet digging through her clothes to unzip my blue chinos and fish my hand through my fly until my hot, hard cock is in my palm.

She steps into a pair of purple panties one foot at a time. I wrap my palm around my cock and pump myself, precome rolling from my cockhead down my curled knuckles.

Her lithe fingers hook the fabric, and... *she bends at the waist.*

The Heavens part, and sunlight and grace rain down on me.

She stays bent over. Her ass splits, just slightly. I don't see what I *really* want to see, but the dark cleft between her cheeks grows, giving me a quick and subtle peek *deeper* inside her.

I stroke myself again, the taste of copper flooding my mouth. I'm *really* fucking biting my lip. Her spine straightens as she tugs the fabric up her hips. Elbows out, I watch her shimmy into a nude-colored bra and clasp it. *I would clasp that for you baby.*

She spins, and it's then I notice the clothes on the bed. How did I not see that before? *Maybe because I rushed in here like a fucking assjacket with a less-than-stellar plan in place.*

I'm getting sloppy. My growing obsession with this wide-eyed gorgeous woman is making me irresponsible. I need more of her so I can calm the fuck down and be smarter.

The bra is un-padded and... *lace*. Those delicious nipples poke through the delicate filigree of the fabric, so of course I pump myself again... painstakingly slow and *perfectly tight*.

Tight... how I know my girl is between those perfect godly good thighs.

Before she picks up the clothes she's laid out for herself, she returns to her dresser to dig around some more, pulling out some lifeless undergarments the color of sand.

What are those? She holds one next to the other before rummaging around, her small fist coming up with another brown sock thing inside of it.

Scrunching the item between her two hands, she leans forward, lifting one foot towards her arms. *Nylons.* She's got nylons.

My cock pulses in my palm, so I stroke it again because *fuuuck*.

It's when she snaps the lacy band at the top that I realize they're *thigh-highs*.

Sliding my fist to the base of my dick, I grip myself like I'm fucking Stallone in *Cliffhanger*. My jaw flexes so hard my teeth are probably grinding to powder, and my spine is snapped so straight and tight that I worry with the lack of oxygen in this fucking closet, I *may* pass out.

Snap.

The other thigh-high is in place.

I lick my lips, feeling the marks from my teeth. They're deep and sore. It's when she slides that fitted black skirt over those grabbable hips that I can't hold back anymore. Two quick and silent strokes, and I'm biting into my bottom lip as my come rockets out of me.

I turn my hips in time for it to miss the door. The first rope of Violet-inspired goodness spurts onto the carpeted floor below. Thick and abundant loads make for loud coming. Thank god she's zipping her skirt, then wrestling with the direction and fit of her blouse–her dressing noises serve as a buffer to my come attacking and drenching her carpet.

After her blouse is tucked into her skirt–god, she looks like some sexy ass news anchor I want to fuck the forecast out of–she toes into some black flats tucked under her bed. Then she stops, hands on hips, white painted fingernails drumming against the black fabric of her skirt.

Raising a hand to her face, she taps her chin, humming with thought. My lips curl into a satisfied smile, my orgasm drying on my hand–still holding my dick.

Still hard, too, by the way.

Like a ton of fucking bad news-bearing bricks, it hits me why she's paused.

She's looking for her notebook.

My other hand is still pressed to the book, under my uniform. I fan my fingers over the fabric, the spiral of the spine dragging against the tips as I do. *Don't worry baby; it's safe*, I'm shouting to her in my fucking sick head. Fucking sick because this plan wasn't thought through very well.

Yes, I want to get to know her. Yes, this will help.

But I didn't think of how it would make her feel. See? This is the shit I gotta fucking get better at. Think about shit from her perspective.

My heart races again, and I feel like I just shotgunned a warm beer after a day of golf. Shitty.

After a minute-long moment passes, she grabs her bag and huffs out. Even her huff is cute, though.

I smile from my private, sticky spot in her closet as I watch her leave the bedroom.

Chapter Seven

VIOLET

Outside of that house, everything is so beautiful.

Rose's commitment to being a witch is impressive.

The *yellow* cardigan didn't even look good with her baby spice mini skirt and stupid pleather jacket, and yet, the outfit is now burned into my corneas. Why? Because she's worn that outfit–or a variant of that–all freaking week.

Whatever.

She doesn't hate me, she's just a stupid yes-man to my father. She's just like a pet, in a way. She snarls and he pats her head in reward. It's sick.

I have to get out of here.

The perfect, amazing, sculpted-with-care nest egg edges its way into my consciousness this morning as I get dressed for school. I'm running late because Rose borrowed my car this morning without telling me. When I went downstairs to grab my pre-shower coffee, I noticed it was gone.

"She'll be back soon; cool your fuckin' jets; it's not like you're the goddamn principal," dad said when *I* had the audacity to ask where *my* vehicle was at. I called Sasha and told her I'd be an hour late.

"Thorn?" she asked, knowing that if it were just me, I'd never be late.

But I had to call Mr. Wheeler and tell him that I needed someone to run my class for an hour. I told him I'd Uber to work if it was going to be any longer than that. He, of course, offered to give me a ride. I declined, and then he told me that he needed to see me after school today to talk about this tardy.

At that exact moment, Rose came back with... a Starbucks latte and a breakfast sandwich in her hand. Yeah... a really important errand that made me late for my *career*. And now I have to "talk" to Wheeler over it.

I wish I had that nest egg. Freedom was so close. I could taste it. Sometimes I dream about that little house. Sometimes after school, I drive by that little house and my eyes get watery.

I don't let myself linger. The accident happened, I paid my medical bills, the money is gone. That's that.

This morning sucks already.

First, Rose took my car. Second, the anticipation of talking to Mr. Wheeler. And now? The cherry on top of the shit cake I'm shoveling in is *I can't find my notebook*.

I know twenty-five is too old for a blankie or a stuffed animal. Obviously, but I'd be completely lying if I said my notebook didn't comfort me the way a blankie comforts a toddler.

My thoughts are in there.

My struggles.

My frustrations... the ones I keep inside because what good does complaining do if you can't do anything about it yet?

It's all in there.

And I can't freaking find it. I could've sworn I put it on my desk last night before falling asleep but because I was flustered this morning, I didn't stuff it in my school bag right away. And now that I'm beyond late, I don't have time to hunt for it.

With my hands on my hips, I survey the room one more time before abandoning the cause (temporarily) and heading down to grab my lunch from the fridge.

Dad's at the table, newspaper spread across the surface, his suit jacket draped across the chair next to him. He doesn't leave until half past nine, which means we'll be leaving at the same time today.

Goody.

He cocks a grayish bushy eyebrow at me, his eyes narrowing to a point, prodding me as I enter. "You're late."

Um, yeah, no duh, asshole. "I'm leaving now," I say, deciding always on the most careful, calm, least-aggressive words. I mean, I could easily say *'yeah, because Rose took my car without my permission to go sit in the drive-thru line at Starbucks for thirty-five minutes'* but it's pointless. I know it makes me weak to never stand up to him, but then again, the last time I stood up to him, it cost me nearly fifty-grand.

My mom drifts in, her blonde hair in a braid down her back, just the way dad likes it. Sometimes I wrack my brain to remember a time when my mom was stronger. To a time where she had a dissenting opinion, or was *allowed* to have an opinion at all. The sad thing is... I have no memory of that.

Sometimes I convince myself that I just can't remember.

Because me having a bad memory is far easier to stomach than having a weak woman for a mother.

The apple doesn't fall far from the tree, huh?

"Good morning, sweetheart," she says to me as she tops off my dad's travel mug.

"Morning," I smile at her, because hating her isn't easy. Sometimes I do. Because she turns a blind eye to a lot of what happens inside this house, but I know that if a mother lets her child suffer, the pain she's in must be far greater. *It must be.* Because mothers don't let their children get hurt. Over and over.

I try to build her up, too.

"I was thinking of sending a letter of interest to the school board," I say, grabbing my silverware from the drawer and tucking it into my nylon lunch bag. "Expressing interest that I'd like to be considered as a future member."

Mom strokes her bony hand down my back as she watches me fill my bag.

"You'd be a won–"

My dad's bitter laugh snaps our conversation right in half. *Did I ask your opinion, asshole?* I think to myself as he rises from the table, pushing away from it the way a king shoos away a peasant. Stomach acid rises in my throat as he stands over me.

"You think you have something to contribute to a school board?" he snorts, and his belly jiggles a little. If Santa were real, his belly like a bowl full of jelly would completely trigger me into a panic attack because I've seen dad's beer belly jiggle enough for a lifetime. "Those are *grown-ups* with *smart ideas.*" He taps the side of his head and bends before me, getting in my face.

I should get an award for not poking his beady eyes out. Seriously.

"I've been teaching in the district for over five years," I defend, though I don't know why. Defending yourself against a narcissistic clown really is pointless.

"Teaching, babysitting, same thing, right?" his lips curl into a satisfied smile, and my mom begins her mindless humming. I think she thinks if I hear her humming, then I'll think she can't hear him.

"Third grade isn't like kindergarten. Third graders already know how to read and do multiplication," I continue to defend, stupidly.

He slings his coat over his arm and smooths a fat hand over his remaining strands of hair—which are pathetically combed over his shiny bald head. "Any career where you can be almost two hours late and things keep going without you isn't a career. It's a job. You're replaceable. And they don't appoint replaceable people to board member positions."

My mom continues humming as she disappears into the garage, loading my dad's car for him. She always does that. She puts his tumbler in the cupholder, his lunch in the seat, his briefcase on the floorboard, lying sideways so his papers stay organized. I have a feeling she learned that the hard way.

As if the asshole-signal has been flashed into the sky, Rose appears in the kitchen, clutching her precious coffee. Her coffee that will cost me a hand up my thigh later. My stomach burns with unease.

"You can't be a school board member," she snorts, rising to her toes to give my dad a goodbye kiss. Seriously, a goodbye kiss.

"I disagree," I reply stupidly.

I know it's stupid, for a myriad of reasons. The first one

being it supremely, utterly, completely makes no difference what either of them think. But I'm late, and I'm missing my notebook, and ugh. My frustration is driving this conversation... I know better. I need to get out of here.

With my lunch under my arm and my keys in my hand, I move past Rose and my dad, cracking the garage door to say goodbye to my mother. Before it closes, she says, "I think you'd be great." She turns back to the car and continues smoothing the lint roller over dad's seat.

"Have a good day, everyone," I say over my shoulder. Met with radio silence, as usual, I leave the house and breathe for the first time all morning.

Before backing out, I search my entire car but... no notebook. Did Rose take it? As much of a little witch she is, I don't think she cares enough about me to read my thoughts. Plus she's taking classes at the junior college right now, and I don't think she has time in her busy schedule of "studying" to read my notebook. Oh, and studying *most definitely* means doing keg stands for frat boys at a party in an orchard.

No sooner is my house in the rearview mirror does my stomach normalize. I smile to myself as I think about how nice it will feel to be on my own.

Outside of that house, everything is so beautiful.

The vast, cloudless blue sky. The soft crushing of leaves hitting leaves as a breeze moves through the trees. A bright orange and slightly disgruntled looking tabby cat licking his foot on the sidewalk. The zingy bright yellow of the electrical company logo on the truck that passes me.

I can't wait to feel this way all the time. I just need to rebuild that nest egg.

Sasha messages me as I'm pulling into the parking lot,

both anxious and indifferent to get inside as quickly as possible.

Sasha: *Hell-on-wheelers has been teaching your class for the last hour and a half*

Me: *Seriously? Miss Egars couldn't stand in?*

The librarian, Miss Egars, loves standing in for teachers when they're late or have meetings. It's my personal belief she wanted to be a teacher, but has slight public speaking anxiety. She loves reading to the class, but when it comes time to discipline students or chat with parents, she's a pink-cheeked clam.

Sasha: *Prepare yourself. He's been smiling all morning.*

For the umpteenth time today, my stomach rolls in on itself. He's happy I'm late because he thinks it will justify his itchy, meandering hands.

With my bag and purse on my shoulder and my lunch tucked under my arm, I push my hair behind my back, hold my chin high and head up the steps.

The familiar smell of pencil shavings and day-old meatloaf flood my nose as I make my way down the long, tiled hallway. I stop at Sasha's door, pressing my face up to the rectangular strip of window.

I give a small smile and then a wave, which she returns before mouthing 'good luck.'

Then, with an inhale in my gut and resolve in my shoulders, I enter my classroom.

Mr. Wheeler has a social studies video about President's Day running on the TV, and the students are restless in their chairs. I want to roll my eyes–the principal couldn't even be bothered to teach for an hour–but instead, I smile.

"Thank you; I can relieve you now," I whisper to him as I approach my desk.

He's sitting in my chair, knees spread wide, leaning back in a way that's almost inappropriate. His fingers are laced together, resting on his lower belly, like he's trying to draw my eyes to his crotch or something.

Yuck. Wait, is there a word greater than yuck? Because if so, insert that word here.

"Come by my office with your lunch today, Miss Carlisle. We can go over our attendance policy again." He doesn't attempt to vacate my chair, and his eyes don't attempt to hide the fact they're crawling over my tits.

A sea of murmured *"she's here"* and *"Miss C is back"* washes over me, and it's the first really good feeling I've had all morning. The kids want me. The kids love me.

"Okay," I respond, still holding a forced smile. "May I?" I ask, motioning down to the chair without my eyes leaving his. I refuse to look at the way he's sitting; I refuse to buy into this.

"Certainly," he draws out, finally standing. I fiddle with the calendar on the wall and swap the sun covered by a cloud with just a sun for today's weather chart. When I'm done, my seat is open, and like a creepy Vanna White, he holds an arm out towards my chair.

Another eyeroll is stifled, and again I deserve awards for tolerating this shit.

Smiling broadly, I thank him before sliding into my seat and waking up my computer. After a few minutes of ignoring him by clicking the attendance and opening my email, he finally goes.

I send Sasha a text.

Violet: *Wheeler is making me eat lunch in his office. Run interference? Pretty please?*

I add several praying hand emoji's.

Sasha: *I'll be there.*

By the time I pull into the driveway of my parent's house at four on the nose, I'm exhausted. After my lunch meeting with Mr. Wheeler—which only lasted four minutes due to Sasha needing me with a "student issue", my focus shifted to my missing notebook.

I tore the house apart from four to five looking for it. As soon as dad got home from work, I locked myself in my room, not wanting him to enjoy the fact that I'm missing something so important to me.

What a great guy, right? Taking pleasure in his daughter missing something she loves.

Depressed that today felt pretty normal, I get in bed at seven o'clock and give my worries over to my down pillow and sleep.

Chapter Eight

DONOVAN

A girl I like lives here.

The camera footage was supposed to make me feel *better*—not *way* fucking worse. Because having a fish-eye lens view of Violet's bedroom for the last week has made me realize one thing: my girl needs me more than I realized.

Watching her all this time I've grown to *know* her.

She still lives at home with her parents, and I don't know what that's about. Most women can't live under the same roof as their mother for that long—too much estrogen and shit.

Six months back, on one of the *only* days I didn't idle near the school playground in my cruiser after the bell, she got hurt.

I don't know what happened and it fucking kills me that I don't know. All I know is that when I was covering for Mally in court, something happened to my girl.

The next morning, after telling Mally he owed me, I went back to my comfortable spot four houses down. But I sat there. And kept sitting there. Her car never left her rectangle of pavement in the driveway.

Or the morning after that.

Or the one following that.

I lost my fucking mind those days where I didn't see her.

Held some blonde woman by her scalp against the bricks in the alley behind the sports bar. She made the most awful noise when I yanked her head back. I realized she wasn't even scared for her life–she was worried I'd pull out her weave.

I ripped up some of her bills before dropping them on the ground around the corner. However, she earned it; her priorities told me she didn't fucking deserve it.

I pressed two knuckles in the back of a man in the grocery store parking lot. He dropped his half-gallon of milk when my words crept over his shoulder, into his ear. "Freeze, don't turn around, don't say anything unless you never want to talk again."

The milk was sticky. I remember my shoes squelched the tile floor in the police department for like, three days before it wore off.

I left his money in the spilled milk.

So, yeah, those days where she was inside that house and I didn't know what the hell was going on... they were dark.

I parked on her street for as long as I could in the morning and came back in the afternoon and evening if I didn't have work. If I was working, I didn't bother fabricating some bullshit story about a kid I wanted to keep an eye on or whateverthefuck else. I told Malibu a version of the truth.

A girl I like lives here.

For two days, I watched her place, grouchy, pissed, ready to lose it.

Her father kept coming and going as usual, and I even saw her mom check the mail and prune some flowers, too. Her younger sister went to class like usual. If Violet was supremely ill, they wouldn't just go on as usual. Nothing made sense. She was home but not teaching, not leaving, not *surfacing*.

Just as I was prepared to take matters into my own hands, *I saw her.*

I was just turning onto her street, prepared to take up my usual parking spot exactly four houses down, my binoculars in my lap. Ready to hurry up and wait. I usually wait on her street for an hour in the mornings that I don't have to work. I see her for less than a minute after all that waiting, but it's the best forty seconds of each day... until I see her again after school.

She slipped out of the house with dark bags under her muted green eyes, one of her arms *casted and held by a sling.*

I think I blacked out for a second when I saw her, honestly.

How the fuck did she break her arm? Was she in an accident? If she was, why wasn't her car wrecked? If she was attacked, why did her family keep going to work and school as if nothing traumatic had just happened? I tail her so often that if *any of that* happened, the likelihood that it would've happened when I wasn't around was slim to none.

The downtrodden expression on her usually soft and impassive face put a boiling in my bones.

Someone did that to her. Who and where I don't know.

I watched her more after that. The stalking became

completely and utterly justifiable in my mind, while I also kept track of the fact that I was indeed pacifying myself by justifying myself.

Yeah, *I'm fucked in the head.*

Even with watching her get her hair cut at the salon, sitting at a table near hers when she brunched with Sasha, waiting outside the grocery store, sneaking into the women's fitting rooms, and taking the stall next to hers so I could see her toes up close. Of all the places I followed her, all the places I'd wedged myself just to see her–I never knew her as well as I have gotten to know her the last week, after installing the camera.

For a few hours from after school until her bedtime, I watch her.

She gets home from school around 4:06 every afternoon, or at least, the ones I get to watch her. When she locks her car, she clicks the lock button once from the driveway and another time after she's locked the deadbolt on the front door. Double-checking. I like that.

What she does until her dad gets home around 5:30, I don't know. The blinds to her house are always shut, and the light in her bedroom doesn't come on until... around 5:30.

And then she doesn't leave her room again until the morning.

She carries a tray up with her everyday, wears her purse and bookbag on her back, and knees the slanted door handle open. She eats her dinner in her room.

Maybe her family doesn't eat family dinners? I guess that's pretty normal. Mally was raised by a single mom who worked all the time and never had a family dinner once in his life. Or maybe their family isn't even close? Bran's a prime example of a weird family. They all love each other or whatever but no one talks and everyone is kind of just... cohabitating emotionlessly. That could be the Carlisles.

After she eats, she uses her laptop. She puts it right on her lap, her legs outstretched and crossed at the ankle. Her back rests against her wall. That's always how she does it.

She has a TV hung on her wall. It's small but nice. It's always off. Sometimes she follows a yoga class on a YouTube channel from her laptop. Other times she reads, and often she talks on the phone. If she had her notebook, she'd be writing in it in the evenings. But once that door closes at 5:31, it doesn't open again until the morning.

She closes her blinds a bit after seven.

She hasn't touched herself yet. *I know.* After her broken arm six months ago, I shouldn't be thinking of any of that shit. All I *should* be worried about is finding out who did that to her.

Or what happened.

And *I am.* I mean, I'm fucking *going to.*

But in the meantime, being a fly on the bedroom wall of an utter fucking queen will *do things* to your cock *and* the dirty mind it's connected to.

I've been beating off so fucking much.

Watching her get out of the shower every day has been murder on my dick.

Instead of wishing that one of these days, she'll spread her legs and part her lips and touch her creamy little pussy–and don't get me fucking wrong, I do wish for that–the thing I wish for the most is to be there with her.

Arrange her bath towel between my outstretched arms and wrap her in it when she gets out of the shower. Smooth the terry–I'd get her better towels–down her creamy skin until she was completely dry and warm.

I'd brush her hair then kiss her lips before smoothing lotion up and down her legs. I leak a little at the notion of it. My fingers stir at the idea, too. God, how soft must her skin feel?

This morning, I'm lying in bed, hugging the surveillance that fills my laptop screen. In a few minutes, her alarm will go off, and then I'll get more of her.

I close my eyes and stretch my legs through the cool pockets of undiscovered sheets. I imagine my leg tangling with one of her soft, slender ones. Her feet are cold so I loop my thick arm under her waist and tug her towards me.

I press my lips to her hairline, sucking in a morning lungful of her hibiscus shampoo. It makes me hard. All of her smells make me hard.

She snuggles against my bare chest, running her fingertips through the thatch of dark hair on my chest. She traces one of my tattoos. Because she loves my tattoos.

"Good morning, baby," I whisper down to her, my fingers laced together at the small of her back. Her nipples harden against me as she wiggles a stretch free from her legs.

"Good morning," she groans, her sexy little voice thick with sleep. Because she sleeps well now. No more of that tossing and turning bullshit she did at her parents' house. I fuck her into the mattress every night, and when we're done, she's done. Just the way she likes it.

I open my eyes when I hear her covers stirring through the laptop speaker. Like a complete psycho, I smooth my fingers down the screen, over the curve of her exposed hip. The blankets are lowered, her tank top has risen, and her bare belly is on display. Part of her thigh peeks out, too. Somehow, this gets me fucking hotter than when she's getting out of the shower.

It's intimate, waking up with someone. Seeing them in their purest form, first thing in the morning.

Like she's with me, I close my eyes again and listen to her early morning coos and whimpers of exhaustion. She tossed and turned a lot last night. I push that from my head, an issue to be solved once I have a plan.

Back to her in my arms. She fishes an arm between us, and I know what she's doing. Her palm slides beneath my heavy sac then her fingers curl into me, the tips grazing my taint.

She doesn't ask me to empty them inside of her with words because the affectionate touch is her request. Rolling her onto her back, I hover over her as she slides her hands up the columns of my arms. Her knees fall apart, and before we've even been awake more than a minute, I'm thrusting my hips between her thighs, and her breathy moans are filling our room.

White-hot pleasure rockets up my spine and my cock pulses in my fist, come coating my belly and chest in thick jets.

I open my eyes, and my girl is sitting on the edge of the bed, wrapping her golden hair into a bun. I move my fingers through the come on my torso and imagine it's her tongue, because I know my girl loves my come.

"Good morning, baby," I say, this time aloud, to the on-screen Violet.

She looks sad as she makes her way to the door, going downstairs for her pre-shower cup of coffee.

I can't keep watching her much longer.

She needs me.

I need a plan.

Chapter Nine

DONOVAN

It's out of my system.

I'm itchy today. My face, my knuckles, my arms, my insides. Everything twinges with discomfort. And my irritation is at an all-time fucking high. I'm rolling with Malibu, we're on days together this week, and I'm already over it.

I fucking love partnering with Mally, it's not that.

It's the lack of Violet that's making me mental.

Now that I have a pipeline to her bedroom on a live feed, I hate waking up and leaving before I get to watch her wake up and leave. Not to mention the fact that we're busy on calls, so I haven't had the chance to drive down her street, or past the school.

I fucking hate it.

What's worse is now knowing how poorly she sleeps, how much time she spends alone when she's home, and how sad she's been because I stole her favorite thing in the fucking world. Her notebook.

My fingers carom over the keyboard of the laptop mounted to the dash. Information overwhelms the screen. Expired registration, and I'm thankful for that because I'm itching to light someone up.

So I do.

"Expired registration," I say to Mally who is pushing his aviators up his nose.

"10-4," he replies as he radios dispatch with all pertinent information.

With my flashers going, the compact silver car edges to the curb. The driver—a thirty-two year old man, according to my computer—eyes me through his rearview. Lines of irritation wrinkle his forehead, and that makes me smile.

Oh, I'm sorry that your choice to break the law is now an inconvenience to you. Fucking people. They never cease to amaze me. You break the law, there are consequences—pretty simple. Yet everyone thinks there should be some exception to the rules… just for them.

This is why I do what I do.

People need to be shaken up, woken up, alerted to how lazy and lackadaisical they are. How much time they waste being thoughtless and selfish.

My boots crunch the poorly paved shoulder as I edge up to the passenger window, which is still rolled up. I roll my eyes and thump the heel of my palm to the window. Then he rolls it down. Jack-off.

"Your registration is expired," I tell him, no greeting or anything.

"No, it isn't," he retorts, his hands still on the steering wheel. I don't like that.

"Put your hands on the dash," I order him as Mally approaches my backside, ducking down to see in the back windows.

"Why?" he asks.

"Because I told you to, and I have the gun, and you don't."

Mally sends a private kick to the back of my foot.

"You know what? Get outta the car." I'm not in the mood for this shit today. This rotund asshole picked the wrong day to talk shit.

"No," he says defiantly, and I'm grateful as shit he's argumentative, because it turns Mally from *concerned I'm being a prick* to *let's both be pricks to this prick*.

Mally manages his way to the driver's side and opens the door.

"Hey, you can't open my car door!" the man protests, his head swiveling on his fat neck, back and forth between Mally and I.

"Oh no?" Mally asks, his hand across his chest in the manner of pearl-clutching. He feeds it through his sun-bleached hair before tipping his sunglasses down the bridge of his nose, giving the man a peek of his blue eyes. "Looks like I just did."

Then he reaches in and yanks the keys out of the ignition, giving me time to go around the back of the car and meet him at the driver's side.

"Get out," I tell the man.

He does, but grumbles the entire time.

This isn't the normal scenario for me. I don't assault people while working, as I'm on three different cameras right now and am wearing a nameplate that says D. DRAKE. It would be pretty fucking stupid.

But that's me right now. Stupid from anxiousness.

When he reaches for his wallet, I grab his wrist, spinning and pinning him to the vehicle. He tells me I can't do this, he tells me it hurts him, he tells me lots of things. He sounds like a fire engine in the distance. I can hear the noise, but I'm not really concerned with it.

Mally takes the wallet from me and returns to the cruiser before leaving me with the warning, "remember the body and dash cams."

Stepping to stand adjacent to him, so that the dash cam can't see me, I pull my taser from the holster at my hip and press it to him.

"You like being an asshole to cops, huh?' I nudge the device into his back with more force. He winces and promises to have my badge.

Mally returns with a ticket, which he shoves into the man's pocket, along with his returned wallet.

"Pay your registration or don't drive your fuckin' car," Mally warns the man, then grabs my elbow to pull me back. I get in one more twist of his wrists before I release him. He jumps back, turning to face us, wagging a chunky finger.

"I'll fucking have your badges. You can't just tear people out of their fucking cars. I'm going to remember you two," he says, his tone full of conviction but his body telling another story. He edges back toward his open car door.

"I'm Officer Donovan Drake, I go by Van, my badge number is 1895. And this is my friend, Officer Christian Miller. We call him Malibu. His badge number is 1905. The number to the Willowdale PD is 848-755-2143. The dispatchers on duty this morning are Shondra, Keith, and Donna."

I smile at him, and his face goes blank, and kind of pale, too. "Call them, by all means."

Mally lifts two fingers in the air to the man before both of us pace back to the cruiser and slam our doors.

"Don't," I say, because I can feel Mally's eyes on me. "I'm fine. We're good. It's out of my system."

He knows that even though the man was an asshole, my behavior walked the line of reportable. But I know men like the one we just pulled over; he won't call and report us. He probably can't risk any inquiries into himself.

Mally lifts his hands in reaction. "I didn't say anything," he says, drawing out the words.

I wait for the man to drive away, and after he does, I flip a bitch and gas it. Mally lets it go, and we drive in silence to our next call that dispatch has alerted us to.

After that one, Mally drives us to lunch at the taco trucks. "You wanna grab dinner with me, Bran, and Batman tonight?"

I do want to catch dinner with the guys. It's been a couple weeks since I've seen Batman, our other bro from high school. He lives in the area, but he's got a wife and two kids now—the morning pumps and late night drinks have all but disappeared.

But... I also want to watch Violet in her room all night, too. Especially since these shifts have me seeing less and less of her. This morning, though, I promised myself I'd pull back on the *following and watching*, and seriously start making a plan to meet her.

"Sounds good," I agree, because if I eat with them, by geography and physics alone, I can't watch her. I mean, sure I'll rewatch the feed when I get home (and get my pants off), but at least I'm not rearranging my night for once. Just like a salad, I hate it... but it's healthier.

We finish our shift with Mally driving the remainder of

the day. He doesn't say it's because he wants to be the point-man on all stops, but I know from the way he keeps side eyeing me that he's thinking I'll do something stupid. Normally I'd fight him over the driver's seat. Put him in a sleeper until he concedes. But today, I don't care.

My ears are steaming from how hard I'm trying to work out a way in which Violet and I can meet. Seems easy, I know, but I don't want to just run into her at the grocery store and *hope* I catch her eye. No fucking way–I've watched my girl for far too long; I have to know for sure she'll want to talk to me, and the only thing that makes women want to talk to strange men? If you save them from something.

Up until I meet my guys at the chicken wing place down-town, I'm trying to concoct a situation where I can save Violet without drawing major attention or seriously scaring her. If she sees I only want to help her, that I'm a good, trust-worthy guy–that's the only way I'll have a chance in the long-term. Because once I come clean about all this? I might be fucked.

I may have to save her a few times.

"Bodfather, there he is," Bran claps his hand where my neck and my shoulders meet, squeezing hard. I wince away and shove him in the ribs.

"Fuck you, that hurt," I whine, rubbing my trap out dramatically.

"Because you aren't working out your shoulders enough," he teases, even adding a playful wink as he pulls me into a hug.

"Is that right? How about we have a push-up contest, my man?" I pinch the back of his neck as he twists his lips to the side, whistling. "You said it yourself. I'm the Bodfather, not you."

Mally slaps us both on the back, with Batman on his heels. "Why don't we just get out a ruler, my dudes?"

We drift towards our table, which is in the very back of the restaurant. The floors are sticky, various sports flash across different TVs, and the air is dense with warm beer and vinegary sauce. It makes my nipples hard.

Batman waits at the counter, working seriously hard to avoid the fuck-me eyes the girl behind the counter is offering. Batman doesn't fuck around about his marriage. He loves his wife, and he's not doing anything to jeopardize that.

I respect the shit out of him.

Bran and Mally slide in on one side, and I take the other, leaving a spot for Batman near me.

"So how much you payin' Mally to open Paradise every day? I mean, he's on the payroll, right?" I ask, a shit-eating grin on my face. Bran's been deep in this chick lately—he won't even bring her around us yet—and those sleepovers are making his 4am opening pretty hard.

Or easy, I guess, because he isn't even trying to get there. He's just letting Mally use his key and punch in the code. Paradise is a lifting gym, so there doesn't really need to be any employees around. Dudes walk in, nod their hooded heads, then do their thing with a jug of water and headphones. All Bran really needs to be there for is mopping up stank and sweat, and that's better in the evening anyway.

Still, I can't resist giving him a hard time.

This is the first chick he's really into, and we all know that Bran never expected to find someone.

I'm a big enough man—with a big enough dick—to admit when another man is handsome. Bran and Mally both give me a run for my money. Okay, maybe not a fucking run but at least a jog.

Bran's over six foot, like me, with shaggy dark hair and a full, but fucking beautiful beard. His pores are soaked with ink, skulls with snakes, topless mermaids, words of wisdom, an important date–your typical bodysuit of ink. How could a guy like that worry he wouldn't find someone?

Of all the things Bran has–a good fucking heart, a solid work ethic, compassion, empathy, and an appetite that blows even me away–there is one thing he is missing, and that thing has made him self-conscious.

Dudes don't say shit like that to each other, though. But Mally, Batman, and I know our boy, read him like a fucking Playboy. We know what he's thinking.

What dope chick wants a guy with a fucking eyepatch?

See, Bran's *actual* name is Brian. But when you lose an eye and your friends are assholes, well, your name loses the i, too. He wears a black patch over it, and while it's been a few years, he still ducks his face away from women. Even though he's a walking thirst trap, and I'm fairly certain women don't give a shit about the patch. *He* does.

There was an incident between Mally and Bran and a group of dudes. The night he lost his eye is now simply *"that night"* and we hardly talk about it. It changed the four of us. Our bond went on fucking steroids. A never-ending cycle.

"I know, I know," he groans, tugging a palm over the top of his messy hair. I don't call him out on the pink that colors his cheeks at the first mention of his secret girl.

"So what's up man? I don't mind opening Paradise but come on, we want to meet her." Mally nods like an eager puppy waiting for a bone. I love his golden retriever energy. Happy for everyone, all the time. I mean hell, he loves me and he knows my dark side. That's a special fucking guy.

"Ehh," he says, nodding to the waiter who slides four

beers onto the table. He takes a long pull then burps, which I wave away. "Not yet. *I'm not ready.*"

Those three words—we've learned they mean something when Bran says them, so we back off.

"Well, my old lady is anxious to have another female in this group," Batman adds, taking a drink of his beer in a way that allows him to glance at his watch. Kids bedtime and shit, I know he can't stay long.

"What, Robin doesn't like hanging out with us all the time?" Mally asks with a grin, thumbing a finger between me and him.

"No, she fucking doesn't. Last time you guys came over, one of you taught Fiona how to make fart noises with her armpit and she got a timeout in kindergarten the next day."

Mally's face scrunches up stupidly as he shoots a straw wrapper across the table.

I tip my head in his direction, my lips pursed. "And you're even *considering* that it was me who taught her that when *he's* here?"

"And," Batman continues, "Fiona started calling me Batman." He shakes his head, his eyes wide with the fear of pussy withholding. "Robin doesn't fucking like that shit, you guys gotta quit."

I look at Mally, who looks back at me, then over at Bran. "*We* can still call you Batman when it's just us, right?"

Batman nods. "Yes, even though it's fucking stupid, *yes*, yes, you can. I know change is hard for you idiots."

Bran pushes a thumb into his pecs. "Hey, you fuckin' think I want to be Bran? Half the time, I don't even remember my real name is Brian!"

We all laugh way too hard at that, just as the waiter comes back with... *one hundred hot wings.*

We tuck our napkins into the neck hole of our shirts because we are classy fucking guys.

"Bran at least makes sense," Batman adds. "My fucking name is Henry."

Mally points a finger at him and, through a mouthful of habanero chicken wings, says, "when your old lady has a dope name like Robin, you absolutely do not walk away from the opportunity to be Batman."

"I'd love to sprint from that opportunity actually," Batman says, also with a full mouth. These fucking guys. No manners.

"That's why you have us," Mally grins, and both Bran and Batman roll their eyes. "And hey, maybe Van will get a nickname soon. Bodfather is fine but personally, it makes us look weak." He washes down his too-big bite with the last drink of his beer, then wiggles it in the air for a refill. The waiter nods. "He's got a girl. We could work him up into a new nickname."

"Oh really?" Batman asks, pressing his fists together under his chin like we're about to talk about our first kiss at the lockers.

"It's nothing yet. I just... I like her."

"We drive by her house all the time," Mally adds with a grin, which earns him a sock to his side.

Saved by the tired mom. Batman's phone skitters across the sticky table as Robin's face and name illuminate the screen.

"Fuck, I gotta go. It's bedtime, and Fiona has a cold, Jack is teething. I just, I gotta go." He grabs his phone and answers, and the guys and I officially don't exist.

He throws down two bills, overpaying as usual, and

waves us off as he coos promises of bubble baths and wine to his wife.

As if not wanting to be the first one but nonetheless eager to flee, Bran follows suit. "Going to my girl's. I'll see you fuckers at Paradise tomorrow morning."

"With one eye."

"Yes," he smiles sarcastically, "with one eye."

They leave us with too many wings, and because we're not quitters, we keep eating.

"So tell me," Mally says eventually, a ring of orange around his lips. "You been active in your extracurriculars? That expired registration stop today you seemed... *stressed.*"

I take down two more wings, giving myself a chance to formulate a good answer.

I really don't like lying to Mally but equally, I'm not exactly proud that a seriously fucking deranged stalker is living inside me. I mean, if I told him what I'd been doing and for how long, he'd probably have me fucking committed. I stick to the extracurriculars he's referring to instead of going full-confessional. The only person I'll ever spill it to is my girl.

"I've slowed down some," I admit, thoroughly pleased that for the most part, that's the truth. It's been months since I've really been on a bender. Those days she wasn't leaving her house, and I couldn't see her–that's the last time I really binged on assault. Sure, I still partake here and there but keeping my eyes on my girl has shifted some of my sour energy into anticipatory energy.

I really don't know if that's a good thing because now I want her so bad.... I don't know what I'll do if she isn't mine. Soon.

"Good, that's good," he says, pushing out a relieved

breath. "So who's the girl? You know I can just run the address, right?" he smiles, and I grin back because he isn't threatening. He's just nosey as fuck.

"You get yourself a lady, Mally, and then you won't have to sniff around mine." I lean back, my spine cracking loudly against the stiff vinyl booth.

I don't have the details worked out with my plan, but I need to know that if I need help, I'll have it. And I'm itching to get home and rewatch the feed of Violet this afternoon. "Hey, listen," I say, changing the subject as Mally hopelessly wipes at a buffalo sauce stain in the middle of his v-neck shirt. Fucking Mally and his white v-neck shirts. Women love them. You can see his nipple piercing through it.

"I may need your help with something, I can't give you any details yet but I need to know if you're in."

One of his blond brows slowly raises, and he leans back like he's the guy on fucking *Shark Tank* deciding if he's going to fund me. I let him irritate me and feel powerful, though, because he's the only one I can be this vague with. Mally *gets* me.

His lips twitch a little as he drapes his arm over the back of the booth. The moments tick by, and I roll my eyes at his drawn-out indecision.

"You gonna buy me something nice after?" He bats his eyes at me, and I roll mine again.

"I'll buy you one meal depending on your performance."

We put down the rest of the wings because they're wings and they're there. And after Mally pulls out of the parking lot, I speed home, anxious as fuck to catch up on my girl.

Chapter Ten

VIOLET

I've had enough.

Things that don't walk: anything that doesn't have legs.

With that knowledge, where in the *freaking crap* is my notebook? It's been missing for a week and honestly, around day two I decided to stop being in denial and accept the fact that I've lost it.

The thing is, though, I've been writing in notebooks for a long time. And not once have I ever left one anywhere. Because if I'm anything, I'm careful. Double-check, all that.

The thought has passed through my mind that maybe someone took it, thinking it was theirs. Did I leave it out in the teachers' lounge? Did I bring it to Sasha's classroom and leave it? I don't go anywhere else and–holy crap that's a sad realization.

Or did someone... take it?

I cannot think of one single person that would want to

read my notebook. And no, it is not a diary. Because I am too old for a diary therefore we don't call the notebook a diary.

(But it is.)

And someone could have it right now.

I'm trying not to lose my mind while I continue the hunt for it. I've upturned every couch cushion, emptied every drawer, and looked under everything–why do we look in places that we've literally never put anything, still hopeful we may find *the thing*? So stupid. But I'm *stupid* for this freaking notebook.

With the extra time I had all week because I was unable to pour my soul between the lines, I decided to do something positive instead of sulk. Well, I sulked a ton, but I made room for one positive thing.

I wrote a letter to the school board asking them to consider me for their upcoming membership. Because even though I let my father talk to me in a way that makes me dream of him taking a long walk on a short plank over a shark-infested black sea, I don't always let him get in my head. Not about this, at least. I know I would be good on the school board.

Unrelated, school board members get to vote on tenure-track, administrators, and instructors. Another unrelated fact, Mr. Wheeler is up for tenure in three years.

But in my gut-twisting, soul-wrenching ongoing hunt for my notebook, I forgot the letter on my desk this morning. On my drive into work, I call my mom at home.

"Hey mom," I say when she answers with her rehearsed "Carlisle House" greeting.

"Hi sweetheart. Is everything okay? Aren't you on the way to school?" she asks, and it always sends a chill through me when she's so concerned. It's genuine, the concern a mother should have for her child. And yet, how easily she turns it off when my dad is destroying me... She's either soulless, crazy, or brainwashed; aren't all of those just terrifying options for the person who is supposed to be your role model?

I swallow, and smile at the woman in the gold sedan waiting at the crosswalk. I wave her to go, and she edges out.

"Yeah. I'm fine, on my way to school. Listen, I was wondering if you could do me a favor?" I hate saying those words to anyone, even Sasha. I hate being the girl that needs help.

Can I dictate my lesson plans to you? My hand is broken, and I can't type or write.

Can someone watch my class please? I'm running late because my sister took my car.

Can you bring me a sweater? I don't have mine.

There will be a time when I'm out of my parents' *hellhole* and on my own. That's the crux of my change; a brand spanking new environment. With room to breathe, I can just... be. It's hard to be anything when someone is always telling you you're nothing.

"Oh, sure," she draws out sweetly, and there's that chill vibrating through my skin, leaving goosebumps in its wake.

The old woman completes her turn, and I accelerate, noticing a police officer turn out behind me. I'm glad mom's on speaker–the last thing I need to do is get pulled over, too.

"My letter to the school board is on my desk. It needs to go out today, can you grab it and pop it in the box before pickup? I was running a little late this morning, then I forgot."

"Oh course I will." The next words she speaks are in a low, private voice. It makes me sad. "I'm glad you're going for it."

"Thanks. Can you text me when you've done it?" I press a palm to my belly, exhaling. "I'm nervous about it. I just want to know it's done, so I don't have to think about it."

She laughs this weird, boxed-up laugh that makes my skin kinda crawl a little, if I'm being honest. I don't know whether to be angry with her or sad for her... or both?

"Sure, sure, of course. Now you drive safely, okay?"

"Okay, thanks, mom. Bye." I look into my rearview mirror before I reach forward and tap the red end call button. The police cruiser is gone now.

Thank goodness, *no one wants to be followed by a cop.*

The morning goes by quickly, thanks to my favorite "Nuts for Synonyms" unit. I spent more time than I'd like to admit cutting acorns from construction paper, then drawing four horizontal lines across each. Well worth it though. I write one word in each nut and the students have 3 minutes to fill out the other three lines with synonyms. It's really freaking fun.

The kids get really into it, and when they learn I'm happy... but when they have fun learning? It's really freaking special.

When my phone vibrates against the tile through my thin bag resting on the floor, I tell the class to turn their nuts over and think of their own word, then switch with a neighbor to fill in the synonyms.

No one ever calls or text messages me when I'm working, so checking feels vital.

It's a text message. From my mom.

I open immediately, not knowing what I'm wishing or hoping to read.

Mom: *Violet, I'm so sorry. I spilled coffee on your letter. By the* *time I noticed, it was saturated. I'm sorry sweetheart. Can you print another tomorrow?*

My stomach free falls into a disappointment I'm well acquainted with, unfortunately. It had to go out today. Letters of consideration cannot be late. Today was the last day. The last mail pick up was... I look at my watch. Shit. An hour ago.

Me: *It had to go out today.*

Three dots ripple with indecision across my screen, but I lock my phone. There isn't anything she could say that would change the outcome. She's sorry. I'm sure.

The back of my eyes prick with heat, and my neck grows sweaty. I try to remember if I ate this morning because I feel light on my feet, my head a bit woozy. I slump into my desk chair and take a breath, then take some sips of the Diet Coke on my desk.

I'm okay. I'll try again next year. Or hope for someone to kick the bucket. Okay, not that.

I don't make my way to my car until two hours after the bell rang. I searched my entire classroom for my notebook, and made Sasha help, too.

"Are you going to mop my classroom for me because that's what I'm supposed to be doing right now." She pats her voluminous dark hair, thick and curly.

"You don't have to mop," I say, nudging her towards another crate of Highlights Magazine. I've literally NEVER walked over here with my notebook from home, but I'm at that stage of loss. Utter freaking denial and completely unwilling to accept the truth. It's a goner. "We have a custodian, remember?"

She raises her eyebrows, her lips pursed in difference. "I would not make that poor man deal with what's going on in my class right now. We did glitter today, Violet. Second graders and glitter." She shakes her head. "He doesn't make enough."

I snort. "Neither do we."

We search high and low, bathroom to wastebasket. And repeat it again in her classroom, too, because I'm an actual crazy person like that. She leaves, and I linger in the halls a bit. I don't want to be here, but I don't want to be home. I don't have anywhere I want to be.

By the time I'm headed home, it's almost sunset. I decide to stop at the grocery store for a bottle of wine–I don't normally even drink wine–but stop in the first parking spot because of what I see.

Mr. Wheeler's car. I have to see it every single day at work, so I wouldn't miss it for the world. And his subtle "Willowdale Wildcats PRINCIPAL" plate frame was also a tip-off.

What I did, as tears made of anger and frustration poured endlessly from me, is a bit… shocking.

I carry a knife in my purse.

It's a small one. Folds up. Nothing fancy. I was bringing apples with me to lunch for so many months, unable to cut them but despising just raw-dogging right into the side of one. Finally, I got a small pocket knife and used it daily.

I didn't know if I'd be strong enough to puncture the thick rubber of his faded, balding Goodyear tires. I wasn't sure if the small pocket knife would be sharp enough.

I guess small and sharp can do more damage than you'd know.

And the sound of air rushing from all four tires as I walked calmly back to my car made me so high. My scalp tingled with satisfaction so acute that I couldn't help but grin.

As I drove home, I had adrenaline. And it turned into courage. All the courage.

My dad probably took my notebook. He sees me with it. I try not to let him but hell, it's hard not to slip up in your own house. He eyes it when I hold it, too, like he's willing himself to see through it and absorb its contents to use against me. And he would.

I don't know why I didn't let myself accept this before. Maybe because I didn't want to face it. Because I knew I wouldn't face it. But now, my sharp little blade showed me even the most underestimated can take down the strongest things.

That's what makes me realize.

It's him. It's clearly freaking him, and I've had enough.

Chapter Eleven

VIOLET

I need out. Or I'll explode.

I think I understand crazy people a little bit more now.
Seriously.

I never thought I'd slash someone's tires in broad daylight
but here we are, a deep groove in my palm from the handle
of a pocket knife. And I feel good.

Okay, I feel a little bad because now someone is going to
have to help him. A tow truck driver, another man who'll
have to stay late at the tire shop, he may even distress a poor
Lyft driver. But I don't feel bad for Wheeler because he has
deserved worse than that for way too freaking long.

And another thing that has gone on way too long? Letting
my dad walk all over me because he decided that I'm less
worthy. Notebooks don't grow legs. If he took it, he'll give it
back to me tonight.

By the time my dad is home from work, my mom is a

literal basket case. Like the charge in the air before a tornado, my mother is circling around me in the kitchen, wringing her hands.

I never sit at the table in the kitchen this close to when dad gets home. My mere presence in my own house makes her anxious because she knows what a freaking asshole he is. Yet if Rose and her yellow stolen sweater were out here, he'd probably pat her head. She is, after all, a piano genius. *Eyeroll.*

"You're breaking your routine," mom says finally, carefully selecting those words as a way of saying, *"you aren't normally doing this and I don't like it."*

For some reason today, my voice comes easy and sharp. My cheeks tingle as I speak, and I think that feeling is... pride. "Should I slink up to my room, and hide because my dad hates my existence? Or can I sit at the table like a normal person does in their home?"

My blouse clings to my lower back as my skin breaks out in an adrenaline-fueled sweat. I've never stood up for myself in this salty manner. Normally I'd skip the salt. Bloat and all that. But to my family—it's about time they see I have a backbone.

"Are you upset about the letter, Violet? That was an accident, and I'm sorry, sweetheart."

"I'm upset about the letter, yes, mom."

"It was an accident," she says, taking a seat next to me, her hands worrying with the table cloth.

"Do you know where my notebook is?" I ask her, leaning back to show her I'm not nervous. I want to know, and my mom is intimidated by body language.

"What notebook?" she asks without meeting my eyes.

"The notebook I always carry around."

"I thought there were many. Don't you have many?" She

smooths invisible wrinkles from the red and white check-ered print.

"One at a time. Always the same color. So you know what it looks like. Have you seen it?"

She shakes her head staunchly, like I've asked her if she's ever seen an alien or something.

"No, I haven't, Violet."

I twist my lips together, hating that I almost feel guilty about putting pressure on her. But the yes-man is just as much of the problem. "If I went through Rose's room, I wouldn't find it?"

She smiles, impassive and soft. Her voice is unwavering. "Why would she care about what you write in your note-book... sweetheart," she adds that last word in an effort to turn down the scoville units, but it's too late. My body tenses and I find myself swallowing.

At that moment, the garage door gears churn and I know dad and Rose are home. He picked her up from her last class today on his way home from work because she wrecked the car they got her.

I saved and bought my own car, *for the record.*

Dad and Rose come through the back door, both of them looking surly. Can you inherit a surly demeanor? I swear no one does surly like the two of them.

"Hi sweetheart," my mom says, taking the jacket and briefcase off the floor where my dad dropped them when he came in. Growing up, I thought her love language was a dutiful mom–picking up, cleaning, organizing, always *doing.* Only after my accident did I realize she was afraid not to be busy.

"What's the smell?" my dad gruffs, wrinkling his nose a few times as he sniffs the air. Mom rests her hand on the slow cooker lid, smiling catatonically.

"Pot roast."

"You need something?" Dad asks, turning his attention to me as he flops down in a chair at the table, waiting for my mom to bring him his first after-work beer. "You're usually too good to hang out with your family."

Gaslighting. Okay. A technique I know he cherishes more than his own daughter. *Rise above, Violet.*

"I wanted to ask you and Rose something."

Rose slams the fridge door closed and sits next to dad, cracking open a La Croix. When I buy La Croix, I think I'm "too good" for tap, but when Rose buys it, it's not even a conversation.

"What if I don't want to talk to you?" she says, sipping the lemon-flavored drink. I bite the inside of my cheek so as not to reply, *likewise asshole.*

"My notebook is missing. I've looked everywhere, and the last place I had it was this house."

Dad blinks, taking the beer from my mom's hand without so much as a look of acknowledgment, especially no thank you. Rose smirks.

"You mean, your *diary,*" she sing-songs teasingly, her brows pinched to make sure I know it's not playful banter.

"You're too old for a diary. Maybe you lost it because it's God's way of telling you to grow up," dad says as he cracks his neck and loosens his tie.

"You know what grown-ups do? They move *out* of their parents' house," Rose adds, as the kitchen fills with mom's humming. She fiddles with the pot roast before putting the lid back on, and I stay focused on her while I choose my words carefully.

This is the point where I'd normally slink away–

unwilling to ruin my evening because I fought with jerks. But as mom opens the valve on her pressure cooker that's cooking tonight's potatoes, the escaping steam gives me a heady dose of deja vu.

Just an hour ago I was slashing Mr. Wheelers tires because he is a sexual predator and absolute filth bag. And it felt good.

The steam finishes releasing and a rush of courage moves through me, remembering the high I felt in the parking lot earlier.

"I would move out if I didn't have an *accident* that required me to use all my savings. And last time I checked, just because you don't have a job doesn't mean you aren't an adult. You're over eighteen, Rose, so why don't you move out?"

Holy shit. My head spins, blood and excitement soar through my veins. I stood up to my bullying little sister. *Go me.*

Then my dad does something to surprise me, which is hard because old dogs and new tricks, you know? He gets up from the table... *before* his second and third beer and before his meal has been served to him.

I hear my swallow as I look up at his round, cherry face. "Your sister is in school working towards an *actual* career," he says through clenched teeth. "Don't talk to her that way."

I can't believe I do it but I get to my feet and match his position, fingers fanned out over the table as I lean forward. "So, don't say to her exactly what she said to me?" I lift my brows, and watch as the pressure builds in his brain. His eyes are buggy and wild.

"Why are you always bringing up your accident?" The table squeaks under his weight as he leans further across; an intimidation tactic I'm sure. It's working, but for freaking once, I don't let on. "You think anyone here cares?"

Mom's humming grows louder, and I snap.

"Would you stop humming? I know you can hear this. You don't have to put on some act for me. You hear it, and you don't care. Stop freaking humming!"

God, it feels good to finally say it. To say what I said to Rose, to mom, and standing up to my dad. The high I felt when I slashed Wheeler's tires returns, but like most balloons of happiness in my life, it pops.

Mom slowly turns to face me, and I just shake my head because I honestly don't know what else to do anymore. I start back in with my original point–because, really, my notebook is all I care about now. It's too late for the school board letter, and fighting with these strangers is pointless, despite the rush it's given me.

"I just want my note–"

The heaviest of hands comes down across my face, connecting first with my eye socket and then against my cheek and jaw. An open-handed heavy smack.

I've been grabbed. I've been shoved. A few times I've even been pushed. I've had a bad... *accident.*

But I've never been hit.

His strike knocks me back, so far back that I stumble a few times. The back of my head connects with the door jamb of the pantry, and then the fluorescent tube lights of the old kitchen are all I see.

Then I see nothing.

Blacking out is so strange. When I come to, a few minutes of my life are missing, but judging by the setting around me, I didn't miss much.

Dad's not standing there, hand on forehead, pacing,

saying, *'what have I done?'* In fact, dad isn't even in the kitchen. From the living room, I can hear a football game on TV and the slow sip of his beer.

He hit me. And I fell and blacked out, and he's watching TV and drinking beer.

I raise my hand to my head, trying to assess the damage. The pain in my eye is piercing, radiating through my face, down to the base of my skull. It's lumpy and hot to the touch, and I'm in excruciating pain. Putting thoughts together makes my brain sore.

Mom's on the floor, scrubbing my blood off the tile as she... hums.

Rose is blowing on a piece of meat pierced by the tines of her fork, scrolling through her phone with the other hand. Eating dinner as if I didn't just get freaking decked.

I don't know who got me in the chair and put my chest and head on the table, but I don't care anymore.

"You ruined the letter on purpose, didn't you?" I ask the room full of enemies, the room full of my family. "You didn't want me to get it."

My mom continues humming.

How this house hasn't exploded from all the gaslighting— it's a freaking miracle. But I need out. Or I'll explode.

Rising from the table, still wearing my cream-colored blouse with a large silk bow at the neck, my tweed pencil skirt, and black flats, I walk straight to the front door. I don't grab a coat, my purse, or bookbag, I don't say another word. I just open the door, step onto the front porch, and close it behind me.

Step by step, I move down the driveway, between my car and mom's, and make my way to the sidewalk. My pace grows quicker and despite my aching skull and seriously shaken brain, I go faster and faster until I'm running.

My low, loose ponytail is the first thing to give up, and a block from my house my hair is whipping around wildly behind me. I run and run, understanding Forrest Gump a lot better. You may not really be able to run away from your problems, but sometimes you can.

Sometime later–I have no idea how long because I'm fairly certain I have a concussion and should definitely not be exercising–I'm at Sasha's house. I always go to her back-door and knock before just walking in. It's what best friends do.

But for some reason, I go to her front door and ring the doorbell and wait.

When she answers, her face moves quickly through a series of emotions–surprise, shock, horror, worry. She loops an arm over my shoulder as she repeats my name over and over, along with the question "what happened?" and "are you okay?"

But the hit, the fall, and the run settle in as I pass out face down onto her couch.

Waking up to a freaked out Sasha leaning over me freaks me out, and after I scream, she screams, then we both laugh as I hold my head in agony. The laughter is short lived as it turns to tears.

Lots of them.

I tell Sasha what happened. She knows about my *accident*– she's the only one–so I know I'm safe with her. She doesn't make me feel weak or badger me about why I don't report him or call the police. She listens and she loves; that soft place to fall is the only thing keeping me going these days–knowing I have her.

Finally, when I'm done recalling the entire thing, she sighs. And I sigh, too, because there just isn't much to say.

After a few minutes of pensive silence wherein I think we're truly both trying to figure a way for me to move out and get away from them, Sasha clears her throat.

"You could sleep on my couch," she says, and I can tell she's thinking aloud. "I mean, it's not a great one, but we could buy a new one?" she says, and just the suggestion makes my heart warm.

Sasha lives in a tiny house. It's adorable, an absolute dream with a skylight in the kitchen, low sitting windows, a path of stepping stones through her lawn to the sidewalk, a wall of exposed brick adjacent to a wall lined with shelves. It's the sweetest dream of a home ever.

It's also less than a thousand square feet, and her sister lives there, too. Being a flight attendant, she's not there much, but the home is small enough to still feel full, even when she's gone.

"No," I wave a hand down through her suggestion. "No, Sash. You and your sister live here. I can't rely on other people to solve my problems. I have to figure it out."

"When have you ever relied on anyone to solve your problems?" she asks, sounding irritated with me. If I tear myself down, she is my personal construction foreman. "You can stay here until you can get something else."

I shake my head, but it freaking hurts, so I stop. Adjusting the bag of frozen peas that Sasha put on my eye earlier, I smile softly at her as tears roll down my cheeks. "No, I can't. I don't want to feel like I don't belong in another space, you know?"

She opens her mouth to defend, but I rest my palm on her knee, kneading her to calmness. "I don't mean you will make me feel that way. But I know myself, Sash. *I'll* feel that way. I need my own place."

She nods with understanding.

"I'm working on another nest egg. But after tonight, I think my goal should just be enough for first, last and security deposit at an apartment. Just to get me out."

Sasha presses a hand into her chest as her eyes flutter closed, and she sighs. "Oh, thank god, Vi. I really do not want you under that roof with *those fucking people.*"

I snort at that. "My family," I say, really just for laughs. Because we share blood but are we really family? I am alone, aside from Sasha.

"I'm just going to ask one more time because I feel like I'm a bad friend if I don't." She winces a little. "We're sure we don't want to call the police?"

I barely shake my head because it's really starting to hurt now that the shock and adrenaline are wearing off. The peas are getting warm and mushy inside of the slick bag.

"No. If he gets arrested, he'll lose his job."

Sasha's face says, "so?"

"Then all four of us won't have a place to live." I shrug because that hurts less than any facial expression. "I want out. His karma will get him. I just… I want out."

"Okay," she says, taking the bag of peas from me. "I'll run you a bath and bring you a new bag of peas… or maybe riced cauliflower. I'm not sure what else I have in there. But I'll get you something cold to put on that. I'll leave some clothes for you on the bathroom sink, and I'll put your clothes in my machine so you can wear them to work tomorrow."

I smile, grateful that I can stay with her but also that she's literally thought of everything.

My eyes grow fuzzy. She loops her arms under mine and lifts me up off the couch into a hug.

She's warm and familiar, the smell of her Marc Jacobs perfume making me feel like everything is okay.

At least right now, everything is okay.

Chapter Twelve

DONOVAN

I don't feel good about it.

I enter my house like someone whose had to take a shit for the last leg of a long drive: drop everything on the floor, kick the door shut, and fucking bolt down the hall. Only it's not the toilet I'm rushing toward. It's my laptop.

Usually, I like a nice hot shower, some comfortable pajama pants, a few push-ups, and maybe a beer before I watch Violet on the screen. Set the mood, all that shit.

Tonight, though, nervous energy crawls through my veins. I boot up the laptop and go straight into the footage from today. I don't even kick off my fucking sneakers–that's rare for me.

The footage ticks past 5:32. Violet is punctual. I scratch the side of my jaw then pull at the end of my trimmed beard. Where is she? I skip ahead until the footage clock reads 5:41. Violet's bedroom is still dark. My knee bounces.

I skip to 5:55. No change. I yank the laptop off the bed and rest it on my thigh, scrolling forward to the current time of 9:14.

The room is dark, so I zoom in on her bed to see if it's turned down, even if I can't see her. But I don't need to zoom too far, because after my first click I can see her pillows are exactly where they were just a few frames back at 5:32.

Where are you, Violet?

My chest is heaving, and the edges of my vision grow fuzzy as my heart abuses my ribcage. *Calm down*, I coach myself. She could be home. Maybe she fell asleep on the couch.

It's possible. Not even that far fetched of an option, either. A lot of people fall asleep on their couches after long days.

But the anxiety in my veins is in control of me completely. It tells me *no, she's not asleep on the couch, something is wrong.*

Before I can shut the laptop, I'm back in my SUV, headed toward Violet's house.

Four houses down, like a well-worn glove, I settle into familiarity. Violet's car is in the driveway, in her usual parking spot. A few windows glow, telling me they're home and someone is awake.

Maybe she just fell asleep on the couch.

I scratch the side of my jaw, then pull my palms down my face, releasing a frustrated groan. I still just... I don't like it. *I don't feel good about it.*

See, now if I hadn't been watching her for the last year I wouldn't know that her co-worker Sasha is also her best friend. And I also wouldn't know that Sasha lives a few blocks away, next to the school.

Luckily, I have been watching, and I do know those things.

I drive to Sasha's not really having a plan. I really need to fucking stop that shit. Going into things without a plan has proven not to be so smart for me recently. Parking a few houses back, I get out of my SUV and tread quietly towards the small house.

The house shows signs of life, orange leaking out around the closed mini blinds. Slowly and intentionally, I make my way down the side of Sasha's house, stopping at every single window to look in. First, I raise just the corner of my cell phone up, so the camera has a full view. I take a photo, look at it, and keep moving.

Finally, I get around to the back of the house where a large sliding door eats up most of the wall. Yellow light pours onto the lawn, and I can see two muddled shadows moving. I don't like to get on the ground and crawl–makes it much harder to get away. But in this case, I have no cover in the yard.

On my belly, I pull myself to the glass door and slowly, with my heart in my fucking throat, peer in.

Sasha, donning a large Rolling Stones t-shirt that hits just above her knees, is standing in front of Violet, whose back is to me. She's laughing hysterically, using the inside of one wrist to wipe away tears. Now she's jogging in place and reaching out, pausing with a hand on her hip to laugh hysterically. Violet must be laughing, too, because her shoulders are shaking.

Near them, there are two empty wine glasses and… two empty wine bottles. Looks like it must be a girls night. Violet's wearing a big, loose t-shirt. It must be Sasha's.

I guess it's a sleepover.

I didn't know grown women still did that shit, but... I sigh as I shimmy my way back to the side of the house, hop to my feet and get back to my SUV.

On the drive home, I expect to feel calm but am irritated to discover I literally feel worse.

If Violet was going to spend the night at Sasha's house on a work night, why didn't she have her own car? She'd need a way to get home tomorrow after school, and Sasha doesn't have a car.

And if she were spending the night with someone, she'd be prepared. My girl is fucking prepared. Why is she wearing what looks to be like Sasha's clothes?

In the year I've had eyes on her, I'd never really seen Violet drink, either. Definitely not enough to get drunk or even tipsy. And tonight, it looks like Violet and Sasha drank a full bottle each.

I saw her. Granted, I didn't see her face because of the angle, but it was her. I recognized her hair, the beauty mark on the inside of her wrist that she exposed for me to see when she was wiping away a tear of laughter.

They were both laughing, though. They wouldn't be drinking and laughing if something were wrong. Maybe it was just a spontaneous, random girls' night.

Yeah, that's probably what it was.

I can't make myself believe it, though, and I don't know why.

Chapter Thirteen

VIOLET

Fighting back just isn't that gratifying.

Turns out, frozen riced cauliflower makes a great ice pack because it disperses the cold more evenly.

Sasha helps me get my hair done, wrapping it into a bun on the top of my head. It's the first time in my teaching career I've worn a bun. I hate to wear it off my face–I need any cover I can get–but it looks like shit, and I didn't have the energy to wash it last night. She irons my washed clothes and packs me a lunch–I end up crying into my coffee because it's so freaking sweet, and I love her so much.

My face doesn't look as bad this morning as I thought it was going to. I mean, my eye socket is fifty shades of bruised, and it's still a little swollen. After some foundation–which I never wear–it looks decent. Noticeable, of course, but not horrendous. My story is that I fell.

God, how cliché.

I get why people say that, though. Who can dispute a fall? It has so many factors. Like, the type of shoes I was wearing, what I was standing on–Converse on sandy concrete is a fall *waiting* to happen. Or if you're standing on a curb or didn't see the "wet floor" sign at the supermarket–location matters, too.

Falls are definitely hard to dispute. So I become a cliché and tell students and other teachers that I fell. And no one asks for more details, and that makes me both happy and incredibly sad.

On our lunch break, Sasha comes to my classroom, and we sit on the ground, our backs against a poster of action words.

"You know what you need?" she asks, a piece of provolone stuck in the crease of her lips.

"Money," I deadpan, taking a long drink of the sweet tea she packed me.

She laughs, covering her full mouth with a hand. "Yeah," she says, swallowing a too-big bite. "But what else?"

I shrug and bite into my sandwich. Peppered turkey breast, thinly sliced red onion, sprouts, crisp romaine, banana peppers, and provolone cheese on toasted sourdough. I moan as I take bites, my eyes closing in ecstasy as I chew.

Saving money means not buying the freshest, best food. It also means not eating out at restaurants either. This sandwich is orgasmic.

"You alright over there?" Sasha asks, her eyes wide. She nudges me, and I smirk through the bite I'm finishing.

"It's just so good." I smile, wanting some levity since I've been such a heavy friend for what feels like so long now. "It's the best thing I've had in my mouth in a really long time."

She tips her head back and howls, slapping her hand to her knee. "Oh girl," she says through her laughter.

I take another bite, and she calms. "Seriously, about that. You need to start dating. Get yourself a boyfriend."

With my head cocked irritably, I roll my eyes. "Yeah, because I need to add more stress to my life right now." I touch my bruised eye. "And this isn't exactly sexy."

She gives me a sad smile. I could go a lifetime without being the recipient of another sad smile.

"You're still beautiful, Violet. You know that." She runs her hand over my head, smoothing back the flyaways before adjusting my bun.

"I'm no Rose," I say sarcastically, the inflection on her name sending home the theme of my life: *Rose good, Violet bad.*

Sasha pushes a dismissive huff out. "Vi, that thorn doesn't hold a candle to you. You've got the blonde hair, and even longer legs. Thorn and your devil dad can keep their sewer-water brown hair gene, thank you very much." She sizes me up, eyes narrowed. "And you know you have good tits."

I press my palms to my chest, pinching the rest of my sandwich between my palm and thumb. "I do not."

She knocks my hands away. "Shut up. Seriously, just shut up."

She smiles at me, and I'm softened by the moment. "I'm thankful for you, you know?"

She shakes her head staunchly, wagging a finger at me. "No, no mushy shit right now. Back to the issue at hand."

I raise an eyebrow.

"Dick," she deadpans. "Now, hear me out." She counts off on one finger. "First, it would give you another place to physically hang out, so until you can move out, you don't have to be home as much."

That's actually a good point, but again, I don't like to feel like I'm somewhere I don't belong. Where I'm imposing.

"Secondly," she says, pushing another finger down. "Protection."

I blink. "The only place I need protection is the one place where a boyfriend wouldn't be. I wouldn't bring any guy home to my parents' house." I shake my head even though it's sore, despite the three Tylenol I've taken. "No way."

"I mean," she starts, but goes quiet for a moment. She sets her waxed paper on the floor, resting the remnants of her sandwich on top. Angling her body towards me, she says, "if you date a guy who falls for you—he'll want to defend you." Her eyes are trained on mine, and the subtext of this conversation feels important.

"I couldn't have someone I care about hurt my dad," I tell her. "Like I said, I just want to get away."

She nods. "I know you do. But until you can, it doesn't hurt to have someone around. You know… in case."

I'm all too familiar with "*in case.*"

WE'RE JUST twenty minutes from the bell ringing, and the students are thoroughly engrossed in their assigned chapter in *Indian in the Cupboard*. Gosh I love that book. Today has gone way better than I expected. Yeah, I got asked what happened, but no one pushed, and Sasha went above and beyond to make me feel good.

Before our lunch was over, Mr. Mathews, the sixth grade teaching favorite, graciously offered to give me a ride to my house to get my car–so I could get home from work. Since Sasha lives next to the school, and rides a bike everywhere else, she couldn't. And I'm a bit too old for riding the handlebars.

All in all, I feel good about the day.

And then Mr. Wheeler pulls open my classroom door, right as I'm having the kids organize their desks for tomorrow morning's lesson. When the students are stirring, he's bolder. I pull my chair out and busy myself with my desk drawer, creating a barrier between us.

When his shoes drift by my desk and his shadow looms over me, I look up. Mr. Wheeler's lips twitch, his beady eyes narrow in on my face before he tips his head to the side.

"Turn into quite the *rough girl* in the evening, huh?"

Though I'm still crouching there, I feel a part of myself float away. It doesn't have to be a hand on my ass to make me feel intensely uncomfortable.

"I fell." The words slip out, feather light.

"What?" he leans forward, and it's all I need to scramble to my feet and move around the other side of the desk.

"I fell. I'm not a rough girl in the evening." I repeat his disgusting insinuation back to him, and he just nods like he and I are in on some secret together. Just us.

"Right, okay, Miss Carlisle," he says with a grin that makes my skin crawl.

He knocks on my desk–his annoying trademark good-bye–and makes his way out of the classroom. After the kids are dismissed, I tell Sasha I'm going home. She asks me to promise on my life and Henry Cavill's life (we do not swear or promise against our man HC) that I'll call her when I get home and stay on the phone with her until I get into my room and lock the door.

I told her I'd compromise and call her once I was in my room with the door locked. Though when I promised it, I knew I'd only text, because calling felt a little too dramatic. A text would be just fine, and I know it will satisfy her.

I stop off at the drug store near my house, grabbing a new notebook. I guess dad and Rose have some big plans for my notebook so whatever. Let them have it. Let them read about how awful they are, and get mad at me for being honest. It's no different than real life.

I chose a green notebook this time. They were always black before.

When I get home, my mom tries to talk to me, but Rose and dad are still gone. I could talk to her–but last night was eye-opening. Truly.

What does it matter what she says when she isn't on my side? I ignored her, grabbed a few of my items from the refrigerator, got my stuff, and went to my room. I locked the door, however much protection that provided.

The first thing I did was sit down at my desk, flip open a new notebook, and start writing.

As it turns out, fighting back just isn't that gratifying.

Chapter Fourteen

DONOVAN

A tie can be a gag, too.

I'm off today. I should sleep in. I should take my car to get detailed. Resod that part of my lawn that died last winter.

But more important than any of that is seeing Violet.

Her girls' night thing is still throwing me off. Three months ago, Sasha and Violet went to this painting class and drank wine, but that was the only time I'd really seen my girl drink or partake in girls' night.

I didn't go by the school or stake out Sasha's this morning—Paradise was getting new squat racks, and Bran needed someone there with him for the delivery. And since I'm already cutting back on my Violet binges, I convinced myself it would be okay to just drive by the school and see her leave her classroom. That seeing her once today—not including the camera feed—would be okay.

I've been irritable all day.

The equipment delivery was running late, so of course I decided to read those fuckers the riot act. I went for a run–I don't even fucking like cardio–and while catching my breath on the pier, I watched some twenty-something prick throw a soda can over the railing. Who the fuck still litters? I mean, seriously?

I don't like to attack spur-of-the-moment. It's not my style. And I usually watch my surroundings for a while before I pounce, too. But this tapering–shit, it's not easy. This must be what junkies feel like when they fucking detox. I can't cut back on Violet *and* my hobby.

I followed the *litterer* four blocks down the pier, into a parking lot behind a shipping center. He headed toward an old Honda, and that's when I pressed my knee into his tailbone and held his wrists behind his back.

I didn't give him my normal spiel, and I definitely didn't bother taking his money, either. Instead, I held him against the car and told him that if he littered in Willowdale again, I'd find him, cut all but two of his fingers off and put a gun to his head and force him to use his two remaining fingers to pick up all the garbage on the pier.

I didn't hurt him, though, and when I released him, he didn't even try to see my face. He just stood there, breathing loud and making promises.

On my jog back home, I feel a bit more settled. Getting my hands on that fucker on the pier took away some of my immediate jitters. Now my irritation is turning to excitement because the bell is going to ring in one hour, which means I get to see my girl.

I only got to see the back of her fucking head yesterday, and that doesn't sit right with me.

After trimming my beard, I take a long, hot shower,

letting the water release some of the tension from my shoulders and traps. The stress of last night is tight in my neck, and honestly, I don't think it will go away until I see her.

I've been working on a way to meet her–I have. I know the more obsessed I get, the scarier I become, and I don't want that. I don't want to be like this. I want to have her in the daylight, in my arms.

I don't want to lurk and watch.

The best I've come up with is letting the air from her tires then, after school, *happen* to be driving through when I spot her at the same time she's spotting her flat.

Lame, I know, but Mally could back me up. I could say we patrol the area frequently and whatnot.

I know–my plan needs work. Like, requires a scaffolding type of work. But at least I'm actually working towards it. I hate that I'm learning more about my girl through her notebook–I don't want the most intimate of details to be learned dishonestly, but I'm desperate. The idea that she'd turn me away–I can't fucking stomach it.

She has to want me, and the way I see it, understanding her is the best way to get her. That means–guilty as fuck or not–I've read the notebook.

Cover to cover. I've run my fingers over the bubbled-up ink; I've held the paper to my nose and inhaled, hoping to suck up some of her scent.

I've read a lot of things, but surprisingly, I still don't know what happened to her arm that night six months ago. I still don't know why she's always in her room at home. I have no better understanding of her family life.

The notebook seems to focus on her goals and dreams, and it makes me realize if that's what is in here and that's what she's always writing, she's probably leaving those dreams on those lined pages.

And why would that be?

What would have a smart, responsible, beautiful woman in her mid-twenties journaling dreams only to stack them in a closet and forget them? Why isn't she going after them instead of writing them?

I'm learning about her, but it still feels like there's so much I don't know.

With just twenty minutes to the bell, I sit in my SUV in the parking lot parked several cars back. It's the closest I've gotten, but I feel like I need to be closer to her today. I can't explain it. It's not me getting bold because I'm going crazy. It's just that I need to be closer to her.

I survey the parking lot of cars, wondering how she got her car here when it was at her parents' house last night? The girls' night feels more and more off, but I can't figure out what's what. The car doesn't have new tires; there's no service tag taped inside the windshield—no signs that it was at a shop or impound or anything. Fuck I don't know.

But I'm temporarily relieved from wondering because the bell rings.

Floods of kids come pouring out of classrooms, running along the grass with too-big backpacks shaking behind them. They climb into cars, wave wildly at other children, drop things, trip, high-five... and after ten minutes, the school is completely silent again. Everyone is gone—there aren't even any stragglers.

That's when the teachers start coming out.

Some look happy, chatting actively as they trail to their cars. Others look like they're walking away from doing battle, bags under their eyes with shirts partially untucked. Teaching is a confusing career.

Sasha waves to a male teacher who looks a lot like Mister Rogers. When she wanders down off towards the dodgeball courts, I know she's taking the shortcut off campus to her house. And she's alone.

Which means Violet should be alone.

And she is.

"Holy fuck, baby," I hear myself saying when my eyes land on my girl.

Her silky blonde hair, which she normally wears down, falling well past the ends of her luscious tits–is up in a bun. A few wispy pieces frame her face, which is currently turned away from me as she chats with another teacher.

The slender curve of her delicate neck makes me touch myself through my jeans. I'm hard and aching for her–as if that's not normal. But holy shit. I want to bite into that milky flesh and taste her sweetness.

Her tits bounce beneath her silk blouse, and I leak a little when I see those perfect nubs harden with the breeze. I know what those tits look like naked. Those tits are going to be mine one day. My offspring is going to fucking *feed* off those tits.

I grind the butt of my palm into my cock, and groan in the privacy of my SUV. She's so goddamn beautiful. I don't even understand how she's single, honestly–and living at home like... such a *good girl*.

Fuck me.

I'm shoving a hand through my hair, dragging my nails against my scalp, choking on the groan of arousal and frustration that's fucking clawing its way up my throat when—

The entire world falls away around me.

Literally, everything around me goes blurry *but* her.

She's facing forward now, the other teacher in their car. She's approaching hers, only about twenty feet away now, but that's when I *see* her.

Her face.

Her beautiful face.

The one that makes me want to quit my bullshit and be a good man. The one that I would sell my soul for to make her happy. The one that brings me to my knees. The one that makes me stalk. The one that makes me blow in my sheets, and install fucking cameras in a private residence assuming someone else's identity.

The one that makes me risk it all.

Bruised and fucking swollen.

Bruised.

And.

Fucking.

Swollen.

My vision tunnels further, existence around me going completely black. Her face–trampled and inflamed. Her beautiful, perfect face.

My girl's face. *My future wife's face.*

Something happened to her. Someone hurt her. Something is fucking wrong. Something is going on. I can't just follow her down to her street and watch her on a screen. Someone fucking hurt her. I can't stand by. I just fucking can't.

In a split second I decide I'll revert back to my plan from the day in the closet.

It's not perfect. It's not ideal. Fucking *fuck!* It's not even close. But what am I supposed to do? Fucking sit here with my thumb up my ass and let her potentially go back to a bad situation? I have no idea what happened therefore I trust nothing and no one when it comes to her.

From under the seat, I grab my cuffs and a black necktie. I actually keep the tie in here in case I have to show up randomly at court, and I have a suit jacket at the station.

But a tie can be a gag, too.

This is the only way I can make sure she's safe. And she has to be safe.

My feet are quieter than a whisper as they trudge along the asphalt. She doesn't look at me until we're nearly toe-to-toe because she walks with her beautiful head tipped down.

That's something I'm going to change.

I grab her quickly, so fast that she doesn't even have the chance to make a sound. I've got her cuffed and gagged in just moments and in the back seat of my SUV just as quick.

It's true how it's always recounted; it always happens so fast.

She struggles against my hands, which pin her into one of the captain's seats by the shoulders. I hold her until she's out of fight, which only takes a minute. Her shoulders droop with fatigue, and I fucking hate that I'm scaring her right now. But I'll make it right. And this is for her own good.

She *will* see.

Violet with the emerald eyes.

I keep my eyes tamped down on hers until she lets herself look at me. When she finally does, my chest catches fire. Those green eyes are even more brilliant and complicated than I imagined. Shades of moss and lilies, ombreing towards the pupil. Her lashes are thick and dark, and *god,* she smells good. Like sunscreen, with chapstick, and vanilla. The groin of my jeans tightens uncomfortably. I crouch down in front of her on my haunches.

I keep her cuffed because I have to, but I take my hands from her shoulders and carefully pull the seatbelt across her chest. I do not let any part of my knuckle touch her body. I clip her in and find her eyes again.

For some reason, I don't think she's looked away from me yet.

Her chest is rising and falling quickly. I know she's worried, possibly even terrified. I didn't plan this, and while it makes the most sense to get the fuck out of here as soon as possible, I can't drive her away from here with her thinking she's about to get ax murdered.

I put my palm on her knee, and her bare skin is like velvet against my hand. It takes a lot of goddamn strength not to slide it further up and sink my fingertips into her inner thighs.

I don't, though. I give her knee one single squeeze before I take my hand away. I smooth some of her stray hairs back into her bun.

"I'm not going to hurt you," I say, hating how fucking bad that sounds because isn't that how every creepy kidnapper starts his sentence? But it's true. "Do you need anything out of your car? Purse or anything?"

She blinks, and a tear slips through those seductive eyelashes.

"Do you need anything?" I look out the window to where we just were and see her purse lying there, strap broken. I don't remember doing that, but of course, it was me.

"I'll get your purse, okay?"

She doesn't move; she doesn't blink. She swallows, and her chest bobs heavily. My girl is terrified. Fuck! This was a bad fucking idea.

But then I look at her eye– rich purple, swollen and tender.

I *had* to take her. I couldn't risk someone hurting her again.

I get her purse as I promised and put it on the passenger seat up front, next to me. I drive us to my house, keeping my music off and all the windows up. The car is quiet, but I can feel her gentle, panicked sobs piercing me as I watch her in the rearview mirror.

Red-rimmed eyes, those beautiful shoulders slouched in defeat. Those fucking marks on her face. My blood boils, and just thinking about someone hurting her sends me into a silent rage. By the time we reach my house, I'm glad I took her. I have no doubts.

I cannot let my girl be out there with some fucking psycho that will hurt her.

I *had* to do this.

When the garage door closes, I go right to her door and yank it open. Twisting her in her seat I slip the key in the cuffs and release her wrists. She brings them to her lap, taking turns on cradling a wrist with her hand.

I reach behind her head with both of my hands and release the black silk tie. I tug it away from her gently and drop it to the floorboard. She exhales, lurching forward a bit but stopping herself so that our spaces don't collide.

I wish they would collide.

I cup my palm to her cheek, and she doesn't shirk away from it. Her eyes stay trained on mine, intense and wide. Smoothing my thumb over her bottom lip, I move my hand up her face, gently brushing over the swollen and bruised skin. I hold her face in my hand, my thumb stroking her cheek as I focus my eyes intently on hers. Her pupils are full moons of darkness.

"Who the fuck did this to you?"

A tear slips down her cheek, colliding with my skin. A flutter moves through my chest, and I bring her tear to my mouth and kiss it from my skin. She shudders, then blinks a few times, catching her breath.

"I'm not gonna hurt you, baby. Okay? But I gotta fuckin' know. Who the fuck did this to you?"

Her lips part, and for a second I think she's going to say something. *Fucking please say something.* Then her eyes flutter closed, and her body goes limp in the leather seat.

Chapter Fifteen

DONOVAN

Try again.

I know I can't put her in my bed, so I lay her down on the couch, propping her head up with a few pillows. As soon as I do, her eyelids flutter, and she awakens.

Startled, she jerks back against the couch; one palm pressed to her breasts, the other braced against the seat.

She still hasn't spoken.

"Who hurt you, Violet?" I ask, and god, my cock goes to steel saying her name aloud like this, so casually... *to* her. This isn't how I wanted us to meet, but now that I've met her, I really don't care. I'm so fucking hard being next to her.

"Wh, why do you care?" she asks, her bottom lip trembling. I sit next to her on the couch, giving her a comforting one-cushion buffer.

I raise my palms in a safe surrender. I need her to trust me.

"I need to know who's hurting my girl." I take a pause, and scratch at the side of my beard, trying to work out the best way to put this. "One day you will be mine, and no one fucks with what's mine."

Her pupils dwindle, their mass draining away to mere points. Her pink lips fall apart and her tongue darts across her bottom lip.

"You, your girl?" she stutters again, those intricate green eyes wide with surprise.

I can't stop staring at her lips. They're so perfect. Ripe. Ready to be taken with my mouth. Ready to slide down the veiny length of my cock. To slide up the seam of my ass. Because my girl gets dirty, and isn't shy.

She licks her bottom lip again, and my cock leaks a little more in my briefs. My chest is twisting with... fucking... pleasure.

"You kidnapped me," she says finally, her bottom lip trembling, this time more in shock than fear. Her brilliant eyes are wide, thick lashes guiding every blink.

"I saved you."

She stumbles through an exhale. "You saved me?"

I nod. "I saved you." Then I volley my head between my shoulders because I always told myself I'd be honest with Violet. We'd be honest with each other. "We saved each other."

She licks her lips and swallows. "How did *I* save *you*?"

I like that she asked that question. I can't help but smile at her. She doesn't smile back, and that's okay.

"Knowing someone hurt you, if I had to let you go and be out there alone," I shake my head, slice a hand through the air. "Fuck. I wouldn't have made it even an hour. I didn't make it a full minute from the time you turned your head, and I saw."

"You saw?"

I lift a curled knuckle. "Your face."

She cups her hand to her face, fingering it softly, stifling a wince. But I can see it in the way her lips just barely twitch. It hurts.

"I would've gone crazy, so taking you saved me from that."

She swallows again, and then... she slowly nods twice. "Okay."

"I'm not crazy," I say, then immediately feel the need to clarify. "I am passionate about things when I care. There is a difference."

She loses control, and her lips twitch, then tremble. Biting the corner of her mouth, she pushes out a slow, intentional exhale.

"Who did that to you, Violet?" I ask again because the original question is still the most important one right now.

"I fell."

I slam my curled fists into the table near the couch. Her body lurches forward in reaction. She whimpers gently.

"Try again."

Chapter Sixteen

VIOLET

I want more of you... more than I've ever wanted anything.

Oh my god. *Ohmygod.*
 I got kidnapped.
 I was kidnapped.
 I *am* kidnapped.
 Wait, no, I'm not a kid. I wasn't kidnapped. Stolen? Taken? *Abducted.*
 But the man who took me carefully put me in the back seat of his Tesla. And then he made sure not to touch me, and he went back and got my purse.
 He held my face. His skin sizzled against mine. I felt him between my thighs when his dark eyes overtook mine.
 This man abducted me.
 And he could be crazy because he said I'm his girl and one day I'll be his, and that's... well, that's absolutely freaking

crazy. He doesn't even know me! But he knew my name. And he was watching me.

He said I saved him. If he didn't take me, just wondering who hurt me would have made him do bad things.

His admissions put goosebumps over my skin. It made my nipples hard.

It freaked me out. And the fact that it freaked me out for all the wrong reasons only further freaked me out.

This man is a work of art.

Chiseled cheekbones with a strong nose, commanding dark eyes sit behind black glasses. He has a beard, trimmed short and neat. His hair falls into a hipster category, shaved in a clean fade up the sides, falling into a tight part until a wave of dark hair topples over the other side. Ink up both arms, muscle writhing under the ornamented skin. He's muscular every-where–his chest, even his neck is thick. My mouth tingles a little, looking at the striations of muscle running up his throat.

Then I spot his Adam's apple, thick and heavy, dipping below his collar as he swallows.

I'm *attracted* to this man. This *stranger*. This man who took me *without my permission* and brought me to *his* home. In *handcuffs*. Real ones, too, I think.

Something about this man makes all of my nerve endings scream, *yes, yes, yes!* But I know it's rationally, completely, and utterly freaking *wrong*.

I don't want to be here. I need to try and get away.

I force myself to repeat that. *I need to get away. This man abducted me. I need to get the freak out of here!*

"I want to leave," I say, my voice wavering.

"You don't sound sure," he says, his temperament even keel.

"I, I want to leave. I don't want to be here." I swallow, and only look him in the eyes for a second before they go back to my feet and the floor. I can't look at him. My head is confused from the other night, still sore, and maybe concussed. Too much emotion after everything with my family.

I am *not* attracted to a man who freaking *kidnapped* me.

No way.

He nods, smoothing his wide hands down his solid thighs. "Okay, how about this? You can leave under three reasonable conditions."

I can't believe I ask. "What are the conditions?" It's my right to leave, but for some reason, saying that doesn't seem important or pressing.

"You let me feed you."

I blink. Then blink again. "Feed me."

He nods, and remains expressionless as I try to figure out what... or *why* he's saying that.

He scoots closer to me on the sofa. Close enough to feel his warm breath against my lips as he whispers, "I know you eat ramen alone every night." His thumb travels the line of my jaw, ending under my chin. "I want to feed you good food. I want you to eat more."

A chill breaks out over my skin, and my thighs draw together.

What is wrong with me? What does it say about me psychologically that I want this man, *who abducted me,* to feed me? Taking in his expansive chest, pecs bubbling with muscle, and his arms, braced against his legs by the palm, are mountainous and large. His discipline and dedication to his physique comes across as intense, which... well, fits, considering.

But I like intense. Sitting near him makes my pussy clench in appreciation.

"What are the other two?"

He smiles, and I feel it between my thighs, warm and wet. He nudges his glasses up with a thick, curled knuckle, and I gush a little, I swear I do.

"You sleep. At least eight hours."

My heart skitters. My forehead feels misty. "I sleep," I defend, but why? He doesn't know *how* I sleep. Wait. He knows what I eat for dinner.

He knows what I eat for dinner.

"You toss and turn. I don't like that. I want you to rest. You work hard in that classroom, you need your rest."

My mind temporarily freezes. Goes on hiatus. I just sit there, mouth agape, staring at this orgasm in the flesh, this hunk of a man, saying all of these incredibly romantic and exceptionally creepy things.

He knows I don't sleep well. He knows what I eat for dinner. He... watches me.

And yet, my body magnetizes to him in a way that is really hard to refuse.

But he's... a stalker, I think.

I have a stalker?

I have a stalker.

And it's freaking *this guy*?

"Say last one," I stammer, my mouth dry and sticky. "My mouth is dry," I say, pressing my hand to my throat. "What's the last one?"

He lifts a bottle of water from the side of the couch and twists the lid off before handing it to me. I sip and feel relief right away. "Thanks."

He just stares at me, the espresso of his eyes so intense.

107

"You talk to me for an entire hour, and answer every question that I ask."

I arch a brow. "Why would I do that?"

He leans forward, and rather than intimidate me; he rests his palm on my knee the way he did in the car.

Squeeze, release.

"Because I'm desperate for you. It's making me crazy to see you hurt." He shakes his head, strands of dark hair slipping over his glasses. With his palm, he smooths it back, nudging his glasses up.

"This isn't how I wanted us to meet. But once I saw you were hurt, I couldn't wait a minute longer. So..." he smiles, and it's timid like he's looking to me for reassurance. Utter psychos don't need reassurance. "I want you to talk to me for an hour. You have no reason to do it, but I want it. I want more of you, Violet, more than I've ever wanted anything."

"Can I just leave without those things?" I ask, rolling my lips together. As if the setting is growing comfortable, my eyes leave him and move around the room. Gray walls, white molding tracing the rooms along the ceiling and floor, oversized Edison lights hanging over a long bar, the kitchen made of exposed white cabinets and swirled blacks and whites in the marble counters. I look down to my thighs, resting on a large, overstuffed sage couch. This room is a variation of green hues, mixed with creams and grays. It's a man's home but... nice.

Really nice.

"Tell me," he says, snapping me out of my investigation of his home. I mean, I'm guessing it's his home. It smells like his car; cedary but lemony, notes of spice barely perceptible. He smells like I want to bury my face in his chest and inhale him until my lungs can't hold a single molecule more. "That you don't need those three things. And if you can look me in the eyes and tell me honestly that you don't, then you can go."

I laugh a small, humorless laugh. "You'll just let me go. Walk out of here in broad daylight?"

He leans back over the couch, peering off to something in the distance behind me before bringing his mysterious eyes back down to me. "Not really daylight, and I definitely wouldn't let you walk in the dark to your house. But yes, I would drive you home and let you go. Free and safe."

He looks like he wants to touch me or say something, his hands fidgeting along his thighs as he chews the corner of his mouth. "Fuck, I really didn't want us to meet this way."

"With you abducting me?" I ask because I am so freaking confused right now, I don't know what to say or do. I'm *terrified* that I'm *not* absolutely terrified of this man. What's wrong with me?

He gives me a sad smile, and it makes me feel... strange. Like I want to hear his worries, and give him a reason to really smile.

"Now, can you tell me you don't need a good meal, a good night of sleep, and good conversation?" He stands, outstretching his mitt to me as he awaits my response. I study his calloused palm before slipping my hand into his. The callouses abrade my soft skin, igniting a spark between my legs.

He walks me into the kitchen, and then he's grabbing my hips, sitting me on the countertop. My legs swing childlike since they don't reach the floor. I've never been handled by a man or any boyfriend in the past. Being tossed onto the countertop is, *I'm learning*, quite the aphrodisiac.

In his fitted black t-shirt and fitted black jeans, I watch this man move seamlessly through his kitchen for a minute before a spread of ingredients appear on the counter. The ignitor clicks as he turns the burner on and smothers the flame with a pan.

"So, I can make you fried bologna, sweet pickles, and tabasco on wheat bread, but I can also make tacos."

At first, my pulse rockets at the mention of my favorite lunch. Because at first, I think he likes that, too. But then I remember… he's my stalker.

I still cannot believe I have a stalker.

Me. Violet Carlisle.

Not Rose Carlisle. Not Sasha, the goddess that she is. But me. Writes in a diary, lives with her parents, me.

I should hate it. I should at least dislike it.

But I don't hate him or dislike him. In fact…

"Tacos," I reply, forcing my stupid brain to stay on track. I'm sure at some point every woman who was moments away from being murdered by a man thought, *hey, this guy isn't so bad. Maybe I finally found the one.* Then whack. An ax to the head or rope around the throat or… whatever it is.

He nods, and returns the bologna, tabasco, pickles, wheat bread, and butter to the fridge. The layout of the kitchen allows him to talk to me as he cooks; breaking up ground meat in a skillet with a kitchen tool I've never seen before.

"So," he says, glancing at me through the steam rising from the cooking meat. "Let's talk. I'll start. Who did that to you?" The black in his glasses frames matches the intensity in his eyes, and the cimmerian hue of his hair. He screams *broody and dark* but the tenderness with which he stroked my lip and uncuffed my wrists… he *cares.* I can feel it.

I swallow hard, because… I want to tell him who hurt me.

Chapter Seventeen

DONOVAN

Are you scared of me, Violet?

For as much as I've thought about Violet, for as much as I've followed and watched her, the one thing I never really did was wonder what we'd be like together. Wonder what she'd be like in person, right in front of me.

I'm glad I didn't.

Because everything we're building now is organic. And that's what we need. A connection beyond my one-sided knowledge.

"Are you crazy?" she blurts out as I chop bell peppers and jalapenos. Her green eyes flit between the knife and my eyes.

I place the knife on its side, on the cutting board, and twist my fingers in the dish towel that's hanging from the waistband of my jeans. Bracing myself against the counter, I lean forward and push out a breath.

"Here's why I think the answer is no," I start, and I

fucking love that a tiny little smile twists her lips at my response. My heart slams into my ribs in jolted beats. Beats that tell me... there's hope.

"I know that following someone isn't right. I mean, I'm a cop." I push off the counter, and weave my fingers together behind my head, elbows out. "I think because I deal with actual crazy people, I can safely say I'm not crazy."

Her lips waver only slightly, maintaining their straight line of indifference. Her eyes are wide but not in fear, more like curiosity.

"Here's why." I hold one hand out to the side of me, the other out to the other side. "A crazy person," I lift one hand, "doesn't think anything they're doing is crazy." I wiggle the hand that represents me. "And a *not crazy* person doing questionable things knows those things they are doing are questionable, but does them anyway. Not because they're crazy but because they're passionate."

She swallows, and moves to tuck her hair behind her ear, forgetting it's up in a bun. My eyes go to the slope of her bare neck, and my lips burn to press against her. "And you're the *not crazy but passionate* hand?"

I wave with the hand that represents me, and she smiles.

She smiles. My chest tightens, my dick comes alive, and my entire night has meaning now.

"Does that answer your question?" I ask, returning to the cutting board where I scoop up the diced veggies and toss them into a bowl. I start on the avocados, slicing, de-pitting, and scooping out the meat. "You like guacamole?"

Her green eyes hold mine for a minute before she nods. "Yeah, I really do."

"I didn't know that," I admit, but I don't know if she knows it's an admission. Because I really don't know how much she really understands about me. About me when it comes to *her*.

Then, before I can shape or guide the conversation, she blurts out, "how long have you been watching me?"

Smashing the avocados, my eyes go between her and the dip. "Over a year."

I thought coming clean would be terrifying; I thought she'd try to flee immediately –I figured it would push her away, and make me lose my mind.

But coming clean to her feels good. Relieving almost. I don't have to sneak around anymore. I don't have to look and wish. It's over. All the waiting and watching is over.

And she doesn't seem terrified at all.

"Why?"

Why? This is one question I never considered her asking. She is the proud owner of at least four mirrors that I know of, so clearly, she's aware of the answer.

"Seriously?" I ask, tossing the finely diced tomatoes into the guacamole mixture.

She bites into her bottom lip self-consciously. "Why did you *stalk me* for a year?"

"I wish I could give you an easy answer, like I'm crazy and that's what I do," I admit. "But I'm not crazy. And I don't know what made me think I should follow you, but... the first night I saw you, you were at the park off G Street, at the movie night."

She nods with recognition immediately, and I know it's because she doesn't go there often– of course she remembers.

"You were there?" She questions, because after the recognition fades, confusion takes over. "I didn't see you."

"I didn't want to be seen."

"What does that mean?" She narrows her eyes as she asks. I like that she isn't chewing her lip, and keeping her questions inside. She can be shy and timid with the rest of the world, but she's blooming for me. And my hope blooms a bit more, too.

Fucking listen to me. Blooming hope.

Not wanting to detour when we haven't even attempted the main road, I shake my head, and steer us back. I'll tell her about my hobby. But *later*. After she knows the more important shit.

"I was walking up the path, leaving. I saw your eyes. They were the most unforgettable shade of green. You mouthed 'I'm sorry' because you bumped into me. Your dad was dragging you by the elbow, and he was talking shit to you."

I'll never forget those motherfucker's words. *They don't give a shit about you, so tell me why people who don't fucking care about you are more important than your father?*

My attention goes from the cooked meat straight to her face, studying the bruised eye socket. It hits me. It hits me right then the way he *clearly* hit her. "It was him, wasn't it?" I drop the spoon which is currently loaded full of meat. Crumbles of crisp ground beef topple to the counter and floor as I rush around to her side of the bar, and spin her seat to face me.

Her bottom lip trembles, and her eyes well. She doesn't answer. I close the sliver of distance between us with just one step, and wrap my arms around her. She remains seated because I'm that close to her, but doesn't jerk away when I press her cheek to my chest in a tight hug.

Then I feel her arms— *she's hugging me back*. Her nails barely press into me, and heat surges through my cock. I shake away the image of her nails digging into the bare flesh of my back while I pound that pretty pink pussy of hers.

But right now, she's falling into me, letting me see her broken, giving me all her shattered pieces with trust. I smooth my hands up and down her back as her sobs wrack deeper and deeper, hampered by the wall of chest her face is pressed into.

Her tears soak my shirt, and I hate that she's crying, but I fucking love that I'm the one absorbing her tears. I'll always be that man, I will never be the man who causes them.

I give her endless time, just holding her, smoothing my hands up and down her back. She moves her grip from behind me to my chest, where she clings to my shirt before finally pulling back.

The tip of her nose is red, and her eyes are puffy with fatigue. Some of her blonde hair has broken free from her bun around the crown of her face. The green of her eyes shimmer under the low light of the bar pendant.

My breath catches.

She's gorgeous. She's perfect. She's mine.

"I can't believe any of this," she says, bringing her fingertips to her temples, massaging. Back at the stove, I clean up the spilled meat, and wash my hands, taking *very* deep breaths.

I'm not going to fucking trip out about this information right now. Nope. I'm not. Because that isn't what's best for Violet.

I even lower my mouth to the sink and take a drink of water like a heated fucking dog.

Once I feel cool enough to face her, I turn and begin assembling tacos. "How do you like yours?" I ask, lifting a soft flour tortilla in one hand and a folded crunchy in the other.

She winces a little. "Crunchy, what kind of monster wants a chewy, pliable, soft taco?"

The anger that I thought I'd not be able to control seems to melt away, as I find myself grinning at her. "Same."

I point to the pinto beans and then the black beans.

"Black," she says. "I just casually told you, the man who abducted me, that I'd prefer black beans in my taco. Oh, and my captor is making me tacos." She shakes her head, eyes glued to me, palms pressed to her cheeks now. "What the freak?"

Language, idioms, phrases, slang, expressions—all things you can't know from watching. The heat in my chest grows wider, swallowing more of my simmering anger, as I realize my girl doesn't curse.

I don't mind a dirty mouth on the right girl, but it's so fitting on Violet, my wholesome third grade teacher. My lips twitch with satisfaction, but she's still just shaking her head in a daze.

"Hey," I say gently, and the shock in her eyes begins to wane. "I did take you, yes, but I'm not a captor. I'm not a fucking kidnapper." I lean down over the food, bringing my face close to hers over the bar. "I couldn't let you go back to him after he hurt you."

She touches her eye, and I pull back and begin making her taco.

"Lettuce," she nods as my hand hovers above the glass containers of assorted toppings. "Cheese," she agrees when I come to the shreds. "Guac," she says, and I scoop her a hefty amount onto all three tacos I'm making for her. She says yes to the remaining garnishes–cilantro, onion, homemade salsa, and fresh lime juice.

When I pass the plate to her, she makes eye contact with me as she thanks me for the meal. But she doesn't dig in. She waits, watching me make mine.

I scoop both black and pinto beans into the shells first.

"Why do you eat both kinds?"

My lips twitch with an unexpected smile. She's asking *about* me. I'm doing an endzone dance in my head because women only ask about shit when they care. This much I know from Batman's wife. If a woman asks about something it's because it's important.

"If I do just black beans," I press a palm to my lower stomach, and I take pleasure from her eyes going there. I like that she sucks in a little extra breath as her eyes briefly move over my groin, before going back to my hand. "They fuck up my stomach. I can hear everything digesting for like, three hours."

She wrinkles her nose. "I hate that. I know what you mean. My stomach does that with oatmeal. A bowl, I'm okay. But if I have oat milk in my latte, too–I'm digesting like a freaking loud speaker." She swallows, and shifts in her chair, her hands smoothing nervously around the edges of the dinner plate of tacos. "I just told my stalker *slash* captor that too many oat products give me IBS." She shakes her head as her eyes fall to the tacos. "*Oh my god.*"

"Hey," I say softly, which brings her gaze up to me so slowly and beautifully that my heart actually twitches a little. I keep my voice low and romantic when I say, "you didn't say IBS. You just said digested really fucking loud."

She stares at me a moment before bursting out into laughter, and I join in. See? This is how I knew it would be with my girl. Natural, seamless. We're meant to be together, that's why.

I continue assembling my tacos, and to my delight and surprise, she keeps asking about my choices. "You don't like cheese?" she asks when I bypass the glass dish of shredded cheese. "I do," I say, adding a healthy topping of lettuce, "but I like it after the lettuce. I don't like it to be melted and if I put it on the beans, it melts."

She nods then looks at her plate then back to me, any traces of playfulness or ease now completely drained from her face.

Her voice is a whisper when she speaks, even though we're inside and alone. "How did you know what I eat?"

I finish assembling my fifth taco, and then take a seat next to her, leaving an empty barstool between us. "I'm going to tell you everything, Violet, and I'm not going to hold anything back. Because..." I rake a hand up the back of my head, then pull my glasses off and pinch the bridge of my nose.

There's no going back from this now.

Pushing out a breath, I swivel a few degrees on the barstool to face her. She's done the same, and is facing me. If I was one seat closer, our knees would touch.

"I really do think you're meant for me. I really do believe that if you give us a chance, you could love me, too."

Her lips move but she isn't really speaking. Just sort of mumbling.

I can't have her spinning out, so I cut off her train of thought right at the knees. "Let's eat and... I'll tell you everything you want to know."

"How will I know you're telling the truth?" she asks, a

tremble to her bottom lip. I can't help myself, I reach across and smooth my thumb over her lip.

"Because the answers will scare you." I stroke her lip again before returning to my side. I have to move slowly with Violet, and touching is too fast. "But you'll know they're the truth. Because they won't make me look good."

After a moment, she nods then turns reluctantly to her plate of tacos. "Before we eat, I need to text my friend Sasha." She stares at the food, but it gives her no answers, because she sighs. Barely looking at me, she adds "you can read the message as I write it."

My nerves burn through my shoulders and neck. "That's alright." I get up, grabbing her bag for her. She taps, but I don't watch, and then it's over and she willingly gives her focus back to me.

She lifts it to her mouth but pauses, twisting her neck to look at me as she holds the food steady. "Why me?"

I nod to her food. "Take a bite. I need to see you eat."

Immediately she does, and the way her eyes roll closed makes my balls tingle. She crunches and chews, and I begin.

"Like I said, at first, it was just… your eyes. I'd never felt something from *eyes*." I take a bite of my taco, chew and swallow. "Usually, it takes big tits or even a few times hanging out for me to *really* notice a woman. I've never been big into dating." I take a drink of the La Croixs I've set out for both of us while I made the food.

"But your eyes, I don't know. I just wanted more."

"Did you follow me home that night at the park?" she asks, her mouth staying open.

"Yes."

She nods, and enjoys another few bites before asking

another question. "Then you just started following me everywhere?"

"Yeah, because when you went inside your house that night, I was worse off. I wanted more of you, you were—you *are*—all I can think about." We eat in quiet for another few minutes, and internally my panic begins to build. These confessions—while I think romantic—can be viewed as absolutely fucking crazy.

Now I ask a question. "How weirded out are you?" I force myself to look at her, but it's hard because I'm fucking terrified. I don't want to see her let me down easy, say *not that much* but see the fear in her eyes. I don't want to make her lie or panic, so I'm about to rescind the question when she answers.

"I think something may be wrong with me."

I rest my remaining taco on the plate and clean my fingers on the napkin as I turn to her. "Are you okay? Are you feeling okay?"

She waves her hand near her plate. "No, not like that. I mean..." she rubs her lips together then looks at me, cheeks pink. "I should be really, really scared. But—and this is where I start to get terrified..." Her lips draw together, and she swallows, her brilliant green eyes idling on mine in a way that makes all the blood rush to my cock and my scalp tingle. "I feel so comfortable here." She looks around the kitchen and back to the living room, where she sat on the sofa. "And you're here. You brought me here. So that must mean that subconsciously, I'm comfortable around *you*."

"What about the conscious Violet? What does conscious Violet feel around me?"

She shakes her head. "I don't even know who '*me*' is."

"I know, and I'm sorry. I want you to know me. I wanted

to meet you. I told myself that night that I wasn't going to follow you." I jump to the barstool next to hers, and dip my head to meet her eyes, which have nervously veered to the counter.

"I've never followed or stalked anyone. I've never treated a woman or girlfriend badly. I'm not a dangerous person. But when I started to follow you I just... I got addicted. I wanted more of you, and the more I followed you, the more I thought... you're so perfect. I can't just walk up to a woman like you and date you. You're out of my league. So I just... I kept watching you, and I knew it was wrong but I promised myself one day, I'd meet you and come clean... if you gave me the chance."

She presses her hand to her chest. "I'm out of your league?" Her eyes move over my bicep, transverse over my shoulders and then to my beard. My lips. My frames. My eyes.

"I'm not even in a league," she whispers, still just gazing into my eyes.

I rest my hand on her knee, even though I said I wouldn't touch her. I give her a squeeze, and goosebumps break out along her neck as I do. I think I hear a little sigh or... whimper, too.

"See, that's another thing I'm realizing having you here." I swallow, the anger resurfacing at the remembrance of her father. "If I would have known you weren't getting treated right... Baby, I would've taken you ages ago."

I squeeze her knee again before releasing it.

"You're in a league of your own; you're so fucking beautiful."

Her mouth falls open, her tongue swiping over her

bottom lip. I face forward and finish my LaCroix, but feel her eyes searing into me.

"I can't believe this is real." Her voice is quiet, and when I wipe my mouth and turn back to face her, I find her staring forward.

"I know it's... weird. It's definitely not cool that I've been following you, and that I kind of... well, fucking, snatched you. But I swear to you, Violet, it's not because I'm low-key some fucking rapist or some shit." She turns to meet my gaze. "We belong together. I really believe that."

She regards me for a minute, then asks, "how would things have ended if you wouldn't have nabbed me today?" She swallows, and out of nowhere, I think she's... scared. "Would you have followed me more? What if you would have seen me with a man? Would you have killed me?"

I jerk back, nearly falling off the barstool. "Kill you? What the fuck?"

She matches my reaction, jerking back from me slightly. "I don't know! You say you're this good guy, and that you aren't a rapist, and you're making me tacos and crap, but dude–you freaking took me. I'm kidnapped right now."

I smooth my hands through my hair and place them face down on the counter, needing to tap into some reserve of chill right now. Because if I lose my cool, she'll rightfully be frightened. *And we do not frighten our girl, Van. No, no.*

Reaching into my back pocket as I lift the side of my ass from the stool, I fish out the leather bi-fold that looks like a wallet. Flipping it open, a silver police badge is revealed. My silver police badge.

"Don't be scared, but" I say, my tone one smooth wave-length of calm. Her eyes are huge now, so I drape my mitt on her knee and give her another reassuringly soft squeeze. "I'm a police officer with the Willowdale Police Department. I really am a cop. That wasn't a joke."

She swallows thickly, and even in the tense situation my cock hears her swallow and hardens a bit. The nerves of my admission and what it's doing to her start to gnaw on my cool. My knee bounces.

"Why would that scare me?" she asks, her voice delicate and soft like a whisper between the sheets.

"Because I have connections. Resources. I don't want you to feel like I can do anything and get away with it, and then have you be more scared."

"You'd be scary without a badge," she says, but it doesn't feel like an admission. More like a benefit.

She rests her hand on my knee, now, and stills my bouncing. My dick leaks when her nails curl into me. Even through denim she makes me leak. Stifling a groan, I force my gaze from her lips to her eyes.

"Are you scared of me, Violet?"

She licks her lips while staring at mine. "My dad is right. I'm an idiot. Because you should scare me. This whole situation is the stuff of horror movies and nightmares. But you don't scare me." She swallows through a dry mouth and throat. "You really don't."

Chapter Eighteen

VIOLET

I've tried to be invisible for so long, I didn't realize how starved I was to be seen.

His knee presses into the side of my thigh, and my breath catches. We're close. His body is touching mine. And I'm not scared.

After establishing that fact, I hit this man with questions, and he wasn't lying when he said he wouldn't be lying. Because some of these answers are... hard to hear.

And to be consistent with the theme of my life the last three days, those answers were hard to hear for the *entirely* wrong reasons.

When he said he drove behind me to school, that his cruiser tail lights were the ones I always saw–I didn't feel panicked. I felt *good*. Really freaking good.

Because this man is beautiful. *Yes*, men can be beautiful, and he is that. He speaks with intelligence and eloquence, his home is clean, he's a good cook and, oh yeah, he's got a freaking good body and handsome as hell face. The kind of man that if you saw in a shopping mall, you'd take a picture of him and text it to your girlfriend.

I want to take a picture of him and send it to Sasha.

Sasha.

Real life. *Reality.* Okay. The reality, though, is that this man stalked me. *Yes, Violet. Be smart.* Don't let the loneliness between your thighs make you fall for a stalker. Even if he's the love child of a gorgeous business man nerd and the most alpha, feral muscle head alive. Even then, *be smart.*

With the decision not to romanticize him, I continue listening to him come clean about all the ways he stalked me.

Peeked in Sasha's windows. That one makes my pussy throb, and I hate that I love it. He admits to having bumped into me once in the grocery store. My nipples get hard and the back of my neck goes hot. Then he tells me that he sat near me at the movies once when I went with Sasha. That makes my belly flutter.

So close, but I didn't get the chance to know. I never even saw him. Why didn't I see him? If I would've seen him, we could have met. Things would be different.

He wouldn't be an abductor.

But he is. And I need to remind myself of that.

After he is done coming clean, he asks me one simple but powerful question. "How are you feeling?"

I swear to God, no one has ever asked me that before. I'm not even being dramatic.

"I, I don't know," I admit, finding my mouth so dry. All the moisture has flooded to the spot between my thighs. "I'm not afraid," I tell him because his emotional security has somehow become incredibly important to me all of a sudden.

He nods and slips his glasses back on. He's incredibly intense and so sexy, and I know, he grabbed me from the parking lot. I know he has followed me, invaded my privacy, crossed moral and ethical boundaries time and time again, but... I don't know.

I've tried to be invisible for so long, I didn't realize how starved I was to be seen.

His affection, his attention, his care is feeding a hunger burning a hole in my soul.

And for once in my life I think, maybe don't plan. After all, the last time I planned to save and buy a house, well, look how that turned out. I spent my nest egg on my broken arm surgeries and related bills, not to mention the out-of-network therapy required to use my finger again. One of my fingers was nearly crushed.

I decide to just... see what happens. I mean, I'm not going to do anything completely stupid and like, run away with him today... but I'm not rushing to get home either.

Why would I?

"Are you full?" he asks, his tone moving like a rake through my nerves, leaving me feeling sweaty and a bit rustled.

I swallow then take a sip of LaCroix, needing moisture in my arid mouth. "Thank you, I'm full."

He smiles, mindlessly feeding the napkin through his fingertips, over and over. His dark eyes settle on mine, and he... just looks at me. I don't feel like cringing or shirking away. I don't feel weirded out like I have in the past when moments were supposed to be deep but weren't.

My whole body seems to float, weightlessly pleased with

everything about the moment. For once, even with a bashed head, and in a technical stranger's house, I like my life.

"I want to know more about that," he says, giving a quick tip of his forehead toward my bruised eye. "But I want it to come from you when you're comfortable." He crumples the napkin and drops in over his plate. "On your terms."

I study him as he clears our plates, puts away the leftovers, and begins cleaning his kitchen. "I don't know your name," I tell him. And how this hasn't been a bigger thought to me before now, I have no clue. Maybe it's a good sign. Some part of me was actually worried about the fact that I was abducted... even though I'm far less concerned at the moment.

He turns, suds to his wrists, and it's then I notice how much intricate ink takes up both of his arms. Tons of color and detail. A mandala spanning his broad tricep that must've taken many sessions and plenty of hours. Over his shoulder he says, "Donovan. But my friends call me Van."

"Van," I find myself repeating aloud, because I wasn't expecting it, but god, do I freaking like it. An image of me with my head thrown back, neck pink from beard burn, my fingers deep in his hair with his mouth tucked between my thighs flashes through my mind.

The one eye exposed to me winks, then he returns to his dishes.

"What's your last name?"

Facing forward he says more loudly, "Drake."

A moment passes where I don't say anything. A thrill rolls through me when he says, still facing forward, in a more private tone, *"Violet Drake."*

My pussy clenches, and I suck the last drops of LaCroix clean from the can because I need something in my throat and mouth. Van takes me by surprise when he asks, "do you need to tell your parents you aren't going to be home?"

My face pulls up tight with confusion, sending sharp glints of pain through my hurt eye. Van turns the water off, spinning to face me. Leaning against the sink, I enjoy the veins bulging in his forearms as he grips the edge of the counter.

"This isn't a captor thing, Violet." He stops himself mid-sentence and walks until he's at my side. My heart beats a little bit faster, and his musky clean scent sweeps through my veins.

This is a man who makes women dizzy.

He tips my chin up to face him, and gently cups my face in his very large hands. "They can know exactly where you're at if you want them to."

What is happening right now?

But then again.

It makes sense.

I don't really want Van to be in trouble, and if my dad called the police, I'm sure someone somewhere would find footage or a freeze-frame or something to figure out that Van was at the school. That Van wrapped a silk tie around my face and slapped cuffs on my wrists, and had my back to his bulbous chest in a matter of seconds, carrying me to his SUV like I was a notebook.

Still, he took me because he panicked. He saw my face and panicked, and no one has ever even raised an eyebrow in concern for me before now. It could be wrong. I could be digging deeper in an emotional pit rather than filling it, but the truth is, he makes me feel seen. And the fact that he's sexy and dominant doesn't hurt.

When answering my questions, his truths are so pure that

I know his actions are undeniable. He didn't have to tell me everything that he did.

"I don't want to tell them. But I'll tell Sasha."

"Your best friend," he says, but I can't tell if it's a statement or a question, so I clarify in case.

"She is my best friend, yeah. She's the only one that really knows me."

He sits down next to me and takes one of my hands with his. The air in my lungs seizes, his touch holding me captive. When he pulls my fingers to his mouth and presses his warm lips to my knuckles, a small breath escapes me.

"Does she know?" he asks, his voice like crushed velvet on jagged rocks, both terribly raspy and incredibly smooth. "That he hurts you? Does she know all of those secrets?"

I bite my bottom lip to keep it from trembling. Hell, to keep me from sighing out the dreamiest and most sickeningly smitten of sighs.

I nod. And he nods, too, bringing my knuckles to his lips again. A rush of heat and wetness seeps into my panties, and my face warms. When I try to tip it down and hide the pink in my cheeks, he uses my hand to nudge it back up.

Our eyes meet. My world changes.

"You don't know this yet, but you can trust me. And I'll never hurt you, okay?" His lips dust my knuckles again, sending heat and lust barreling up my arm, into my shoulder, then down...to my heart.

I don't say anything, because I can't agree. He's right, I don't know him yet. Not at all. I only know I *want* to trust him because I feel so good with him.

"You can sleep in my room tonight, that way you'll have your own bathroom and the only bedroom in the house with a lock. You can be sure that I can't get to you. So you can sleep soundly." He releases my hand back to my lap, and disappointment floods my belly. "You need sleep, especially after the last few days that you've had."

I nod, because agreeing to what's best for me feels good. It's foreign, but good.

He stands in front of me, folding his palms. "Up."

Nervous and unsure, I stand. Without warning, he's scooped me up, one arm under my knees and the other around my back.

I cannot help it, I hate myself for it considering the deplorable circumstances but... I grin. "I can walk you know," I say, burying my face into his... pec. And *holy pec*. His chest is big and solid, and... what does he look like without a shirt? I bet he looks like my panties on the floor, that's what.

"You got hit in the head last night. And kidnapped today." His lips turn up in the slightest of smiles that makes me grin. "You should at the very least be carried to bed."

I can't believe I'm enjoying this.

I have some serious issues. And for the first time ever, I don't freaking care.

I love the way it feels to be pressed against his body. I love how permanent and solid his arms feel flexed around me. As we get further down the hall, the lights from the kitchen fade away, and the air becomes cooler, darker.

He nudges open a door with his foot, and after a few paces, I find myself lowered and placed on the center of a very comfortable bed. The absence of his arms overwhelms any comfort the bed brings, and it disturbs me how comfortable I am with him. Seriously. Like, *what?*

Lights flicker on, and his bedroom comes into focus. I blink a few times as things become clearer. The first thing my eyes connect with is his dresser. Drawers closed, nothing hanging out –good job, Van– with a couple of books and a candle on top. Next to that, a family photo. Van with his parents.

He follows my gaze, I feel it in my peripheral vision. "They were killed in a car accident when I was sixteen." He looks away from the photo, studying a spot on his hardwood floor. "They were really fucking good people. And I know people always say that about dead people, but they really were." His gaze meets mine, and he swallows, eyes shiny. "I miss them every day."

"I'm so sorry, Van," I whisper, and I want more than anything to crash into him, feel his arms around me, and press my lips to his. Bring him comfort.

But I don't.

Because I have to maintain some level of smartness here.

Seriously.

He smiles, then turns to his dresser, rummaging for a moment before coming up with a Willowdale PD shirt that honestly makes my stomach flutter and my pussy so freaking wet. It's *his* shirt. His police department shirt. And it's going to smell like him. He sets it on top of the dresser, then sneaks a pair of pants from another drawer.

"What time do you need to be awake? We have to go to the school to get your car, then you need to go home, shower, and get ready for work." He pulls his phone from his pocket and opens what I presume to be his alarm clock app. "How much time do you need?"

I'm overwhelmed by the level of thoughtfulness he's put into my morning, my routine, and what I need. I'm speechless for a moment, but when he looks up from his screen, I begin counting backwards. "Umm," I say, "I think 6:45 should be good."

He nods, smiling as he keys in the time. "Great, I'll knock a few times." He locks his phone and slides it back into his pocket. "Soap, towels, and a new toothbrush are in the bathroom. It's," he pauses to glance at his watch, "only eight so you should get some good sleep."

I smile, a rush of embarrassment hitting me at the fact that my eyes are now damp and misty from his care. My abductor's kindness is making me cry, and that, ladies and gentleman, is pathetic. He notices, *of course he does,* and comes to the side of the bed, dropping to his knees.

"What are you feeling, Violet?"

"Confused," I say, because it's true. Partially. I don't say how good I feel with him. I don't say it because it's crazy.

SNUGGLED in the middle of Van's bed, swallowed by his scent—masculine and heady, I sleep so well. I mean, I really didn't think I would. I thought I'd wake up, forget where I am and freak out but I didn't wake up until he knocked gently at the door.

"Violet, baby, it's 6:58. You gotta get up. You slept through two alarms."

Waking warm and content, Van's thick voice rumbles through my chest as my toes sweep through the cool sheets. Coffee drifting through the air, sun flanking the curtains–a perfect morning. I feel... good.

"Oh my god," I gasp, sitting straight up in bed. Looking around, I press my hand to my mouth. I'm sleeping in Van's bed. The man who kidnapped me and stalked me.

He knocks again, and my eyes fly to the door. "Hey," somehow he whispers through the closed door. "You're okay, alright? Everything is going to be okay. I'm yours, Violet, and I'm not gonna hurt you."

I'm yours, Violet.

Those three words slither up my spine, giving me confidence.

Yeah, I slept over here because in addition to being a *sort-of-abductor*, Van is also a police officer and a really nice, tender man.

"You gotta get your clothes on so I can drive you to your car, okay?"

"It's open," I tell him from my spot in the center of his bed, knees curled up to my chest. He pushes the door open, and there he is, bare-chested.

The back of my brain goes hot and fuzzy, my mouth goes dry, and the excitement intensifies between my legs. His chest is chiseled, disciplined perfection. Striations of hard work twist down his sides, bleeding into a poignant six-pack. A faint trail of dark hair trickles down said abs, disappearing beneath the waistband of his athletic pants.

I pull the sheets up to my knees, to have something to do with my hands. Because I really want to reach for him. Like, so badly.

He's technically a stranger.

"You didn't lock it," he says, looking down at the door handle that he easily opened.

I shake my head. "I had no reason to."

We stare at each other, and an invisible charge zips and pops between us. Then he looks at the photo of his parents and back to me, his face serious. "I didn't appreciate them. I mean, I was sixteen. Do teenagers appreciate anything? But I didn't. I have to live with that.

And because of my extreme anger and guilt I have for

that, I roam the park off G Street every so often, follow people, and assault them." He drags a hand down his face nervously. His dark eyes are gentle behind his black frames. "I don't hurt anyone, and I don't have a weapon. I make them think I am going to hurt them, though. I make them think I do have a weapon. And then I steal their money. I tell them to know they're lucky to be alive. Once I get a few feet away, I drop their money and disappear." His eyes never leave mine, his voice never wavers, and his steady calm should make me uneasy, but it doesn't. He's unflappable; he can be vulnerable and honest but also strong and unrelenting, and… I freaking love it.

"I just want them to see how good they have it. Appreciate it, you know?"

"What's it?" I ask, wanting to understand.

"Life."

I nod. "Is that why you were at the park that night when you saw me a year ago?"

He nods now. "But Violet with the green eyes stole me away." He smiles, and all of me burns for this bearded man with the glasses and the chest of a Greek God. "Now, get dressed so I can drive you to your car." He closes the door, and I get dressed with a smirk on my lips.

———

I SIT in the passenger seat on the drive to the school, and Van asks if he can kiss me before I get out. "Just on the cheek," he clarifies, his palms out in innocence.

And I say yes. I say yes because I already feel like I don't know how to say no to this man who I've known for less than twenty-four full hours.

Oh my god. I've become a woman on *Dateline* that goes away with some catfish from Hinge and disappears. I'm *that* idiot.

Except.

I feel more like I'm being rescued than anything else.

He kisses my cheek, and then he drives behind me the entire way to my house, staying parked four houses down. I don't turn around when I'm on the porch, but somehow, I know he's still there.

No sooner does the front door shut than my dad is in the foyer, hands on his hips.

"Where the fuck have you been?"

I never texted them that I wasn't coming home. I texted Sasha. If they gave one shit about me, they'd know she is my best friend, and they would have texted her.

I thought I'd be scared to face him. Or nervous. But the last sixteen hours have changed me, and even though I don't know if I can trust Van yet, I'm not scared this morning. For the first time.

"Wanting to know if I was at the police station, huh?" I ask, folding my arms over my chest. "You can just wonder all day while you're at work if you're going to get taken away in cuffs or not." I push past him, my shoulder bumping his, and make a beeline for the stairs.

He calls out after me as I head to my room. But I block it out. Why listen? I need a shower, and I need to get to work. So I do just that, and when I'm dressed in my favorite black slacks, a chardonnay-colored silk tank top, and my hair air-drying behind my back, I head back down. He should be getting ready to leave soon, but he's dressed as if he's not going to work.

I chew my lip, so he doesn't catch sight of my grin. He's

probably worried I *did* report him. Doesn't want to get arrested at work. So I let him writhe, and when he asks me, "if I wasted the police's time or not," I don't answer and simply smile as I pull the front door closed behind me.

When I am securely locked inside my little car, I send Sasha a text message.

Violet: *Can you talk?*

Chapter Nineteen

DONOVAN

I don't regret the punches.

Now that I've been with her–and I don't even mean fucked her–but just *been* with her... Sat with her, talked to her, made her laugh, watched her cry, felt her tears burn my skin... I know I'm right.

We belong together, and if that makes me crazy for believing it, well then, put me in a fucking straight jacket.

She needs me. She needs a real man in her life to help her see how fucking smart and gifted she is, how hard she works in the classroom, how effortlessly beautiful she is.

I haven't gotten to whatever happened or is happening or... whatever the fuck is going on with her family. With her fucking father. I can't even let my mind wander off to that dark corner, or I start to go a little haywire.

Point is, she needs me. And I need her.

She makes me a better man.

Though I didn't ask her for her phone number, she must know that I already have it. Because I do. I've never used it, but it's programmed in my phone.

I can't believe I finally get to use it.

I've had to work this morning, so I haven't been able to check on her. Mally and I had some calls on the East side of town—we couldn't even zip past the school to get eyes on her car. I'm assuming she made it, and that fucking prick of a father left her alone, but when it comes to my girl, *assuming* isn't good enough.

Mally's bullshitting with the gas station clerk when I glance up through the windshield. His surfer boy charm works on everybody.

The FaceTime call dings, and to my surprise and pleasure—two feelings that come together often around Violet—she answers. Her blonde hair has a little bit of body, forming loose waves around her face. She's free of any and all makeup, and because of it, her eye looks a bit worse today. I grit my teeth so hard my jaw clicks.

Her green eyes seem so fucking bright with the sun illuminating her from behind. She's sitting at her desk, in her class. It's her lunch break. This I know.

"Hey beautiful," I answer, the greeting feeling so natural. Her pink and completely fucking tantalizing lips curl slightly. "You do look so beautiful Violet. Do you know that?" I glance up to make sure Mally is still schmoozing and busy. He's currently demonstrating a one-handed push-up. Yeah, I'm good.

"Thank you," she whispers, a blush crawling up her cheeks. She looks around the room nervously, then back down at me.

"What did he say to you when you got home?" I ask.

She shakes her head, and bites her thumb nail nervously. "He didn't do anything."

I swallow, and give her a smile. "What did he *say* to you?"

"He asked where I'd been, but of course," she smiles, chewing at the corner of her mouth. "He didn't ask quite that nicely."

I take my jaw in my hand so she can't see me grinding my teeth. "Is that right?"

She nods a little.

"Where are you going after school today?" I ask, my gut knowing her answer before she even gives it. I feel fucking sick.

"Home," she answers, and *fuck*, that's what I was afraid of.

I lower my voice, and glance up, checking on Mally again. Now the clerk is trying a one-handed push up, too. With my attention back on my girl, I say, "you can come stay with me, Violet. You know that, right?"

She blinks, tipping her head forward, her hair curtaining her face before she tucks it back behind her ears. My stomach flips casually watching her, knowing she knows I'm watching her. I'm so used to her not knowing.

"You're a stranger to me, Donovan Drake."

I've been shot—a bullet grazed my shoulder in a traffic stop gone wrong. I've pulled my groin working out; that is something I'd love to never experience again. I've put the only two people I loved in the ground.

But those seven words tear through me like a virus, infecting every part of me with a sick, burning feeling, leaving me fucking paralyzed.

I knew she'd say no, because my girl is smart, and as much as it pains me, she's not wrong. I *am* a stranger to her.

And while she isn't one to me, that doesn't bring her comfort. Not yet.

"Get to know me then. Can I take you out?"

She looks away from the camera, and even though she's still on the screen, it feels like I'm losing her. Like she's drifting away.

"I'll take you out tonight, or you can come back to my place and have dinner." I swallow, trying to control the desperation in my voice. It's hard. "Please, Violet. I don't like you being there with him." Panic rises up in my throat, but I control my tone. "I need you."

She gives me a small smile, and I know I've lost this one. "Thank you for last night." She pulls her bottom lip under her top teeth, her expression pensive, and for a second I wonder if she isn't battling her choice, too. God, I fucking hope she is. "Thanks for checking on me."

I start to panic as I feel the end of the call near. "Violet," I say, open-ended; anything to keep her on the line.

"Lunch bell is going to ring. Take care of yourself, Officer Drake. I hope you find a more interesting way to fill your time."

She ends the call, my screen goes black, and rage consumes my vision. I'm looking out the windshield, but I can't see anything. I can't hear anything. Fire churns in my gut and rips through my veins, my hands curl into fists and my jaw tightens.

"Fuck!" I slam my fists into the steering wheel, and the cruiser rattles. "Fuck! Fuck! Fuck!" I beat the wheel like it's Violet's dad's face, I beat the wheel like it's my fucking poor choices. Why did I think coming clean about everything I'd done was smart? Did I seriously think she would value my honesty more than fearing for her own safety? Violet is fucking smart.

My mind spins like a top. Scenarios and likely possibilities zip around my brain, colliding with worries and fears.

Take a breath; I advise myself, because when you're a little fucking off your rocker–just the slightest–you gotta be your own cheerleader. I mean, Mally can handle my *hobby*, but a mental breakdown and emotional spiral because the woman I stalked and kidnapped just "broke up" with me? Yeah, that's one to keep to myself.

After a deep inhale and a slow exhale, I focus on what I know.

Everything was okay last night. She didn't even lock the fucking door. And this morning, I think back to kissing her cheek. She let me kiss her cheek. I didn't force it.

She was home for a short amount of time, and I don't think she'd share details about me with them, then she went to work. I stroke my beard with my palm, scratching the edge of my jaw as I think.

Sasha.

She saw Sasha at work, and with whatever her asshole dad said to her this morning, paired with the intensity of last night–she probably came clean. Sasha, having no idea about me and who I am–simply heard "stalk" and "snatched" and made a judgment.

I mean, I don't need to know her to know her judgment.

Girl, hell no. A dirty cop? Leave that man behind.

She doesn't know I'm not a dirty cop. I'm not even dirty in any other way. I just... I know what I need, and that's Violet.

Mally waves off the clerk he has thoroughly impressed,

and flips up his shades to wiggle his eyes at me. He slides into the cruiser, biting into a footlong stick of jerky. "See how impressed they were?" He lifts a curled arm over the center console and flexes. "I don't see anyone asking you to do push-ups, I'm just saying, maybe I should be the Bodfather."

"You know you went in there and offered," I say, putting the cruiser in drive.

He denies that, then rattles on and on about our lifting day later. We didn't work out this morning–for once, Bran wasn't spending his morning buried in his lady's pussy so he could open his own fucking business. Mally and I took the morning off, both agreeing to sleep in a little before our mid-morning shift started and workout tonight. I told him I slept in, because what else would I say? I had to wake up early to take my fucking stalking victim home? Uh, no.

We go on calls, and I tune out Mally as much as possible so I can make room for my issue at hand. If I'm right, and Violet poured her heart out to Sasha, what did she tell her? It feels like I'm fighting the advice from a best friend because Violet wasn't turned off to the idea of us this morning.

She didn't kiss my lips or attempt to hug me, but she was open to it. I can read people. I read her. She was.

And now she's telling me to basically leave her alone, and that's she fine living with her dad? I can't accept that. I can't let Sasha talk Violet out of giving me a chance.

I'm no closer to figuring out the mess in my head. How do I get Violet to trust me? Can I find Sasha and talk to her? That feels like it would work against me; stalking the friend. But this can't be it.

It takes every goddamn bit of me to go to the gym with Mally instead of staying home and waiting by my laptop to watch her get home. If I want to win her, I have to stop doing creepy shit. This I know. Fuck, I'm a police officer. I always tell people, if it's something you could get arrested for, ask yourself if it's worth it.

I need to take my own advice, and give her space.

I work out with Mally and Bran, and the day catches up to me when some fucking amateur doesn't rerack his weight on the bench press. I put my finger into his chest and tell him to show respect to Paradise. He scoffs.

I've been set off from far smaller things than a scoff, but that's all it takes tonight.

I only connect with his face twice before Bran's on my back and Mally's between us, pushing the kid back.

"Hey, hey!" Mally shouts towards the kid, who is actually pretty innocent. He didn't rerack, it's not cool, but does it deserve a two-hundred-and-twenty pound man driving his fist into your face a few times? Definitely not. "He's a fucking police officer, bro," Mally says, yanking the kid by the neck of his stupid Gymshark shirt. We're fucking lifters, and this assclown is wearing *men's Gymshark*.

I don't regret the punches.

"He hit me!" the kid yells, pulling said shirt up to his lip, blotting it like he put on too much fucking lipstick.

"That's not what I saw, so unless you wanna get arrested for assaulting a police officer, I'd get the fuck out of here," Bran adds, releasing his hold on me to join Mally standing in front of the kid.

"Fuck this gym," he says, but he never meets my eyes. He grabs his milk jug full of water, and storms out. I just cost Bran a customer.

I still feel angry that Violet won't see me and I can't figure out a solution, and now I feel fucking guilty and that only makes me feel worse.

Mally faces Bran, putting his hands on his shoulders. "We're good, it's all good. But we need a minute, okay?" Mally nods to Bran until he nods, too. He gives me a quick glance, and I can see concern in his eyes, and that makes me feel even worse.

After he walks me out into the parking lot, Mally holds me by the shoulders, and I want to fucking shrug him off, but I don't.

"Van," he says my name so low and quiet that I feel obligated to meet his eyes.

"Is this about the girl?"

I regard him for a minute, his hair slicked back with sweat, his chest heaving from the set my outburst interrupted. He's almost as tall as me, almost as strong as me. He's inked up his arms like me, too. He takes the back of my neck and squeezes, and he's never felt like more of a brother until this moment. "You gotta slow down and relax. Use your head, Van. Okay?" He grips my neck more tightly and with his intensity and seriousness, commands my eyes to stay on his.

"Be smart, Van, okay?"

I nod. "Alright."

We finish our workout, and my mind finally slows enough to realize Mally is right. I need to relax and slow down. I can't jump to any conclusions about what Sasha may or may not have said to my girl.

First I have to give Violet some space, so that's what I'll do.

Chapter Twenty

VIOLET

I met someone.

It's been a week since I last heard from Van.

The morning he dropped me off at my house, I'll admit, I was really confused. And the thing is, it wasn't necessarily how I felt for him that was confusing me. Because my feelings for Van are strong, and they are real, and I don't even want to deny them. Really, I don't.

But that's the thing tripping me up.

I'm smart. I have a career that I love, teaching kids how to love learning. I'm not a woman who gets backward in the head when she gets the panty-tingles from a hot man.

Hot doesn't do Van justice.

It's not just physical, either.

I know I shouldn't be saying this because of what he's done, but Jesus! Freak! The way he talks to me makes my head spin. No man has ever lowered his voice to a calm octave just to tenderly ask me how I'm feeling. He doesn't just stare into my eyes when I talk, rehearsing what he's going to say in return. He *sees* me.

No man has ever even asked me how I'm feeling if we're getting into details.

But Van stalked me and defiled my personal safety in so many ways. And *that* is wrong. The Violet inside of me that *isn't* busy drawing VC + DD inside of a heart on her desk is saying, *stop! Red flag!*

And you have to stop when a red flag is on the play. I know little about sports but plenty about men with red flags. I live with a freaking red parachute of a man.

When I got in my car that morning after I'd spent the night at Van's, I texted Sasha to talk. Can you keep a secret, I'd said because, at that moment, I was ready to spill.

She didn't text back; she called to say she was filling in for the 6th grade teacher, and that she had to get a lesson ready for her class, since her favorite sub was easy to get. Long story short, Mr. Mathews got a stomach bug and he was out all week, meaning the rest of the teachers had to pull some extra weight, as two subs ended up calling in at the last minute.

I haven't really got to talk to her yet.

I don't really know what I'm going to say to her either. I don't know if I should come completely clean, if I should get a little clean, or stay downright filthy. Lying to her feels wrong, but telling her the truth feels dangerous, and that leaves me torn.

He called me that day on my lunch, and I still hadn't vented to Sasha or even shared a word of it to anyone. I didn't even have my notebook to pour myself into. It was hard.

He'd asked me to come stay with him, then have a date with him, and every single stupid part of me wanted that. I wanted to go to dinner with him. I wanted a lot more than that.

But I couldn't allow myself to be a dumb female and run into the arms of someone questionable. As much as I want him, and as much as my gut tells me he's good, my brain is pulling rank.

Damn you smart brain.

It's Friday night, and as I drive to meet Sasha for dinner, I wonder what Van is doing. But that's not new, because I've been thinking of him and the entire situation all freaking week long.

Van was stalking me.

Me!

It's flattering, you know? I know I should worry for his mental health, and I do, but… it feels good when I imagine him seeing me, and having something about *me* strike him so hard that he can't let me from his sight.

Something about me is special enough to make a man like him follow *me*. And I believe him when he told me I'm the first woman he's followed or stalked or… really cared about.

After I park and head into the small wine bar and bistro, I know I have to choose.

Tell Sasha the complete truth and run the risk of her never accepting Van; which means, I'm leaving the door open for him to be in my life. Or I could tell her that I met him in a different way, lie to my best friend all for the hope that he feels the same way about me.

Risky stuff.

"Hey girl," Sasha waves without rising, and I slide into the booth on the opposite side of her.

"This place looks nice," I tell her, smoothing my hands across the fabric tablecloth. When I say nice, I mean expensive, but I don't say that. I never go out. After the few weeks I've had, I deserve a freaking splurge.

"I ordered you a glass of red wine," she says, giving me "don't say a word" eyes over the top of the menu she's perusing.

I sigh, dipping my head to rest on her shoulder.

"I need it today."

"You've needed it for a while."

I sigh again because it seems like it takes less energy than words at the moment.

She wiggles her shoulder to shake me off her. She takes my chin with her thumb and curled finger and turns my head. Studying the healing bruises on my eye socket, she purses her lips and shakes her head. When she releases me, the waiter brings us our wine, and we both take our first, long sip.

"I don't make you talk about it, do I?" she asks, taking another long drink of the burgundy wine. She makes a point of dragging her eyes to my injury, then back to me.

"No," I say, "and thank you for that."

"Okay, well, I want you to seriously think about what I said, Vi." She gives me a serious look that makes me nervous, the wine already tasting more bitter as I drink.

"About what?"

She rolls her eyes, and a good looking waiter approaches our table. His name tag says Antonio. He has dark hair, and I think of Van. He is tall, and I think of Van. He smiles, revealing a mouth full of metal, and I stifle a laugh.

We order, and I don't skimp when I get a calzone. If I'm eating out, I may as well get a few lunches out of it, too.

Sasha gets fish, but the wine is kicking in so I don't worry about the repulsive smell.

When the waiter walks away, we both giggle. It's a little immature, but it feels good. And also, yeah, that's the wine, too.

"I thought he was kind of cute and then-"

"Metal mouth!"

I snort, bringing the back of my hand to my nose to stifle the laughter.

"Okay, but seriously," Sasha says, circling back to the issue at hand. She takes another drink of wine, and it's gone now, but she traces the top of the glass with her point finger nonetheless.

"I wish you had a guy. I mean, I know your man hunt is like your moving out hunt; you don't want a stepping stone, you want the final deal." She slices her hand through the air. "And I get that. But… in this case, I think you get the apartment, and you get the temporary man." She nods fervently in an effort to get me nodding in agreement.

I giggle again because I've finished my first glass of wine, too, and the woman with the bottle wrapped in the towel is coming our way. And I like that woman. She has the booze. My life hurts, so I wave her over.

Sipping the second glass, I turn to Sasha.

With liquid courage, now is the time. And I don't know what version of Van I'm going to give her until I start talking.

"I met someone." My pulse booms in my eardrums as I study my best friend. At first, she gets immediately gleeful, her eyes lifting then going wide, her lips pulling up on the edges in a grin. But then, her brows dip and her grin slides into a look of disapproval.

"When?"

Shit, that one word is a really good freaking question, because I've been with Sasha a lot recently. Even though we've both been busy at school, still, we've been in the same building. And before that? We had that impromptu sleepover.

"He's a cop," I say excitedly, in an effort to at least temporarily divert her attention to the idea of a hot man in a tight uniform.

And it works, long enough for me to nod and smile through her pleased open-mouth expression to come up with a lie.

It's as I'm amending my statement with "and he actually pulled me over on the way to work the other day," that I add, "and you've been busy this week so I haven't had a chance to fill you in."

She rubs her palms together, and this news must really make her happy because she sets her wine down to listen. "Ooh, girl." Her dark eyes widen as she fluffs her soft, curly hair. "Does he have a friend? You know I like the badge."

Chewing the corner of my mouth, I swirl my wine as I try to hide a grin.

She pokes me in the arm. "Spill it."

I box up and stash away the fact that I'm lying a bit to Sasha, and instead allow myself to indulge in the massive surge of happiness hitting me. I get to spill to my best friend about the supremely hot guy I'm crushing on. I'm going to forget the rest of the details for now, I'm going to sip my wine, gossip, and have a nice freaking night.

And I do.

Describing him with so much detail that Sasha claims she has a vivid sketch of him in her mind, I relax into the booth and enjoy way too much calzone. We talk about Mr.

Mathews and the the rest of the school that got taken out by the stomach bug, Sasha updates me about her sister and how she's staying in Germany for three extra weeks, we giggle at some of the ridiculous Hinge profiles that she's been alerted to as a match, and after two hours of much needed catching up, we pay our check and peel ourselves from the booth.

My belly is full of awful red wine and delicious calzone. My soul is full of a good session with Sasha. I do feel guilty about omitting some... *pertinent*... details about Van, but... I don't even know what's going to happen between us. No use in freaking Sasha out if I'm not even sure what's going on.

I did kind of blow him off earlier this week but... I was being smart. I *am* being smart.

It was fun to tell Sasha about something exciting and positive... but the truth of it is, even through the booze I know I need to be smart.

"Your face just got really fucking depressing," Sasha says, feeding her arms through a taupe teddy bear-style coat. She's trendy with her ankle booties, crop jeans, and off-the-shoulder sweater. Sasha looks good in everything.

"You're so pretty," I tell her through a hiccup. She shoves a cardboard cup of coffee in my hand.

"Well, my beauty shouldn't depress you," she says, popping the lid off my drink so it cools more quickly. We had walked around the corner to the coffee shop so I could get some coffee in my belly before I drive back home.

God, it really feels weird to call my home *home* now. And it feels even weirder to say that Van feels like home because... I don't even know him.

Still. I want to be with him. I just don't think I can. It was fun sharing the excitement but sobriety brings the realization that this is just too crazy.

"I'm just… I'm realizing how it can't really work out with that hot cop I was telling you about." I wrinkle my nose. "I'd worry too much."

That part isn't a lie. If my husband was a police officer, I'd probably never sleep. And holy shit, I just jumped to him being my husband in my fake dream scenario. I didn't even go for *my boyfriend*, I went straight for *my husband*. Shit.

"I think I may have gotten a concussion last week, when my dad, you know," I say quietly through the steam wafting off my cup. I take a few really long, big drinks, and even though my tongue burns and my eyes water, I want the wine out of me now.

I need control and clarity. I need to really focus on how *not* smart it is to like Van.

"Yeah?" she asks, coffee almost to her lips. "Your head still hurting?"

I nod and rub the fading bruises. "Yeah, and I just… I feel different."

She narrows her chocolate eyes at me, her lips pursed. "You need to see a doctor. You don't play around with your brain, Vi."

I take the last few drinks of my coffee, wondering if I'll have any taste buds tomorrow that aren't charred. But I just want to down this and get home, and get to my room. I hate that I envision locking the door. I always did it before the incident, but now I see the act clearly and it helps me breathe.

"Yeah, I'll make an appointment and say, *hey, remember me? Welp, I'm back. Start up a new tab!*" I wrap my sweater tightly around my core and hold myself as we walk to our cars. It's getting cool out, and my legs are bare.

"Thanks for a fun time tonight, Sash. I needed it. Even

though it cost me nearly fifty freaking dollars," I scoff teasingly.

"Sometimes you gotta treat yourself." She winks, and gets on her bicycle, settling her helmet over her voluminous hair as she tells me goodnight.

I don't worry about her. She's been riding her bike everywhere since I've known her. And the main street in Willowdale, where we're eating dinner, is connected to a very well-lit and populated trail running behind a residential area and the school. She'll be home before me.

"Don't give up on that cop," she says, pointing her finger at me as if it's a command. Little does she know my arm doesn't need to be twisted. My brain, however...

The coffee soaked up the wine, but its usual effect of waking me up just isn't working. And as I yawn for about the fifth time in the last two minutes, blue and red lights fog my rearview, an angry cruiser behind me.

"Shit," I say as I flip my blinker towards the curb, a streetlight right overhead. That's lucky at least. Could I pass a breathalyzer? Oh shit. My heart starts to race so fast it makes my already queasy stomach swirl. I swallow as my car hugs the curb, and I crank the gear into park. In a minute that feels like years, finally an officer approaches the driver's door.

Do I want it to be Van?

I have my answer when the cop leans down, bringing his face in line with mine, nothing but the rolled-up glass of my early 2000's commuter car separating us.

I look at his nametag. C. MILLER.

I take him in for a moment before I pull the lever, letting the window roll down. This man is quite possibly the opposite of Van.

He's blonde-haired and surfer-skinned, his eyes are bright blue and his teeth are freaking white. He's both built and lean, but with his crooked smile and floppy hair, he kind of makes me want to laugh. No burning loins here.

"Hi," he says, and even with just two letters spoken, I can tell he's a total bro. The way the *hi* rears up at the end, like he's laughing at a joke or something.

"Hi," I respond because it's now that I realize I don't need to worry if I had enough coffee. Officer Miller... this is Van's partner. His friend.

"Are you following me, too?" I ask, absolutely no inflection in my tone as to get a read on him.

He stares at me, his forearm pressed against the top of my window as he leans slightly down. I stare back, not a ripple in my surface. Internally, I'm so nervous, and I don't know why.

"I knew it," he says, still holding my eyes while shaking his head just barely, in subtle disbelief.

My face scrunches.

"I knew something was up by the way he was being about you and..." he trails off, and his eyes do, too. Glued to nothing off in the distance, Miller's mouth snaps shut as he drags a hand down the lower half of his face.

"He's been different. And I didn't know what was up, but I knew it had to do with you."

When his head swings back into the open window, and his eyes meet mine, I literally secondhand vibrate from the concern that wracks this man's face. "So he's been following you?"

Swallowing down my instinct to lie to protect Van, instead I nod. "Yes."

Mally's head falls between his shoulder blades as he grips

the side of my car, laughing without humor. Finally, he looks up at me. "Are you scared of him?"

Without hesitation, I shake my head. "No."

He chews the corner of his mouth, head partially turned away from me but his eyes still on mine. He says, "I don't know if that should make me more or less concerned."

I lick my lips, and find the courage to ask what I really want to know. I turn and face him. "Is he a good man?"

Miller blinks a few times quickly before pulling back from the window, straightening to his full height. With a sincere expression he says, "the best."

Chapter Twenty-One

DONOVAN

Van is the Bodfather, the man, the greatest of us all.

I'm putting in extra workouts this week, and it has nothing to do with needing to take my mind off the fact that I haven't watched Violet in six days and everything to do with my love of the gym. Even on Friday at eight o'clock at night.

Yep, hanging with Bran on Friday night is *great*. Bran's new lady friend had to work, and I'm just trying not to stalk anyone.

Who knew quitting would be so hard.

I don't miss stalking. I'm not a fucking psycho.

I miss *seeing* her.

"So, what do you think?" Bran asks, hands on hips as he edges closer toward me. "You think it's too soon?"

I lift my head from where it's hanging over my knees and swipe over my face with my towel. I didn't need another leg day, but if I didn't do this, I'd be at home holding that fucking laptop in one hand and my cock with the other.

And I'm trying not to do that.

"What?" I ask. I'm an asshole. I need to be listening to Bran because the guy is sensitive as shit and hardly talks about the hard stuff. When he opens up, it's rare. And he's doing it now. With me, not Mally, so I need to treat this moment a whole lot better than I am. *Fucking focus Van.*

"Do you think it's too soon for me to meet her daughter?" Bran doesn't look impatient with me, and I know it's because this matters to him so much. Instead of arguing that I wasn't listening, he simply wants my advice.

Returning the bar to the rack, having just finished my last set of box squats, I turn to face him and clap a hand over his shoulder. "I think it's pretty cool you're worried about if it's too soon or not," I admit because that tells me he cares enough about this chick that he doesn't want to hurt a kid he's never met. "You care."

He scratches at the side of his cheek, a thousand-yard stare into the empty gym around us.

I tighten my grip on his shoulder. "What are we worried about here, Bran?"

I can see now the real concern is something I haven't considered. "Brian," I say, using his real name which I can't honestly remember when I used last. Real-naming your bro is like being full-named by your parents. It's serious. His eye comes to mine.

"She's four," he says, with vulnerability in his voice. He raises a rough, tattooed hand to his face, letting his fingers trace the edges of his eye patch. "What if she's scared of me, man?"

I nod. "Very valid concern. But I think there's a way you make it cool."

His good eye rolls. "There is nothing cool about losing your eye unless you're like a vet or something."

I guide us toward the bench in front of the free weights, and we take a seat. I massage my quads as I talk to him, in an effort to make the conversation feel more casual. I can sense Bran is highly stressed. He's been pulling on the ends of his hair and pacing between sets.

"Kids are cool, man. They're a blank slate. They don't have all these predisposed ideas of shit. They see something and they're willing to learn whatever. You know?"

He nods a little, but insecurity wracks his shoulders.

"If she's scared of me, her mom won't see me."

I clasp his shoulder again, this time using my hand to force his head my way. For bros, this is as intimate as we get.

"Stop. Okay?" I say it firmly, and he's bubbling with emotion now.

"Brian, you're a good fucking dude. This chick really likes you if she wants you to meet her kid. Okay?" I thump my closed fist to his chest. "She really fucking likes you, man."

He blinks. "I love her."

The back of my brain tingles with relief and happiness for my friend. I smile at him. "It looks good on you."

He smirks just a little. "But her kid." He adjusts his eyepatch without even knowing it.

Still holding his neck I tell him what I believe to be the truth. "You explain you were in a situation with a bad guy, and that the bad guy hurt you, but you won."

I release his neck and he leans forward, putting his elbows on his knees, holding his head in his hands. "I don't know," he sighs.

"You don't need to know. *I do.* That story is absolutely true, and the kid will think you're a hero. Then all you gotta do is bring books that have like, good pirates in them and shit like that. Then all she'll associate with an eyepatch is heroes." He twists his head to peer at me. "And once she gets to know you, she'll know a real hero."

He turns forward again. We sit in silence for a moment. I meant every word I said.

"I want to be over it, man," he says finally. "I don't want my whole life to be about losing my eye."

"Then don't let it be," I tell him, feeling fucking rotten as hell because I'm the biggest hypocrite. My entire life has been about inflicting pain on people because I haven't healed the chasm of darkness inside me that was born from losing my parents.

He looks at me again. "Thank you."

I give him a smug grin. "I'm glad you didn't take this to Mally. That fucker's head is getting too big. You know he thinks he's the best looking one in the group, right?"

Bran stands from the bench shaking his head. "Everyone knows it's Batman."

I wag a finger of warning at him. "Careful or I'll arrest you on your next date."

He holds his hands up in surrender. "Van is the Bodfather, the man, the greatest of us all."

I wink, and flex my thick thigh. "Better."

IT'S AN ESPECIALLY DARK EVENING, the moon behind a wall of gauzy clouds. The lights that line my street haven't come on yet, so the only illumination comes from windows and porch lights. The night feels peaceful to me, but I'm sure to some it would be eerie.

I'm enjoying the somewhat peaceful darkness of my street when I see the back of a very familiar car. Without knowing why or how, my chest goes into overdrive. Heart racing, mind doing the same, I gun it in my SUV until I'm at my house, parking hastily in the driveway, not worrying about the garage.

I jog to the street where the car is parked; in front of my house along the curb; and right when I see it's empty and panic rises in my throat, I hear her.

"Hi," Violet says, stepping down from my porch.

Violet on my porch. Violet came to my house. Violet is here.

Her name echoes through my veins as I meet her in the middle of the walkway to my porch. Without permission, I take her face in my hands and move her head around, trying desperately to analyze her in the limited light. The once comforting darkness is now irritating. I can't see well, so I smooth my thumbs down her cheeks, then move my fingers along her nose and eyes.

"Are you okay? What's wrong? Where are you hurt?" My voice is panicked because if she's here, she's hurt. That's the only reason a smart girl like Violet would come back to me, her admitted stalker.

But she shakes her head, the bleary moon shining against her eyes, making them glow. "I'm not hurt," she replies, sending a huge wave of relief through me. All my muscles unclench from the way they seized up the moment I saw her car.

"But you're here," I admit hoarsely, both happy and

worried. I want this woman, but I have no idea where her head is at. She's been through so much already.

"I had dinner with Sasha tonight, did you know that?" she asks, without any attitude or inflection–she genuinely doesn't know if I've still been following her.

I want to tell her that I haven't followed her since I dropped her off at her house last week, but I don't. Instead I say, "I didn't know." She studies my eyes, really analyzes them. Then after a beat, she nods. "Okay."

I let go of her face, and both of us seem hollow when I do. "So you had dinner with Sasha," I say, trying to get us back on track. The more I just stand here staring at her, the more lightheaded I get. Because I can't believe after all this time, Violet is actually in my life. In a curious capacity at the moment, sure, but something is better than nothing.

"I did. And I had wine." She wrinkles her nose, and I notice now that her normally straight hair is a bit wavy, gaining body from the cool fall evening. It's so sexy. Everything about her is so sexy. "I felt good tonight, and I didn't want to go back home after because when I do, I won't feel good anymore."

I nod because I understand that. After my parents died, home felt worse than just an empty place. It was like walking through shattered glass on bare feet. Every step was a painful reminder that the safety, warmth, and security of the space never existed in the house. It existed with my parents, and without them, I'll never have that again.

I *get* Violet so much, even more than I thought I would. We're perfect together. She's my other half. I just wish she'd see it.

"I'm sorry," I say, not knowing what else to say. Her lips twitch as she stuffs some of her golden hair behind her ear.

On a thick swallow, she says, "so I thought of you."

"Oh yeah?" My heart drums in my ears, my stomach catapulting into my throat.

She nods. "That's a lie."

I don't know what to say or what's happening, so I just stand there.

"I've been thinking of you all week."

My head pounds with noises–my heart, my thoughts, everything.

"What are you thinking now?" I ask.

Her lids droop a little, and her demeanor shifts from nervous and timid to something new. Something I haven't seen in Violet's face before. Not in an entire year.

"I just want to feel good. And you look like someone who could make me feel *really* good."

"Violet–" I start, and I guess I'm on the cusp of warning her. Telling her that if she goes down this road with me, I won't be able to turn back. But I can't speak. She doesn't let me. She clearly doesn't want to talk, and I only want to give her what she wants.

"I want you to make me feel good, Van." She steps closer to me and rises to her toes, bringing our faces so fucking close together. "Make me feel good."

A car drives down my street, I hear it behind me but I don't turn. I don't look anywhere but into her eyes. She isn't drunk. I know because even in low light, I can see her pupils are normal. And I can smell the coffee on her breath.

Violet leads a life of not being heard, no one trusting her opinion or valuing her for anything, really. I'm not going to insult her by asking if she's sure. She's here, she knows what she wants, and she wants it from *me*.

My blood slowly begins draining from my brain, heading south at the entire moment unfolding before me.

My eyes still on hers, I outstretch a hand, fanning my fingers open. Keeping her gaze on me, she weaves her fingers through mine, and we both fold our hands together.

Her gentle squeeze moves up my arm and vibrates down my spine, leaving a trail of heat and need in its wake. My cock stirs. Her skin feels like silk against my rough, worn hand.

With our hands linked, we walk the remainder of the way up the steps. I don't usually go in the front door since I park in my garage, so it takes me a moment to fish my house key from my wallet.

"Did you leave your keys in the car?" she asks, watching me shove my huge finger in the leather bifold, bringing a silver house key out with it.

"No, my car doesn't have a key. It uses a card, like a credit card." I slide the car key out from behind my driver's license, tipping it down to show her. "See?"

She drags her fingertip over the letters etched into the card. Why the fuck is this woman touching my key card giving me a fucking hard-on? "I can use my phone to unlock it and start it, too. I don't use this much."

She looks back up at me, her eyes wide and hazy. "That's pretty cool."

I shrug. "I could act like it's not cool and say I just got the car to do my part for the environment," I say of my electric car. "I wanted the car for that reason, but once I test drove it, I wanted it because it goes fast, and it's badass."

She laughs at that, a small, simple but organic reactive laugh that makes my chest tighten. My cheeks even burn a little.

She takes the house key from my hand, surprising me again. For as well as I know my girl, she still has a variety of surprises, and I fucking love that. I want them all; I want everything she has to give.

"I'll go in the front," she says, stepping past me, her arm grazing my belly as she slides the key into the grooves. "And you can put your car in." She looks down the yard over at the white SUV parked haphazardly in the driveway. "It's too pretty to sit out in this cold."

She likes my car. It's small, but I can't help but fucking grin at the small victory as I'm parking my Tesla in the garage and closing the door behind me.

Once I push inside, I see Violet standing behind the barstool she sat at the last time she was here. Her attention is on the go, moving over the items on the fridge, the running shoes tucked against the wall by the front door, she tips her head to the side to read spines of books on the shelf, and finally, her attention is back on me.

"Violet," I start, but she doesn't let me finish. She pads her way to me, that sexy hazy look in her eyes. When she's in front of me, I notice how the vibrant emerald of her eyes looks a little mossy tonight.

"Make me feel good, Van," she repeats the phrase from the sidewalk.

A year of stalking, and now she's here, begging for me. Stomping down any fears of becoming a regret, I grab her by the hips and lift her easily, tossing her over my shoulder.

She squeals with shock, but when her fingers curl into the fabric of my shirt and my skin burns under her slight graze, all worries and hesitation fall free from my mind.

She wants me, and I'm going to make her feel good. I'm going to make her feel so fucking good.

By the time we're in the master bedroom, and I've tossed her onto the bed, I'm so goddamn hard that any more walking will be difficult. Turning on the light, we blink through the adjustment then our eyes idle on one another.

Her wavy hair is wild, her pink lips full and parted, her chest heaving. She's nervous but excited; she wants this but is fearful it's going to be a mistake. I can see it all in her body language, in the way she gnaws at the inside of her cheek as we stare at one another.

I lift my glasses from my face, setting them on top of the dresser. Reaching behind me with one arm, I tug off my sweaty shirt in one swift pull. She gasps a little at the sight of me.

Now's the time to be the Van that makes her feel like the most beautiful, important, special fucking woman in the world. And I can do that very easily. Because to me, she is those things.

"I just worked out, I'm sweaty as fuck, so I need to shower."

She nods eagerly, and fuck her anticipation is sexy as shit. I'm not stopping to wonder where her change of heart came from. I'm just here to embrace it and make her see that I'm hers.

I jerk my head towards the bathroom door behind me. "Come on."

She brings her hands to her chest, pressing them into herself as her eyes go wide. "I can't shower with you."

I love that a beautiful woman like Violet is modest, but one day there will be a time when modesty is left at the bedroom door.

"You're not ready for that," I agree, thumbing the waist of my athletic joggers. Slowly, I peel them down, leaving them next to my damp t-shirt. "But I want you in there with me because I'm going to get you ready."

She swallows hard; her eyes fixed on my erection which strains for freedom through the fabric of my boxer briefs. She nibbles at the inside of her mouth, her eyes on the prize as she slowly scoots to the foot of the bed.

I expect her to ask how I'm going to get her ready because I can see Violet probably isn't a surprise type of girl. And yet, as she gets to her feet, she surprises me. With one hand delicately placed against my pec, she reaches down and moves her fingertip across the dark spot on my briefs.

Her voice is so fucking sultry when she licks her lips and asks, "what's this from?"

I growl out a laugh and grab her by the wrist, and close my hand around hers so that she's squeezing the head of my cock. My answer is simple. "You."

She whimpers, her lids growing heavy. I groan and fill my chest full of air to steady the heady sensation coming over me. She came here for the alpha, dominant, tattooed, muscled man to make her feel good. She didn't come here to see me go beta-male and come in my pants.

Remembering that, I move her hand to fit in mine, and lead us into the bathroom where I lift her to sit on the counter. Positioned between her knees, my cock leaks a little when her legs close around my hips.

"It's always from you," I tell her, loving that I can finally be honest. And she seems to like that answer because she reaches for my cock again, but I step back.

"Not about me tonight, Violet." Then I thumb off the briefs, shove a hand through my hair, and twist on the water to the shower. She swivels on the counter to face the shower, her eyes racing up and down the length of my bare body. I love that she isn't trying to hide it, that she's blooming from her shyness right in front of me.

I grip my cock and stroke my tight fist up the hard length just once, loving the unmistakable moan that slips past her lips as she watches me.

"You're letting me just like... stare at you and watch you in your private space." She tucks hair behind her ears, and grips the edge of the counter, her body magnetizing towards mine as she lurches forward. I love it.

I step in the shower and close the door, swiping my hand through the condensation on the door so she can see me when I say, "this body belongs to you, and you can look at what you own anytime you want."

Steam clouds my vision as I roll the bar of soap between my hands and begin washing.

"Van," she says over the noise of the shower. "I told Sasha about you."

I freeze in the stall, hot water pouring over me. I don't know what this means because if she told Sasha the truth–

"I told her you pulled me over, that it's how we met."

I get light headed at the admission.

Violet protected me from her best friend. You don't lie to your best friend for nothing. You lie to them when it's *something*.

I am something.

I find my voice after clearing away the cobwebs that have crowded my throat. "Why?" I ask because I know what I think it means, but I need to know what it means to her.

"You make me feel alive," she says just loudly enough to be heard over the spray of water. "And I need that."

I swipe the door so I can see her, so I can find her eyes in this vulnerable admission, and let her know that she isn't alone in this scary part of figuring us out. But she won't look at me, so I turn off the water and step out, her eyes whipping up to meet mine. Dripping all over the tile, I take her face in my hands and bring my forehead almost to hers, not quite touching.

"If you let me, I will make your life so good, baby," I tell her, but still, I don't kiss her lips. That part isn't for her; it's for me. I don't want to know how good her kiss makes me feel because it will ruin my resolve to do this right. Or, as right as I can at this point.

"And telling Sasha what you told her?" Now I press my forehead to hers, guiding her hand between us to my naked, wet, and very erect dick. I close her hand around me for the second time in ten minutes, only this time, it's her skin against mine.

She swipes her thumb over my swollen head as I squeeze her hand tighter around me. "What you did for me–that's how it makes me feel." Then I pull her hand off my dick and press it to the center of my chest, where my heart is losing control beneath my ribs. "This, too."

Her cheeks and neck go crimson, and she bites into her bottom lip. She wants me to kiss her; I can feel it. "You gonna finish your shower?"

Putting necessary space between us, I reach for my towel and shimmy it through my hair, down my chest, and up my legs. She watches me dry off like she's watching Monet paint the lilies under the bridge.

"Your legs," she says, watching me dry myself. "They're so big." Then her wide eyes roam over the mountainous span of my shoulders and chest. *"You're so big."*

I cock a brow to her as I tie the towel around my waist. When she's finished checking me out and meets my eyes, she blushes when she realizes her choice of words. Tipping her head to the side, she smiles at me. "That's big, too."

"Well, you don't need to make any room for that yet," I tell her as I lift her off the counter and carry her against my chest to the bed. After putting her right where I did earlier, I go for the light switch. But she stops me.

"Leave it on." She plays with the comforter, busying her hands as she looks at me shyly. I don't question her–hell, with the lights on *is* better. Then I can see everything. I just figured she'd be shy. Most women want the lights off.

Coming to the edge of the bed, I take a moment to just... look at her.

Long wavy hair strewn about my pillow as she makes herself comfortable in the middle of the bed. Her fair skin and bright eyes captivate me, but her soft curves and tight lines make my lower half hot and needy.

Violet is here, in your bed.

I lower my voice. "I'm going to make you feel good now, Violet."

She just nods. Climbing onto the bed, I straddle her, one knee on either side of her. Her breathing quickens, and her bottom lip trembles a little.

"You're not scared, are you?" I ask, hoping like fuck the answer is no.

She shakes her head. "I'm..."

"Nervous?" I offer as I move my fingers to the top of her slacks. She's still dressed in her work clothes which, today, consisted of black slacks and a matching cardigan and sweater tank set the color of a daiquiri. The backs of my fingers graze the warm, private strip of skin under her pants, and she whimpers.

"Ready," she says instead, and with that one word, I tug

her slacks until she's kicking them free from her feet. Her panties are plain white cotton, and I fucking love them. She didn't change herself into something she thought I'd like before she came here–she just came as she is, knowing I'd want her that way.

I've never fucking wanted her more than I do now.

"Van?" she asks, her voice a little nervous. I loop my arms behind her back to sit her up, and she shimmies out of her cardigan knowingly. With my fingers at the hem of her tank, our eyes lock as I slowly lift it up and off of her.

"Yeah?"

"Are you going to kiss me?"

"Everywhere," I tell her, tossing her clothes onto the floor near mine. I want to take a picture of that, evidence of us being naked together, so I can remember it forever in case I'm just a temporary event on her timeline. "But your lips have to wait."

"Why?" she asks. Scooting closer to her on the bed, I loop my arms behind her back. Her breasts press against my bare chest, and both of us heat at the contact. I know she does because she looks down at her breasts against me. And my cock rises under the terrycloth, reminding me he's ready for her.

Unclasping her bra, I keep it held together behind her. With my face tipped to hers, we're just a few inches apart. "Can I take this off of you, Violet?" I don't tell her why I can't kiss her.

Her eyes study my lips as she nods.

"I want to hear that I can take it off."

"Yes," she breathes out, "take it off me, Van."

Tucking my fingers under the straps, I lean back, taking

the garment with me. When it's all the way off, I wrap one arm around her back to lie her down gently.

Nestled in the middle of my bed practically naked, I climb over her, caging her against the mattress. She runs her hands up my arms, grabbing at the flexed, tight muscle. I love that she loves it, it makes every hour I spend at Paradise fucking worth it.

Lowering my face down into her hair, I inhale slow and deep, committing her sultry scent to memory. Then my lips are on her neck, and it's begun.

As I drag my mouth down the column of her neck, kissing and licking along the curve of her throat, she moans, and her body vibrates. Her pleasure already fills me with pride–that I can make her feel good–that's the fucking *best* feeling.

Better than holding my hand to someone's throat while they beg me to stop.

Better than handing a prick a ticket when he could've been let off with a warning.

Better than watching her get out of the shower from the privacy of my laptop screen.

Her hands are everywhere–up my back, nails dragging down my sides, tickling my ribs, through my hair, grating against my scalp. Every touch infuses me with more. More passion, lust, need, and love.

Leaving a trail of bites and kisses along her collarbone, I make my way down the creamy valley lying between her breasts. Her skin is more than soft; it's buttery and pliable against my lips, molding to my kiss like her body is made for me.

When I move my palms over her breasts, covering them

in entirety, kneading them softly as I kiss along her sternum, that's when I notice.

A tremble running up her spine, down her limbs, making her whole body shake just slightly. "Baby," I say, my lips trailing tender kisses up her chest. I don't stop until I'm over her face, my hands tangled in her hair. "What's the matter?"

She presses the heels of her palms to her eyes and shakes her head, blonde hair tangling against my pillow.

"Violet," I say softly, and she lets her hands fall away, exposing her red-rimmed eyes to me.

We're alone in my room, in my house but… it feels like we're alone together in the universe. Because all that exists right now is Violet Carlisle in my bed. That's all that matters.

"Tell me how you're feeling," I say to her as I stroke her temples with my thumbs, combing her hair away from her face.

She reaches up and runs one of her hands through my hair, then drags it slowly through my beard. My eyes shutter closed because the tips of her fingers touching my face are strangely and unexpectedly intimate.

I expected intimacy with Violet… just not yet. I thought she'd need time. And lots more of it.

"Scared," she says, a familiar tremble to her bottom lip. I fight the visceral reaction to stop it from shaking by capturing it with my mouth, kissing her raw and hard, making her enjoy and not worry.

But I'm not ready.

I kiss her stray tears instead. And then I rise to my knees between her legs and stare down at her beautiful body. Swirling circles along her inner thighs with my thumbs, I smile at her.

"Talk to me about why you're scared."

She pushes out a shaky breath, then stretches her arms out, linking our fingers together. Tugging our hands, I pull her up, lie down behind her, bringing her cheek to my chest.

Then I take her hand and press it to my heart, keeping mine on top of hers.

"I'm scared," I start, trying to make her comfortable. "Because I care about you so much, Violet. I know I'm intense. That the way we met was… fucked up and intense."

She doesn't say anything, but her fingers have stopped stroking my chest as she listens intently. I hope this is working because if it isn't, I really don't know how to help ease her fears… the fears that *I've* put there with my choices.

"I'm scared of it scaring you off." I can't calm my nerves for the next part, but it feels like it's gotta be said. For her sake, and I mean every word. "If you ever feel scared of me, Violet, I want you to go. And if you want me to go away because our past is too hard to move on from, I'll go. Because that's how much I love you, Violet. Whether it's weird for you to hear or not."

"How can you love me if you don't know me?" she asks, and I can hear how badly she wants a satiating answer in the way her tone wavers.

"I have so much to learn about you still," I tell her, and I take note that her fingers still aren't moving. "But I *do* know you, Violet. More than I should, more than I have the right to, but I do."

"Tell me about me."

I smile and place a kiss into her hairline as she tips her head up, grinning at me.

Almost completely naked Violet is smiling at me.

"Okay." This will be easy. There are so many things I

know about my girl. "But I'd like to look at you while I do. Is that okay?"

She pushes up to one elbow, placing a hand to the center of my chest while leaning slightly over me. "Like this?" She smiles, and an explosion goes off inside of me, leaving traces of heat popping inside me everywhere.

I wrinkle my nose, and give the tiniest of head shakes.

"I was thinking more..." I tip my head toward the wall where my dresser is, and her whole head turns toward it. Towards the wall. Where there's a floor-to-ceiling mirror affixed to the closet door. I find her eyes in the reflection, and then at the same time, we take in the sight.

I don't know what she's thinking with any certainty, but it can't be far off from my thoughts because her mouth parts with a soft sigh, chest going concave. Me on my back, the soft dip of Violet's waist folded into my groin, her blonde hair pooling on the mattress as she peers over her shoulder– what a fuckin' sight. Only one of her green eyes revealed, the dark split of her ass complimenting the dark ink along my limbs–we look like a painting. An erotic fucking painting.

She looks back to me and nods. She doesn't ask what my plans are; she gets up off the bed and stands next to it, wrapping her arms around herself. I take my time getting up because my cock is like steel, and I'm so close to Violet, the flavor of her skin imprinted on my lips, I don't need to be a hero.

Once I'm up, I see her smirking, and it lights me up. She's relaxing, and I know that's a step in the right direction. A step towards me. And not just in this bedroom tonight.

"Stand here, and I'll make you feel good, Violet." Positioning her directly in front of the mirror, I drop to her feet on my knees. "Let me make you feel good," I whisper, adding, "and I'll tell you how well I know you."

She swallows through a dry mouth, the smack of her lips pulling apart making my dick twitch. She nods, pushing her hair back over her shoulders. Her breasts–plump and perfect–are on full display now and *goddamn.* Better in person by a million times.

"Okay," she rasps in a voice much quieter than a whisper.

Bending over this low is hard for a guy my size, but I manage to lower myself down to her feet. Pressing a kiss to the top of her foot, she giggles. I twist my face up to her, still low by her foot. "You don't like being hot. You always use the AC in your car, even when it's like seventy-five degrees outside."

Her lids droop with my first confession, and her body shudders as I press my lips to the inside of her ankle. "You have six skirts, the kind that are tight down to the knee." She swallows again, and I kiss her calf, letting my tongue discover her skin there. She's sweet and tangy, and my aching cock leaks a little at the discovery.

All discoveries about Violet do that to me.

She makes a noise–a cross between a whine and a moan and goddamn. I reach through my thighs and give my dick a squeeze, hoping to disperse some of the mounting pressure. But when has that ever worked?

"You drink coffee before work and again around two o'clock." I kiss behind her knee, then up her thigh until she says my name.

I tip my head back to look up at her. "Violet."

"Have you seen me naked before now?"

My fingers edge their way up to her hips, and I press my nose to the center of her panties, inhaling slowly. She's damp, and as I'm smelling her, she sifts a hand through my hair to hold me there.

"Yes," I say against her slit, and her fingers knead my scalp in response.

"How many times?" she asks, her voice so fucking low and raspy that I rock my hips forward toward nothing as a desperate attempt to diffuse the pressure brewing in my balls.

I kiss her pussy through her sticky, damp panties as I groan the answer into her. "I've seen you get out of the shower at least ten times," I tell her, and because I don't know the exact number, I guess as close to the truth as I can. Because I won't lie to her. And it seems like she likes the truth.

It may even turn her on.

She feeds another approving hand through my hair, dragging her nails against my scalp before tugging the ends of my hair. I feel it in my balls, and groan into her white cotton panties.

When I slip one finger under the fabric and tug it to the side, she moans my name. Actually fucking moans it. With a quick kiss to her pussy, I slide my tongue through her lips. She slaps and claws at my shoulders as I tuck my face deeper into her.

"Van," she pants, her hands alternating between feral clawing and eager rubbing. "Look."

Craning my head, I take in our reflection.

Violet's gorgeous legs spread, me on my knees between them. Small hands contrast and compliment my broad, inked back. Her arousal is evident in the darkness soaking her pulled-aside panties. Her hands on my shoulders, holding me, owning me. "I fucking love it," I tell the reflection of her before turning back to her puffy, bare cunt.

"You're the best thing I've ever tasted, Violet," I tell her before I dip my mouth between her lips, running tight circles around her swollen little clit. Her hips begin to roll forward as her breathing grows more frantic.

"What else do you know about me?" she asks through many broken pants and moans. I suck her clit into my mouth then tease it gently with the tip of my tongue. Over and over, I flick it up and down, then draw the smooth pad of my tongue against it. A rhythm of movements she likes; she breathes so hard that she can't even speak.

"I know you'd never regret being with me. I'd make sure of that every fucking day." I drop a hand from her hip to slip it between her legs. Her pussy is so wet that I slide two fingers inside of her easily, and she moans with delight at the intrusion.

The noises she makes. They're so different from what I thought she'd sound like. Soft-spoken Violet, I expected a coo here and there but I was wrong. I love learning the things I couldn't watch.

She rasps her moans, her voice throaty and raw. The way she touches me is another thing I never expected, too. She's bold when she wants to be but subtle otherwise. It's a perfect blend of ladylike and cock-killing, and I love it.

Just another thing I love.

"Mmm," she moans, and then I take her into my mouth again, nibbling my way up her swollen lips before flicking her clit with my tongue. Gently I roll it between my teeth, and she slaps at my shoulders, her voice growing loud for the first time.

"Van, *ohgod*, yes."

At some point, the towel tucked at my waist abandoned ship. And my cock is now a steel rod against my belly, the swollen head red and angry, glistening with all my slip ups.

I fucking want her. And after tasting her tonight? It's going to be hard to wait. But I have to. I have to show her that *she* is my number one priority. She is first, then us.

My fingers curl and release, her walls tightening around me each time I thrust deeper inside of her. She eases her feet apart, giving me more room to lick her and fuck her with ny fingers.

She isn't looking at our reflection anymore; her head falls back, the ends of her long hair swiping over the top of her plump ass. Fuck she's sexy. I bury my nose and mouth deeper between her folds, loving the way she fills my mouth and smothers my senses.

Fucking finally.

"Van, Van, *Van*," she hums the only melody I ever want to hear. "It feels so good, it feels so good," she moans, smoothing her palms up her flat belly, over her tits. I strain my eyes for a second, looking up at the sight of Violet grinding my tongue, her own tits in her hands–fuck me.

Hold it together, Van, don't fucking lose it right now, I tell myself as my cock pulses against my stomach. One white-hot spurt of come hits my belly, and I clench my ass as a last defense to keep it together. It buys me a few more passes of my tongue straight up her seam.

"Van, holy crap," she moans, tipping her head completely forward. Her hair fans over her hands which knead and pull at her tits, her hard little nipples poking through. "Yes," she breathes, her hands holding tight at the column of my throat. "Van, Van, *Van*," she chants as I twist my wrist, changing the direction at which my curled fingers stroke her spot.

It's the best position change, because her legs begin to quiver and her spine goes concave as she continues the endless cry of my name.

"Van, Van, oh Van." Fucking her with two fingers in a heavenly combination of pumping and curling, I bury my face in her cunt and feed until she unravels completely.

Sliding my free hand up her backside, I grab her bare asscheek tight as I hold her down on my face while she comes.

"*Ohmygod*," she cries, and her nails dig into my shoulders, and the pain is fucking exquisite. She begins to spasm on my fingers, so I slide them out of her slowly before sinking them into her again.

She holds me tight inside of her, throbbing as she comes against my tongue and around my fingers, each wave of release sexier than the last.

"*Ohmygod* Van yes, *Van yes*," she cries. Then, breaking the last of my resolve, she says, "you make me feel so good."

The final rush of pressure zips down my spine, everything between my legs hard and hot. I can't hold back anymore. I'm fucking lucky it didn't happen sooner.

Bobbing against my belly with each urgent shot, I come hard as I lap up the rest of her orgasm. I groan into her wetness, committing her taste to memory as I suck her juices and massage her clit. My come coats my stomach and drops heavily against the hardwood below, but I don't give it attention. I don't pause my mission to bask in how fucking good it feels to blow with my mouth buried inside of her.

When her hands frantically pat at my shoulders and back, and her rasp turns into a giggle, I know she's ridden my face as hard as she can.

Reluctantly I slide my fingers out of heaven and press soft

kisses to her pussy lips. They're sticky and swollen, and when I roll back to my haunches and look up at her, she's relaxed and sated. And I'm happy.

I've never seen her this way.

She strokes her fingers down my beard, and my cock perks up a little, despite the fact I just emptied myself a moment ago. She does that to me. Fucking drives me insane.

Our eyes idle, and the air between us is dense with the emotional charge that comes with sharing an intimate moment. But when her lips tip up to a small smile, my chest tightens with hope that it's not just the orgasm. That it's her heart, too.

Then her brows pull together as her eyes melt over my chest. She steps back, taking her hands from my beard, and I groan at the loss. She presses her hands to her mouth, her eyes darting to mine.

Before I can get to my feet and explain that I kind of lost control of my cock while I had her in my face, she drops to her knees. We stand on our knees facing one another, and then my girl moves her hands down my naked body, fingers digging into each lump of muscle as she does.

"You came," she says, and my eyes roll closed for a moment as she connects with the come drying on my skin. "Open your eyes."

I do as I'm told.

She worries her bottom lip but holds my eyes. *"You came."*

I tip my head to the side and shrug my shoulders. "I didn't want to. I wanted it to just be about you." I smile at her, and it feels like one of the first real smiles of my life. One I really fucking mean. "But you taste so good. And listening to you ride my tongue and fingers, I just kept thinking how I couldn't believe it." I swallow and spit out the rest of my admission. "Then you kept saying my name." I shove my dry hand through my hair, struggling to explain myself.

"For a year, I dreamed of you saying my name, being in my house, holding my hand, laughing with me. Then you were chanting my name, and flooding my mouth, and I just, I lost it." I chuckle awkwardly at the admission, but I'm glad I said it. Even if she thinks I have the sexual aptitude of a junior high school boy.

Then she digs her hands into my hips, our skin sticky from sweat and come, and she nods ever so slightly. "Can we shower?"

I drop my forehead down to hers. "Baby, you never have to ask. The answer to you is always yes, a resounding fucking yes."

Chapter Twenty-Two

VIOLET

Baby, I get you.

It's kind of strange how fast things can change.

One day everything is business as usual, and less than twenty-four hours later I feel like I've fallen down a human rabbit hole named Donovan Drake and a way out isn't even on my radar.

All the time I spent telling myself to be smart... Well, I kind of wish I would've spent it with Van instead. Because what is smart? Is smart making a traditionally right choice, even if it keeps you freaking miserable?

Maybe I don't know what smart is anymore. Because I know if Sasha knew how I came to meet Van, she wouldn't encourage me to be with him. Knowing her, she'd probably call the cops on him. Call the cops... on a cop? I close my eyes, desperate to rid my mind of the thoughts that don't align with my heart.

I've been a good girl my whole life.

Don't talk back to dad. Don't pick a fight with Rose. Go to school. Got a job. Save money. Pay my own bills. Have a career. Own a home.

I was close to that last part, but the rest of it I did. I did it with a smile painted on, and followed the expected timeline the way the world told me to.

And where did that get me?

I lost forty grand and my future all because I did everything the way I was supposed to and still, I got the freaking short end of the stick.

Maybe if I start doing what resounds in my heart, then I'll be happy. Because doing what's right has left me so underwhelmed with existence.

Van stirs next to me, and it makes me smile. A powerful, sexy man arching his incredibly strong chest against my back, his arms holding me tight–it's *the* way to wake up. I highly recommend it to anyone, seriously.

Between my thighs grows warm and tingly as he groans good morning into my ear, pressing his lips to my shoulder. Electricity pops inside of me, convincing me to roll in the bed to face him.

He props his head up on one hand, elbow to the mattress. With his other, he reaches out, draping it comfortably on my hip. The feel of his calloused palm sluices through my lower half, making me wet.

"Good morning," I reply to him, taking in how rough and sexy he looks in the rising sunlight. Dark hair tousled, eyes a bit puffy from sleep, beard mussed– I can't believe *this* man has wanted me.

This is the type of man that women set their desktop background to at work, who they stare at while they work out. He's beautiful but also hot and very sexy and intriguing and–I mean, really, he's *all the smokin' things.*

"I like you in my shirt," he smiles, sliding his hand over my belly beneath the hem of his Willowdale Police Department T-shirt.

"I like being in your shirt," I say stupidly because I'm realizing, when Van touches me, I struggle with the ability to think and speak.

After he went down on me last night and I exploded at the sight of us, we took a shower together. We didn't touch; I told him I just wanted to get clean. The truth was, as soon as the steam filled the stall, and I saw his ropy muscles coated in suds–I wanted him.

But when I reached for the soap, he'd caught my wrist and pulled me into him. Kissing my wrist, palm, and knuckles, he said, "you said you want to shower and be good, so that's what we'll do." The way he respected me was a first, and it made my eyes warm.

When we got out, he dressed me in his shirt and put me in his bed. I watched his godlike body disappear down the hall and a few minutes later, he came back with water, sliced apples, and a cup of peanut butter.

He knew it was my favorite snack, and instead of feeling uncomfortable because of how he knew it, I felt grateful. And it wasn't the first time that our history comforted me, rather than made me feel icky.

Then I fell asleep in his arms while he stroked my hair and read a paperback book. It was the first time we'd been together in any intimate way, and it felt like I belonged there in his arms.

I slept so perfectly that I woke up this morning panicked at first, thinking I missed work. But thankfully, it's Saturday.

His palm skates over my belly until it connects with my breast. He cups and lightly squeezes me, and when I look down to see his hand fishing around under his t-shirt on me, holy crap. Beads of sweat pop up along my hairline, and my legs are dying to spread.

I've never woken up like this. It's surreal. I love it.

"I feel like I was a kid until this morning," I attempt to explain to him what's going through my mind, but feel like that was maybe not the best opener. "I mean, I'm not a virgin or anything, but... I don't know. I woke up here this morning, and I feel... like a woman."

He studies me, processing, sliding his hand down my belly until its free from the fabric. He cups my face and smooths his thumb across my bottom lip.

I've seen the lip smooth move done in movies. I never thought men really did that. Or that it would actually make a woman tingle. After all, it's just a thumb along a bottom lip. How hot could that really be?

Hot.

The answer is, *very freaking hot.*

"Waking up with you, having slept next to you... I don't know..." I trail off, needing coffee to better articulate myself. "I'm not making sense. I need coffee."

He cups my cheek and places a gentle kiss on the tip of my nose. "I'm gonna go make us coffee and breakfast, but just so you know, Violet, I understand what you're saying."

"You do?"

He nods and kisses my forehead. "Baby, I get you."

"I ACTUALLY DON'T KNOW what you like to eat for breakfast," Van says to me about thirty minutes later. I'm sitting at the bar in his kitchen–in *my seat*–watching him move seamlessly in the space.

"I usually just do something quick so I can get out of the house," I admit, but I don't want to talk about home. Not while I feel so freaking good. "Do you cook a lot?"

He flips an omelet before turning to the carafe of caffeine. He pours us each a cup, both black, then slides mine to me. The mug is worn, the image of a grand castle on the front faded, the lip chipped.

He must catch me eyeing it because he says, "it was my mom's. She loved Disneyland. We went every year growing up."

He takes his glasses from the neck of his shirt where they hang folded, and slips them on. Then he rests his head on his curled fist, elbow on the bar. Facing me, he speaks quietly. "I don't know that I ever really recovered from losing them."

"I can imagine," I say to him, and then because the urge is too strong to deny, I reach into his lap and weave our hands together by the fingers. "I'm sorry. I'm sorry you lost them."

He looks down at our connected hands then back at me. "Tell me what you want for breakfast for next time," he says, changing the subject.

I look down at the perfect omelet then back up into his big brown eyes. "I know you meant food," I say to him, nervously touching the edges of the plate. "But... honestly, all I've ever wanted was to wake up and eat breakfast at a table and feel comfortable. Not feel like I have to watch where my elbows are or how much noise I make or if I made food for anyone else or.... whatever. I just want breakfast to be relaxing. I'd love to start my day relaxed for once."

When I get the courage to look over at him–since I gave that speech directly to my omelet–I see he's gripping the edges of his plate, too, with white knuckles.

"What's wrong?" I ask because his neck is bulging with strain, and his jaw is snapped tightly shut. I can feel his anger over here on my barstool.

"I don't fucking like that you live like that." He faces me, and his passion seems to kinetically transfer to me because my body tingles and burns. "I know we haven't established anything yet, and I'm not going to put any pressure on you. I know I," he presses his thick-fingered hand into his pecs, "am a lot, and our history is a lot. But I just want you to know, if you didn't figure this out already, I'm here for you. You know, when and if you want to share."

He takes a sip of his coffee, and I delight in watching his Adam's apple slide down his throat. "Or if you need my help." His knuckles are white as he grips the crescent handle of the mug.

Squeezing our connected palms again, wetness blooms in my panties as his thumb moves over the top of my hand mindlessly, tracing slow sensual circles. I love how he touches me, sexual, subtle–all ways, I love it.

"I know," I find myself saying.

He starts eating so I follow his lead and– "holy crap! This is amazing," I tell him as I shovel in another bite of perfectly cooked omelet. The egg white is soft but not spongy, and vegetables are tender but not mushy, and the flavor– "and the flavor is so good."

He chases a bite with another drink of coffee. "And how's the coffee?"

I'm nearly done with my mug but I take another drink,

smacking my lips in playful delight as I swallow. "Really freaking good." Like, *perfect,* but I keep that word to myself.

"Good," he says with a single nod.

We finish breakfast, holding hands the entire time. As he clears our plates and washes the dishes, I enjoy the show.

I watch the cords of discipline flex down his back as he bends over, filling the dishwasher. I take note of the way he rolls his neck and stretches his back against the counter. When he tosses the egg crate into the recycling, I watch him write on his grocery list "eggs" with his left hand. I'm learning about him, more and more, and yet I already feel like I'll never get enough.

"Van," I say, and for some reason, I find myself nervous. "Would you want to start dating?"

He sits next to me at the bar again, but swivels us so that our knees are kissing. Taking my hands in his he studies them for a quiet moment before finding my green eyes with his brown ones.

"Violet, I want you. You know this." His eyes bore into mine and my breath catches. "Dating you, taking things slow and getting the chance to do it right after feeling like I've done nothing but fuck up?" One of his hands leaves mine because he cups it to his chest, over his heart. "You just made my fucking year, baby."

I chew at the corner of my mouth so I'm not grinning like a freaking fool.

After breakfast, he takes me into his back yard where he lifts me into his hammock and hands me a second cup of coffee. He mows his lawn, trims the death from his succulents, and repairs a broken sprinkler. All the while, I sway in the gentle breeze, sip my coffee, and enjoy the vibe.

It's quite possibly the best morning of my entire life.

Chapter Twenty-Three

DONOVAN

If she changes her mind... I'll lose mine.

I didn't want her to leave my house that Saturday morning. I was afraid if she left, I'd wake up and find out everything was a dream. Her coming to my house last night, me getting to taste her and touch her, our breakfast, our talks, *our beginning*... but she said she had to go. That she couldn't start not coming home at night or else her dad would freak out.

To that, I wanted to tell her I'd fucking kick his ass. But moving slowly was putting more ground behind me, and that was the goal: move forward together. Attacking–verbally or physically–her dad would be moving to a place I hadn't earned the right to be. So I let her go, and made her promise that she would text me throughout the day.

I wanted to talk to her, of fucking course, but I also needed to know she was okay.

Because the moment she left, I told myself I wouldn't

look at the camera feed anymore. Building things the right way with her meant putting all the watching and creeping in the past. Because if you're dating someone, a normal person doesn't stalk them.

I asked her to text me the moment she was home, and when my phone beeped just ten minutes after she drove away from my house, I knew it was her.

Violet: *Home safe*

Van: *Thank you for letting me know.*

Van: *What are you doing the rest of the day?*

Violet: *Ahh, so you're a full-word texter. Me too.*

Van: *?*

Violet: *I'm just catching up on some laundry and working on my lesson plans.*

Violet: *You wrote "you" instead of "u"*

Van: *Does your principal see your lesson plans before you teach them? Or could you, in theory, teach them the Macarena during PE?*

Van: *"u" is a turn, not a word :)*

Violet: *Yes, Mr. Wheeler reads our plans. We submit them for approval a month in advance. That's why school doesn't start in August for us teachers. Our first month's lesson plans need to be submitted by the first of July.*

Violet: *I agree. My sister only types in emojis and letters. It's crazy. I don't know how her brain reads.*

Van: *Mr. Wheeler is the balding guy with the bushy eyebrows?*

Van: *And if that's him, is he a good boss?*

Van: *I'm still using a colon and an end parenthesis for a happy face.*

Violet: *I noticed that :)*

Violet: *Yeah I forgot... you've probably seen Mr. Wheeler.*

Violet: *He's okay I guess.*

Van: *Just okay?*

Violet: *His boundaries could use adjusting.*

Van: *Do you want to be principal?*

Violet: *I used to think I didn't.*

Violet: *But now I realize that just because someone has had a job for a long time, doesn't make them good at it. It only means no one else has wanted it enough.*

Van: *And now you want it?*

Violet: **shrugs* I don't know but either way, I know I want to be on the school board. I'm sending my letter of interest for consideration for the race next year.*

Van: *You're even fucking cute over text messsage*

Violet: *?*

Van: **shrugs**

Van: *:)*

Van: *Why not this year?*

Violet: *Grr. My mom accidentally spilled coffee on my letter the day it had to go in the mail.*

Van: *Why am I getting the feeling it wasn't an accident?*

Violet: *We play it fast and loose with the word accident in our house.*

Van: *Why would she do that on purpose?*

Violet: *It's complicated*

Van: *Try me*

Violet: *Are you sure you want to hear inter-family drama? We just started dating an hour ago :)*

Van: *I guess I haven't been clear babe but I want to know everything where you're concerned*

Violet: *You've been clear*

Violet: *But I've been conditioned to not share because I'm also conditioned to the people in my immediate surroundings not caring about me*

Violet: *Sorry, that was a little World's Smallest Violin, huh?*

Van: *Tell me about your family. Why did your mom ruin the letter?*

Violet: *I guess it comes down to my dad. We have a complicated relationship.*

Van: *Why?*

Violet: *Honestly, I don't really know why. And I know this is going to sound like something a spoiled brat would say, but the truth is—he's just never loved me.*

Van: *Elaborate.*

Violet: *Well...*

Violet: *I don't know. I just typed and deleted a million things because this feels petty. Like I'm complaining about my sister out of jealousy or something.*

Van: *Why does your dad treat your sister better? What about your mom?*

Violet: *My mom hums.*

Violet: *Whenever dad is being an asshole to me or whenever Rose and dad gang up against me, mom hums. I think in her mind she's convinced herself that we don't think she can hear anything but her own humming.*

Van: *Why does your dad favor Rose?*

Violet: *I couldn't tell you. And I'm not trying to be dramatic here but... it's not even that he favors her, Van. My dad genuinely hates me.*

Van: *I hate that, Violet. I'm not gonna lie.*

Violet: *It's been this way my whole life, no need to panic now.*

Violet: *Okay, I gotta get to my lesson plans. When will I see you again?*

Van: *You got lunch plans Monday?*

Violet: *Sitting on the floor of my classroom with Sasha, eating fried bologna.*

Violet: *So not really, no*

Van: *I'm working a day shift. As long as I'm not on a call, I'd like to swing by the school and eat with you. Is that okay?*

Violet: *I'd love that*

Van: *Can I bring you lunch, too?*

Violet: *Don't! I pack my lunch. It's fine. Seriously. I just want to see you.*

Van: *That's what I want to hear*

Violet: *:)*

Violet: *Have a nice weekend if I don't talk to you until Monday. I really gotta get going on the lesson plans; I'm meeting Mr. Wheeler before class on Monday.*

Van: *Good luck with the lesson plans.*

Violet: *Thanks! Talk to you soon.*

From there, we'd begun texting off and on all day. Later that evening, I texted her to see how her writing lesson plans had gone, and Sunday morning, I texted her early and told her I'd left her a coffee and bagel in a bag behind her car. I wanted to leave it on her porch, but I wasn't sure what would happen if her dad got to it first.

Monday, we met for lunch, and I was officially introduced to a very excited Sasha. She squealed and clapped her hands like a tween at a Jonas Brothers concert when I kissed Violet on the cheek hello.

Violet later told me in private that Sasha was shipping us hard. Before Sasha knew about me, she was telling Violet to get a boyfriend. I didn't ask her why Sasha said that because at the time, I was just fucking happy Sasha was on my side. But not a week later, I'm thinking about that comment.

Sasha is single herself, so why would she push for Violet to get a boyfriend?

We didn't have the chance to meet up for the rest of the

week, though, because I was working nights with Mally, and Violet was asleep most of the time I was awake. We did, however, "drop" text messages for each other throughout our days.

Some of the messages she dropped me were so fucking adorable.

Violet: *For later: You're really big—how many calories do you eat in one day?*

Violet: *For later: What made you want to be a police officer?*

Violet: *For later: TV or movies?*

Violet: *For later: Cats or dogs?*

And this is the way we started building. Of course, in-person conversation would beat out text any day, but with our schedules, that was proving hard. But we found a way, and in one week, I learned more about her than I did in the year watching her.

Like her favorite movie (*Serendipity*), what she's dressed up as for Halloween for her students (the peach from *James and the Giant Peach*, Charlotte from *Charlotte's Web*, Sarah from *Sarah Plain and Tall*, and a bunch of other literary characters I haven't heard about in years), her favorite kind of pie (peach), her pet peeve (people who say *supposubly* instead of supposedly) and she even told me her most embarrassing moment as a teacher—she was explaining swimming and how most people doggy paddle before they learn any traditional techniques. Only... she misspoke and said doggy style instead of paddle. Luckily, none of the kids were wise to it, but she said her cheeks burned the rest of the day.

I'm in love with Violet, but I'm also falling in love with her, too. Because everything I knew I loved before is our foundation, and all these details and nuances I'm learning now are like the cherry on top of the damn sundae.

Each time she'd ask me a question, I'd answer it then ask her a different one. I'd been glued to my phone so much that Mally was getting butthurt.

"Great," Mally gripes as he slams the door on the cruiser. We're back at the station for some paperwork; then we're heading out. I've texted Violet precisely three times since I've been with Mally in the last hour. "Now I'm the only single guy in the group."

I slide my prescription shades off, swapping them for my glasses as we pull open the door to the department building. "You're single because you have the attention span of a fly."

He whacks me across the chest, jarring my radio. "Dude, I once watched a fly go to town on a piece of hotdog my dog barfed up for like, ten fucking minutes."

"Dude, seriously? Dog barf? It's not even nine in the morning."

He stops short, right before the dispatch office, and his eyes go wide as he grabs the inside of my elbow, forcing me to stop.

"Get the fuc–"

"Wait," he says, feeding his fingers through his blonde hair like he's about to walk onto the stage of a dating game show or some shit. "Wait, wait!" he hisses because I don't stop walking. "Hey!"

That stops me. I turn back and see him frantically waving me back to him. Rolling my eyes, I make my way back to him and put my hands on my hips. "What?"

He lifts to his toes, peering around me toward dispatch, then settles in front of me. "I like a girl."

I slap him on his arm. "Well, good. That solves your problem."

He stops me from turning back. "There's a problem, though."

I raise a brow. "Dude. Do not fuck a dispatcher. That has bad news written all over it. You gotta pass her every fucking day. Don't shit where you eat." There, valuable advice was dispensed.

But his face doesn't change.

"It's worse than that."

Stroking my hand down my beard thoughtfully, I try to imagine what Mally's gotten himself into now. Last year, around the time I met Violet, he dated a fucking eighteen-year-old. And she was still in high school.

Yeah, Mally thinks with the wrong head.

"I honestly have no idea what to expect right now," I say, grinning at his visible angst. "But you look like shit, so I'm getting pretty interested."

"Okay, first of all, fuck you." He holds my shoulders, tipping his forehead a bit forward for dramatics. "You know Donna, in Dispatch?"

I roll my eyes and shake his grip off of me. "Uh, no. I've been at Willowdale PD for eight years, and I don't know Dispatch Donna." Sarcasm is my favorite way to bug Mally—he hates it because he never knows when I'm using it or not.

He turns his head fifteen degrees, lines of confusion rippling through his tanned forehead. "Do you seriously not know Dispatch Donna?"

I stare at him. I blink a few times. "Dude, of course, I know Donna."

He nods; his wrinkles vanish as relief moves in. "Okay. Well–"

"Are you fucking Donna? Malibu. She's like sixty years

old," I laugh, trying to imagine Malibu with the ashen-haired dispatcher.

"Her granddaughter."

"Granddaughter," I repeat, doing mental math in my head. "And that would make her how old exactly?"

He swallows, and suddenly, this shit isn't funny anymore. "Christian," I say because this is a mother fucking full-name situation.

"She's eighteen, she's eighteen," he says in a rushed panic, and I sigh with relief. Thank god. Mally's had my back through too much, but I don't know how I could support a man with a girl. That's just wrong.

"Okay, so she's legal. Is she at least out of high school?"

He pulls nervously at the back of his neck. "Yeah."

I hook a thumb over my shoulder. "Dude, we don't have time for a guessing game. We gotta go."

He swats at my thumb. "She lives with Donna. But I didn't know she lives with her grandma because like most kid–most *young adults*," he corrects himself, making wide, serious eyes at me, "live at home with their parents. So when she said she had the house to herself and invited me over, I went. I mean, duh."

I put out a finger. "You have your own house. Why wouldn't you always have her at your house?"

He starts, then stops, his eyes going to the laminate flooring as his brows dip with concern. "Fuck."

Idiot. "Okay, so?"

He brings his gaze back to me. "Okay, so we were, you know, fooling around on the couch, and Donna came home."

My grin could span a football field. "Oh shit. What happened?"

"I panicked because when she saw it was me, she started

yelling and screaming, and I'm pretty sure she hit me with a rolling pin." He rubs his head at the memory. "So I ran out, and I have been avoiding her since."

"How long has it been?"

"Three days." He winces, and I wince in return.

"Okay, so what's the plan here?" I look at my watch. Now we actually can't waste any more fucking time.

"Pop in, say hi; I'll run by the windows."

"Normally, I'd argue that to be the dumbest plan, but I really don't feel like listening to any alternatives, and we're going to be late for the department meeting." I walk ten feet down the hall and pop open the door, greeting the crew. It's not a normal thing I do, but it isn't abnormal either, so they're none the wiser. I bite my cheek to stifle the smirk that threatens when I hear the racing pitter-patter of Mally running in a crouch past me. Fucking idiot.

LATER, on my break, I FaceTime Violet, and Mally cuts in—telling her the entire story about Donna's granddaughter and being smacked upside his head with a rolling pin. He has her in tears as he recounts the "absolute horror" (his words) at thinking his face would be damaged from a rolling pin injury.

It's the first time I've seen Violet laugh hysterically, and my chest nearly splits; it feels so fucking full. The best goddamn noise I've heard. Well, second best. Hearing her say, "Van, yes, you make me feel so good," is the first, obviously.

When Mally's done, I take the phone back and shove him out of view. Violet blots the corners of her eyes with the sleeve of her t-shirt. It's a crop, off the shoulder, and I'm hard from seeing a miniature version of her. "He's got issues," I say as her laughter fades. Left on her face is a sexy little smile, and her eyes cloud over.

"Yeah, well, it could be worse. He could be a stalker." She licks her lips, and my cock leaks a little. I swear it does. This fucking woman. She really is my missing piece—our history is working to curry favor, not the opposite. And what woman would like that you stalked them? Seriously. Diamond in the fucking rough.

"Hmm," I say, narrowing my eyes for just her to see. "You coming over for dinner tonight?"

"Hmm," she mimics, then grins. "Yeah. Six, right?"

"Six."

Our screens could crack from how much our silent eyeing sizzles. Her eyes roam over my uniform—what she can see of it at least—then over my mouth and around my beard. She admitted to me on the phone the other night that she loves touching me—especially my beard.

God, did that make me high.

"I'll see you tonight, baby," I respond, winking. She says bye, and gives a little wave. No sooner have I ended the call than Mally is sing-songing *"I'll see you tonight, baby".* Naturally, I punch him.

He laughs, rubbing the spot where a big ass bruise will most definitely be in a few days.

"Socked by the Bodfather," he teases.

"Talk shit, pay the price."

His smile fades away and he regards me seriously. "I know you followed her."

Whoa, whiplash. That was unexpected. But it's Mally, so I don't deny it. "Okay."

"I followed you, you know." He pulls his hand down his

face, holding his jaw a moment. "A few times actually. And you followed her those few times, too."

I nod. "Okay."

"Dude."

"What?" I position myself in the car to face him, and he does the same.

"What do you mean, *what*? You know *what*. You can't fucking stalk a girl then date her."

"She knows I followed her. She's fine with it."

He nods, and says, "I know that, too." And I grow confused.

"What do you mean you know?" I ask as anger inches through my blood. I don't want to be pissed at Mally, but we're talking about Violet here. "How do *you* know she's okay with it?"

He swallows and looks out the windshield. "I followed her and pulled her over."

I blink. My heart wracks in my chest. "You *what* now?" My palms itch, and I have the strongest fucking urge to grab someone by the throat and slam them into bricks. Not Mally. I don't want to do that to Mally.

I don't want to *have* to do that to Mally.

"I was worried about you, Van, because I love you, okay?" He meets my eyes now. "And I know you. Don't get hot with me right now, man. I know you're gettin' hot. Don't get hot."

His familiarity with me and his words of brotherly affection are ice on my fire, lowering my temperature right away. "I'm sorry," I apologize.

"I wasn't gonna talk to her about you. I was just feeling her out. But she knew me. She said, *you're Christian Miller*. And then she asked, *are you following me too?*"

My hands move up and down my quads. "What else?"

He shakes his head. "Nothing. She asked me if you're a good man."

"What did you tell her?"

"The truth."

"Oh shit."

He laughs. "I told her you're the best." He looks out the windshield again, and it worries me because when we say the deep shit, we don't make eye contact. My throat is thick. "You're like a brother to me, and I want the best for you. So quit with the risky shit, okay?"

I nod, and he nods in return despite the fact he doesn't turn to face me.

"I came clean with her, man. And she's giving me a chance."

He nods. "Good, good. She seems like a sweet girl. But it's only been what, a few weeks? Just be careful."

"I know she could change her mind about me, and if she does, well, I'll deal with it."

"With your little hobby?"

"I'm... giving that up." It feels good to say. It feels even better to mean it.

He sighs out a breath then meets my eyes. "She's a keeper if this is her influence."

I nod. "She's definitely a keeper."

ON THE MENU for tonight's date: hopefully pussy.

But the real menu: handmade ravioli, homemade marinara, grilled broccolini, and peach pie for dessert. She's never had homemade pasta; I learned that when she told me more about her childhood on the phone the other night. We've talked on the phone a couple of hours every night…. In addition to constantly text messaging.

It's been a week since I've really seen her. Sure, we've FaceTimed, and sure we had lunch Monday, but shit. I'm having withdrawals. It's just not enough Violet.

When she rings the doorbell a few minutes before our agreed meeting time, I can't help but smile because that's exactly what I expected. And that's who I know Violet to be: punctual.

Pulling open the door, the smell of her skin and hair rushes back into the house, and before I even see her, I smell her.

My dick perks up, and I find myself licking my lips as our eyes meet.

She's changed out of her school clothes into something comfortable–black yoga pants that ride low on her slim hips, a cropped hoodie the same dark green as her sultry eyes, and black Converse. All that long blonde hair that makes me hard is down, over one shoulder, and she's holding her phone and keys in her hands in front of her, smiling up at me.

"I'm a little early," she rushes out, wincing a little. "I was just… excited to see you."

Fuck me.

The words *I fucking love you* are on my tongue and even though I've already said it, it feels a little *stalker Van,* so instead I smile. Looping my arms around her waist, I pull her in for a deep hug right there in the doorway. She knots her hands together behind my neck, and I don't even care that I can feel her keys and phone against my skin too. The way she embraces me is so natural—fuck, I'm so deep into her for real now that if she changes her mind… I'll lose mine.

I reassured Mally that if this didn't work that I'd be okay

but the truth is, I wouldn't be. I couldn't be. Violet is everything.

"You smell good," her lips move against my throat, and my cock lifts, without question.

"You too. You look gorgeous, baby," I reply, kissing her neck, then her jaw before pulling apart. I hold out my hand, and she feeds hers through mine, our fingers linking together in a tight hold. I love that she doesn't just give me her hand but she actually holds mine.

It makes me hard.

What doesn't when it comes to Violet?

Leading her to the barstool, she grips the counter to boost herself up but I take her by the hips and lift her on, and she squeals a little.

"I like how you handle me," she smiles, her voice low, surprising me as I get us each a glass of water.

As she takes the glass, I stretch the tips of my fingers over hers, and she shudders from the touch. Lowering my elbow to the counter, I continue sliding my hand over hers until my palm is flush to the top of hers. I close my hand around hers, which closes around the sweating glass of water.

"I like touching you, Violet."

She swallows audibly, staring at our hands. "I like your hands," she whispers, "a lot."

"Yeah?" I ask, an absolute pathetic glutton for her compliments. "What else do you like?"

I let go of her hand and smooth mine through her hair, wrapping some of the loose golden ends around one of my fingers. Her eyelids grow heavy, and I tug the strands, bringing our faces closer. I want to kiss her, but I know if I do, all my resolve to move slow will be shot.

Because I know how soft and sweet they'll be. I can

already hear the little moans she'll surrender to my mouth, and it will be the last straw–I'll have to have her, officially and for good.

"Van," she whispers, and our lips are practically brushing we're so close. I can smell the Crest toothpaste on her breath; I can feel wisps of her hair catching in my beard. "Kiss me."

I tug her hair a bit harder, bringing her lips just to mine. "Are you sure?" I ask her, my bottom lip meeting hers. Her response is action; she feeds her fingers through my beard and slams her mouth to mine. She leads the kiss, sweeping her tongue over mine, moaning softly.

Her kiss is raw and urgent like she's been suffocating and this is her breath; this is her life. I fucking love it. Holding and kneading my face as she frantically kisses me, lips and teeth, hot breaths and deep moans–our first kiss is better than I ever fucking imagined.

But I was right.

She's fucking mine now. There's no going back. Losing her after this would be fatal.

Breathless, lips swollen and parted, she pushes me back and grabs my shirt in both hands. "I want you," she pants.

Fuck. I thought I'd explode when I heard her say I love you, but I never anticipated hearing these words. A growl sounds in my throat, and I take her hands from my shirt and put them on my thighs. She fans her fingers and moves her palms up and down my quads.

"Say it again," I command as she rubs my legs. I'm completely hard, my dick is becoming way too acquainted with the inside of my fly, and I'm certain that if we don't get this moving, my jeans are going to become acquainted with the load brewing deep in my balls.

"I want you," she says, wasting no time.

"Mmm," I moan, sealing my mouth over hers, licking up the sweet words, taking them off her tongue, and swallowing them down. "That's the fucking best thing I've ever heard."

I kiss her mouth over and over, both of us breathing hot and heavy when– "*ding!*"

The stove timer pings repeatedly, calling for me to turn the oven off. "Fuck," I grit out against her lips, and her hands' stroke the insides of my thighs. "Dinner's ready."

Lengthening her spine, she peers over my shoulder into the kitchen. "Can it keep?"

"Fuck yes, it can," I reply, getting to my feet and grabbing her off the barstool. Tossing her over my shoulder, she giggles as I carry her down the hall to my room. I could fuck her over the kitchen counter, and I will, but not for our first time together.

Lowering her down to the bed, I smooth her hair out around her, adjust the hoodie beneath her and smooth the blankets around her.

"Stuff like that," she whispers up to me, her eyes wide with wonder. "How you take care of me in the littlest of ways." She props herself on her elbows, and it pushes her tits out, her nipples so hard they pierce the thick fleece of her hoodie.

"I want to take care of you in *every* way." My belt hits the floor with a resounding clank, and she bites the inside of her cheek. Those emerald eyes watching me get undressed is the biggest compliment of my existence.

"But tonight I'm going to take care of you the way you want. So tell me... what do you want?" Thumbing my boxer briefs, I'm about to step out of them when she stops me.

"Wait."

Half bent over, cock jutting out under the tight fabric, I stop, and look at her.

"Did you ever touch yourself while you watched me?" she asks, her chin pulled down to her chest seductively.

I nod. "Yes."

"Hmm," she purrs. "Tell me about it." She lifts her hips, bracing her feet against the mattress. "Tell me about it while you look at me." Then she shimmies out of her yoga pants, leaving her in just a cropped hoodie and neon yellow thong.

Holy fuck, yellow may be my new favorite color.

I like this game. I have plenty of content to play this game. The thing is... she doesn't know about the camera yet. But she needs to know before I fuck her. If not, it could definitely create a divide.

Reaching into my briefs, I wrap my hand around the base of myself and stroke once. "Do you remember a time when the electrical company came to your house? A few weeks ago?"

Her face goes from seductive to contemplative for a moment, her eyes studying my ink as she thinks. "I saw a truck on the street..." she thinks aloud, then adds, "and one was behind me on the way to school."

I raise my hand, letting it stay in the air like one of her students waiting to be called on.

Confusion etches her soft face, and I put my hand in my boxers again. Stroking my cock, I come clean.

"I snagged that uniform off a truck months ago. Didn't know exactly what I'd do with it, but I knew it would be a tool to get me closer to you."

She rocks to sitting, then yanks her hoodie off and tosses it to the floor. The soft fleece of the exposed inside hits my foot, and a thrill runs through my spine. Goosebumps rise up on my thighs and all down my arms.

Precome drips from the slit on my cock, and I stroke it into my skin, using it for lube. "Tell me how you used the uniform then," she says, back on her elbows. Her knees fall apart, exposing a strip of dark yellow fabric at her seam. She's soaking that little thong. I stroke my cock again, this time gripping my crown hard to thwart the fucking quick building need to blow.

"In broad daylight, I put a ladder next to your bedroom window."

Her hand covers her mound, lithe fingers spread open over the ever-darkening fabric. "And?"

"With a tool belt and uniform, I installed a camera through the stucco and drywall from the outside."

Her head tips back, blonde hair pooling against the mattress. Eyes closed, she slips her hand under her panties. When she touches herself, I can hear her wetness sticky against her fingers. I squeeze myself *very* fucking hard.

"I went in your room to cover the tiny hole I made in the drywall," I admit, still gripping myself hard as she rolls one nipple between her fingers. The tip of her tongue sweeps over her bottom lip, and I imagine what it would feel like tracing the veins up my shaft.

"And?" she asks, breathy and eager.

"I thought you were gone. You're usually gone by then." A live wire whips around inside my balls, and I hold myself tighter, trying not to fill my boxer briefs with come before I've even touched her.

"But you were in the shower," I continued, watching her bring her mouth to her breast, that pink tongue swiping over the hardened nub. "Fu-uck," I groan, slamming my eyes closed to gain some fucking willpower. "I hid in your closet. I'd been hard all morning at just the idea of getting a camera in your room. Then when you got out of the shower and dropped your towel–I didn't want to, Violet. I didn't want to do it. But I had to."

"And what did you do, Van?" *Van.* My name in her sweet tone is dangerous. It infiltrates my blood, shoving me closer to the edge, which I'm already fucking teetering on. I open my eyes.

"I watched you through the slats," I admit, the memory of that day infusing with the heady reality unfolding before me. "I unzipped, and I touched myself while I watched you."

She swallows, and with her eyes trained on mine, she slides the crotch of her drenched panties aside again. My mouth fills with saliva at the edible sight.

Glistening, her puffy pink folds stare back at me, and I can't help it; I stroke my fist up and down my length just once at the sight, to pay homage to such a beautiful bare cunt. I have to.

"Do it now," she commands me. "Show me exactly how you did it."

I shake my head. "I want to come while I'm buried inside that sweet pussy of yours, Violet," I tell her, stepping closer to the bed.

She tilts her head to the side, and brings her hands back to her tits, which she covers then squeezes.

"You asked me what I want, Van. This is what I want. I want you to show me how you touched yourself while you watched me. Show me how hard I make you come." She taps her bare belly, giving me a peek at one of her beautiful breasts.

"And I want you to finish on me."

Chapter Twenty-Four

VIOLET

Van is an orgasm for my eyes, so when an orgasm orgasms—holy hell.

Van's restraint is sexy–it shows me how important pleasing me is to him. It's the *most* important. But also sexy? Watching a man like Van lose control. I mean, I don't know for sure yet, but I think it's about to be the sexiest freaking thing ever.

Last week, I watched him go down on me. I've gotten head before, of course–just because I teach third grade doesn't mean I'm some freaking prude. I've had boyfriends. I'm no virgin. But I've always kept my eyes closed. Never tried to watch the show.

Van insisted I watch us in the mirror and freakin' A—I came so hard I thought I was going to faint. And to top it off, he came without touching himself just from making me come. I can't. I can't even think about it because it makes me so wet, seriously.

I've touched myself to that memory four times in the last seven days. No shame in my game. Van is an orgasm for my eyes, so when an orgasm orgasms—holy hell.

Now I have him touching himself for me, reenacting something private and dirty. Am I surprised to learn he put a camera in my room? No. Do I feel violated? Again, no. Should I feel violated and yucky? I don't care about shoulds anymore. I've been living on shoulds my whole life; doing what I should do, doing what the world expects of me. And it's held me back, if anything.

"Get closer to me," I command him, and holy shit, *commanding feels good.* I've never commanded anything. Asked politely? Yes. Begged? Yes. Pleaded? Yes. Silently hoped? Yes. But commanding isn't a word I'd ever use to describe myself.

Until I met someone who let me command him. Until I met someone who empowered me to be any version of myself that I wanted to be, and opened his arms to every single version.

Van. Van's done that and continues to do that. And I really don't care if he followed me, watched me, whatever he did. He cares about me. *Really* cares about me.

And I really care about him.

"Now tell me what you saw and what you did." I lick my lips, sweat breaking out on the back of my neck. My lower half squeezes together tightly, my need a burning coil between my legs, waiting to be sprung open.

"I hid in your closet—the side you don't open," he says, his inked flesh a blur as he pumps himself quickly a few times before gripping his thick, broad cock at the base.

"And?" I coax him to tell me more while I simultaneously tease him, bringing my nipple to my lips by gripping and pushing my breast tightly. The tip of my tongue laps around my areola, and he growls loudly in response. His noises vibrate between my thighs, making my clit thrum.

"You were putting lotion on," he groans, his voice thick and deep. He strokes himself again, and I watch as his meaty girth passes through his art-covered hand, the contrast between his private, hot flesh and his inked skin making my stomach flutter.

God, he's so freaking sexy. I almost have a fear that I have a brain tumor and I'm like, imagining him, and this, and maybe even us. That's how good it is.

I bite down hard on my own nipple before releasing my breast, falling back into the cloudlike bed. When I look at him, his jaw is ribbed with strain, his chin tucked to his chest, a trail of excitement dripping slowly from his flushed crown to the floor.

"You were rubbing lotion into your legs, and I watched the cream disappear and just kept thinking about how soft you probably felt, and how I wished..." he bristles as he bites into his bottom lip, letting go of his cock. It bounces proudly in front of him as he pulls at the back of his neck with both hands. His glasses begin to fog, so he slides them off and lazily tosses them onto the nightstand.

"Why are you stopping?" I ask him while my eyes vacation over his thick thighs and knotted core. This man is built like freaking Jason Momoa.

"I don't want this to end." The loose gravel of his tone is so sexy I question if this was a good plan. I want him inside me, really freaking bad.

But this is hot, too. And I want to do it all with Van.

We have time.

He takes a few steps closer to the bed until his cock is a

shadow on my belly like the arm of a clock. Slowly, he brings his arms back from behind his head. With one hand, he grabs his balls and tugs them. With the other hand, he wraps it around his length, gathering the slickness from the head before pumping himself.

Watching a man touch himself has been programmed into my brain as level ten scorching. Seriously. I'd much rather watch a man handle himself, excite himself, and bring himself to an intense orgasm than watch porn with two good-looking people any day of the week.

And watching Van touch himself? I can't help it—my hand finds its way between my spread legs.

"Baby," he moans, his dark eyes keeping my hand pinned to my pussy. "You're not making this easy."

Smiling, I spread my legs further, and his Adam's apple bobs as he struggles. "I'm not supposed to make it easy. I'm supposed to make it fun."

To that, he simply groans, because he is incapable of words. Then several more muffled groans before he pulls hard on his swollen sac and aims his fist towards my bare belly, the curved crown of him barely brushing my skin.

The slightest rub of his cockhead against my stomach is the final straw, and when the first eruption of come spreads over my skin, I succumb.

"*Ohmygod,*" I moan, keeping my eyes on the wide slit at the peak of him. Opening, spurting, over and over, he shoots his come all over my belly, up to my breasts as my pussy clenches tightly. Rubbing my clit, the sounds of my wetness and his groans of completion make the sweetest soundtrack to our orgasms.

"*Yes, Van, Yes.*"

I rub until my entire lower half is numb, and when I open

my eyes in an attempt to float down from the undeniable high that comes with fooling around with Van, his gaze finds mine.

His chest seems to span from one side of the room to the other, and watching it heave as he gasps for breath does nothing to bring me down. It only lifts me up.

He makes me high.

"That was so hot," I admit, my words coming out on a pant as I struggle to catch my breath, too.

"Fuck yeah, it was." He releases his cock and it swings down between his thighs. And even as he grows soft, everything he has between his legs makes me feral.

"I want to be inside you, Violet," he says, lowering his naked body over my almost naked one. He lifts me and our bodies press together, his come smearing between us. "But first, we're taking a shower, and then I'm going to feed your fine ass so you have the energy to spread these beautiful legs for me tonight."

I bite my lip and nod, ready to follow this man wherever. To the ends of the Earth if I have to. He's just that freaking good.

Van slides his glasses on after we shower, and I find myself staring at him. The more I'm around him; I want to watch him do all the things. Mundane, trivial–doesn't matter. I'm quickly becoming obsessed with the man who obsesses over me.

He holds my hand on the short walk down the hall to the kitchen, and though it's just fingers and palms pressed together, it's something. It means something to me, and he knows it. I watch him plate our food–the food he made from scratch, by the freaking way, and bring it to me, complete with a glass of red wine as well as a glass of water.

We eat, and we talk.

He opens up to me a bit more about his parents and how they wanted more children, but his mom wasn't able. He says he'd always thought of Mally, Bran, and Batman as brothers since they'd been close since they were just starting junior high school.

He doesn't ask me a ton of questions about my childhood, and I think it's because he knows I just don't want to go there. One day soon, I'll tell him all the things I'm ashamed of. I'll tell him another time, I will. It's just… tonight has been so freaking good. I don't want my dad to take up real estate in my good times, too.

"Your mom must've been a really good chef," I say, finishing the last bite of homemade pasta. He made ravioli stuffed with ricotta, and the marinara? Homemade, too. And he opened his freezer to show me the jars remaining in the batch.

Officer Donovan Drake with the big muscles and the meat between his legs, makes pasta and sauce, and eats me until I scream. Holy heaven on Earth.

The feelings I'm catching are real… and I'm catching them fast. But when my mind goes all teacher and type-A, I remind myself that doing things the way everyone else does them hasn't worked for me at all so far.

And it's just what I need to bring me down from the panic and put me back in the present.

"She really was," he says soulfully as he finishes his third helping of pasta. "But she didn't teach me."

"No?" I sip the red wine.

He shakes his head and pushes his plate away from him, giving his large forearms room to rest. "The only stuff I kept of theirs was my mom's cookbooks and my dad's baseball card collection. Everything else was just stuff. But those things were special to them, so I kept them."

I reach out and stroke his cheek as he speaks, and when his glasses slide down the bridge of his nose just a little as he shares, I nudge them back up, earning me the sexiest of grins. With his free hand, he brings my foot to his lap and tenderly strokes the arch.

"I taught myself by reading her notes. She wrote her recipes on these cards but then on the back, she made all these notes to herself, like, *if it tastes too salty, add a pinch of sugar; if the celery notes come through too strong, add pepper.* Stuff like that." His lips twist to the side with a mischievous smile. "The first year I was cooking, I was wasting a lot of food. Nothing came out right. It was all just... salty frustration."

I laugh at that. "What changed?"

He catches my hand on his face and holds it there, turning into it for a moment as his eyes flutter closed. My chest tightens when he kisses my palm, then drops his arm back to the counter. "I got one right. It was," he scratches the side of his head thoroughly as he peers up at the ceiling. "I think it was manicotti." He tips his head to one side. "It was a pasta dish of some kind; I remember that much."

"Are you Italian?" He has dark hair and dark eyes, but aside from that, he's one of those deliciously handsome, ethnically ambiguous men.

He wrinkles his nose. "Na, my dad just fucking loved to eat. Loved pasta dishes a lot." He smiles. "She loved cooking; he loved eating."

I stroke my fingers through the sides of his hair, unable to stop touching him. "You're a good cook," I tell him with a smile I cannot get rid of.

"And you need to eat," he says, his voice an octave lower than a moment before. So low I can feel it vibrate through my seam.

Our eyes idle together, and the world around us stops. "I love you, Violet. I know I've already said it, and I know you may think I can't because we just started really dating, but I have to tell you; I really fucking love you."

My eyes grow hot, and I'm not ready to say it back, but the words are there, bouncing around my brain. They just haven't made it where they need to make it for me to say them.

"Thank you," I reply somewhat lamely, because what do you say to something so freaking beautiful? "Thank you," I say again, this time slipping off the stool to stand next to him. We showered together, but he smells so good.

Looping my arms around his neck, I pepper kisses on his lips, along his cheek, into his beard, and down his neck. Before I know it, his hands are under my ass, kneading into my cheeks as he carries me down the hall, my legs cinched tight around his waist.

He's hard and ready; I can feel him grinding against my center as he pads down the hall. With each step, my mind grows fuzzier, my heart bigger, my pussy wetter.

"What do you want, Violet?" he asks me, his care seeping into my bones, making it harder and harder to go without.

"You," I tell him honestly. "I want to feel you inside me, and I want to watch you the moment you empty yourself into me and give me everything."

He sets me down on my feet, and we take off the limited clothes we had on—his basketball shorts and me in one of his t-shirts. His forehead slams against mine, and he grabs me, his thumb and forefinger cradling my jaw.

"Are you on birth control?"

Smiling, I drag my finger through the trimmed barbed hair on his chest. "Something you don't know," I say, "I'm surprised."

Coiling my hair around one of his fingers, he tugs gently. "At the first fucking whiff of interest, I quit all that shit, baby. Because I knew watching you wasn't right. And I wanna do it right."

"Hmm," I moan, "do *me* right."

He grins and takes his glasses off. The glasses coming off is the sign that good things are about to happen—my tummy flutters.

"I will. Once I know if you're on birth control."

I nod. "I am. I've been on it to regulate my cycle since I was sixteen." I realize how it sounds, so I decide now is a good time to say, "I'm healthy and clean. I've only had three partners."

He nods and drags a single finger along my collarbone, then up my throat until it's under my chin. Tilting my face up, he lowers his and slants his mouth over mine. He tastes like heaven, sex, and home.

He doesn't make me ask. "I've slept with more than three women, but I'm clean." He parts my lips with his thumb; eyes tamped down on my mouth. "I had a physical and all pertinent blood tests just two months ago for my semi-annual physical at work."

"So then I guess we're going bare."

He groans. "I love how you have a dirty mouth without actually having a dirty mouth," he says, eyes still on my lips as his tip up on one side just a little.

"I'm going to leave the really dirty mouth to you," I tell him, then I lead him by the hand to his own bed, and unhurriedly, we climb in and get comfortable. Lying on my back, he climbs over me, nudging my knees apart with his.

We kiss.

His tongue sweeps through my mouth, mine twists around his. Our mouths smack together, his fingers move through my hair, mine grip helplessly at his back. Sometimes his top lip rests above mine, and then he kisses me lower, my top lip pressed over his. We kiss with tongue; we kiss without, we kiss with moans, we kiss through panting, we kiss. We just keep kissing until we realize his hips are rocking down between my spread legs, and my arousal is nearly coating my thighs.

"I could kiss you forever," he whispers into my mouth. I eat up his words, kissing him again for another minute.

"Me too."

Then our eyes meet, and our hearts lock as our gaze does, too. He reaches a strong arm between our sweaty bodies and grabs himself. A moment later, his wide crown is positioned at my very wet and very ready opening and pushes inside of me slowly, sealing the first stroke in with a long, soft kiss.

His kisses are the only thing soft right now.

"Are you okay?" he asks, probably knowing that those three guys that came before him were definitely not as big as him. Because he's *big*.

Big like, I googled *"does it ever not fit?"* after I saw his dick the first time.

Even though I'm wet, it does hurt a little. He's got more girth than the other men I've been with but I don't want him to stop. The last thing I ever want is for Van to stop. So I nod, and press my lips to his to reassure him.

"You feel good," I say, not lying at all. "Keep going."

His hips saw slowly, my legs fall apart instinctively, and

before I know it, his groin connects with mine; he's fully seated inside me.

"How does it feel for you?" I ask him, because he hasn't said much, other than to check on me and moan through clenched teeth.

"Violet," he groans, stilling his hips between mine. "You feel so good." His voice is different, strong but cracking. Reaching up, I sift my fingers through his beard and hold his face, bringing our mouths together.

With a smack, his lips lift from mine, and I can see his eyes. The dark chocolate I'm used to has stormed over, leaving them nearly black.

"Are you okay, Van?"

He nods as he pulls his hips back, temporarily hollowing me. "I'm trying to not look like a complete fucking jackass here," he says, sliding his steely length back inside of me. My pussy clenches around him in appreciation. I'm actually throbbing around him, my lower half gulping in as much of him as it can.

"Wh-What do you mean?" I ask, feeling the undeniable zing of my orgasm swimming down my spine, headed south.

"I just, I've wanted you for so long," he says, "I just can't believe you're really here."

He swallows and blinks, staving off the emotion by pressing his mouth to mine, dragging his tongue over mine.

"I'm really here," I tell him, "and I'm really close."

He throws his head back, swiveling his hips a little to alter the position. The head of his cock slams against my g-spot when he thrusts back into me. "Fuck, Violet. That's the best thing you've ever said because I've been trying not to come since like... the kitchen."

God, his sexy little admissions are like fire between my

thighs. Straining away from the pillow, I bury my face into his neck, loving the delicious scrape of his beard against my face as I cry out, begging for him to come.

"Oh Van, come with me. Come with me, *I'm gonna come.*"

His deep moans paralyze me, my hands stop, my lips freeze against his throat, and my pussy clamps down on him like a vise as I come, and come hard.

"*Van, Van, Van!*" I cry, my lower half seizing so fast and hard that my spine goes concave, and I choke on my moans. "Oh, oh, *ohmygod!*"

For the first time since he's been inside of me, he thrusts fast and hard.

His hips roll to a stop and the steel pipe that spreads me wide pulses; heat floods my hips and abdomen as his come fills me.

He pushes as deep as he can as he empties himself, and though my pussy is burning from his size and growing sensitive now that I've come, it feels so damn good. My eyes get misty, so I turn my head on the pillow, freeing the moisture before he can see.

When he's filled me completely, he collapses on top of me, still holding his own weight on his forearms so he doesn't squash me.

We pant, we touch tenderly, he strokes my cheek, and curls my hair around his finger. I rub his lower back and drag my nails up the delicious striations of muscle on his sides. And finally, after he's softened inside of me, he pulls out, rocking up to his knees.

Lying there, sated and dazed, I watch as he grabs a towel from the bathroom. Returning to his place on the bed between my open legs, he begins carefully wiping my swollen, sensitive parts.

His aftercare is slow and tender–my chest tightens with each pass of the cool towel over my hot skin. My eyelids grow heavy and even though I'm not ready for this perfect night to end, I lose the good fight and drift off to sleep.

WAKING up with Van is like waking up in a dream. Seriously. One of his strong arms draped over my hip, the other somehow wrangled underneath me and around me, his hand holding my hip.

"Good morning," he yawns against my ear, and I love the tingle that spreads down my shoulder when his beard grates my bare skin.

"Good morning," I yawn back to him because yawns are *totally* contagious.

"Can I convince you to spend the day with me?" he asks; the hand that isn't on my hip is already playing with my hair. I love it.

Flipping around in his arms to face him, I stick out my lip in a pout. "I can't."

He sighs and gives me a small smile. "I figured." He pinches his eyes and reaches back behind him, grabbing his glasses from the night table. Sliding them on, he smiles. "There, now I can clearly see your beauty."

I can't help myself, I grin. "You want kids one day? Because your dad jokes are on point." I meant to tease him for his comment. But his smile in response is short-lived.

He rests one of his large palms on my arm, his thumb stroking me. "I do want to be a father, Violet." He swallows, and his alpha shield slips for just a minute. I can see the uncertainty flash through his eyes. "Do you want to be a mother?"

The subtext of this conversation makes goosebumps break out along my back. Placing my hands against his chest, I curl my fingers into his muscle and he moans through closed lips, praising me for my touches.

"I do," I tell him honestly. "I mean, not today or tomorrow but I do. One day."

"One day," he repeats. "I can work with that."

As much as I'd adore spending the day with Van, I can't push it. I don't have a curfew because I'm twenty-freaking-five years old. But I do have a prick for a dad, and with the *three whole times* I've left the house lately, it's really irritated him.

I don't give a crap if he's irritated, but I'm also looking to not have anymore "accidents", especially since my last accident left me financially ruined.

After breakfast, I get dressed and ready to go home. Van watches me, and he has the saddest expression as he does.

"When can you come over again?" he asks, and I grin.

"We sound like high-schoolers." Feeding my arms through my bra straps, Van clasps it for me, and drops my hoodie down over my head, helping me get it on. I pull my hair up, securing it in a messy heap with an elastic from the newspaper that Van got this morning. With one leg in my yoga pants and one still bare, I stop. "We kinda are. I live at home with my parents."

He smirks, but doesn't laugh, because he's too sad that I have to go. After my pants are on and I'm toeing into my Converse, I tug his beard and kiss his mouth.

"I just need to save a little bit more money and then I'll be out of there. We're talking weeks, Van."

He chews the inside of his mouth a little. "You could live here with me. Starting right this second."

"Van," I say softly. "That's not a good idea. It's... it's too soon."

I hear my words and hate them because while, on paper, it may be too soon–I want to say yes. I want to go against all the rules; all the shoulds, all the life designs put in place for me by history. I want to say yes and move in today.

But the truth is, if I move out, I can never move back. And it's not like I want to be there but... I have to be *somewhere*. And Sasha and her sister have no room. And I just don't have enough money saved to nab a nice apartment near the school.

Before I move out, I need to have a financial safety net, just in case.

He cups my cheek and kisses me, and though it's slow and tender, the charge between us is there, sizzling. "I love you," he says with a smile on his face. He takes my hand, guiding me to the front door, where he holds it open for us, then walks me to my car.

"Listen, baby, full transparency here." He scratches the side of his cheek as he tugs open my door for me. "I'm gonna hop in my car and follow you home; make sure you get there safely."

I lift a brow his way. "You can just text me."

Anxiety rolls through his shoulders, and he pulls at the shirt over his chest, getting it off his skin for a minute. "I get anxious," he admits, looking at his sneakers. "I watched you for so long, and now I don't anymore because, well, I have you. But when you leave me, it's fucking hard. I'm fucking brimming with directionless energy. So I'm gonna follow you, and I'm gonna make the promise that one day I won't have to. But today, Violet, is not that day."

Sweat dots at his hairline, and I can see he's telling the truth. Me leaving him is physically making him not feel well. My heart flexes against my ribs. A certain word drifts across my tongue, but I swallow it down.

"Okay." We kiss, I get in my car, and then I wait there on the curb for him to back out. His SUV glides from the garage, and I start the drive to my house.

At some point during the short drive, a car separates us, but I know he's there. When I pull up to my house, all of my happiness and excitement from the last day drains out of me fast. Dad is outside, a water hose in one hand, the other on his hip.

He doesn't actually look at my car when I pull into the driveway behind mom's car, but as soon as I open my door, I'm assaulted by his voice.

"Where in the fuck have you been?" He shouts it—*actually shouts it*–as he continues to water the already lush lawn.

Bumping the door closed with my hip, I take a private breath to steady my frayed nerves. My healed eye socket throbs at the sight of him, and I understand Harry Potter's scar situation a little bit more. I smile at how much my students would like that metaphor but am interrupted by yet another demeaning shout.

"If you want to stay out all night and party like a fucking teenage whore, go live somewhere else."

A teenage whore? I want to argue that even if I was staying out late and partying, that wouldn't make me a whore. And why do I have to be a *teenage* whore? I bite down on the inside of my lip to prevent myself from screaming.

"Sorry," I say, but I leave it at that because there is no

224

actual point. I just make my way across the driveway and over the lawn towards the front door. He steps towards me as I attempt to pass him and reaches out, grabbing me around the arm. His grip is tight and painful.

"*Oww*," I hiss, "let go of me." He holds me tighter and jerks me towards him. He starts to let loose a string of curse words in my ear when I hear the heavy slam of a car door, followed by the most beautiful noise.

Van.

"You motherfucker!" he shouts, no, he *screams*. "You better fucking let go of her you piece of shit!"

And the thing is… dad *does* let go.

The only other time he listened and let go of me was the day of the accident, when he held me by my throat over the edge of the basement stairs. I did ask him to let go of me, but not over a flight of stairs with my feet behind me.

Then Van's wall of a body is separating me from dad, his face close to dad's face.

"What kind of man hurts a woman?" he growls down at my dad, but I grab his wrist and yank him back, as hard as I can.

He doesn't budge, but he can feel my desperation in the gesture, and turns to face me. "What do you want me to do here, baby? Just tell me." His eyes are dark and serious.

"He isn't worth you losing your job," I whisper, "seriously, Van." I tug his hand when his head drifts back towards my dad. "He isn't worth it," I repeat more loudly. "And you being here will just make it worse, seriously." The last sentence is just for our ears.

Van presses a finger into my dad's soft chest. "Watch yourself motherfucker."

He hugs me, kisses my lips, and holds my face when he

says, "you call me if he so much as *breathes* on you, you got that, Violet?"

I nod.

"I love you, baby, okay, *I love you.*" His eyes search mine.

I nod.

He hugs me again, then walks back to his SUV on the curb. I watch him until his car is too far away to see, and when I turn around, I'm clobbered immediately by something moving hard and quick, and the crunch of my skull hitting concrete is the last thing I hear before my world goes dark.

Chapter Twenty-Five

DONOVAN

What I see makes me insane

"Dude, you gotta do some negatives. That's how you really get around the mental block. Tricks you into believing you're lifting heavier. Then you actually *do* lift heavier."

I drag my wrist over my forehead as I sit up from the bench. "Who told you that?"

Mally shrugs. "Probably you, *Bodfather*."

I shake my head and vacate the bench. "Negatives help, but it's not a fucking mental trick. That part has your flavor written all over it."

He scratches his head. "Yeah, maybe I added that part."

I slide plates off the bar, and he makes a song and dance about how he could do it but he's just sore. I roll my eyes and spot his lame ass. "You get right with Donna?" I ask as we re-rack the bar after his first set.

His face is beet-red as he sits up to take a drink. "Not yet."

I shake my head at him. "Idiot."

Batman sidles up, adding, "Yeah, idiot." Then he flips a thumb between us. "Wait, which one of you?"

Mally bats his hand away and lifts his leg up, making a lazy attempt to kick Batman in the nuts. "Alright, alright," Batman says, swiping Mally's leg away, trying to take his shoe off at the same time. Fucking idiots.

"I gotta protect myself extra," Batman says, standing up straighter, cupping his dick with his hands. "Robin wants to have another baby."

Mally grows serious and presses his hands to his mouth. "Are you serious?"

Batman nods proudly. "Henry Burke, you are going to be a dad again?" Mally whispers dramatically, and Jesus, I can't help but roll my eyes. He is so fucking soft.

But we love him.

"That's the plan. If my guys can still swim." He grins, and Mally jumps up from the bench and pulls him into a hug. They slap backs and shake hands.

"Good luck," I say to Batman. "You're lucky Robin even lets you have sex with her." Batman's wife Robin is a lawyer, and super fucking hot.

He sticks out a closed fist for me to bump, so I meet him halfway. "No shit."

"You're going to have another baby, Bran's all happy playing step-daddy, you're all in love and shit," Mally whines, tossing his arm towards me before going full wallow, folding his arms across his chest.

"Wait, what?" Batman turns to me, and I am a fucking jackass, I know it, but I grin. I grin broadly because I can't help it.

"I met a girl," I say because Batman doesn't need the

details. I'm close with Henry, and he's like a brother. But he isn't the brother I'm closest to, the one I ride and put my life on the line with daily. There's only one Malibu.

"Violet," Mally lifts from his pity party long enough to spill my girl's name.

"Wait, Christian met her, and I haven't? You always introduce the friend with the wife first so that they know you can get serious. You can't get serious if you have all single friends." He shakes his head incredulously at me. I put my hand on his shoulder and nod to him.

"Don't worry man, she knows I'm serious about her. *Trust me.*"

He is still quite skeptical. "Dude, bring her over for dinner. Robin will love that. She's really tired of..." he tips his head toward Mally, then changes the subject with an obvious and attitude-filled *"anyway."*

"You know what? If she doesn't believe me, *I don't care!* I told her already, I wasn't the one who said tits around your kid." Mally gets off the bench and starts to pull plates off the bar. I help him.

"Malibu, it *was* you. Van doesn't curse around the kids," Batman says, exasperated, using his tired dad voice on Mally.

"That's fucking right I don't," I nod.

"Hey," Batman says, turning on me and toward me, a scary combination. "You didn't tell me you met a girl. And it's serious?" He presses a hand towards his chest. "I'm hurt."

I roll my eyes. "One day, I'll tell you a very good story and you'll understand why I didn't tell you. But you're not ready. Your brain would explode."

He narrows his eyes at me. This guy is thinking something along the lines of a one-night stand gone wrong. Not at all that his best friend is a fucking nut job stalker. Nope.

That's why the day I'll tell him will never come. He can't handle it.

"Violet Carlisle. She teaches third grade at Willowdale Middle School."

He winces. "Oh shit. Robin's sister works there. I guess the principal is a really big fucking creep." He shimmies a palm. "Handsy."

My blood starts to simmer. "Is that right?"

He nods. "That's what I heard." His face falls. "Shit, sorry, man."

I shake my head. "All good."

Silence passes around us for a moment, but Batman catches up, saying, "I'd love to meet her."

I hold out half of a handshake, and he matches it. "Let's do it. I'd love for her to meet Robin and the kids. You can also be there." I grin at him.

AS I'M DRIVING HOME from the pump session at Paradise, I realize I need to take the camera out of Violet's house. I've been doing good on not watching and following her, and that's what I told her I'd do... that I'd stop. So I have to make good on that, on all fronts.

After a quick shower and a protein shake, I decide the best first step in getting rid of the camera is seeing if the coast is clear. If she's not there now, it will only take a matter of minutes to get there, pull it out, and go.

My laptop is slow to boot, so I scroll through some news on my phone, not really focused on anything. Finally, the computer boots up and I log in to the security camera feed.

What I see *does* things to me.

It makes my blood boil. It puts me on my feet, moving toward the door. It makes me insane. It makes me an absolute fucking crazy person.

Violet is on her bed, face visibly darkened–even through my low-quality security footage. A bag of frozen peas is over her face and she appears to be unconscious.

I'm in my car, backing out of my driveway in less than a minute, no fucking joke.

Chapter Twenty-Six

DONOVAN

I should've fucking shot him.

First things first. I send a text to Mally as I'm impatiently waiting at the first red light I hit.

Van: *Here's my location [DONOVAN DRAKE HAS SHARED HIS LOCATION WITH YOU], meet me where I stop in five minutes. Come alone.*

He's only just about to start his shift–we're partner swapping for a few shifts since we're down two officers–and is likely doing paperwork. That means he will come in uniform, and that will bode well for me and my plan.

Yep. You got that shit fucking right. I already have a plan.

Because that motherfucker hurt Violet for the last goddamn time. She's mine, and no one hurts what's mine. That's going to be the mother of my fucking kids.

I choose to park at the end of the driveway, effectively blocking any of the vehicles at the home from leaving. I tuck my things in my pants and quietly close my door, making my way up the long driveway towards the front of the house.

When I get there, I clear my throat and knock gently on the wood door. It's quiet out today. I actually heard crickets chirping as I walked up through the yard. Some other pops and buzzing off in the distance, the trademark soundtrack to a slow fall afternoon.

The door swings open; there is no peephole. Violet's dad answers the door, and just as his eyes go wide, I have him by the collar of his shirt, my weapon shoved up under his double chin.

"Don't say a fucking word. Do not make a single fucking peep," I growl, releasing his shirt long enough to reach behind me, gun still under his chin, and close and lock the front door. His hands are up, and he doesn't attempt to break away from me. I don't know if it's me, the ink, and the size—or if it's the gun, but whatever it is, her dad isn't going to fight me.

At least not yet.

"What do you want?" he asks, his voice low but strained.

"I want you to do everything that I tell you to do. Everything. Not *close* to what I tell you, not *your version* of what I tell you but what *I* actually fucking tell you." I tap the gun to the end of his nose and smile. "Got it?"

"Or what?" he replies, deadpan. "You gonna kill me?"

My grin somehow broadens, and my cheeks burn with delight. I bring my face close to his because I am in control. "Kill you?" I shake my head. "I'm not a killer." I tap the gun against his temple. "I'm smarter than that." Taking his shirt again, he jerks in my grip, and I grab his shirt tighter, getting some flesh and chest hair as I do. He winces.

"I'll start by cutting off your dick, because you won't die

from that. And who will really care aside from you? I figure all in all, it's a pretty harmless crime." I return the gun to its comfortable position beneath his chin. "There are worse things than death," I whisper with my lips next to his ear.

"What do you want me to do?"

"Get your wife and your daughter, Rose out here without any suspicion. If you raise a single fucking red flag of any kind, I'll cut your balls off, asshole." I jam my gun further into his jawbone. "And by the way, I'm Willowdale PD."

I push him back as I let go, wanting to shake the feel of him off my hands. He's fucking disgusting. Like *shoelaces dragging through the wet floors of a public bathroom* disgusting.

"Go get them and bring them in here, and we'll go from there."

"What about *her?*" he asks, his voice growing irritated on the last word. And *that* irritates me.

"I think we know she's not getting up, is she?" I yank him by the shirt collar again and pull him towards me. Why doesn't this asshole just do what I'm telling him to do? "Now go do it." I push him back again, and he goes.

Seven minutes later, the three members of the Carlisle family that are conscious are now handcuffed (well, one handcuffed, two zip-tied) and about-to-be-gagged. Keeping a few tie options in my vehicle for last minute court appearances has come in handy yet again. My mom was right; being prepared will save you from disaster.

I held them at gunpoint while I made them tie each other up, leaving Rose for last, since she'd be least likely to fight me. Then I just sat the gun down and tied her up, and the other two couldn't have done anything even if they would have tried.

Once they were all taken care of in the living room, Mr. Carlisle made a tiny effort to put up a front and act bad.

"You think I'm not gonna call the cops the second you leave us?"

He got brave with his arms behind his back, tied up, unable to actually fight.

With the barrel of my gun, I tapped the crotch of his bland brown Dockers. "I think you should remember our talk from earlier because we're in the presence of females." Then I leaned down and whispered privately, "don't think they want to hear about me cutting off your balls, one at a time, then your dick. Huh?"

He went white, and it filled me with pleasure. That's when I decided to gag them all.

After they were securely gagged, tied, and unable to do anything but give me wide eyes, it was time to get Violet.

I couldn't have gone to her first–there's no way her dad was going to let me in.

Taking the stairs two by two, my heart is pounding in my neck as I push open the door I know is Violet's.

There she is.

Blood rushes through my ears, making me temporarily deaf to anything but the panic echoing through my veins. He hurt her badly. She's unconscious. And then he just tossed her on the bed with a fucking bag of frozen food on her face?

I should've fucking shot him.

I still can.

Rushing to her, I drag her limp body up into my lap and knock the now warm and mushy bag of frozen food to the floor. Her golden hair is tinged with ruby all along her hairline, and I push it from her face, so I can get a good look at her.

A large gash eats away at her eyebrow, moving up her forehead and disappearing into her hair. It's at least three inches long but thank god it doesn't seem very deep. And yet, she's unconscious.

Gently I feed my fingers through the backside of her hair, searching her scalp for signs–trying to figure out what happened and exactly how she's hurt.

My fingers drive over a lump the size of a tennis ball on her head, and everything goes black for a minute as I lift her up and hold her against my chest. With my lips pressed into her bloodied hair, I whisper to her, "wake up, baby, wake up. You're okay, but you gotta wake up."

This motherfucker has some explaining to do.

Chapter Twenty-Seven

VIOLET

I'm not leaving you.

Holy pain balls. It hurts to even open my eyes, but I force myself to do it because of what I smell. *Who* I smell.

Van. The scent of fatigued muscles, aftershave, men's soap, and sex appeal floods my senses, and even though my head feels like a freaking pressure cooker, part of me relaxes knowing he's here.

"You're here," I say before I can even bring him into focus. Blinking until things are fuzzy but there, I say, my voice weak sounding, "I can hardly see."

A moment later a warm, damp washcloth sweeps over my closed eyelids, down my cheeks, and along my jawline. Though it only touches my sensitive, aching skin, it seems to soothe the storm inside me, too. His fingertips smooth over my skin after he wipes my eyes and face another time, and then I can see.

Above me, the features of his face align, dark eyes nearly black in the partial light of my bedroom. I reach up and run my fingers through his beard, finding comfort in touching him. He leans down and for a moment, I can see my face in the reflection of his glasses.

I close my eyes, because I don't want to see what dad did to me. I just want to feel Van's lips against mine. I just want to feel good again.

His kiss radiates through me, and when he breaks away, I'm not ready, so I reach up with one hand and grab onto his shirt, and force my eyes open. His gaze goes to my hand gripping him, then comes down to me. "I'm here baby. I'm not leaving you."

I nod, and close my eyes because it hurts to keep them open. With them closed I ask, "I'm going to be okay, right?"

His fingers feed through my hair, massaging my scalp as he reassures me, his tone low and thick, wrapping around my worries like a reassuring hug. "Yeah, you're going to be okay. I think you have a concussion, but the cut on your head won't need stitches." He smooths his thumb over the cut softly, and I don't even wince because he's so gentle. "I cleaned it up, put some butterflies on it. We need to get some water and pain relievers in you, and get you an actual ice pack."

I attempt to nod, but fire spreads up my neck and floods the base of my skull. I wince, and Van leans over, kissing my lips. And honestly, I really do forget the pain for a second.

"Don't try to do too much, okay?" He studies my eyes and then holds my face with both hands. "All I need from you is to know exactly what happened. Okay? Can you tell me what happened?"

Biting my bottom lip, I think back to the morning. Everything was wonderful with Van, but I had to come home. Dad would be mad if I didn't, I'd said to Van. My lips twist into a smirk at the irony of that thought.

"What?" Van asks, watching me like a hawk.

"I just... I didn't want him to freaking flip out if I was gone too much, but he flipped out when I came home so....kind of funny and ironic." I attempt to shrug, but the realization of my life throws an unexpected lump in my throat. "He hates me."

Van's hold on my face intensifies, but he's still gentle. "Violet, listen to me; he's a piece of shit, okay? Trust me, as a police officer, I know a piece of shit when I see one, okay? He's one. He's a big one."

He wipes my tears away. "And he isn't gonna hurt you ever again, okay?"

I nod.

"But I have to know what happened."

"After you got back in your car, I watched you leave," I tell him, remembering how his tail lights faded until they disappeared. "Then he hit me, I guess." I think back to the sound. The hardest thud I'd ever heard, like a stone colliding with a stone or a boulder doing battle with a rock. "I hit the cement step on the porch, I think." My head throbs as I speak the words, like my body is trying to tell me, *yes, Violet, yes, that's what happened.*

"I think, at least."

"Okay," he smiles down at me, stroking the pad of his thumb over my bottom lip. "I'm going to sit you up now. And it's going to make everything hurt really bad again for a few minutes, okay? So I need you to be tough until I can get you downstairs and medicated."

"Downstairs?" I shoot back, all of my nerve endings alive. "He's down there."

Van swallows, and it's then that I notice a small violet blooming from the eye socket on the skull inked on the base of his throat. I press my finger to his hot skin, and he doesn't ask what tattoo I'm touching. His eyes are tamped down on mine when he says, "I got that when I knew I loved you."

"It's fading." I trace the petals of the once vibrant but now fading purple flower.

"It's been there a year. I need to get it touched up."

Then, before I can swoon anymore over him, he feeds his arms through mine and lifts, shifting me until we're sitting side by side on my bed. My hands immediately go to my head, where I tip it forward and cradle it as it throbs and pounds like never before.

"Oh my god," I whimper as the pressure inside my brain seems to press against the backs of my eyes and burn its way down my nostrils. Everything freaking hurts. "I think I'm gonna be sick."

Prepared, he slides a wastebasket below me just as I empty the contents of my stomach; which aren't much. He takes the warm towel and wipes my mouth, kissing me after.

"I puked," I say, not opening my mouth for the kiss.

He kisses my temple and stands to get rid of the garbage can. "Puke can't stop me from kissing you."

I want to smile, but my whole face throbs. As he takes the bag out of the basket and ties it off, I realize my house is quiet. Silent, almost. Van is here, in my room, taking care of me. There's a Willowdale PD first aid kit spread open on my bed.

"Is my dad in jail?" I ask, confused because Van isn't in uniform, but he's here, and he's a cop and—

"No, and I know you're hurting, but I have to ask you a very important question."

"Okay," I say, confused.

"Your dad, your mom, and your sister Rose are downstairs. They're tied at the wrists and gagged." His eyes flit between mine as he pauses, giving me time to digest. As unpalatable as the information should be–my family is tied and gagged–I feel... nothing.

"Okay," I say, slightly less confused.

"Violet," he says, resting his palm on my thigh, spreading his fingers over my yoga pants. "Do you want these people in your life?"

His eyes search mine, his brows slightly elevated. The moment is thick with the unspoken subtext of his question. He lowers his voice while bringing his face closer to mine, fingers softly stroking my thigh. "I'm asking because there are a few solutions to this problem. But one is irreversible."

I don't think about the question as much as I think about what he's saying.

If you don't want these people in your life, I can make that happen. And somehow I have a feeling this offer has very little to do with rehoming quietly to a small town in Alaska and more of the rehoming six feet deep somewhere.

Carefully, I weave us together with linked fingers, palms touching. With my thumb stroking his hand, I say to him, "I don't want them in my life, but I want them to have *a* life."

His eyes search mine, and we don't say anything for a second. But it's a calm second. A second that seems to span lifetimes as we hold an unspoken conversation of vows, promises, and so much more.

And maybe a better person would try to find a way to make all of this work–without violence–but as it turns out, some assholes are so special they make even the calmest people see rage.

"Okay," he says, and as if we've silently agreed on it, we conclude with a kiss. He strokes my face with the backs of his knuckles, calloused and tough, but it sets off a fire under my skin. His lips are soft and pliable as he slowly parts his lips, letting our tongues coil together before slipping away. "We need to go downstairs and get you some ice and Tylenol."

Without warning, he feeds his hands underneath me and lifts me up, cradling me to his chest.

Pressed into him, surrounded in his safety, I realize as he carries me first down the hall and then downstairs that any hesitations I had about Van–big or small–are now completely gone. He studies me reverently as he takes the bottom step, and mouths the words, "I love you" before placing a kiss on my forehead.

In my peripheral vision, I see a very familiar shade of blue, and I turn my head to see Officer Miller standing in the entryway of my parents' house. Van and his friend exchange head nods, and after a moment, he's carefully lowering me to the kitchen countertop, Miller's there, too.

"Wait," I stumble aloud through my thoughts, confused, my head aching. Throbbing, really. "Did you call the police? Did you call him?" I whisper to Van, and the whisper isn't meant to keep it private from his partner but more from the tied-up family in the other room.

He shakes his head and keeps his voice private, too. "I text messaged him, not as Officer Miller. As my brother."

I look over to Officer Miller, his wild blonde hair looking far more serious under the dayglow fluorescent tubes of my parents' kitchen. His face is concerned and angry, perfectly fitting the role of a concerned brother-like best friend. It surprises me that he isn't worried. Why isn't he worried? If Van texted him to have him come here, to this mess, it could put him in trouble.

But I don't get the chance to pick apart any of the answers I'm given, because within a moment Van is pushing a glass of water to my lips, after setting two white pills on my tongue.

"Tylenol," he says, and I trust him.

Then Officer Miller is searching through my parents' freezer until– "fuck it, just dump ice into a bag," Van says, growing impatient of Mally searching. With the butterfly bandages on my head double-checked, Van pulls an elastic hair tie from his pocket, and stands flush to the countertop, adjacent to me.

"Tip your head this way, baby," he directs, and because everything in my brain is singing freaking opera, I do without question. And then Van, the alpha male of muscle and ink and general badassery, braids my hair.

When he's done, I want to ask him where he learned to do that, but he lowers his mouth to my ear from over my shoulder and says, "you look beautiful."

I laugh a little in response, but stop immediately when I realize that just about any emotion outside of deadpan is going to murder my skull.

"Mally and I are gonna go talk with your family. You stay here, drink all of this water, and keep the ice here," he holds out my hand as he places the bag of ice in my palm, then presses it to my head. "Wrap it in this towel when the cold starts to burn." He kisses my forehead softly, then slants his lips over mine for an equally soft, quick kiss. "We'll be back."

I nod, and as Mally–my brain bump had me forgetting

that Van and all his friends go by ridiculously stupid and pretty cute nicknames–passes by, his lips lift with a bare minimum smile. He really does seem angry, with zero trace of worry in sight.

Once the guys are through the dining room and into the attached living room, I can't help myself, I slide down off the counter and crouch in the doorframe, out of sight.

Before I hear any speaking, I hear the distinct chirp of a police radio. Easing around the corner, I see Mally, his back to me. Elbow out and arm across his chest, it's clear Mally is using the radio secured to his chest.

"Dispatch, a civilian alerted me to a domestic down here on Pine Hill Drive. I'm en route." He releases the buttons of the radio and turns to Van, volleying his head back and forth in a silent count. After about thirty seconds, he turns his chin across his body and awakens the radio again. "Looks like there's a dispute out front. Gonna get out and check it out. Two females and one male. No back up for now."

Dispatch verifies the information, and my jaw falls open as I realize what's going on. Christian Miller is lying on the job for his friend. They're creating a situation to give Van an out for... whatever he does to my parents. I swallow down a lump of... pride.

I'm proud to be with a man who loves me so fiercely. And I'm proud to be with a man so good that his relationships are this solid.

Falling back against the kitchen wall, I stare at the bag of melting ice in my hands. If I would have told Van to kill my parents, he would have. And he has a friend so devoted to him that he would've helped him. I'm sure of it.

And they're police officers.

Now's the time when a normal person would probably be

freaking out. Probably question the entire system because if the bad guys are the good guys then—I stop myself.

As I watch Malibu contact dispatch for the third time, notifying them that he had to subdue the occupants of the residence in order to speak with them safely, I realize that *everyone is both bad and good.*

Everyone chooses, every moment of each day, just what they are. There is no fairy that floats down over a precious newborn baby and denotes them a future bad guy with the swish of a wand. There is no black crow sitting in a window sill, whose presence is so ominous that it turns humans evil.

We all choose what we are. We choose if we're strong or weak, smart or lazy, bad or good. Everything is our choice. And in the case of my dad, he chooses to be hateful. He chooses to hurt me; therefore, he chooses to be a bad guy.

Van makes choices that not everyone would see as good, and he definitely does things that could fit under the column titled "heel." But no matter what, his choices come from love–everything he does comes from his love for his people.

I'm lucky to be one of the people he loves.

I peer around the corner as dispatch finishes their routine response. Mally has stepped close to my father but refuses to crouch down to my dad's level of sitting. With his hands on his hips, he says to my dad, "Does dispatch need to know that a twenty-five-year-old female has been assaulted?"

He looks at Van. "I saw her face. That's prison time if she presses charges." He looks back to my father, whose face is white as a ghost. The shade of his skin brings a tingle of satisfaction.

Van holds a finger up to Mally. "Hang tight, Officer. Maybe Mr. Carlisle would like to have a talk with me?"

Van and Mally look at my dad, and slowly, with sweat

trickling down his face into the silk tie in his mouth, he nods his head yes.

Van smiles. "That's what I thought."

Chapter Twenty-Eight

DONOVAN

It's funny to me when the man without the gun thinks he has a choice.

Mally and Violet are sitting side by side, backs against the kitchen wall, near the doorframe. After I told her dad that we needed to have a talk, I went to check on her. I found her crouched on the floor, staring at the wall.

I asked her if she was okay; if she was confused or anything–I'm fairly fucking sure that asshole gave her a concussion. The vomiting is a sure sign. But when her glassy eyes met mine, I could see it wasn't her injury that had her on the floor.

"Thank you," she whispered, her voice hoarsely torn with emotion. Then she fed her hand through my beard and pulled my mouth down to hers. It was the first time I felt like she kissed me from her heart, not just from attraction.

Mally said he'd sit with her while daddy and I had a talk. I could see that there were things bothering Violet; but this time, I don't think I was one of those things. For once. The great thing about leaving her with Mally is that if there's a person to leave an emotionally tailspun woman with, it's him.

Sensitivity is somehow his specialty, despite the fact he hangs out with a stalker and a guy with a fucking eye patch.

Unexpected, but true.

I don't focus any of my energy on Violet's mom or her sister. They're... just there. Mr. Carlisle is the head of the family, therefore responsible for the problem. Her sister is barely an adult. She's got time for karma to put her ass in check. And her mother? The humming. I think of what Violet told me about the humming.

Fucking sad. And not *"boo-hoo"* sad, but pathetic sad. *Denial, table for one.*

I drag Mr. Carlisle by his bound wrists to the dining room table that sits between the kitchen and living room. Depending on how loud our voices are, it can be private from the rooms around us. I could take him into a bedroom and close the door; have the type of privacy that would no doubt terrify Mr. Carlisle.

But I don't want to be that far from Violet. Not after everything that's happened. I know she can't get hurt anymore; she's with a person I'd trust with my life. But still, I physically cannot be that far from her. My skin burns and itches at the thought.

Folding Mr. Carlisle into a chair at the table, I sit across from him and calmly rest my firearm on the table between us. I sift a hand through my hair, scratching at my head. I slide my glasses off, using the hem of my shirt to swipe them clean.

Secret: they were already clean. They're always clean. It's just a tactic to really make him nervous. And judging by his drenched t-shirt and wet hair, he's sweating it pretty good already.

Motherfucker.

"What the fuck is your name?" I realize that I don't feel like formally addressing this asshole as "Mr" anything.

He tips his bowling ball of a head to the side, making eyes at me. Fuck, that's right. He's gagged. I hop up and untie the silk tie a bit, but keep it on him, loose around his neck. I pat his shoulder and with my mouth near his ear I tell him, "we'll keep it here for now. In case."

When I'm back in my seat, the sweaty, weak, fuckface across from me says, "Michael."

"Michael Carlisle." I test it. "Sounds like the name of a man who beats women."

He snorts, shaking his head. "You don't know what the fuck you're talking about."

Now feels like the right time to reach for my firearm, so I do. I test how it feels to grip it; then I test what it feels like to hold the butt in my palm and aim it. "Don't worry," I tell him as I point the weapon towards him, not more than two feet between us. "The safety is–" I turn the gun and tap the safety down, engaging it. "On."

I keep the firearm in my grip against the tabletop. "Michael, here's what you're going to do. You're going to leave. You're going to leave Violet's life completely. That means you're going to leave your job, leave this home, leave this town, and never, ever, ever come back."

I study his eyes, and this motherfucker has the nerve to look both indignant and confused.

"See, Michael, I'm starting to get nervous now," I tell him, pulling a hand down my jaw, grabbing at the loose ends of my beard. I can smell Violet on my hand, from her hair. A flash of her lifeless on the bed and I'm infused with more anger. "I'm feeling like you don't understand the situation whatsoever." I lean in over the table, and it squeals under the weight of my muscle.

"I have the gun, I am the police officer, and *you* are the one tied up. *You* are the one caught." I scratch the side of my head, and spin the gun against the grain of the table. "Have you ever seen any movies? Usually the guy who did the bad thing, when he gets caught, it's not good for him." I lean further in, spinning the gun so that the barrel brushes Michael's sleeve. "You're caught."

He licks his lips but still chooses not to speak. Probably a good idea.

"I'm not fucking moving," he finally says, and it's funny to me when the man without the gun thinks he has a choice.

When things are funny, I laugh. "Oh," I say through said laughter, "you are moving. You are quitting your job. You are leaving Willowdale. Because Violet likes it here. She has a career here and *we* want to put down roots here."

I tip my head to the side and wait for his eyes to meet mine. "Her roots need a lot of room and you take up too much of it."

"Career," he snorts, shaking his little fat head. Why does this fucking guy not get the whole, *man with gun in charge, man without gun have no power* dynamic.

My palm itches as I curl my fingers into it. *Don't hit him.* Not yet.

Then he says, "being a babysitter who passes out spelling tests doesn't make a fucking career."

In my defense, I hit him with my non-dominant fist so it

doesn't pack quite as much of a punch. And after I sit the chair back upright and shove him back down into it, I apologize.

"I'm sorry that you're a fucking fuckhead and I had to hit you because of that but," I shrug, "quit being an asshole so we can get through this without hurting my hand. I need my hand to lift, Michael."

He licks the corner of his lip where blood drips steadily from the split in his skin.

"You're going to move. And you're not going to say no, you're not going to threaten to tell anyone, or any of that shit. Because not only do we have ample evidence proving your years of abuse, but also because I think you know *I will actually filet you* if you don't leave."

I stand up to stretch my back, my arms going wide above my head. As I do, what do you know—my shirt rises, and Michael's eyes seem to gravitate to the other gun in my waistband. Then his eyes find mine.

"That one's off the books. Not registered."

He looks back down at the gun, then faces forward, staring at a sad painting of a pear on a table hanging on their wallpapered wall. "She's not worth all this. You'll see."

This time I hit him with my good hand, because why doesn't this motherfucker learn?

And this time, when I pick him back up and put him back into the chair, I hold him by the collar and keep my face right up next to his. "That's the last one you get. Next shot you take at her, I'm taking a shot at you." I grab his face and force it back to mine when he tries to look away. "And my fists are tired, but my gun's not."

Leaving him there, I return to the kitchen, where it seems Mally and Violet have had a heart-to-heart. Her eyes are red-rimmed, and she looks so exhausted. "We're gonna pack her up, load her stuff into my car, then she can wait on the porch while we untie them."

Mally doesn't question a word and nods. "She's up here?" he asks as he heads toward the stairs, having seen me carry her down from there earlier. I nod.

Then I lift Violet into my arms, and we head upstairs. Violet sits silently on the bed, pointing to where things are when I ask her. After we get out her suitcase, I tell Mally to get everything from the bathroom, and hand him another, smaller bag. Then I clear out her clothes from the closet and drawers, and sadly fit it all into just one suitcase.

I scratch my head and look at her. "Is this everything?"

She nods. "My computer, the charger, my phone charger, and…" her eyes move slowly around the room, studying each nook and cranny for vital items she can't live without. She comes up short, turning back to me with a shrug. "Since my notebook is still missing, I guess that's all."

When Mally comes back, his bag is overstuffed. I peer inside, finding boxes of bar soap, bottles of shampoo, razors, toothpaste, a retainer case, a loofah, a box of tampons, and a Ziploc bag full of tiny rubber bands. "I took it all."

I nod, and slap a thankful hand to his shoulder. "That's what I'd do."

I add the bag to the top of the suitcase, looping the handles together, and ask Mally to take it down. Then, before I've reached down to lift her into my arms, Violet reaches up for me.

I smile, and so does she. "I'm getting spoiled. I might have to fake concussions just to be in your arms."

Hoisting her up, I kiss her on the mouth, and she moans.

"Spending more time in my arms can be arranged. Concussion-free."

When we reach the bottom of the stairs, Mally is standing with his hand on the doorknob, waiting. Taking the last step, I set her on her feet. She steadies herself using my forearm, and though the gesture is small, I've never felt more important.

"Do you have anything you want to say to anyone?" I ask her, cupping her cheek. I've never been a guy that fucking cups a woman's cheek. The only thing I usually cup is my balls when I'm jerking off. But with Violet, fuck, I can't keep my big hands off her.

"Is this it?" she asks, but her eyes aren't afraid. They're hopeful, and I'm so fucking glad that I get to be the one to reassure her.

"Yes," I say emphatically. "This is it. Once we walk out that door, we won't be seeing them again unless you really want to." I take her hands in mine and kiss her knuckles. "I'll never ever keep you from them, Violet, but I really believe you will be so much better off without them." It feels good to really mean that.

She looks over to the couch, where Mally has moved Violet's mom and sister. Her mom is straining desperately against the gag, and she's been moaning and trying to speak the entire time. It's been pretty fucking annoying actually. Rose, however, purposefully keeps her eyes on her feet.

Disappointment flashes across Violet's face. I don't know what she wanted them to do or say, but I can see she's hurt. And it fucking fires me up all over again, because I'm sick of these fuckers hurting her.

"Do you want them to be able to speak to you?" I ask her,

willing to have her in the room when we untie them. But with one more look at Rose, she shakes her head.

"I'm ready."

I'm so fucking proud when she doesn't even give her father a second thought and instead chooses to follow Mally and me out to the car.

Once her stuff is in the back of my SUV, I buckle her up while she adjusts the towel-covered bag of ice, now holding it to the back of her skull.

"I'm locking you in; I'll be out in five minutes tops." I kiss her forehead as she groans, struggling to get comfortable again after all the movement. When I close the door, she melts against the window, her eyes heavy.

"She needs to get to bed," Mally says, already walking back toward the house. We stop on the front porch. "What's the plan? We really gonna let 'em go, or what?"

I nod. "They're going to leave."

"Threaten them?"

Nodding my head again, I take my glasses, sliding them in the neck of my shirt. I don't expect the guy to get squirrely, but I gotta drive home. I need my glasses. "He may try to act tough but ultimately, he's fucking leaving. I told him I'd cut his balls and dick off if he didn't. And I punched his lights out."

Agreeing, he nods, his blue eyes wide. "Yeah, he'll leave."

Mally goes to open the door and finish this entire shit show when I stop him. "Hey, what were you and Violet talking about in the kitchen?"

He smirks. "Wouldn't you like to know?"

I grab him around the bicep and bury my thumb into his muscle, applying more and more force by the second. "Alright, alright!" he slaps my thumb away. He straightens his uniform, adjusting his nameplate which is already straight.

"Dude."

He clears his throat then rolls his neck.

"Dude, Violet's waiting in the fucking car."

"Fiiine," he sighs. "The one time I have information someone wants, I don't even get to enjoy it."

I blink, and my jaw tightens.

He clears his throat. "She told me something, but she hasn't told you yet, so I don't want to tell you and ruin it." He shifts his weight on his feet nervously, and it's sort of funny watching a muscled-out beach bum-looking motherfucker act nervous. The power of the Bodfather I guess.

"She's going to talk to you about it. I'd assume very soon." He winces a little, knowing this is going to irritate me. "Sorry, man. It was an emotional dump. I just happened to be the one there."

I nod. "Okay." We step toward the door and he pushes it open but I stop him one last time. "Hey, thank you." I don't say for coming here, I don't say for lying for me, I don't say for never questioning me, I don't say for taking care of Violet. I just say thank you.

He pats my chest. "Brothers."

Inside, we untie the silk wrapped around the women's mouths, and cut their zip ties off. They rub their wrists, and Mrs. Carlisle hugs her daughter. I uncuff Michael while Mally stands directly in front of him, preventing anyone from doing anything stupid.

Michael has proved to be a stupid man, so Mally's presence feels smart.

He turns to face us, his mouth agape though he remains quiet. With the tip of my finger against his nose, I remind him of his plan. "Get the fuck out of here. As soon as possible. I'll be back in a week to make sure you're gone."

"I need longer than a week."

I look around the house. "Are you asking a police officer to set your house on fire so you have less things to move?" I step toward him. "I wouldn't set a fire, Michael. I'm a police officer."

He swallows, and attempts to look casual walking away from me, but he rushes.

He's scared.

Mally reminds them of the hazards of calling law enforcement as I take my gun out, make sure all is well, and replace it. Then we leave.

When I get back to my car after seeing Mally off, Violet is asleep.

I drive us back to my house, knowing this is now *our* home.

Chapter Twenty-Nine

VIOLET

His praise is the ultimate freaking aphrodisiac

Holy crap, my head is *really* freaking hurting. I think it hurts worse now than it did a few hours ago. Has it been a few hours? I honestly don't know. I've never been this tired either. I'm the level of tired which makes talking hard. I'm just sitting on the closed toilet, blinking, my body wobbling, Van taking care of me like I'm a freaking toddler.

"That's better," he soothes, pulling off my Converse. He sets them neatly along the bathroom wall and tosses my socks into the open wicker laundry basket in the corner. I put those socks and shoes on here, in this house, happily this morning.

What a day its been.

He's on his knees in front of me, holding one of my bare feet between his hands, rubbing. His thumbs smooth up the center, spreading the ball of my foot apart, sending a relaxing vibration through my entire body. He repeats on the other foot, then brings his hands to my waist, kneading the sliver of bare skin.

"Okay, now I'm going to help you out of your sweatshirt. I'm gonna do one arm at a time, then ease your head out. I won't jostle you at all." He nods after he says it, searching my eyes for permission. His dark gaze is brimming with care. I nod, and attempt a smile, but my head hurts so bad.

He does what he says, and adds my hoodie to the laundry basket. Keeping his eyes on mine, I shudder when his thumbs slide under the straps of my bra, his knuckles sending a ripple of heat down my spine. "I'm going to take this off, too."

I swallow, and my mouth falls open as a hot breath hisses past my lips. My head throbs; my thoughts a freight train screaming through my eyes. I manage a small nod. And a weak, "okay."

Leaning in, he reaches around me, his beard tickling my shoulder. The tickle spreads through my chest, filling my breasts with a dull ache, before pooling like liquid heat between my legs. My head hurts. Even in that pain, I want him. I know I can't right now, but god, do I want him.

His sweat-kissed skin and traces of his cologne flood my senses, and my head tips against his as he unclasps the last clasp on my bra.

His chin drifts toward me, his beard grating my neck. Another heated breath comes out of me, and the heaviness wins over my eyelids as they droop closed.

Then his warmth evaporates as he leans back, pulling my bra down my arms as he does. It joins the other items in the laundry basket with a whoosh. My eyes slowly open.

His head is back just slightly, exposing the length of his thick neck to me. He swallows as he takes a single deep, chest heaving breath. His dark eyes circle my breasts like a hawk eyeing it's prey.

His hands fall heavily on my hips as he rocks forward, closer to me. "Now the pants and panties, baby."

He makes good on his word, lifting and shimmying me to get my pants and panties off with minimal (read: *none whatsoever*) work from me. And then I'm naked. Slouched over on the toilet seat, face partially swollen, blood in my hair, looking like death warmed over.

And he smiles at me, the most beautiful smile. One that lifts his eyes; he even sits up straighter. "You're never going to be hurt again." He cups my face gently in his big hands. "I'm sorry you're hurting, but I'll get you better, okay? And then it will just be us. And you'll be safe."

My chest burns as it swells. A tear slips past my lashes, and I blink a few times. "I love you, Violet. And I'm glad you're here."

I smile, my head feeling so heavy that I start to tip forward, but Van is there, catching me. "Alright, alright, I'm going to get you in the bath, okay?"

I look to the tub, where he's at some point started running a bath, full of bubbles. Now that I think about it, it smells like lavender. It smells amazing.

Easily, he lifts and lowers me, and I've never felt more cared for. He guides my neck to the back of his large, freestanding tub, and drapes my hair over my shoulder, down my chest. He unbraids it, and fingers combs it, and I watch him. It's private and tender, and something I'd never pictured in a romantic relationship. But this man cares for me in ways that crushes and infatuations wouldn't. I knew it before, but I'm so freaking appreciative of him and his love now.

"I'm going to get you as clean as I can with how much I can move you, okay?"

"Okay," I say, immediately feeling some of my voice return as the warm water begins to eat away at some of the nagging ache running through me.

"There's her voice," he says to me, throaty and low, all sexy. But he's not trying to be sexy, he just is, and it's so much better that way. "Is the bath helping?"

I nod, and he steadies me with a hand in the water, on my belly. With his other hand he reaches to the counter where he has another glass of water, and this time two Advil. "You can alternate Tylenol and Advil, so take these, and it should start to take the sting off a little."

I stick out my tongue, and he puts the mauvish-brown, round pills on it. I swallow them with a drink of water, then end up finishing the glass.

"Good girl," he says to me, and his praise lands between my thighs. My pussy clenches tight at those two words. My head may ache, but my lower half throbs. He turns to set the glass back on the counter, and my knees drop apart, sending the water sloshing around the tub.

His eyes are on me when he sets the glass down. My head rolls to the top of my shoulder, and just barely, I bite down on my bottom lip. "Thank you." I don't have the energy to say more.

When he leans down to kiss me, the steamy bath water fogs his glasses. He takes them off and shoves his hand through his messy, dark hair. Then his hand vanishes beneath the bubbled surface. The washcloth sweeps over my skin as he begins washing me. Slowly he rolls the bar of soap between his washcloth-covered hands, then dunks them in the tub between my legs. He repeats this lazily, washing every part of me, including the back of my neck and even my hair.

The way he holds me with one arm over the surface of the water as he uses the faucet and his other hand to rinse my hair–holy crap. I can feel myself getting swollen and achy. He turns the water off and wrings out my hair, resting it on top of my shoulder.

His palm is flat over my knee, his fingers working my skin softly. "How do you feel now?" he asks, because during the bath I dozed, and he let me. He washed me slowly and carefully, being so gentle with me. It was one of the hottest freaking things ever. The parts I was awake for of course.

I only wish my head didn't feel like it got steam rolled.

I nod, enjoying the cool porcelain of the tub beneath my neck. "Better. I love baths."

"You do?"

"Yeah. I've never had a tub. I only ever took baths on vacation. My bathroom at home is just a shower."

His palm slips over my knee, sliding down the inside of my thigh. "Your new home has two bathtubs."

My heart pounds heavily, sending a throbbing ache to my ears, which sears my temples with fresh pain. I wince a little. and then his fingers are tracing the seam of my pussy lips.

My eyes open, and the pain dulls. The pleasure increases; maybe that's all it is, pleasure outweighing the pain. But either way, it's good.

"Yes," I say, because that's all I can say.

I *want* to tell him how I'm feeling. Share just how much tonight and the last two days have impacted me. But I don't want to do it under these circumstances, so it will have to wait. Instead, again I say, "yes."

He doesn't push inside me and he doesn't touch my ass.

Instead, he slides two fingers up, stopping to circle my clit. I want to watch his breathtaking arm– covered in images of beautiful women surrounded by death –torque and twist. I want to watch him make me feel good.

But my eyes are so freaking heavy, so I close them.

He lowers himself so his lips outline my jaw with sweltering kisses. Then his lips find mine. His fingers drive up and down over my clit enough times to make me gasp, then he pinches it gently, firing off new sensations. Amazing sensations.

"I'm gonna worship this pussy every day for the rest of my fucking life, you better believe that Violet." My heart leaps, warmth rushes out of me. My chest hollows as I exhale a raspy moan.

"This pussy belongs to me now, baby. Property of Donovan Drake. It's mine. And I intend to get on my knees for it every fucking day." He slides two fingers inside me, and I gasp at the intrusion. His thumb comes down on my clit, rubbing it side-to-side, fast. It feels... it feels like it's hard to breathe, I can't even think.

"Yes," I say, because *yes* is right. Oh yes, this feels *good*.

Then he curls his fingers and presses down above my pubic bone with the heel of his other palm. I nearly pee. Or come. Or both.

"Van!" I rasp, my orgasm monopolizing me utterly, out of nowhere. Throttling me, making me teeter on consciousness. "*Yes!*"

My head pounds as my thighs quiver... then tremble... and my pussy clenches around his fingers as my spine curls and I lurch forward out of the water.

"Baby, baby, *baby*," he coos, taking his hand from my belly to lower me back against the tub. Reaching forward,

Van turns the hot water on to warm me up. It feels good. *"Relax."*

When I open my eyes, he laughs. "You look stoned right now."

I smile. "I feel stoned. That was so intense. I'm high."

"High off an orgasm," he says with a wink. "Good girl."

I'm overwhelmed with the urge to reach over that tub, pull his pants down and feel that thick, veiny cock all hot and hard on my tongue. *Gahhh.* It literally makes my stomach ache just thinking about it. I want it so bad my lower half actually throbs at the thought.

But I don't want it like this. I want to enjoy every freaking morsel and moment. And I still feel like shit, despite the incredible orgasm he just gifted me.

I want to tell him how much I want him, how much the idea of just sucking him makes me crazy, but the jackhammering in the back of my head has my eloquence in a chokehold. I say to him, "I like your penis."

He laughs heartily, and I roll my eyes at myself, palming my forehead carefully.

"I mean," I start, but then I don't finish.

He just smiles at me, the only grin to make my belly flutter. "Let's get you out and in bed, okay? You can have your favorite penis when you're rested."

I want to roll my eyes, but it hurt last time I did it, and nothing is worth this freaking headache.

Ten erotic minutes later, Van has rubbed his hands all over my naked body when he finally gets to lotion me down. It's been his fantasy for a while. I pouted because I couldn't act on his fantasy and make it better, but he agreed to one thing: he had to lotion me naked, so I could see just *how good* I made him feel.

What a stupid idea that was.

Staring at the monster cock I've been drooling over for the last few weeks while I am right next to it but can't have it? Yeah, worst idea ever.

Now, as he tucks the down comforter in around me, the smell of him all over the pillows and sheets, my cunt aches for him. Literally aches for him. But he's right. I need sleep.

"I love you," he says with a kiss on my lips. Then he turns off the light, telling me he'll come to bed soon. I fall asleep, hungry for him, but also strangely sated, too.

"OH, VAN, *YES*," I moan as he drags his tongue between my wet lips yet again, so torturously slow.

I woke up this morning to Van nestled snugly between my legs, the thick pad of his wet tongue discovering the seam of my body. His hands were at the back of my thighs, nearly touching my ass, holding them up. I'd never let anyone have me in this vulnerable of a position, but as Van feasts on the sweet meal amidst my thighs, I don't feel the least bit self-conscious.

I've never felt sexier.

He groans as he sucks my clit into his mouth, teasing it with the tip of his tongue. My spine begins wobbling, then he shakes his face, sending a ripple of movement through my lower half, making me clench.

"*Ohmygod,*" I rush out, a faint pounding in my temple that I choose to ignore. His tongue pushes into my wetness, making me ache with this feral need to be held down and pounded hard by him. But I don't attempt to take control or change anything.

I just reach down and feel his silky hair between my fingers, and enjoy the suction and strokes of him eating me out.

And when I'm close, I'm so high off of him that I don't warn him. I can hardly speak. I just begin to crumple and convulse as my orgasm clenches me tight. I cry out his name and pull at the ends of his hair, slap his shoulders and keep him pinned to my greedy sex.

He kisses my swollen pussy, telling me what a *good girl* I am for coming for him. For tasting so good. For being so tight.

Holy shit.

His praise is the ultimate freaking aphrodisiac; *good girl* does to me what oysters, Bruno Mars by candlelight, champagne, and lingerie do to a normal woman.

Then he gets up on his knees between my thighs, and I blink him into focus as I catch my breath. He's naked, his cock thick and swollen in his palm. He curls his fingers and pumps himself, the thick slit at the tip already glistening.

"I want to suck you," I tell him from my now only partially sated spot in the pillows.

He shakes his head. "You're not doing that until your head is better."

I push out my bottom lip in a real pout because damn it, I want that beautiful cock between my lips. I want to trace the deep red crown with my tongue and feel those veins throb on my tongue.

He strokes his cock again. "But making you come gets me so fucking hard, I'm so close. I'm ready now, Violet." He lets go of himself, his cock hitting his stomach with a resounding smack that makes me wetter than before.

I curl my pointer finger towards him as he grips himself

at the base, hard. Groaning, he knees closer to me, and I swat his hand away. With our eyes focused on one another, I reach up and whimper as I wrap my palm around him.

My fingers curl into his torrid flesh as I tug down on his cock, giving his crown extra attention. "Violet," he mutters, his dark eyes fixed on me.

"Praise me," I whisper, his engorged dick thrumming in my palm. He *is* close.

"Be my good girl, Violet," he grumbles, leaning down to swipe a thick finger through my slit. I pump my closed fist down his cock again, stopping at the base to drag my fingers over the sensitive skin of his balls. Bringing his finger to his mouth, he sucks me off of him before folding his hands behind his head, elbows out.

He is the Bodfather. All that disciplined muscle and strength; he's broad and vast everywhere, every part of him brimming with power. An Adonis belt melts down to his groin, where a manicured thatch of dark hair rests just above the biggest beast of all.

I stroke the beast again, hungry for his eruption, desperate for Van's praise.

"That's right, baby, play with that dick that belongs to you," he says, and excitement spreads through me everywhere. The way he talks to me makes me high.

With the pad of my thumb, I stroke the underside of his cockhead, validated by the steady stream of precome flowing freely from his slit. Then I bring my hand to my mouth and drag my tongue over my palm slowly, his dark eyes following my every move.

When I grip him again, he shudders when I begin pumping. "Get that come, Violet. Get it like my good girl does."

I find myself jerking him fast, holding my breath, staring at his cock; desperate for him to erupt.

"Yes, baby, yes. Oh, good girl, *good, good, good girl,*" he groans in time with his pulsing cock, his release coming in white-hot jets over my bare pussy and up my belly.

Hypnotized, I hold him, sticky and hard, in my hand, trying to catch my breath. He's doing the same thing, too. When our eyes meet, he smiles and I laugh.

"Good morning," he offers, leaning over me to press a kiss to my mouth. My sweet and salty flavor is on his lips, and that's not something I ever thought I'd want to taste, but tasting myself on Van is next level.

He reaches for his t-shirt and balls it up, using it to clean the pool of come off my belly. "How's your head?" he asks, delicately lifting my breast to swipe the cotton underneath, cleaning me up completely.

After he does, Van pulls my t-shirt back down, covering my body, then lies by my side. He pulls me into him, and a tingle erupts inside me when I feel his big softening cock pressed to my bare ass.

"How long do concussions last?" I ask, my mind going dirty and dark first thing in the morning. Though, to be fair, when you wake up with a tongue between your legs, your thoughts are a lot different than when you start your day with coffee and the newspaper.

He strokes his hand through my probably horrendously frizzy hair; going to bed with wet hair never results in a good morning look. "You should feel better in a couple of days," he says, kissing the back of my neck. His beard is going to leave a permanent wear mark on my shoulder, and I'm here for it.

"Will you make love to me again in a couple of days

then?" I ask, reaching behind me to touch his hip, then slide my hand down the hard muscle in his thigh.

He buries a groan and a kiss in the back of my neck. "I like that you call it making love."

He flexes his quad beneath my touch. "And as soon as you're feeling better, you won't be able to keep me *out* of you." He strokes my hair as our breaths sync.

"You can sleep in if you want. I'm gonna get up and take care of some stuff."

"Yeah? You're not leaving, are you?" Panic stirs in my gut. I don't want to be alone. Actually, I just don't want to be away from Van.

He kisses my ear, then his weight and warmth are gone as he gets out of bed. I roll into his dip and hold his pillow as I watch him slide into clothes. "Domestic stuff. I gotta mop and vacuum." He winks. "Sounds a lot better when I just say "take care of some stuff" doesn't it?" He smiles shyly, and I reach for his hand.

"I know this is really dumb but I find it sexy that you take care of yourself and your home."

He looks a bit puzzled. "I'm glad you find it sexy but I'm thirty. If I can't cook and clean my house, well shit, that would be scary."

I stroke the hard ridges on the top of his hand, tracing the tail of a snake up his wrist. "My dad never took care of anything or anyone, including himself."

Van sits on the bed, keeping my hand in his as he kisses my knuckles. I love when he does that. "Fuck your dad," he offers softly, and it's somehow just what I needed to hear because it makes me grin. "I tried to organize your bathroom stuff, but I wasn't sure what a lot of it was, so I put it in the cabinet by the sink." He cups my cheek and presses a quick yet electrifying kiss to my lips. "With my stuff."

"Thank you," I say with a smile. He jumps up and makes his way to the door, sliding his glasses on as he does.

"Sleep, shower, take a bath, whatever you want baby; just rest. And when you're ready to get up, I'll be out here, okay?"

I nod but stop him again before he escapes. "You don't have work?"

He scrunches his nose. "Sick day. I won't go back until you're okay."

My mind goes to school and Mr. Wheeler. There's no way I'll be up to teaching thirty third-graders in a day. I'll need to call in. For a few days, at least. As if he were reading my thoughts straight from my notebook, he smiles. "We'll get you squared away with work. It's Sunday morning. Don't worry about that now."

I snuggle into the covers and watch the sliver of the hallway grow smaller and smaller as he quietly seals me into his bedroom. And though I'm full of excitement to be with him, my eyes are still so heavy. I fall asleep with my hand drifting across the still sticky skin of my belly, traces of a smile on my lips.

WHAT FEELS LIKE YEARS LATER, I'm woken by an angry howling in my belly. I'm hungry; hungrier than I've felt in a long time. Slowly, I sit up from the bed, and am only slowed down a bit by the ache that reverberates in my brain, pinging the backs of my eyes.

As hungry as I am, I know a shower is the first thing on the agenda. Seeing all my items laid out is as good as a hug, honestly. It wasn't organized but it was with *his* stuff, and that gave me major feels. I cried a little in the shower, remembering how Rose didn't even look at me yesterday. And here I am, in a home with a man who has loved me so much that he's followed me without so much as a glance his way... for a year. The tears are short-lived because the hot water feels freaking amazing, and through the vent I can smell coffee brewing in the kitchen.

Ten minutes later, I'm wearing a pair of pajama pants and a mismatched tank top from my suitcase, which lays unzipped and open on the bedroom floor. With my hair combed and wet, I pad down the hall, my stomach crying loudly at me.

"Hey, baby," Van greets me, immediately setting down the cluster of items in his hands. He stands in front of me, running his hands up and down my arms, analyzing the injury on my face. "Let's get some new bandages on you, yeah?" He kisses me, and when he pulls away I'm grinning.

"Feeling better?" he asks, guiding me to a barstool by my hand. He flips open a first aid kit that was already on the counter, and sits across from me.

"I am, actually. Starving though."

He tugs gently, smoothing his thumb over my sensitive skin to trap in the ache of changing Band-Aids. Then he replaces them, disposes of everything, washes his hands, and stands before me in the kitchen, hands on hips.

"What sounds good? I'll make you anything."

He's wearing athletic pants with a white stripe down the sides, and his gray t-shirt is glued to his mountainous chest, though I think everything probably fits him that way. I'm hungry and sore, but staring at him in his space, his scent still on my skin somehow; I'm freaking starving... but food isn't on my mind.

His lips twist to the side. "Violet, we're talking about food right now."

I snap. "Damn. You know me."

His eyes grow serious. "I really do."

Just then, there are voices growing nearer and then the front door opens, connecting with the wall. Van rolls his eyes, drifting around the corner so the front door is visible to him.

"Dude," Van whisper-hisses, attempting to keep his voice down for the sake of my headache but also scolding whoever is walking in. "I told you, open the door *gently*," he draws out the last word for effect.

"Bro, you need that spring thing down here. The one that stops the door."

Mally comes around the corner, behind Van. He nods when he sees me, like we're old friends, and the gesture is so nice. Being treated like I belong. It's probably how he treats everyone–how *these guys* treat everyone–but it means something to me.

The door closes, and then another burly, bulky man appears. This one is as tall as Van, and just as muscular. Jesus, these guys must eat everything.

"Violet," Van says, swiveling my barstool to face them. I go to stand but Mally stops me with a short but emphatic head shake and an outstretched palm.

"Don't get up; we're not worth it."

"Violet," Van continues, "you know Malibu, and this is Bran."

One of Bran's eyes is covered by a black eyepatch, but as a teacher I'm used to avoiding the things that most people stare at. We shake hands, and he smiles. The wall of men stand before me, blinking.

"Nice to meet you, Bran."

"I've heard a lot of nice things about you," he says kindly. Mally saunters into the kitchen and jerks open the fridge.

"Dude, you need food."

Van turns back to me, ignoring his friends raiding his pantry and cabinets. Bran pours himself a cup of coffee and slides it onto the glass plate in the microwave with a clink. Irritated, he says, "dude, she's got a concussion. Be quiet."

He winces with recognition then gives me a bashful glance. "Sorry Violet." Mally shuts the fridge with a resounding clunk, "sorry Violet," he adds, when Van slams him with a stink eye.

"Bagels," I announce, "I feel like a really good bagel."

Mally snaps and points at my words, as if he can see them. "Oh yeah, bagels. Bagels sound good."

Bran grabs his keys. "I'll go."

Van shrugs into a police department jacket. "I'm going," he says, "and you guys keep it down." He presses a kiss into my temple, and I can't help it–I feed my fingers down his beard before he goes. What is it about this man? I want him tattooed into my *being*. Seriously. Is that a thing?

"Text me if you think of anything else you need. I'm going to the bakery because they have the best bagels, but I can stop anywhere else if you think of something."

Emotion runs through me, staining my cheeks pink at his offer. So simple, just to go to the store for me if I need anything. I don't want his friends thinking I cry over bagels. It's not just the bagels, though. It's *everything*.

"Thanks," I say, swallowing a drink of reheated coffee that

Bran slides to me. "Thank you," I say to Bran, who nods off the gesture like it's nothing.

After Van leaves, for a second I wonder if it's going to be awkward. The kind of silence that falls between three sort-of-strangers who know just the uncomfortable bits about each other, but surprisingly it isn't.

Mally rubs his palms together. "Alright, let's dish some fucking dirt on Donovan."

Bran shakes his head with a chuckle. "I'll leave that to you." He rubs his shoulder, a memory flashing behind his eye as he does. "He packs a punch."

Mally slides onto the barstool next to me, smelling a lot like wind and sweat. My nose wrinkles. "We just got a pump in, sorry if I stink."

I smile at his honesty.

"But get used to it. Van smells like sweaty balls, like, ninety percent of the time."

Bran offers complimentary information to Mally. "To be fair you're with him when he's the sweatiest, therefore the stinkiest."

I smile at Bran, and realize I'm just a smiling fool in the presence of Van and his guys. The realization that a stalker is kinder and more gentler than my own father swipes the smile from my lips, and my eyes drop to the coffee. I take another sip, swallowing down the thought with the bitter, lukewarm drink.

And because I know I don't have too much time, I decide to go for it. Ask Mally the things I wanted to ask him last night, but didn't have the energy for.

"Why did you do it?" I ask, and I hate that both of their faces drain of happiness, that my shit is heavy enough to bring down a whole room. But I need to know. I have to

273

understand this kind of love, because I don't know anything about it.

Mally nods for Bran to take a seat, and I'm glad he obliges because his lingering in the kitchen was making me uneasy.

"Be more specific," Mally finally says, his blue eyes focused intently on me.

"Why did you come last night and help him?" I don't like how those words feel in my mouth, so I try again. "Why did you help us?"

He sifts through his hair with one hand, then closes his palms together on top of the bar. "The thing you need to know about Van is that he's loyal. And when you have someone in your life that is loyal to the point that they're willing to give up their life for your benefit, you return that loyalty." He nods, clearly satisfied with his response, but I'm definitely more confused than before.

"It's not just being best friends," Bran pipes up, and I'm assuming by now he's familiar with the things that transpired at my parents' house. Or maybe not. I really don't know. But it's clear that Van's loyalty clause extends to him because he quickly amends his statement, "we're all brothers, and you go to the ends for your brothers."

Mally pats a closed fist across his chest. "To the ends."

I swallow, trying to figure out what they're saying through the fuzziness swimming around the edges of my brain. "You could lose your job if my dad reports you and Van."

"No disrespect to you, Violet, but the thing you need to know about boogeymen is that they don't tell. Because boogeymen have closets full of skeletons, and they won't do anything that draws attention to their skeletons, you know?"

Do I know? I think of six months ago when my father

274

kicked me in the ribs and held me by my hair over the basement stairs. All because I wouldn't go to work later in order to give Rose a ride to her final. Her final that had been rescheduled because she slept through the first one, on "accident."

Accident. What a blanket of a word, right? Rose sleeping in is an accident. My dad holding me by the throat and making me very well acquainted with what my hair being ripped from my scalp sounds like is also an accident.

"I know," I nod because I've been on-guard protecting those skeletons for years. For what reason, I don't know now. Because I should? Because people shouldn't know? Because... because... because.... There's not been any reason other than that's what I've been made to feel I had to do.

"So you aren't worried he'll report you or... try to get revenge?"

To that, Mally laughs. Hearty, loud, heart-felt, with tears. When he regains his composure, he places his palm over mine. "Violet, your dad will never be a problem again. Okay? And like Van said, if you ever wanna see him again for any reason, you can. But it's up to you now."

Bran's eye is on me, and he smiles when I catch him staring. "You're in good hands now Violet."

Then, doing the thing I'm so good at not doing–that I just bragged about not doing–I blurt out, "what happened to your eye?"

Mally doesn't miss a beat. "Oh, it's under there. He just really likes pirates."

Bran throws a hook into Mally's arm, and that starts a scuffle between them, full of groans and grabs. I take that time to reheat my coffee. When I come back, they are panting, straightening out their shirts, both of them sweaty.

"It's actually a good story," Bran says, sliding onto the barstool next to mine. Mally stands on the other side of the counter, his arms folded over his chest. He nods in support of the statement, giving permission to Bran.

"We went out drinking one night a couple of years ago. We pulled straws for DD, and Van got stuck with it." Bran recounts the story piece by piece. "We got pretty fucked up, shot pool with these dudes from Oakcreek. It was a good time."

"Where were you guys?" I ask, wanting a setting to the story unfolding in my mind.

"The Seedy Seal."

I make a 'yeesh' face, and everyone knows what that looks like, because the Seedy Seal is one of those places with sticky parquet floors, bathrooms that are always damp, and beer that is never quite cold enough. It definitely fits the setting of a bar fight.

"Bar fight, huh?" I say, wrapping my hand around the now much warmer mug. I take another drink of the coffee, and like the magical drug that it is, I feel it in my veins, warming me, pushing out the fog inside my head.

Bran smooths his fingers over the elastic hidden in his dark hair. I think he's going to adjust his eye patch, but he flips it up instead. Lifting it off over his head, Mally and I stare at the patch on the counter before we slowly, respectfully, look at Bran.

I don't know what I expected. I can't begin to speculate what I expected. But there really isn't much to see. Bran has been fitted with a glass eye, the iris matching the shade of his other eye. When he holds his eye closed, a large raspberry scar eats up part of his lid. The skin is damaged and almost purple in some spots, but he opens his eye before I can study it too closely.

"I don't like the glass eye, that's why I wear the patch."

I nod, because I really wasn't going to ask. "Everyone asks that, huh?"

"They used to. But he doesn't take the patch off anymore, so new people don't know," Mally adds, rocking on his feet from behind the counter. He hits the start button on the coffee, having just assembled all required parts for a fresh pot.

The percolator pops and bubbles, an ambient white noise to the serious conversation happening.

"More than a bar fight but yeah, a bar fight on steroids," he says. "The guys we played pool with had been flirting with these chicks all fucking night. My sister was with us, she's a couple years younger, but these guys know to not be an asshole when my kid sister's around."

I nod, thinking that sounds good, though I have little to go on where good sibling relationships are concerned, since my sister is Rose and all.

"They weren't cute anyway," Mally adds, then instantly looks like he regrets his choice of words. "I mean, I'm not shallow it's just–"

Bran shakes his head. "Not what this story is about, man."

Mally surrenders his thoughts, and hands the attention back to Bran.

"Anyway, Van went to get the truck. We were waiting outside, our other buddy Batman was having a cigarette."

I bite into my bottom lip. I know the story is about to take a serious turn but– "Batman?"

Through a bite of apple which he snagged from the fridge, Mally says, "his wife's name is Robin."

Oh, that makes much more sense... I guess?

"Anyway, the dudes we played pool with came out and kind of like, took off real quick. And we thought it was weird. But we were drunk, so very little critical thinking takes place after six Jack and Cokes, you know?"

"I can imagine."

"Then these dudes came barreling through." He zips his arm between us at the counter, indicating the quickness. "I don't think any of us even saw them inside. To this day, I don't know where they came from. Turns out, they thought we were the other guys. And apparently those guys had said some things to a woman... who ended up being one of their girlfriends."

"Eek," I say, then I realize Bran is missing an eyeball. Eek is an insulting reaction to whatever is coming. So I press my curled fist to my lips, shut the heck up, and just listen.

"My sister was by the door, and one of the guys grabbed her." He reenacts the movement, grabbing his own arm with a hand, showing me. "Lifted her up and grabbed her. They were holding her, and when I went to get her, I took a pop."

"They shot you?!" I gasp, my hand now draped over my collarbone, eyes wide, temples pounding.

But he shakes his head. "No, thank fuck." He presses his fist to his temple. "Hit me right here, knocked me out clean."

Mally leans against the counter, his light and jovial personality now in the backseat. Driving is serious Mally, the one that looks like he goes by Christian and drives his truck with the radio off.

"Batman and I just jumped in, you know, trying to get Sammy back. That's his sister," he says, "Samantha. Sammy." He smooths a hand over the top of his hair, still staring into the rippling curls of the crushed granite countertop. "It just got out of control really quickly, and at one point, they had a bottle. They broke it, and that's when it got real."

"I leaned away as best I could, but my reflexes were drunk, too. I knew as soon as it happened that I was going to lose my eye. I just, I fucking knew it. I held my hand to my face and kept fighting with my other, you know, because they still had Sammy," Bran says, emotion thick in his throat.

"It all happened so fast. She hit the ground with a thud, and I couldn't hardly see anything. I was over her, trying to see if she was okay, but there was so much blood between the two of us," he continues.

"That's when Van came back from getting the truck." Mally looks up, his blue eyes overcast with pain. "There was so much fucking commotion; they didn't notice him. He took the first guy by the collar and knocked him out in one swing. Then all he did was pull his gun out."

Though the story is crazy, I am a woman, and my brain is processing a trillion things at once. So while I hear this, I do some backward math because, didn't Van tell me he's only been a police officer for eight years? How did he have a gun before then? "Why did he have a gun?"

"Van's always had a personal firearm," Mally responds, almost defensively, but we're on the same team. I want him to know, so I nod easily.

"We didn't know if Sammy was okay," Bran says, pulling us back to that night. I can see it all, too. The Seedy Seal sits on a quiet corner, narrow streets, lacking adequate lights. The perfect place for a fight, and even better for an easy getaway. "We had no idea. She wasn't conscious, I was losing consciousness. Christian," he says, surprising me by using Malibu's real name. "He was hit in the leg with the same bottle, and couldn't walk. Batman was freaking us out. He was fucking massively disoriented from having his head smashed against the stucco."

"Van grabbed the guy who dropped the bottle. We don't even know if it was just that guy who attacked us or some of the others." Mally's head falls forward in despair remembering that night.

"He held him by the shirt, looked down at Sammy then pressed the gun under the guy's chin and said to me, *Brian, if you want me to kill him, I will.*"

We all fall quiet, and I try to bear the weight of the information on my shoulders. Van would've killed their attackers. Van also, I think, offered to kill my father. My head begins to spin. Is the pattern Van being a hero or Van hoping to fulfill some deep-seeded urge to murder someone?

"Sammy started to stir, coughing and shit. So I said to Van, *she's alive, it won't be in defense anymore. Don't do it.*" He strokes a hand down his face, his eyes growing moist. "And I'll never forget it. He said, *I don't care if I spend the rest of my life in prison. He hurt your sister. If you want me to end him, I will.*"

"Was she okay?" I croak out, almost afraid to meet Bran's eye. "Please tell me she was okay."

He nods, and the relief that fills me is incredible. Everest size relief, seriously. "She's fine. A pain in my ass. Doesn't even have a scar. And I'm the one who lost a fucking eye."

"It was a scary fucking dark night. It's part of the reason we became cops after."

Bran clicks his tongue. "Don't lie fucker. You became a cop for the pussy."

"Well," Mally says, "that, too."

"You know my name is actually Brian," Bran says as the

noise of the garage door opening drifts through the wall. Van is back. "But once I lost my eye, my name lost the i, too."

I can't help it. A broad grin spreads like wildfire across my face. "I kinda wondered what mother names their son after a muffin."

Mally screeches out in laughter at that, and then the back door opens. Van's large frame swallows the doorway, and my heart flutters a little.

He would kill for the people he loves. That's all it is. He isn't some crazed killer. If he were, he would've killed my father. No doubt. I exhale the doubt and inhale the loyalty that fills the space between us, left behind from the harrowing story.

Van looks to his friends, lifting his hands up. "Get the rest of the shit out of my car you deadbeats," he orders them, and they snap to it, Mally placing a soft palm on my back as he passes.

When they're out of earshot and in the garage, Van slides his knees between mine accordion style as he takes the seat by me. His hands come up to my face and his lips are all over my face as he kisses my aching, marred skin.

"How are you feeling? I got your bagels."

"I'm feeling like I missed you." Then I add truthfully, "and my head really hurts."

"Bagel then back to bed," he orders.

When my dad ordered me, it felt like taking orders from a backward dictator. But being told things–being praised–by Van feels like winning the freaking lottery. I'm cashing in on a surplus of emotions I've been starved of my whole life, and it feels good. I'm rich.

"They eat breakfast here every Sunday," he says as the two

guys come back in, setting the other bags on the counter. "If they annoy you, I'll make them eat on the lawn like animals."

"Ho!" Mally says, a hand across his chest in mock anger.

"I like them a lot," I admit.

"Not too much," he says, and his nostrils flare with a momentary flit of jealousy that burns me up inside. This man is so passionate about me in all ways. Gah. I'm gushing, in multiple ways.

"No, not too much." We kiss, and they coo, which earns them the middle finger from Van.

Then we eat carbs. We eat carbs like we're about to run six marathons. Truthfully, I don't know how much they normally eat, but they keep going, and at one point, I think they're just sympathy eating so I don't feel like an absolute glutton.

But the bread is so soft and flavorful; once I start, I tear through freaking three bagels, each slathered thickly with fresh cream cheese. When I'm done, Van feeds me more white pills, and kicks his friends out, sending them each home with a bag of bagels.

Once he's cleaned up the kitchen and watched me drink another full glass of water, I find myself curled up next to him in his bed. I don't want to fall asleep right away.

I want to stroke his chest and ask him questions about his childhood, get inside his brain and find out how he got to be him; but he's so comfortable and warm, his capable body fusing to mine like the piece I never knew I was always missing.

And I doze off.

Chapter Thirty

DONOVAN

The combination of filthy words in a honeyed tone is dizzying.

Napping with Violet is the greatest fucking thing ever. I don't nap. Usually, naps are meant for people who wear diapers: toddlers or seniors. But when her breathing evens out and her body goes calm next to mine I can't help but join her in what seems like the most peaceful, comfortable sleep.

She's still out cold when I wake up, the sun drawing harsh lines on the ceiling from the upturned blinds. I slide out of bed, an agenda of things rolling through my head. First, I need to call Sasha.

Quietly, I take our phones from the night table and make my way outside, so as not to wake Violet. Sitting in the hammock, I find Sasha's number in Violet's phone, and call her from mine.

She answers with curiosity in her tone. "Hello?"

"Hey, Sasha, this is Donovan Drake, Violet's boyfriend."

"Ohhh," she sighs, and then a moment later, "oh no. Is she okay?" My skin crawls because her instinct is to ask that. My girl has been getting hurt for far too fucking long if her best friend automatically assumes danger. But I don't get mad at Sasha, because she seems like a good friend to my girl. These situations are tough, I see it on calls all the time. To the outsider, things are always so simple but when you're inside the eye of the storm, getting out or helping someone get out feels insurmountable. I get it.

"She moved in with me this weekend," I supply, not knowing exactly what Violet wants Sasha to know. I amend the statement, so that when and if Violet dishes the complete story, I won't have lied. Not lying to the bestie–that's important. "Her dad wasn't happy. There was an incident. But I handled it. She's here now, resting."

Sasha pushes out a heavy breath, and we both sit silent on the line for a minute. "She's safe now, Sasha, okay? I'll take care of her." I swallow, and look into the window at the back of my house where Violet rests on the other side. "I love her."

She sighs again, this time from contentment. "You're a white knight, you know that? You're saving her."

I shake my head even though she can't see. "I'm showing her that life can be anything you want it to be, but it's ultimately your own choice." I look up into the cerulean sky and actually find it beautiful.

"Hmm," she harrumphs, thinking over my words. "I like that. And that's a whole lot more feministic than being a white knight."

"I'm no white knight; I promise you that," I tell her, though she has no idea how true those words really are.

"You're a cop. That in itself brings me so much peace, Van. Someone that won't let that man hurt her–"

"No one will ever hurt her again, Sasha, I promise you that. And actually, I was calling for your help." Including the best friend is crucial, and I want to because Violet would want that, and Sasha is cool.

"Oh?"

"Violet's going to take the week off from work. She's a bit stressed about dealing with Mr. Wheeler, so I thought I'd do that."

Sasha lets a strangled noise slip, then clears her throat. "Please do." I hear what she doesn't say. Mr. Wheeler must be a really fucking piece of work. I cannot wait to talk to this motherfucker.

"I was wondering," I say, not wanting to linger on Wheeler and draw any attention to how much I want to fucking kill him. "Could you help make up some crafts for her class for the week? And maybe help me find a sub? I'll call whoever; I just need a list."

It takes us some time, but after we divide and conquer, Sasha and I have a good handle on crafts and art projects for the week for Violet's class. The only thing left to do is notify Mr. Wheeler, which I'll do later. I thank Sasha, but she seems to want to thank me even more.

And when we end the call, I see a sleepy-looking Violet standing at the sliding glass door. Her blonde hair is now a tangled heap contained by an elastic on the top of her head. I maneuver out of the hammock—ever want to feel emasculated? Have the woman you love watch you try to get your big ass out of a swinging netted seat. Only minorly cringy. After I stand up from the lawn where the hammock has vomited me out, I make my way to my laughing girlfriend and slide open the door.

"He attacked me," I say about the still swinging hammock.

"I saw that," she smiles. "Who were you talking to?"

"Sasha." We go inside and fall into the couch together, my back to the couch cushions, Violet topping me on her belly. She stacks her fists and props her head upon my chest. Her eyes are so clear right now–tenderness floods my ribcage. "Baby, you look so much better. I'm so happy."

She kisses me.

"We got a substitute lined up for this week." I pause. "Well, Sasha's going to text if it falls through but as of now, everything is taken care of and a substitute is most likely a go, too. She just needed to reschedule her kid's dentist appointment or some shit."

"Mrs. Gomez?" Her eyes light up.

I nod. "Yeah, that's who Sasha said you'd want."

She wiggles her head on her fists. "Yay. I love Mrs. Gomez." That earns me a wet, slow kiss, and a whispered, "thank you."

"She also told me you'd need to call the principal, but I'd like to do that for you. I don't want you stressing anything."

Our eyes linger. She hasn't told me about Mr. Wheeler being an absolute fucking creep, but from Sasha's reaction to me saying I'd handle the man, I'd say it's not much of a rumor. Plus, Batman's wife's sister is a forty-seven-year-old woman. That's not the standard rumor-spreading age.

Now's her chance to tell me anything or everything about her principal; to share with me. Staying quiet, I glance down my chest at her as my hands discover the swell of her warm back. She chews her lip a little before saying, "thanks."

A lot just happened, man, I tell myself as hurt wedges into my heart. *She's just not ready. She will tell you about shit when she's ready.* I smile, and she smiles, too. Then she rests her head on my chest and I stroke her hair, and we enjoy the afternoon sun warming our toes through the large glass door.

The week we spend together is fucking amazing. Seriously, it feels like a honeymoon, and we haven't even discussed the fact that we are living together now, bypassing many traditional steps.

We spend most of it talking. As a rule, I prefer sex to talking, but with Violet, I could listen to her explain third-grade math all fucking day.

She tells me why she became a teacher–she loves kids and had so many happy memories of elementary school she wasn't ready to say goodbye to the place. She tells me about her last three boyfriends, all of which sound supremely douchey, with names like Tate, Trenton, and Jonathyn–with a *y*–I really wish I would've just introduced myself to her at the park that night a year ago. Sure, she would've still had to date Trenton, but Tate and Jonathyn were all colleague hookups, and I could have spared her.

She only dated Tate for a few weeks and Jonathyn for two months–both ended because she said no to them over something, and they didn't like it.

"What did Tate want?" I asked her, my curiosity nearly eating me alive. I also need to know what this fucker wanted from my girl in the event I come face to face with him.

"Well," she said, "it's not really what he wanted as much as when he wanted it."

I cocked my brow.

"We were at the movies; it was like our fourth date or something. Anyway, he held my hand during the movie. Then he put it on his, you know," she alludes, unwilling to say the word crotch or dick. While some men would find it immature, I like that my girl isn't eager to be vulgar. She can save all the dirtiness for my dick.

"I really didn't like him enough to do anything with him, but I *really* wasn't going to do anything in public at a movie theater."

"So you dumped him?"

"Oh yeah, as soon as we got into his car, I said, yeah, no thanks."

I couldn't help but chuckle at that. Good girl. "What happened with Jonathyn with a *y*?" I asked her, and she laughed hard at that because that's a fucking ridiculous made-up spelling.

"We dated for two months," she said, "but then I caught him jerking off in the middle of the night. I don't know, it was just weird. Doing it next to me in bed while I was sleeping. I just kept thinking, *where are you going to like, you know?*" She shook her head. "To this day I think he was just going to splurt in the sheets and go back to sleep."

"Splurt?" I laughed at her choice of words, but found it fucking cute.

"You know what I mean," she said, going red.

And then, in the midst of learning about one another, things turned hot. Because all that good girl talk was unmasking the deplorable side of me.

I pinned her to the kitchen wall, and lifted her thigh, grinding my groin into hers. I could feel her hot little pussy through her clothes, wet and eager for me. "You don't want dirty sheets because you're a good girl, aren't you Violet?"

She nodded, going breathless and boneless all at once. Coiling my arm around her back, I pulled her against me. She cinched her thighs around my waist.

Like that, I carried her down the hall and took her into

my room. I stripped her naked, laid her down, and rolled my hips between her open legs, driving in and out. The whole time I fucked her slow I told her what a good girl she was.

"You'd put your hand on my cock at the movies, though, wouldn't you?" I slammed myself into her, bottoming out with a resounding groan as my hips began to lose control. Being to the hilt in Violet felt like the heavens were opening, a holy light pulling me up to a better place.

The best place.

"I would," she panted from beneath me, her fingers digging into my asscheeks as she tugged me deeper inside of her with each feral thrust.

"Because you're my good girl, aren't you Violet?"

Her eyes rolled back, head tipped on her neck, her begs for approval entwined with wild moans. "Yes, please, *yes*."

And that wasn't the only time I had Violet chanting affirmations.

All week, I've been digging myself deeper into the boundless hole of loving Violet. Every single thing I uncover is better than the last.

Her favorite action movie is *Die Hard*, and how the fuck am I supposed to not love that? When she really cracks up, a dimple appears on her left cheek, and god, it makes my balls fucking tingle. She had braces when she was thirteen, and I bet she was cute as fuck. She doesn't know how to drive a stick shift, and I obviously couldn't resist the "I'll teach you with my dick" joke. She caught chicken pox at a *One Direction* concert, and when I questioned her on *One Direction* and if she was still in their age range to be a megafan, she pressed a finger to my lips and simply said, "we don't disparage *One Direction*. May their greatness rest in peace." Fucking adorable.

But there were these insanely private moments, too, where I'd hold her so close to me that I swear our hearts beat in sync. She'd stroke my chest, her little leg thrown over my big one, her long blonde hair fanned out over the bedding behind her. She'd whisper things to me. War stories of her past. And I'd stroke her spine, press my lips to the top of her head, and absorb her pain. Let her purge and fall asleep, sated and satisfied.

She told me about her accident six months ago. She'd said how she shared this particular story with Mally the night we came and got her.

She told me how Michael fisted her hair at the scalp and dangled her past the edge of their basement stairs. He kicked her twice before releasing her... and that was the night my anger grew roots.

Before then, I knew Michael was a piece of shit and certainly an awful father. But as she recounted the action followed by the equally deplorable reaction of making her pay her own ambulance and medical bills with her nest egg? It's the only time in my life I've ever experienced regret.

Because I should've killed him that night when I got her out of there.

I should have shot him in the dick and let him suffer before sinking a slug into his fucked up brain. Clearly, he's wired all wrong, and what's the point of having some fucking psycho on the loose?

But she didn't want me to, and I have to remind myself of that in case I ever run into the fucker. And from everything I know, he's not the brightest. He's liable to come back.

Violet also apologized for not telling me sooner. But I understood. In my line of work; I see plenty. It's partially why I have the hobby that I do. People need to fucking clue in on how good they have it and quit being petty over ridiculous shit that has no actual bearing on their life. Live and enjoy, for fucksake. Some don't get that chance.

But Violet had been ashamed. She kept it from everyone except Sasha because she felt like somehow, she must've asked for it, or deserved it. It's how every victim feels.

I know that from being a police officer, sure. But I also know that from personal experience. After my parents were killed, there was one long year from age seventeen to eighteen where I honestly believed that I'd put some bad fucking karma mojo shit in the universe. I thought I was being punished for cheating on tests and sneaking out at night.

It was a hard, confusing year for me. And truthfully, it took me seeing some shit on the beat to realize how stupid that was. How much my pain drove my decisions.

That was Violet.

But it isn't Violet anymore.

The week off has been a utopian blend of heavy and light, and on Monday morning before she's slated to go back to school, I find myself supremely fucking anxious. It's not like I expected her to quit her job. Hell, that's not the woman I fell in love with. But the idea of me plucking her from one creep only to hand her off to another? It doesn't fucking sit well with me. Not at all.

Luckily, she lets me drive her to work and pick her up.

My hand is settled between her thighs the entire drive. When we go places, she loves my hand between her legs. She always clenches her thighs together. And because I can't keep my hands off her, I love that she loves it.

We've been holding hands, her lips have been on my neck, my tongue has explored all of her, and she's mewled secrets in the dark. I've had a fucking hard-on for nine days straight, I fucking swear.

Letting her out at the elementary school suddenly feels like I'm releasing her to a den of lions. Or pushing her next to an active volcano, never knowing when it's going to erupt. It feels wrong, but I don't know how to make it right. I can't be controlling when it comes to her career, she doesn't deserve that disrespect.

And we've all learned through Batman's marriage that "if you don't have a solution, you don't complain"—*Robin's words.*

So I stroke her inner thigh then take her hand, pressing her knuckles to my lips as I park my SUV.

"You've been quiet," she says, perceptive of my pensiveness.

"It's been the best week of my life, baby," I tell her honestly. "I just don't like leaving you with people I don't know. People I haven't vetted."

She leans over the console, sliding her fingers into the coarse hair on my cheek. I've never had a woman worship my beard the way Violet does. Now it can never not be worshiped because it gets me so goddamn hard when she touches it.

She kisses me, then strokes my lip with her thumb in a way usually only actors can get away with in high-budget movies. But somehow, we pull it off, too because this current that buzzes between us is strong, all-encompassing, and undeniable.

She's not ready to acknowledge it. Not yet. But I make sure she knows how I feel. Before the day I took her, I didn't think I'd say it so much. But now that I know what makes Violet bloom, I shower her with love.

That's all she needed, and it's all I wanted to give her.

Well, and my dick.

"I'm excited for you to pick me up. When I look out my window and see your car, I'll probably get wet," she whispers sweetly, and the combination of filthy words in a honeyed tone is dizzying. My voice rises an octave as my cock stiffens.

"*Fu-uck*, baby. That naughty teacher shit makes me wanna blow." She grins, abandoning me for her side of the cab.

"I should probably take my car out tonight, to get gas so I don't have to go on the way into school tomorrow," she says, swiping on some baby pink lipstick using the fold down mirror. She says it all casually, like she's going through her mental to-do list, but I don't like it.

"I can drive you."

She turns her head to face me. Violet with the emerald eyes. Fuck she's so gorgeous. Her hair is wrapped into a bun, sitting low at the base of her head. It's librarian; it's porn star–I fucking love it. I wanna grab that bun and watch those cottony lips clench around my cock.

The week off was full of a lot of things, but Violet still has not graced my cock with her little mouth.

I'm not pushing.

"I can drive. It's safe." Her tone is soft and understanding, not at all defensive or irritated like I feel I deserve. I don't want her to think I'm smothering her. It's not about that. It's that motherfucker Wheeler.

"As long as that asshole Wheeler is in charge, I want to be here as much as I can." She opens her mouth, her brows forming a straight line. I raise a hand to silence her, because I will go insane if I have to stand back a second time.

"Violet, listen. I love you. And my love isn't a casual love based on greeting cards and run-of-the-mill once-a-month missionary sex. I love you like I'll fucking cease to exist without you. I'll evaporate." I nod, because it's frighteningly true. "So when you have to come to work with a man who I know is a fucking creep, I'm sorry, I can't just kick back like it doesn't fucking bother me." I find that I've grown fucking angry mid-speech and by the time it's over, I hit the steering wheel with my clenched, white-knuckled fist. "Fuck that, Violet. I'm gonna be here as much as I can with my eyes on Wheeler. If he looks at you a second longer than appropriate for the boss to look at an employee," I shake my head. "He's *done*."

Her jaw drops, then closes up tight. Then that happens again. She blinks. My fears are throbbing in my ears, soaring through my senses. My heart is fucking jackhammering.

"How do you know about Mr. Wheeler? From following me?"

I shake my head emphatically. "No. I have no reason to lie to you, Violet." My eyes hold hers. "Batman's wife's sister works here." I nod up towards the school, it's flat, low roof lines, and avocado-colored trim screaming seventies.

She narrows her eyes at me. "There are only thirty-six teachers here, Van. If you're lying–"

"I haven't lied to you, Violet." The back of my throat burns at the thought that she could possibly think that after *everything*, I'd lie to her. About someone as trivial as Wheeler, no less.

"I told you I stalked you. I kidnapped you, Violet. I'm not dying to make you remember those things, but I don't know. Right now it feels like maybe you need to hear it. Because it should be clear that I do not fucking lie to you."

She stares at me for a minute. The air is so thick I don't

even attempt to take a breath. Finally, I say, "Violet," and she cuts me off.

"Okay."

Wait, what? "Okay?"

She nods, exhaling a long breath pregnant with emotion.

"Violet, I think this is finally the first normal boyfriend thing I've done. I learned through my buddy that your boss sucks. And now I'm making sure a sucky person doesn't hurt a fucking great one."

A tear breaks past her lashes. "Boyfriend?"

I shrug, a huge grin slinking across my lips. "I mean, we *live* together."

Her eyes go wide and she turns to the side. "Oh my god we do." She laughs but turns back to me, her green eyes brimming with happiness. And God does pleasure absolutely tear through me. My spine is a trail of flames as her fingers sink into my thigh. She leans over me, giving me one small kiss. A single swipe is all her tongue gifts my mouth. But it's all it takes for my blood to abandon all posts and march straight to my dick.

"Thank you for letting me do this," I tell her, as she returns to her side of the car, opening the door.

"See you at the bell," she smiles, all pink lips and sunny hair, making my chest swell.

"I love you."

She smiles, then before she closes the door she says, "I slashed Wheeler's tires in the grocery store parking lot a few weeks ago."

I love her even more now.

Finally, it feels like we're really just a normal couple.

Chapter Thirty-One

VIOLET

I'm kind of obsessed with him.

The first week back at school is an absolute freaking *bitch*. And I don't use that word often.

But my head. Holy crap. I thought I was ready to be back in a classroom full of nine-year-olds but at nine am on Friday morning, the entire week comes crashing down on me like a million plastic blocks clanking against a hard surface.

Oh, wait.

That's what's *actually* happening.

"Miss Carlisle! Miss Carlisle!" Their chants hammer my brain like an actual freaking hammer. Reactively, though it doesn't help, I press my fingers to my temples and rub furiously.

On top of the headaches not pairing well with a bustling third-grade class, Mr. Wheeler has *really* had it out for me. I know that sounds like a line from a 2000s Hilary Duff movie, but I swear it's true.

And it has everything to do with Van waiting outside my classroom door, leaning up against the stucco in his Willow-dale Police Department uniform, which fits snugly on his vast, commanding biceps. I swear, my nipples got hard when I saw him. Then when I got a whiff of his sun-drenched skin with traces of his cologne–I gushed. I had to clench my thighs together because of how aroused I became.

It's been well worth it, but I've been paying the price of having Officer Drake as my boyfriend all week. Mr. Wheeler hates it. But finally, I'm really not afraid. Sure, I'm still going to do my best to avoid him. But if he comes at me, if he touches my knee or any of that crap from before–no. Just, no.

I'm not going to run to Van, though I know that seems like the clearly obvious choice. But just because I have him now doesn't mean I should never learn to stand up for myself.

I have to do better.

If I had ever stood up for myself, maybe I'd have family. Maybe my parents would have considered me more, if I used my voice. I don't know, but I plan to tell Wheeler to cut the crap if he tries anything again.

Something I should have done a long time ago.

I'm almost home-free at ten minutes until the bell, having not run into our wonderful principal for the entire day. Van wasn't sure if he could pick me up today because he had some paperwork to catch up on after his shift. We have restaurant reservations tonight. Van likes to take me out. We make promises to only order things we've never ordered or things we wouldn't normally try.

It's fun.

And as it turns out, *having fun* is something you *should* do. Who knew?

The door to my class swings open, and as soon as I see Mr. Wheeler striding between the aisles of desks, desperation pulls my eyes to the window.

Van's white SUV is not outside. He isn't here.

And that puts some new breed of panic inside me because as much as I tell myself I have to do better and stand up for myself–*now* I actually have to.

He makes his way to my desk, stopping to tap on some papers and drop some words of wisdom to the kids. Being principal brings automatic adoration and respect, none that he deserves. After years of teaching and adulting, I've come to realize education and titles do not make a person worthy of respect.

Quickly I slip into my chair–though I'd normally stand to usher the kids out when the bell rings, it seems like keeping up a barrier is the best choice here. The desk creaks as part of his ass swallows up the edge as he takes a seat, my papers ruffling under his slacks. That's annoying.

"How was your first week back, Miss Carlisle?" he asks, his contrived smile worrying me. His thin lips twitch as he awaits my response. My head throbs, so I look away to avoid the reflective glare of the bright classroom lights off his bald head.

"Good. Tiring."

He touches my pencil cup. He removes a pencil from the cup, sliding it under his nose. "All these years, and I still love the smell of freshly sharpened pencils."

I nod with a small smile. *Give him nothing, Violet. Just sit there. He will leave if you give him nothing.*

"So tell me, you're what, twenty-five?"

How this is relevant to anything, I don't know, but not answering doesn't feel like an option, so I say "yes."

"Hmm," he acknowledges my answer, sliding the pencil back into the cup. Note to self: sharpen that pencil until it is nothing more than a pile of shavings, then burn said shavings. "At what age do you call your boss on your own then, when you need time off?"

I swallow thickly because of all the things that are clearly bugging Mr. Wheeler, it somehow hadn't occurred to me that Van calling me in was one of them. Then again, when I'd asked Van what he told Mr. Wheeler he'd just said, "I told him you had a small accident when moving out, and you needed the week to recover." I was proud of that answer because it included the truth that I had an injury–one that even a week later I wouldn't be able to completely hide with makeup–and it also made Wheeler aware that I was no longer living with my parents. A fact he'd been aware of since he hired me.

He could only assume where or who I'd moved in with, and maybe that was part of the problem, too.

"I'm sorry that I didn't call in myself last Sunday," I reply, keeping an expressionless look fixed to my face. "But I could barely function. I hit my head pretty bad."

His beady eyes narrow, and he grabs a different pencil before snatching up my very favorite pen. A student got it for me a few years back. It's black ink with my name in cursive along the body, a large gemstone on the end. It's cute and fun, and *someone thought of me.* Oftentimes, I slide it behind my ear just so it's on me. I like it *that* much.

Women love office supplies. It's in our DNA, I swear.

"That's my favorite pen," I spit out in defense of the

item. When I reach out for it, he clutches it to his chest, away from me. His lips curl into the most taunting grin, and the back of my neck goes hot, my palms getting clammy.

Ignoring my comment, he slides the pen under his nose, smelling it. A swell of sickness turns over in my belly. "Smells like your shampoo," he says, voice disgustingly low.

"May I please have it back?"

He drops it into the breast pocket of his sports coat, and I want to cry. It's just a pen, I know, but it's mine. First, my notebook and now my pen. My fists ball beneath the desk, but he gets up, and though I'm angry, he's leaving, and that's all that matters.

"Next time, be a big girl. Call yourself in. Don't have your current boyfriend do it." He tips his head to the side, giving me a passive-aggressively sour parting glance. And he would never take a possession from a male teacher. It's... such bullshit. Then the bell rings, and the students filter out, and so does he.

As I'm slamming my stuff around, packing up for the day, Sasha pops her head into my class, knocking on the wall. "Got a minute? I feel like we haven't got to catch up."

I roll my eyes. "Wheeler took my favorite pen. Just to be a freaking prick," I tell my best friend, knowing full well I won't get caught since Wheeler is already on the steps of the school. I can see him from my window.

Sasha walks in, adjusting the construction paper caterpillar that lines the wall by the door. Grabbing a stapler from the supply desk, she slams the paper bug a few times, better securing it to the wall. "How's it been with Van this week?" She sits on my desk, right where Wheeler sat but moves my papers out of the way first. The way you should.

The mention of Van immediately overtakes my annoyance with Wheeler.

Van. My possessive and protective boyfriend. I never knew I wanted a man like him, but now I can't believe I've wasted so much freaking time without him.

"So good," I reply. "I mean, I can't believe I live with him already but..." I shake my head because I can't find the right words. I can't make these thoughts sound prettier or saner. "I'm kind of obsessed with him."

She whistles. "Girl, I do not blame you. That man is fine."

"He is so fine," I say, grinning, fangirling.

She quirks a manicured eyebrow my way. "Are you in love?"

"It's only been a few weeks," I say quickly in response because my real answer is yes, I think, but I don't want to admit it to her first. Van should be the first to know.

Before I can answer, Sasha reaches out and grabs my wrist softly. "Girl, the morning he called me to get work figured out for you–I thought, *this man wants to wife up my friend*. Because the amount of thought and care he put into all of that–"

"He puts that amount of thought and care into everything when it comes to me," I say honestly, a broad smile stretching my lips. Normally I'd worry that sounds boastful, but Sasha has been riding my rollercoaster alongside me the last few years. She knows my lows.

"I bet he does," she says with admiration in her tone. Then she smiles, her cocoa lipstick complimenting her thick, dark curls. "Well, I gotta get going. My sister's in for two days. We're doing sushi tonight, then some movie in the park tomorrow."

"Have fun," I say with a smile.

We walk out to the parking lot together, but Sasha breaks away, walking to her house as I get into my little car. On the drive home, I stay focused on Van.

But I keep thinking about my *favorite* pen and how Wheeler always has to get me. Always has to one-up. Get under my skin, hurt me even if he can't touch me. I gnaw my lip the entire way home, trying to tell myself it's only a pen. It was just a notebook.

I can get another pen.

The notebook is gone.

But really, the end goal is to just surround myself with people who don't strip me of the things I love.

Van put a garage door opener in my car this week, and he's had the guys help him install racks along the ceiling to free up ground space. Now both of our cars fit.

I've never had my car in a garage before. Dad and Rose always parked there. Then at some point, our garage became so full of crap that only Dad parked in it, and that always bugged me.

Not even a full week after moving in with Van and I have a permanent garage spot. *With a clicker.*

I close the door using said clicker, and after my eyes adjust to the newfound darkness of the garage, I see him. Van, eating up the doorway, his muscular arms up on either side of him, his head slightly tipped forward. His lips curl into a grin that awakens my lower half, and I smile back at him.

"How was school today, baby?" he asks as I close my door as gently as possible since my head is still kind of hurting.

"Honestly?" I say, unable to choke back another complaint. All week I've been trying to stay positive, down-play my headaches, skip over the Wheeler-related annoyances, and just be grateful I'm back. But after the pen incident, I feel so deflated.

I fall into his chest in the doorway, and his arms are around me so fast. His fingers inch down my spine as he massages me, dropping random kisses onto the top of my head as he does.

"It sucked," I say, the words muffled, my lips trapped against his hard chest. "Mr. Wheeler passive-aggressively accused me of being a child because you called me in for the week." An unexpected sob breaks free, and I bring my hand to my face to catch it. "Then he took my favorite pen," I cry, unable to stop the frustrated tears from flowing.

Crap, I must be PMSing. It's just a freaking pen. It was just a freaking notebook. Why am I sobbing into Van's chest over a diary and an office supply?

He holds me tight as he walks us through the house to the couch. The first place I ever sat in his house was his couch, the afternoon he kidnapped me. That seems like someone else's life now.

"Why did he take your pen?" he asks, stroking the loose strands of hair out of my face, his fingers sliding through them until the ends. He adores my hair. He loves playing with it. And truthfully? I love it when he plays with it, too.

"Because he's a jerk," I sniffle, and Van uses the pad of his thumb to wipe away my tears. Need crawls up my spine at his tender touch.

"Well," he says, staying calm. Another thing I've noticed about Van is that he's actively working on his anger. Trying not to fly off the handle over every little thing that happens to me. I told him I'm not made of glass and I'm no angel—there's a certain amount of crap I have to and should have to deal with. He can't hold the world by its throat and make everyone play nice. It just won't work.

And he's heard me. And when a man shows he can change, it shows he's committed to you; that he'll do the work he needs to in order to keep you.

My own family couldn't even do that.

"I have a little surprise for you. One that might cheer you up." He rubs at the back of his neck, his dark hair messy from being stuffed under a Willowdale PD baseball cap all day.

"Yeah?" I ask, having no clue what this could be because when it comes to Van, what he's capable of is limitless. And I like that.

He slides me off his lap onto the couch, and I relax into the cushions as he grabs an envelope from the kitchen counter. He hands it to me but doesn't sit. "What is it?" I ask, staring at the long blank envelope.

"Open it."

Unfolding it, my heart begins to race as a business card falls into my lap from the envelope. I hold the folded letter between my knuckles as I grab the dropped card.

"It's a two-part surprise," he adds, smiling. The dark frames, his hair styled to the shove of his hand, those piercing espresso eyes—my lady parts stir as I take him in. I am lucky to have an honest, good, protective man. But also, yeah, he looks like *that*.

I lift the card.

Dr. Angela Richards

Superintendent, Lakeside Schools

She has two phone numbers, an email, and a physical address there. Dr. Richards is on the board here in Willowdale. She's highly respected in the state, even. She's done great things for the elementary curriculum. I've never had the privilege of meeting her.

"Do you know Dr. Richards?" my voice is hollowed by disbelief.

He shrugs. "The Chief does. I told him my girlfriend is a third-grade teacher trying to get on the board, but she missed the deadline to submit her interest letter. He told me he'd talk to Dr. Richards. Turns out, the deadline is just to weed out the less serious. But he contacted her, told her all about you, and she said you could send your letter directly to her office. That she'd read it herself." He smiles. "The paper is your reprinted letter, ready to send."

Holy crap.

"Holy crap," I mutter, staring wide-eyed. "Van," I say because I'm thinking so many things, I don't know which to choose. Affection is thick in my throat, and I want to tell him that I love him, but I don't want it to be on the heels of a favor or nice deed.

He needs to know that what he's built with me has made me fall in love with him, not the things he does but who he is.

I want to say it, but I want it to have a *moment* of its own.

"Thank you" are the lame combination of words I land on, and I know they aren't grand enough, they don't cover enough ground, but now I feel like crying. "Thank you so much, Van."

He sticks his arms out, wiggling his fingers for me to take his hands, and I gladly do. Pulling me into his arms, I melt into his hug. His lips soften against my temple, then my cheek. "Anything for you."

My hands glide up his chest beneath his t-shirt. My fingers explore the bristly hair on his pecs before coiling around to his back. Tracing the hollow of his spine, he groans appreciatively into my head. "That feels nice."

It's been a long week. Today sucked. But within a moment of being home, I feel good. Like, *really* good.

Everywhere.

"You make me feel incredible." I tug at the hem of his t-shirt, and he knows what to do, whipping it off over his head within a moment. I tap his belt as he strokes my hair back from my face.

"I'd like to make you feel even more incredible right now," he says with a smile in his tone. His belt hits the floor with an electrifying clank.

Stepping back from him, I lift my skirt and bunch it around my hips, showing my bare legs and nude thong. "I want to pretend we're over my desk," I tell him, pulling the crotch of my panties to the side. He growls when his eyes meet my slick, shaved lips, and I know how wet I already am. I can feel the arousal sticky between my thighs.

Without any more words—who needs them–he spins me around and bends me over the couch. The quickening evening darkens our backyard, and with the kitchen light on, the sliding glass door serves as a mirror to our intimacy. I watch our reflection as Van grips his cock and feeds it to me, sealing his hips tight to my ass, sinking himself fully inside me.

With his heavy sac hot against my bare ass and his big cock buried deep, we both moan. Watching his reflection, my heart beats hard as he lovingly drags a hand up and down my back. "Good girl, getting that pussy ready for me," he whispers before he fucks me from behind. In the slider, I can see his pants banded around his ankles, and his urgency to have me brings my orgasm to the surface.

The slippery, hot sliding of his steely cock filling my soft channel over and over makes my mind melt. I'm all wordless moans and desperate noises until I can't hold back anymore. I don't warn him because words are hard when you're this high.

Gripping the couch, squeezing my eyes shut, I succumb to the pleasure. I tighten around him repeatedly, and he curses and moans, still trying to stave off his own release.

"My sweet, sweet good girl," he praises, as my orgasm brings him deeper inside me, milking his engorged cock for every last drop of my pleasure. "Taking my dick so good. Coming for me so quickly."

Then his calloused hands are gripping my hips, pounding me hard for a few strokes until he holds himself deep inside me. His grunts sync with the hot pulsing I feel inside me, and I know he's coming. Fingers curled hard into my flesh at my hips, he grunts and groans, each noise met with a thrumming, then a rush of heat inside my body.

After he empties that beautiful part of him into me, he leans forward, dropping kisses down my spine. The gentle scratch of his beard along my sweaty skin makes me shiver hotly, and I reach back to touch him.

"Thank you," he says, kissing the back of my neck, making my brain go woozy with how tender and dirty he can be in the same breath. "I love you."

We get cleaned up by taking a quick shower together before heading to dinner. We go to a new Pho place around the corner, each going with recommendations from the waiter. On the way home, Van runs into the drug store and buys us a pint of Ben and Jerry's to share, and we eat it together in bed while watching *The Office* on Netflix.

A perfect domestic night.

Chapter Thirty-Two

DONOVAN

On her face is the worst kind of pain. Betrayal.

This is not even the first Saturday we're waking up together.

We have actual time behind us now. Time that isn't just me lurking in the shadows of her existence like a fucking creep. Time together, as an us.

I usually wake before her, but I don't get out of bed unless I have to. I love the feel of her breath flanking my skin; I take solace in knowing she's okay. And I really hate that there were so many days where she wasn't and that I was right under her nose but didn't have a fucking clue.

We fell asleep naked last night—something Violet's still getting used to. I get it—if you live at home with your parents, pajamas feel important. I gave her a back massage last night while we watched Netflix. Rubbed oil into her skin, broke up some knots of tension, tried to knead out the stress of the week.

Gliding my hand over her still slick ribcage, her eyes slowly blink open. Propped on my elbow, my head in my hand, we stare at one another. She blinks and yawns, hiding it with the back of her hand. I smile lazily at her, enjoying the ease of the smile I get organically in return.

My hand skates a bit higher over the ridges of her ribcage, coming to rest on her breast. Round and soft, I close my hand slightly, loving how plump it feels. She makes a noise of approval from deep in her throat, and my cock fattens.

Her green eyes are still trained on mine, and my chest has never felt fuller. I rest my thumb next to her nipple, and she inhales a sharp breath as I begin strumming her.

Her pouty lips part and her eyelids grow heavy. My thumb ticks back and forth, her little nipple tightening with each pass.

The sunlight drips over us, and I feel like we're the subject of a beautiful love song. Her silky hair now tangles between my fingers as I dip down and suction my mouth around her nipple.

Her back arches off the mattress, and her hand falls to the back of my head, fingers sifting through my hair. Sucking harder, I take more of her breast into my mouth, my cock hard against her leg.

"You're mine," I tell her, releasing her perky nub, running my thumb over the damp, erect skin. "I love you, Violet. And one day, you're going to marry me." I roll on top of her, and her legs welcome me.

I guide my cock through her folds then push into her without warning. Her head tips back, and she tightens around me, needing a moment to accept my girth. Once the burn of the initial stretch subsides, her face softens, and her feet fall to my ass. She likes to pull me in deeper with her feet, and I fucking love it.

My hips oscillate as I tunnel her from different angles. Our mouths collide, breathing wild, emotions feral, touches carnal. A sensually slow touch to the nipple has evolved in an absolutely vital, urgent fuck where we both need to be as lost as we can in each other to fully combust.

I rise to my knees and yank her up by the legs, holding her to me by the thighs. Only her back touches the bed as I tunnel my aching cock deep inside her. She's slippery and warm, and fuck, I want to come as I stare down at her jiggling tits and hazy eyes.

I hold her legs tighter and fuck her harder, her cheeks pinkening as her pussy clenches my dick. She's about to come already, too.

So I give her a push over the edge.

"I'm gonna fill you so full that my come will be slipping down your legs all day." My balls slap her ass as I collide into her again, hard. "Are you going to keep my come inside you like a good girl? Huh?"

Her moan is something fierce. Loud and window-shakingly raw. She pulses and throbs, her channel tightening all around my cock. That's when I stop, press my face to her calf and bite down as my cock pulses, flooding her insides with my hot, thick come. With each eruption, I fill her more and more, and when I finally slide out, our cream leaks out of her onto our bed.

I could lay down and twitch and bask through my orgasm, but I know women don't like to lie in a sticky mess first thing in the morning. Grabbing a towel from the bathroom, I return to our bed and slide the terrycloth between her thighs. She thanks me with a kiss, and then somehow, we both fall back asleep.

I wake up to the sound of Violet's sleeping stomach howling for food. Seriously, I'm going to have to overfeed this woman for years just to make up for all the times hunger had to wait because she was too nervous to go downstairs.

Pressing a kiss to her forehead, I slide out of bed and grab my glasses from the nightstand. Once I'm in the kitchen, I take out an assortment of things. Her growling stomach and the way she curled so naturally into me last night–my chest is exploding. I tell her I love her all the time.

I'm going to show her this morning.

IN AN HOUR, I make protein pancakes, cut up fruit, scramble eggs, saute some greens, make a fresh pot of coffee, and even fry up some bacon. The house smells and feels like a home, the intoxicating blend of breakfast and sweet skin etched into the place.

I fucking love it.

Finally, things are just as they're meant to be.

My pulse quickens when I hear Violet padding down the hallway. Her feet sound like they're moving slow, so I pour a mug of coffee for her and stand at the edge of the bar, waiting for her to round the corner.

But she isn't moving slowly because of sleep.

Her eyes are red-rimmed, the tip of her nose pink, too. But her brow doesn't say confused; her lip doesn't tremble with fear. It's worse than all the terrible ways I've seen Violet look–it's so much worse than a bruise to the eye socket or a cut through the eyebrow.

On her face is the worst kind of pain: betrayal. Emotional hurt.

When I see what she's holding, the mug slips from my hands. The porcelain clatters to the counter, shattering into a trillion pieces, dark liquid pooling and steaming on the surface of the counter.

"I can't believe you didn't tell me."

Her fingers fidget with the metal spiral of the notebook. Her notebook. The one I took weeks ago, the one meant to be a tool to get closer to her—not to hurt her. The one she'd accused her father or Rose of taking.

"Violet, listen—"

She shakes her head, a tear slipping down her cheek. *"It should be clear that I do not fucking lie to you."* She repeats the harsh words I handed her the day I told her how I knew Wheeler. When, after everything, she doubted my honesty. "You lied to me. You hid this, Van."

And yet... this omission. I know she will see it as a lie.

I know it because she steps backward, moving in reverse down the hall. A moment later, the bedroom door slams, and I know—the same way I feel my love for her in my marrow—it's over.

Chapter Thirty-Three

VIOLET

This is it

Never reply when you're angry. Never make a promise when you are happy. Never make a decision when you're sad.

But the problem with those rules is that when you need to hear them the most, you're at your least capable of good decision-making. So while I know I shouldn't throw a bunch of clothes into my bag and jump into a pair of jeans and a hoodie, I still do.

Because he knew what the notebook meant to me.

He knew what not having it meant to me.

I shove clothes into a bag, toiletries, make-up, and my phone charger. I just... shove things into the bag, including my notebook. As I pull the door open and make a break for my keys—he's there.

"Violet." That's all he says. And his voice bears a chasm so deep; it hurts me because even *he* knows this is bad.

"You could've told me. At any time, weeks ago, you could've said you took it." My fingers massage my temples, but it's not really where the pain is. "Omission of something like that..." I trail off because it hollows me to talk now. My chest aches.

"I know," he rushes out, steps towards me, reaches for my elbow. But I pull back. I have to.

"Don't, Van."

His face drains of color, and those two words are a cement boot. He opens his mouth, struggling with words.

"I knew you'd be upset and I kept putting it off because I didn't want to upset you." He chokes out a breath, and takes another small step. I glide back, too. "I just didn't want to upset you. I swear I just didn't want to upset you."

"But I'm upset now, Van! I'm hurt now! I was dying to get this back! I picked a fight with my parents over this thing!" I wave the spiral-bound notebook back and forth in front of me, kind of crazily. But I can't stop myself. It's like slashing Mr. Wheeler's tires. I just... have to.

"And let me guess," I say, feeling my top lip curl with anger. "You read it."

"Please don't leave, Violet." He steadies his hands in front of him like he can physically will the situation to slow down. "Please, stay and talk to me. We can talk about it. Please. Violet, *don't go*."

I snort, shaking my head ruefully. "You should have told me." Because truthfully, I don't care that he read it. Because I know now that I love him. And that love earns him the privilege of knowing my thoughts and feelings.

But I was *hurting* for that notebook. That slice of peace.

He let that happen.

And I've had no trust in my life aside from Sasha. I cannot

314

be with a man who lies to me; no matter what else he's done for me.

"Goodbye, Van." Snatching my keys off the counter, I blow past him, straight to the garage door. I don't know if he's protesting, speaking–I don't know. Because blood is rushing through my ears. My cheeks are on fire. My back is sweaty.

Oh my god.

Oh my god. We're over.

This is it.

The door bumps the backs of my heels, knocking me from my momentary daze on the garage step. Oh my god. Wait. I almost put my hands out to brace myself. Am I over-reacting?

Van is so many good things.

He's strong both mentally and emotionally. He's thoughtful and sweet, his heart is big and his intentions are always the best. He loves hard–his friends included.

But he took something that mattered to me and didn't have any intention of giving it back. And that just... feels manipulative and a bit like betrayal, too.

I take the steps down, get in my car and drive away.

I don't look in the rearview mirror because I'm afraid I'll break. I'm afraid I'll decide that my own self-respect isn't enough because I love him so much, I want to forgive him. I really do.

I've never felt safe or cared about until Van. And it fills a void in me so deep, so profoundly deep, that without him, I don't know if I can exist.

And I didn't know that until I was driving away.

But now I need to remind myself that he didn't tell me the truth. And honesty is the crux of a good relationship. I pull over a block away, and send him a text, because I would want a text at least.

Violet: *I'm going to Sasha's.*

Three blue dots keep me in suspense for a soul-sucking moment and then:

Van: *I'm sorry Violet. Please forgive me.*

With the back of my wrist, I wipe away my tears then roll down the windows and gulp fresh air for the remainder of the short drive. By the time I get to Sasha's place, I remember her sister is actually in town and home right now. Why am I always the complicated friend? I never thought I'd be the complicated anything, but here I am.

Leaving my bag in the car, I knock on the door, really trying to swallow down all the emotions.

The door opens and as soon as I see my best friend, I break.

Years of pent-up frustration and hurt seep out of my every pore as I bawl, sob and talk gibberish through a snotty nose, in Sasha's arms. After way too many minutes of unintelligible snorting into her shirt, I finally pull it together to sip the water that Sasha's sister is passing me.

"Cadence, I'm so sorry," I snort, "I'm crashing your home time with my drama."

She nods, her curls mirroring Sasha's bouncy ones. "You are, but honestly, whatever is happening here," she waves her finger up and down my body, "seems way more interesting than the handjob I gave in Germany three months ago and that's basically all you interrupted."

Sasha slides a glass of water into my hands and I take a sip. Her wide eyes search mine and I know it's time to come clean. About Van–about everything.

"Sasha," I say, my chin trembling. "Remember how I told you I met Van?"

My eyes go to Cadence and I can see her interest is through the roof. Stress gnaws on my calm, and I fidget until I'm at the edge of the couch cushion. My knees touch Sasha's from where she's perched on the coffee table.

"Yeah, oh shit, this is about Van?" her face goes sad. "I was hoping this was just more Michael Carlisle bullshit. I mean, not hoping but you know."

Suddenly, the story is crowding my mouth and the desire to purge is so freaking strong.

"That's *not* how we met."

Cadence looks at her sister, then back to me. "Oh snap."

Sasha's soft eyes study mine. "Talk to me, Vi."

For the next thirty minutes, I am met with dropped jaws and wide eyes as I relay the real story of how I met Donovan Drake.

My guts spill, telling both Sasha and Cadence how Van snatched me from the parking lot and took me back to his house. I make sure to capitalize on how he cared for me tenderly in the process and how confused I was. How I wanted to hate him, because you know, *kidnapping and everything*. But then I explained to them how careful and sensitive he was with me, emotionally and physically. The word "stockholm" is tossed out by Cadence, but it isn't mentioned again when I tell her how he brought me home the next day, safely.

When I'm at the part in the story when I tell them that he watched me for an entire year, I'm scared. I'm scared because I can't get a read on Sasha's face and her opinion–it matters.

I fight the urge to stop every three minutes and ask her

what she thinks because if I do, I may lose the confidence to continue.

I spare zero details at this point. Nothing gets left out. I tell Sasha and Cadence everything that has happened and everything I know to be true about Van, including the night outside the Seedy Seal.

When I'm done–empty of information, the emotional equivalent of a crumpled tissue–they just stare at me.

"What?" I wring my hands together. "What are you think-ing?" I ask Sasha, turning to Cadence for support, backup, anything at this point. I need one of them to say something, or I may seriously spontaneously evaporate.

"I…" Sasha's voice trails off as her gaze drops to the floor. She cradles her head in her hands, leaning forward. "That's a lot, Vi."

"I know," I whisper.

"So… he didn't tell you he took the notebook, and that omission felt like a lie, a lie is a betrayal, and now you're here." She states it all back to me, emotionless, only fact. I nod to agree.

"Wow."

Cadence adds, "Jesus."

"I'm really sorry to crash here again," I sigh, slipping deeper into the soft couch.

Cadence throws a blanket over my legs, knowing full well from my body language that I won't be changing clothes or doing an elaborate skincare routine. Nope. I'm going to melt into this three-seater and stay here until I absolutely have to peel myself off for school in the morning.

Note to self: get Sasha a really freaking good birthday gift.

"You sleep on it because I sure as hell know I need to."

She grabs my arm and wiggles it affectionately. "What time do you need to be up for school?"

"Six."

Another arm wiggle and a smile then, "alright, I'll get you up then. Just... rest." At the same moment, Cadence puts a box of tissues, a glass of water, and some Advil on the table.

"Thanks Cay," I smile, tears still flowing freely despite the fact that this house is calm, these people are safe, and I am okay. Still, I can't stop crying.

And that's how I drift off to sleep. A life apart from the way I woke up.

Chapter Thirty-Four

VIOLET

Love is a little crazy

Life is full of stuff I really don't need to know about. For example: waking up from *nights* of viscous sobbing feels *worse* than waking up with a hangover, and worse than the day after being hit even.

I wish I didn't know from experience.

"Sorry girl, but if you want to shower before school, you gotta get in now," Sasha says softly, her smooth hand running up and down my arm.

Sasha's caring touch is how I've woken up every day for the last week.

I blink, my eyelids feeling like a trillion freaking pounds. My forehead aches. My temples pound. My throat feels like I swallowed shattered freaking glass.

But all of that feels good in comparison to the way my chest feels.

Vacant of all warmth and fullness. Taking up residency in place of love is this awful, sick feeling that spreads beyond my chest, throughout my entire body. This new sour feeling burns the back of my eyes and bubbles over inside of me. Instead of an abundance of love, there is a world-shifting chasm dividing my heart.

The last thing I clung to before crying myself to sleep was hope. Maybe, I thought, when I wake up in the morning and my emotions have settled a bit, maybe I'll see that I completely overreacted. Maybe I will realize that I was just scared or something.

Except this morning, I don't feel scared. I don't feel any different. He had something I love and he hid it. He didn't tell me. He left me in pain, in a way, and just hoped I'd forget about it.

Even though I've cried myself to sleep every single night this week, I'm angry with him, I'm hurt but I'm also sad.

"Thanks," I reply to Sasha after she's already in the kitchen, packing herself a bagged lunch for work. She always brings a bagged lunch. I usually do, too. I did, until Van. He packed my lunch all week. Bento boxes with fresh salad, sweet fruit, sandwiches or mini charcuterie assortments.

"You want a peanut butter sandwich for lunch?" she asks. Peeling myself from the couch, I pad to the kitchen then slouch down into one of her wicker-backed chairs. Her dining set is from the seventies. She loves thrift shopping.

"Yeah," I replied, "please and thank you."

Then she gives me a cup of coffee, and I swear I chug it. Even though it's hot and it probably will scorch off my taste-buds, I slam that freaking coffee because I need to feel better.

I can't go to school an emotional mess with a headache

that feels like my eyes will pop out and my chest feels concave. I have to *human.* Coffee should help.

"Listen, Violet," Sasha begins, rolling the top of our lunch bags down. "I love you and support you, whatever you choose."

Growing nervous, I chew the inside of my lip. I made the choice to come clean to Sasha; now if she hates Van, I have to accept that. And she very well may hate him.

I could never be with a man my best friend hates.

But then...

"I'm not supporting dishonesty or lying or... *not supplying information,*" she amends, and those three words definitely sound more palatable than the previous two. Even though it's all the same, isn't it?

"But, girl, this man... he loves you." She sips her coffee, her eyes still on me over the top of her mug. "He's *crazy* about you."

"But I told him how sad I was to lose the notebook. I even told him how I accused my parents of taking it. He had so many opportunities to tell me, Sash." I sigh, curving my hands around the mug. "Why did he keep it from me?"

She smiles, her head tipped, eyes soft. "And *you've* never done that?"

"I–" oh shit. I cup my hand to my mouth, and a bucket of steaming hot guilt swallows me–at least that's what it feels like. "I'm an asshole."

Her small smile grows into a grin, and I am out of that wicker chair faster than you can say avocado. Hugging her tight, I tell her how sorry I am. But it doesn't compare to how badly I feel.

"Here's why you get a free pass," she says, stroking my

hair as I ugly cry for the millionth time on her shoulder. I may need to get her a nice birthday gift, but I also need to get her some stain remover from the mascara I've gotten on her clothes this week. Seriously.

"Because you're amazing," I sob, "and I'm a hypocrite!"

She holds me by the shoulders and stares into my eyes. After a moment, the softness of her skin and the calmness of her breathing start to soothe my nerves. "You good?" she asks, watching, waiting, still gripping me. I nod.

"Okay," she starts. "Love is complicated at best. It's not easy. And even when you get butterflies and tingles and all that crap, it's still real. You know?"

"I kind of do now."

She laughs. "Well, this week while I was at work, I was thinking about you two, and... your whole foundation of love comes from a completely messed up place, so it's hard for you to see what it *can* look like."

I laugh, glad that snot doesn't bubble out of my nose. That's happened this week. Like I said, it's been rough.

"I haven't dated much," I say, agreeing with her sentiment. Because how could I be this mature, wise relationship person when I act like I am when I have had less boyfriends than most high school seniors?

"Vi, that's not at all what I mean." She swallows, and chooses her words carefully. "Your parents should be the basis in your heart of what love looks and feels like."

Tears prick at the back of my eyes, but I don't want to cry anymore and I especially do not want to cry about freaking Michael and Judith Carlisle. If there is anyone so not worth my tears, it's them. And Rose.

"Your parents are cruel, cold, confused people. And they

did a little number on you." She says it softly, delivering the obvious truth in a way I've never considered.

Maybe I am broken. And maybe not everyone else is as broken as me. And like the amazing, mind-reading, lunch-packing goddess that she is, Sasha reads me like... a notebook.

"Van hurts, too, Vi. And the way I see it, he loves you. He may be a little crazy but... I don't know. The world is hard. Real love is even harder to come by. So he's a little crazy? Well, love is a little crazy."

"Love is a little crazy." I repeat that because it's something I never considered. Why? I have no idea, because I watched Michael puppet-master my mom for my entire life, bouncing her on marionette strings to make sure it all went his way.

That's not what Van did.

Van took the notebook I'm sure to get closer to me. Everything he did was to get closer to me. I know that. And he knew how hurt I'd be.

He was scared.

The same way I was always scared to step up to Michael or Rose. Not because I couldn't handle it but because I knew it would hurt, I knew it would cause temporary chaos and I didn't want to disrupt things. Didn't want to get hurt.

That's how he felt.

"You processing?" Sasha asks, and I realize I've been quiet a moment, chewing the inside of my mouth nervously as I finger the loose ends of my ponytail.

"Yes."

"It's good to think. It's good to really assess things yourself. Don't be with Van because I think you guys are equal parts damaged. Be with Van because you see his love outweighs his mistakes."

I nod. Then a truth so real slips out of me before I have the chance to keep it in. "The people who were supposed to love me have always hated me, Sash."

Holy shit. I've officially become one of those people that hurts other people because they're hurt.

"I think we should call them."

My mouth goes dry, and my stomach immediately grows uneasy at the thought. "Call them?"

She guides us back to the wicker chairs, and I follow her lead when she takes another drink of her coffee.

"Listen, Violet. They moved, right? Van made them leave?"

I nod. "Yeah, I mean, I don't know if they're actually gone because I didn't check but I would assume they would." A small smile pulls on my lips when I think about it. "Van scared my dad, the guys seemed very unconcerned with the idea that dad would stay or report them or... take any revenge."

"Bad guys don't call the cops on other bad guys."

That hits me. "Do you think Van is a bad guy?"

She sits back in her chair, the wicker squeaking as she does. Taking a sip of her coffee, she analyzes the faux-marble of the green table. Then finally she says, "I don't think he's bad. I just don't think he minds being bad for people he loves."

"Yeah?"

She nods. "Yeah."

"I think you're right."

She finishes her coffee and glances at her wrist watch. Normally I'd need to leave by now but since Sasha lives right next door, I have fifteen minutes. "I'll call them with you. But Violet, if you're going to feel safe giving and receiving real love, you need to be at peace with the people who gave you the love complex in the first place."

"Freaking Michael."

She snorts. "*Fucking* Michael."

Chapter Thirty-Five

DONOVAN

And another day goes in the book of life without Violet.

It's been a week without her.

Okay, not a week. She left Sunday morning, and it's now Friday. But it fucking terrifies me that it's already Friday afternoon because honestly, I thought we'd have talked by now.

She told me she was going to Sasha's, but that's all I've heard from her.

I wanted to really give her space. Because I think that's all she needs, but who the hell knows? I've got issues from losing my parents—fucking clearly—and she's got issues from being treated like the bottom of a fucking boot her whole life.

I'd hoped she'd reach out.

But now, as I stare at my gray reflection in the large paneled mirror lining the wall at Paradise, I'm beginning to think I was being hopeful. Maybe she won't call. Maybe she won't change her mind. Maybe the notebook was the final straw–the stalking obviously being the first issue.

Mally pinches his hand around my neck, giving it a tight squeeze. "Let's do it, bro."

Leg day. Normally we fucking drip excitement and energy on leg day.

Leg day *is* a vibe.

But the vibe today is *fuck this* because that's been the general feeling since Sunday. What's the fucking point? Mally slides plates onto the bar as I position myself under it, supporting it with my shoulders.

He counts off as I do my first set of box squats; the fire tearing up my quads is the best feeling I've felt all week. When I'm down, lifting is the only thing that brings me up. But after the first two sets, I'm losing steam. Losing momentum.

It's the first time that fitness hasn't rescued me. That lifting and slapping chests and measuring dicks in the form of "how much weight can you crush" hasn't solved my problems.

It scares me, because this is what I thought it would be like without her.

Imfuckingpossible to move on.

"It'll get better, dude. It just takes time." Bran offers advice softly, so that Mally doesn't hear. I just give him a nod, because I don't want to talk about it.

This week I've been itching to watch her. Have some small fucking glance into her just to see if she's okay. But then... I know she's okay. I'm trying not to fall back into easy, unhealthy habits just to have a glimpse of her.

And even though she may never come back to me, I know

I can't revert back to all that shit. I know that all that shit is wrong and unhealthy.

I won't do it.

Because one day if she does want to talk–at the very least–I want to be able to tell her with all honesty that I was good. That I kept my word to give her space, that I kept my promise to myself to be better. That I can be a good guy.

"What's the report from Sasha?" Mally asks as Bran racks weight for his set next. I take a long pull from my gallon jug, and Mally does the same with his.

They know I've been in contact with Sasha all week.

I said I'd give Violet her space, and I did. But with a volatile father somewhere in this town, a handsy prick of a fucking boss, and a stressful life situation–I couldn't go no contact. I had to at least know she was okay; eating, sleeping, working.

Sasha didn't cold-shoulder me the way I thought she might. The way I expected her to. She never made me feel like I was wrong or dangerous or bad–all the things I'd assumed she thought about me.

Instead, after I texted her asking for a favor, she wrote back, "I'll let you know how she's doing, okay?" She *knew* why I'd contacted her.

Then I apologized to Sasha. I'd told her that I fucked up, and that I was sorry that I hurt her friend, and I was sorry that my stupid choices were now impacting multiple lives. Her response?

We're straight.

She didn't even tell Violet that I'd contacted her but her response gave me hope. Like, if this smart woman doesn't hate me... maybe there's hope for me with Violet?

I turn to Malibu. "She's okay, I guess."

Malibu drags a towel across his forehead, his blond hair darkened from sweat. "Well... okay is better than bad."

"Yep."

"Yep."

And another day goes in the book of life without Violet.

Chapter Thirty-Six

VIOLET

Why do you hate me?

This is how freaking messed up my life is. I'm nervous over a phone call with my dad. Most people are nervous to bring boyfriends home to their fathers. But here I am, just nervous to converse with him through the freaking ether.

That's not healthy.

Thus, the phone call.

"You'll be alright, okay?" Sasha says, her hand gripped tight to my thigh. She has this chill demeanor that I love, but I know she's nervous right now. Her manicured toes tap against the hardwood floor of her living room.

We're sitting on the couch. It's Saturday afternoon. Yesterday, I sent my father a text message. Well… Sasha and I sent the message, for all intents and purposes. I asked him one simple question: *can we have one single conversation? It would be the final, I think, but I need answers.*

To my shock, surprise, nerves and relief... he said yes.

And now it's today. The day of the call. And it's really terrifying how nervous I am for a phone call.

I don't have to see him.

I don't have to be afraid of him. He can't do anything to me. Not from over the phone. And anyway, he can't do anything to me anymore.

That opportunity is gone.

Still, I feel sick. That second cup of coffee I ambitiously gulped earlier now feels like a horrible idea... as does this call. "You'll be okay, okay? I'm here so if he tries any verbal jiu jitsu, I'll verbally murder him."

I laugh at the idea of Michael Carlisle knowing any form of jiu jitsu, verbal or otherwise. Bullies are weak, that's why they bully.

"Thanks," I reply, then I rip off the bandage. I press CALL on the contact page listing my father. One I haven't yet deleted from my phone.

It rings, my stomach rolls, my back sweats, my palms itch, my throat goes dry. Sasha smooths her hand down my leg, and I love her, I do, but I can't ignore the pulling in my heart that wishes I were with Van right now. That he could be here for this experience, to bond us.

But he's not. And she is. And that's that.

"Hello?"

Just the one word sends a shock up my spine. Hairs all over my body stand on end.

"Hi, dad, it's Violet."

Rose is gone. We planned to call him when we knew Rose would be out of the house. Sasha said the best call with my dad would be if he was at home, but if Rose was gone. So that's what we did. Called right after she left.

"I realize that."

Well hello to you too, asshole.

Sasha's grip on my knee tightens. Confidence and comfort pour into me through her reassuring touch.

I don't waste time and I don't mince words. "Why do you hate me?"

He just makes a noise. I'm not worth more than a freaking noise to this man.

"Why do you hate me?" I ask again, growing freaking irritated. If this is it, the last contact between us, why can't he just give me this one freaking thing?

"You were conceived, and that's enough."

I hold the phone, staring at the clock counting up on the screen, timing this phone call. That's an awful thing he's just said, and I have no words. I look at Sasha, whose expression matches mine; confused, angry, bewildered.

"I was conceived and that's enough? What the hell does that even mean?" It's pretty sad that I get a rush of adrenaline from standing up to him over the phone in such a limited way but still, I take that rush and ride it.

"Why, my whole life, have you hated me? Seriously, dad, why? Because you're my dad. And even shitty dads love their kids. But you—you don't love me at all. You love only Rose. And whatever. I don't need your love. In fact, I don't need anything from you ever again. Because I'm never going to find you. I'm never going to reach out and want you in my life. Or mom. Or Rose." I take a breath so that I can keep going, not because I've lost momentum. Finally, I found momentum. "When I have a baby someday, I won't find you guys. When I have a family and home, and things to celebrate, you will never know. So don't worry about that. I'm done. I'm gone. But the least you could do now is just tell me why. Why, dad, do you hate me?"

The smallest, most ridiculous sliver of me wonders if he'll say "no, Violet, I don't hate you", but of course, I know he won't. And he doesn't.

"You came from your mother and a bad choice she made. And I had to live with and look that bad choice in the eye every fucking day when I raised you."

Sasha's hand slips from my thigh. My mouth falls open and if I thought my throat was dry before, it's really fucking dry now. My jaw burns. "What?"

"What do you mean, what?"

There's an exchange of hands, I can tell because there's muffled talking and then... my mother comes on the line.

"Violet, sweetheart," she says, already crying. Most of the time when people cry, it makes me want to cry.

"Why do *you* get to cry?"

Sasha pumps a fist in the air while silently cheering. "Way to stand up for yourself," she quietly cheers. There's a feeling in my chest... tingly and exciting. That's... pride.

"I–" my mom starts, but this is not the call I'm making. If she wants to right her wrongs, that's on her, but that's also on her own time. She has work to do. Changes to make.

"What bad choice did you make, mom? What's he talking about?"

Sobs wrack up her throat, but she catches them, managing to speak. "I had a slip. It was years ago... I made a mistake that resulted in... getting pregnant."

Oh my god.

Sasha mouths, "*oh my god.*"

Oh my god.

"Your dad forgave me, thank god, but I couldn't terminate. I just… I couldn't. Not after I heard your heart beating."

I've read online that when you're dying, your life flashes before your eyes. It's not fake. I've seriously read accounts of people who were revived, brought back only to recount what the dying process feels like. Darkness, they say, then a flood of your life. You see it all, they say, within mere seconds. Every smile, tear, laugh, pain, explosion, fall, break, fear, blink, hug, drink, kick, swallow. They see it all.

I'd always been skeptical of that. Even with so many people recounting the same stories.

Am I dying? I hold the phone in one palm, the time still counting away as my entire existence plays like a sped-up movie behind my eyes. I swear an abyss opens up inside me and like water down a drain, my entire life circles, spins, and disappears.

"Michael isn't my father."

Sasha is watching me like she's just disconnected the blue wire and doesn't know if it was supposed to be the red or not.

"He is your father, Violet. He raised you," she argues, but the last few words come out weak and spineless. A lot like her.

The facts click into place in my mind, my mother's entire life now looking completely different. My mother now looks completely different.

"Why didn't you just leave him, mom?"

She sobs, but I wait. "I love him."

"How can you love a man who hates you? And your child?"

She clears the sob from her throat. "It's more complicated than that."

Rose. I think of Rose. "Rose." I just say her name, no

prompts other than that, but it's enough.

"We had Rose together," she says.

"He punished you your entire marriage, mom. He's still punishing you. He punished me my entire life for my DNA, which I didn't even have control of!"

"Violet," she starts, and I can just see her worn hands worrying with the end of her braid.

"No, mom. No." What could she say? One day when I have a child of my own, this will come crashing down around me and I'll really have to deal with it, but right now, I can't.

"It was hard for your father to move on from that hurt, Violet, you have to understand that I hurt him."

Sasha is pacing now, practically burning a trail on the floor. "Unfuckingbelievable," she says, more in general than to me. But she's not wrong.

"So he had to hurt me because you hurt him?"

She sighs and somehow, I feel like that sigh is the precursor to something that's going to completely devalue my experiences. "Violet, you've always had everything you need. You've always been taken care of."

Sasha can't help herself; she snorts loudly and shakes her head. I wish my mom could see Sasha shaking her head, to give this moment an outsider's look.

"And I don't appreciate being made to feel like we're awful humans. I didn't have you tied up at gunpoint."

Defenses rocket up around me like a flare gun. "Why do you do that? Why do you rewrite history to benefit him?"

"I'm not rewriting history, Violet. Did you or did you not have your boyfriend tie us up?"

The freaking gaslighting. I don't have to take it anymore, so I don't. "Did you call the police? Did you report him?"

"No, we–"

"No, you didn't. And not because what he did wasn't wrong, but because Michael knows who he is and a man like him has no place on the *victim* side of a police report. He belongs behind bars."

"I'm sorry you feel that way."

I snort. I laugh. Then I go diabolical and laugh until I cry, until my sides feel like they are splitting, until Sasha sits down next to me, nudging me.

"I'm fine," I say to Sash, not trying to shield my words from my mom. I don't care if she knows I'm not alone. Her secrets aren't safe anymore, and neither are mine. Secrets are what got us this far.

"If there's any part of you that cares about your kids, you'd convince Rose to move and go far, far away."

"Rose has a good relationship with your father." *Slap.* An unneeded backhand across the face.

"He's making her a toxic bully, just like him."

There's a pause, and I wonder if she's hung up, but then, with desperation strangling her she says, "if you cut us out of your life, you'll never meet your birth father."

"Are you serious?" Sasha says aloud before she can stop herself. I open my mouth to tell her I can fight my own battles, but she gets on a roll before I can. "You're really going to gaslight your daughter into thinking she hasn't been treated like absolute shit after telling her that the man she thinks is her father actually isn't, and then you're gonna go and hold her real father over her head... all to get her to stay in your life."

Sasha blows out a breath, and damn, hearing it that way really helps make a choice I'd already almost completely made.

These people do not deserve space in my life.

"Judith, we don't need you to tell us who her father is. If she wants to know, we'll do an ancestry swab." Sasha turns to me, her face still lowered to the phone in my hand. "You good?"

Actually, I think I finally am. "I'm good."

With her finger hovering over the end call button, Sasha smiles sweetly while holding a middle finger to the phone. "Bye!"

When the call is over, we don't erupt in laughter or sighs of relief because, again, the moment you dream of is never quite as sweet in the flesh.

"That was a lot," Sasha says, leaning her head onto my shoulder as we relax back onto the couch. "How are you? That news about Michael, yeesh."

Letting my eyes close, I think about everything. The call, my mom having an affair, my dad punishing all of us for said mistake, the mistreatment, the *ignoring* of the mistreatment. It makes me sick to think I kept loving my mom when all along, no matter who gave me half my DNA, she should've protected me.

That was her job.

"It makes sense. Why he hates me."

Sasha palms my cheek, the one not resting on her shoulder. "Don't say that. No one deserves to be hurt the way he has hurt you, inside and out."

"I know," I say, cupping my hand over hers. "But he was hurt and he's too incapable of growing to work through his hurt. So he just hurt everyone around him."

"He's a fucking prick."

I sigh. "It's relieving, in a way. Like, not that I ever

thought that it was me or anything but now I really know… it's them. They're supremely fucked up."

She nods, and we sit in thought. That's what I love about friends that feel like siblings should–they know when you need a break, they know when you can handle more.

After a few minutes, she broaches conversation again, softly. "Are you going to try to find your real dad?"

I shake my head because there isn't even a question. "No. Michael did raise me. He is my father." Finally, I push off of Sasha and rub my temple. "It doesn't feel like I lost anything. It feels like I gained something."

"Yeah?" she rubs her hand up and down my back to soothe me.

"Yeah. I mean, now I know. And now I'm out of there, away from them, for good."

"Hmm, that's true." She smiles, tucking hair behind my ear. "That's really true." Then, "you have Van to thank, you know."

Tomorrow will be one full week without Van. Since the notebook incident. Or what Sasha has lovingly been referring to as "notebook-gate".

"Where are you standing on all that, anyway?"

"I think I made a mistake."

Sasha smiles. "The great thing is that you've both made mistakes. He's made some big ones. But you know what? I think you guys needed this. I think you needed to realize what love really is."

I've spent the last week upset and confused, but with the clarity that I have more by actually having less, things seem pretty clear to me now.

Van risked his happiness in order to not hurt me.

That's love.

Chapter Thirty-Seven

DONOVAN

Crazy or not, it's fucking who I am—her protector.

"Well, I have to say, I'm proud of you, dude." Mally grins so large that it pisses me off.

I've been fucking depressed all week, obviously. I'm not going to try and muscle my way through having a broken heart. I work out. I go to work. But that's all I've been giving.

Mally, Bran, and Batman have attempted to make me feel better. Last night we split 100 wings, but I stopped after a mere twenty. I'm so full of fucking depression that in the last week, there hasn't been a lot of room for much else. Not even chicken wings.

"Shut up," I reply to him as I slide into the passenger seat of our cruiser. He's been driving all week, so of course he likes me sad. "You just like driving."

He presses a shocked palm into his chest, flipping his aviators onto his head. "That hurts, Van."

I roll my eyes.

He throws the vehicle into drive, looking into the side mirror before pulling out into traffic. "But seriously," he hedges forward, despite the fact that I've shut him down on touchy-feely talks all week. Mally just can't help himself. "I don't know if you've been... good... when you aren't around me but shit, bro, with Violet and all that... you're doing good."

Slowly I turn my head to face him and eyeball his profile while he drives. "You mean I'm not being a fucking crazy person, stalking and assaulting, so therefore I'm good."

He lurches forward with a sigh. "What I mean is, I'm proud of you for not letting this shit set you back, drag you down into a place you can't get out of."

Outstretching my arm, I squeeze his arm in a rare show of affection while on duty. "I know what you're saying. Thanks, man."

He nods, and we drive the rest of the way to the station in complete silence.

Once we're parked, I'm heading through the lot, towards the station when Mally grabs me by the wrist. I literally stop in my tracks and stare at his hand around me. "Dude," I say, shaking my hand free. But he doesn't keep moving. "If it's Donna, you should jus−"

"It's not Donna." He smiles, but he gives me his charming, sweet smile, one he reserves for coming onto women in bars or supremely sweet moments, like when Batman's first kid was born. "Catch up with me?"

My eyebrows furrow, ready to ask what he's talking about until he nods over my shoulder, repeating, "catch up with me."

When I turn around, there's Violet.

Her long hair is behind her back, she's wearing yoga pants, Converse, and an oversized shirt–*my* Willowdale PD shirt. I didn't know she took it. And I walk towards her so fast that I'm a little out of breath when we're face to face.

"What's the matter, baby?" I ask, falling so easily and comfortably back into the role of her boyfriend. Because that's who I am at my core. Crazy or not, it's fucking who I am–her protector.

Tears spill over, falling down her pink cheeks. She presses her fingers to her eyes, shaking her head. Instinct kicks in, and I wrap my arms around her, bringing her to my chest. Fuck, my entire body softens with her pressed against me. No, my entire existence relaxes, and the world makes sense again.

Then she pulls away.

"Violet, what's the matter? Are you okay?" I take her wrist and lift her arm, the large sleeve of the t-shirt slipping down to her shoulder to expose her skin. Smoothing my hand down the length of her arm, I repeat on the other side while she chokes on a sob. "Where are you hurt? What's the matter?" Panic floods my veins. She was hurt about the notebook. And now she's here crying–she has to be hurt.

"Violet, are you hurt?"

I pull her hands away from her eyes when she puts them there again. "Talk to me."

She swallows then swipes under her nose with the back of her wrist. I don't want her to cry, but she sure as shit looks beautiful doing it.

"I pushed you away, and you still want to fix me and take care of me," she cries, her emerald eyes glossy from tears. Using the hem of my t-shirt on her body, I blot her cheeks softly, and I don't miss the way she leans into my touch.

"When I said I love you, I didn't mean I love you today, but I can grow out of it. I meant I love you forever until we're both six feet under the soil." I twirl my finger in the end of her honey hair because God in Heaven have I missed doing that.

Her bottom lip trembles, but our eyes hold together. "I love you, Violet. And I'm sorry I didn't tell you I took the notebook. I was afraid of losing you, but I can see it was a fucking foolish mistake." I wet my lips. "I hope it wasn't *fatal.*"

"I love you," she says, and it nearly knocks the wind out of me, I swear to fuck it does.

My lungs burn as oxygen leaves me. My vision blurs and my heart fucking pumps. "Say it again," I tell her because she's never said it before, and I have to know this is real.

"I love you. And I'm sorry, too."

Pressing my body to hers, I lower my mouth until we're kissing. Her fingers slide through the back of my hair, her other hand already deep in my beard. She moans into my mouth, relief and pleasure twisting together to make a potent cocktail that goes straight to my dick.

When I pull back, I stroke my thumb over her plump bottom lip. "Can I pick you up from Sasha's tonight? I'm off in forty-five minutes."

She nods. We kiss and part ways, and I swear I walk backward until I'm in the building so I don't lose sight of her.

I won't lose her, not again.

I float for the rest of my shift.

Chapter Thirty-Eight

VIOLET

My gut and heart were screaming at the top of their proverbial lungs: risk it for him, he'll be worth it.

"Oh yes, *oh yes*, oh yes, Van, *ohmygod don't stop*," I moan like a freaking porn star, because *Van*.

I can hardly catch my breath, and its been that way every day for the last *three* weeks.

After the day I learned the truth from my mom, things suddenly made sense.

And I had the good sense of Sasha on my side, reminding me that the very thing that hurt me was the exact way I'd treated her.

Realizing you're a big, fat hypocrite is one thing, but doing it while you're torturing the heart and mind of an incredibly selfless, amazing human being? It lights a fire under your ass, trust me.

I'd wanted to rush out that moment and find Van, but

Sasha told me to sleep on it. Not because she thought I'd change my mind but because I'd been crying for a week straight. My face was looking... big. I wasn't able to bring it down to normal, but I did manage to get rid of the cherry-face I'd had.

I'd tossed and turned all night, finally getting up to flip through the notebook. And not the one that Van had taken. The one I'd begun writing in after I'd accepted that the first one was gone.

Turning through, angry words leapt forward from every page. Heated words bearing so much hurt and fear that I'd left sentences unread, words hanging idly as I flipped on. I'd been so angry about the old notebook being gone but the emotions coloring all the pages before Van tell a story I don't want to remember.

The notebook I'd been desperate to have back wasn't really important to me, and neither was this one. It was my security blanket; where I put that hurt and pain. I wrote when I couldn't bear my struggles anymore.

Filling page after page, notebook after notebook, I wrote. A false sense of security is what it gave me. Like burying a smoke alarm that won't turn off. It may be hidden but the alert is still sounding, regardless.

After meeting Van, he became the place to store my fears and feelings, he became the place to tuck away the inadequacies and vulnerabilities. That's what partners are for.

I don't know why I didn't see it then. But after the conversation with my parents I realized that if I want to move forward, then I needed to let go.

Everything in the old notebooks, the new one... it doesn't matter. That was how the old Violet lived, not the new one.

Morning took forever to come. After all the epiphanies in

the last twelve hours, Van was the only thing on my mind. Getting to him and apologizing for how selfish I'd been. How quick I was to storm out without explanation. Almost like... I wanted us to fail.

Maybe I didn't think I deserved a man like Van.

Or maybe I was scared to be hurt the way my family had hurt me.

Whatever it was, it didn't matter. Because being happy and loving required taking risks. And my gut and heart were screaming at the top of their proverbial lungs, *risk it for him, he'll be worth it.*

The next day I waited at the station, knowing he had a shift but not knowing when it ended. Sasha had come clean to me over breakfast that Van had been texting her multiple times a day to make sure I was okay, that I was eating, and that Michael had stayed away. He also asked how I'd been at school because Batman's sister-in-law was well acquainted with Mr. Wheeler; he knew that school could be a battle zone for me sometimes.

He asked my best friend about me daily, even after I'd hurt him, after he'd gone above and beyond for me, body and soul. If my ovaries weren't exploding for him before, they certainly were after learning that news.

I wore his shirt as a peace offering, hopeful that even if he didn't take me back that he'd see I appreciated him and that I was sorry.

But he took me back in a heartbeat, and I cried in his arms until he had to finish his shift. That evening, he picked me up at Sasha's. We were essentially crawling in our skin not being able to tear into each other. But he didn't want to get his hands on me until everything between us had been discussed; until we were "straight."

That's another thing I love about Van. He cares about the bones of the relationship, it isn't just physical, and it surely has grown well beyond curious obsession. He loves me, and he cherishes us, and that has always been visible; I just had to let myself see it.

Once I did, I swear I started seeing stars. Every morning, sometimes on my lunch break, and a lot of stars filled my skies at night. Tons.

And tonight is no different.

We're in a happy routine of making dinner together–Van is teaching me how to cook some more complex dishes since I didn't comfortably have access to a kitchen before now. He helps me cut construction paper crafts for the students when I don't have enough hands for the job, and a few times, he's gone with me to my classroom after hours to help me set up lessons.

He reads paperbacks in bed while I scare myself watching true crime. When I end up scared, he makes sure I know how safe I am by caging me to the bed and feeding his cock to the place between my legs he calls heaven.

Admittedly, that's how we got here again tonight.

"Yes, I can feel you, yes, yes," Van moans from above me.

We like having sex in missionary position. I love running my hands up and over his muscles–if your boyfriend was nicknamed The Bodfather, you would too. But also, I've grown to love his sweat raining down on me as he writhes and thrums inside of me. It does something crazy, like a palm to that sensitive spot above my pubic bone, making me want to come on the spot. The muscles, his feral and throaty groans, his sweat on my skin, salty and tangy...

"*Oh baby, yes, I can feel that,*" he rasps, slowly hollowing me as I clench down on him, my body trying to keep him inside of me. He reaches between us, grabbing himself by the base. The generous breadth of his crown massages my clit before he carefully slides his cock through my folds. "Oh, *good girl,*" he groans as he tunnels inside of me again, this time with more force. "Fuck, baby, *let go already.* I know you want to. I can feel you want to."

With his permission, I release my ironclad grip on the edge and free-fall into orgasmic oblivion. I fight to keep my eyes open because I want to see the beautiful dark-haired man straining and groaning over me. I want to see the moment when he falls over with me. I want to see his eyes as he drowns my hunger with his release.

Now who's crazy for who?

My spine rolls as my mind blacks out, my chest gravitating toward the ceiling while my ass hugs tight to the mattress.

"*Ohmygod, ohmygod,*" I cry out, voice broken and needy. When I'm *right there*, he slows his strokes, drawing the orgasm out of me, making it last, forcing me to come harder. He's the only one to do it that way, and I don't know if it's *his* style, our bodies fitting together, the size of his dick, or what, but *ohmygod* is right.

I've never come so hard.

Clenching, pulsing, moaning, aching—my fingernails dig into the tops of Van's structured shoulders as I come. I wanted to keep my eyes open, but they fall closed as I hold tight to the tail end of my orgasm. But when I reopen them, our gazes hold.

His broad hips stop between my open legs. He holds himself all the way inside of me, our bodies as connected as they can be. The corners of his lips curl in the most sizzling of smirks. He pairs it with a wink, then his cock expands inside of me. Pulsating sensations, a ripple of warmth, spreading rhythmically inside of me as he comes in long, hard bursts.

When his chest goes concave and his face softens, I know he's emptied himself. Reaching down between us, I begin massaging the base of his cock. I love feeling him slippery from us, and I love touching the place where our bodies fuse.

And he loves when I do it too, dipping his face into my neck, licking at my sweaty throat.

"I love you," he says right next to my ear.

"I love you, too," I say easily because it is easy now. I love Van with everything I have.

―――――――

"SO," I say to Van when walking into the kitchen after my very quick shower. Even before work in the morning, we have sex. Maybe there will be a time when sleep is more important—like when we have a crying baby—but for now, nothing is more important than getting lost in us. What a way to start the freakin' day. Beats coffee in my bathroom at my parents' house any day of the week.

"So," he says, looping his hands around my waist to pull me into a kiss.

I can taste the freshly brewed coffee on his tongue, and somehow, it tastes better coming from his mouth. Feeding my fingers into his beard, I rise to my toes to kiss him again, and then again.

"I've been living here for three weeks."

He swats me on the butt, and I take the coffee he's poured me. My favorite barstool calls to me, so I sit. "You have," he agrees, plating up my breakfast. He doesn't work today, but he still gets up while I'm getting ready and cooks my break-fast and packs my lunch.

Seriously.

"I was thinking…" I trail off, pushing around a piece of fruit on my plate, the tines of my fork suddenly very inter-esting. When I finally look up, his lips are pursed, head tilted.

"I don't like it when you're shy with me. Whatever it is, tell me. Okay?"

I nod and swallow down my nerves. "Well… I thought maybe we could have a housewarming party. I mean, I know housewarmings are usually thrown when people buy their first house together, and I know this is your house but… it's the first place to feel like a home for me. And I think it would be fun for Sasha and Cadence to come see it and… meet the guys." I take a drink of coffee that's meant to steady my nerves, but caffeine rarely does that. "A party to celebrate us living together and for our friends to meet."

I take another bite of fruit, and meet his eyes again. Talking around the cantaloupe in my mouth, I add, "I'll pay for the whole thing. I know it's a lot to ask since–" He silences me with a raised palm and a broad smile.

"I love it. That's perfect. Let's do it."

"Yeah?" My heart dances behind my ribs. Friends meeting friends is serious, which is funny to me since you know, *I live with him already*. But Van and I don't do things the way they're usually done. We don't follow any *shoulds*. We are categorically and beautifully out of order, and it works.

"Yeah," he smiles, then zips the top of the neoprene lunch cooler he bought me. "But you need to eat because it's time to get you to school."

FIFTEEN MINUTES LATER, Van and I are making out in the front seat of his SUV like we're high schoolers with a curfew. When I peel myself off him, breathless and kind of sweaty, he grins at me. That grin twists my insides and melts me. He takes my hand and presses it to the fly of his jeans, where I find him thick and proud.

"That's just mean," I say, knowing I have to get out of this car and into the real world.

Out of the corner of my eye, I see Mr. Wheeler shuffling through the parking lot, looking particularly cross. There's no way he didn't see Van and me making out, and I swallow down the grimacing thought that he will most definitely confront me about my "uncivilized" behavior on school grounds.

He'd done that twice already. Once after Van kissed my neck after dropping off lunch. The other time I'd been pulled aside, demeaned and lectured after he'd seen me napping on Van during my lunch break. I'd had a headache that day–something the Dr. told me could happen as a repeat concussed patient–debilitating headaches. I'd texted Van that morning that I wasn't feeling well, and he'd shown up on my lunch hour with a coffee (one for Sasha, too), Advil, and his alarm set. He'd reclined his seat and pulled me onto him. He stroked my hair until I fell asleep, and he kissed my eyelids until I woke up. At some point, Wheeler noticed and decided he wasn't a fan. Shocking, right?

I'd kept his complaints and comments to myself, though, *not* to protect him. I could honestly give a crap less about Wheeler anymore. I'd spent so many years protecting my father, hiding the abuse, making excuses for my mother and Rose, but it was all only hurting me worse.

The only reason I hadn't reported to Van how Wheeler

had been treating me was for Van. I love him, and I don't want him to twist with angst because the truth is, Van would teach Wheeler a lesson that would probably leave him bruised. And I didn't want Wheeler, the vindictive, petty asshole that he is, to report Van.

Wheeler isn't worth him getting written up or losing his job, so I kept it to myself. And it was tolerable. He hadn't touched me or said anything sexual to me. Anger I could stomach. Lectures I could take. As long as we stayed in that lane, I'd be fine.

"Don't worry; I'll be hard as stone when I pick you up after school. You can sit on my lap then." He winks, and my insides go molten. So this is what it's like to be absolutely enamored with someone... I love it. "Have a good day," he adds, giving me a goodbye kiss on the cheek.

I bound out of the car, eager to get to work.

Eager. I'm so eager these days. I want to work; I want to be home, I want to get groceries, I want to clean, I want to read, I want to cook. I want to do and be, and experience because finally, at my core, *I'm happy.*

It's five minutes before the lunch bell when I realize what an idiot I am: I'd been so wrapped up in our makeout session that I left the lunch that Van packed me in the car. Shit. I considered texting him but the thing is, I know my man. He will drop whatever he is doing to bring it to me, and I don't want that.

Instead, I tap into my stash of protein bars in my desk drawer. I have a reserve of them for the times that Wheeler is lurking in the break room and I don't feel like risking it. And just as I take my first bite of chocolate chip cookie dough flavored faux food, my classroom door opens, and Mr. Wheeler is there.

His face brightens when he sees me at my desk, and I'm pretty sure he's happy to see me alone. Freaking predator.

"Miss Carlisle, just the person I was looking for."

I can't help myself. "I hope so. You're in my classroom after all."

The way he so easily walks behind my desk, into my private space—he's way too freaking comfortable being him. There has to be a stop to it. I don't want to lose my job because I love this school and this district–freaking a, I'm trying to get on the school board after all. Being fired would not be something they're looking for in a board member.

But what's the alternative? My internal debate is raging a la Bush v Gore when it happens.

Mr. Wheeler's hand slides down my shoulder, his fingertips at the curve where my breast slopes. My insides pull tightly together into a protective yet shriveled ball. *Get your hand off of me*, I scream inside my brain but obviously, he can't hear it. Neither can anyone else, and I know Sasha is next door still.

"I'm not comfortable with your hand on me," I finally spit out in a rush, proud that finally I'm speaking up. My body is slinking away from the touch, but to pull off my words, I force my back to straighten against the chair. I won't move. He has to take his hand off to *get it.*

His hand doesn't move.

His laugh falls down the back of my shirt like ice cubes, my eyes jerking open wide as my body tries to lean away from the awful noise.

"You have no problem making a scene in a vehicle in the parking lot. A hand isn't nearly as bad as that." Clearing his throat, his fingertips dip lower, into the top of my bra. He fans them out, feeling the detail of the top of my bra cup through my silk blouse.

I swear it's the first time in my life I've wanted to projectile vomit. Seriously, I've never understood how people can have vomit rocket from their stomach but this moment right here, it puts it all into perspective. And this is why you don't judge someone else's experiences. Because you never know.

And I'd love to be back in that spot of never knowing about projectile vomit.

But it's too late; acid soars up my throat, burning the back of my nose. His fingers move, and I want to swat him away, I do, but I don't want to touch him. I don't want my hand to connect with his while it's on my body.

I need to do something but I'm paralyzed with fear and nerves, and I taste acid on the back of my tongue when my classroom door opens.

As soon as my eyes meet Van's, tears I didn't know were lying in wait fall down my cheeks, and immediately my bottom lip shakes. But I suck it under my teeth and brush away the tears.

Mr. Wheeler withdraws his hand, but not instantly.

From the doorway, Van's broad chest heaves as thick lines of strain appear in his neck. His jaw clenches, obvious he is exercising control, which for a man like Van in a situation like this has to be hard.

"You should leave this classroom immediately if not sooner," Van says, his voice rough and low.

Mr. Wheeler's confidence deflates now that Van is here, and he slithers out of the room, Van barely letting him pass.

His eyes follow Wheeler down the hall, presumably, and then he steps inside the classroom. I'm on my feet and around the desk moving toward him when I realize he's closed the gap. He brings me in for a hug, and against his chest I start to say– "I told him to get his hand off me, and he moved it down further. I didn't know what to do. I didn't want to touch him, I–"

Van cuts me off with a kiss, then drapes his soothing palms over my shoulders. "You don't have to explain or rationalize or justify. And do not fucking apologize, to me or him, Violet. You're the victim. You hear me? What he does to you is not okay, and none of your actions should or will be under the microscope, got it?"

I nod, fresh tears slipping past at just how right he is. And just how long I've gone needing to hear that. "Thank you," I say, pressing my face into his chest to find comfort. And God, do I.

He strokes my back then places a kiss against my temple before he hands me... "you forgot your lunch."

I take the bag, and hug him again. "I'm sorry about that, and thank you for bringing it to me."

With one more stomach-swirling smile, Van knocks his knuckle to his frames, pushing them up his nose, then gives me a kiss. "You should have Sasha over tonight for dinner."

We hadn't planned that, and Van isn't working, so I'm curious. "Really?"

Back in the doorframe, he nods. "I'll be a little late, so start without me."

I want to ask where he's going and what he's doing, but for some reason... I don't.

"Okay. We'll pick up something. I love you. See you tonight. Thanks again for bringing my lunch."

I feel his grin between my legs. "Love you too, baby." And then he's gone.

Chapter Thirty-Nine

DONOVAN

No one wants a snake up their ass.

I'm turning over a new fucking leaf.

Instead of feeling guilty about what I'm about to do–since I'm trying to be a better man for Violet, I'm going to let myself feel grateful.

Grateful that I am here and in Violet's life to provide her with protection. I know she's a grown woman who can handle herself, but there are some things no one should have to handle.

And those tasks are for The Bodfather.

I'm also grateful in other ways. Going from having a bustling hobby, and a full-time gig watching Violet to being a normal guy in a committed relationship has been a big change.

One I'm mostly good with.

I say mostly because seeing Wheeler's hand on Violet

today stirred up a lot of shit inside of me. Brought some deep-rooted desires to the surface.

So I'm grateful to the fucking handsy, disrespectful potato because he's given me an actual reason to release some of the pent-up anxiety and anger left over from the last few crazy weeks.

He's given me an outlet.

I don't lie to Violet and tell her I'm with the guys at Paradise or tell her I had to stop by the station to follow up on paperwork. I don't lie; been there, done that. So when she texted me a minute ago, I write her back quickly before stashing my phone away.

Violet: *We decided on burgers and fries. I got you the one you like—the one with the fried egg—and sweet potato fries.*

Van: *Sounds fucking bomb. Be home in an hour or so. Love you. Tell Sash not to touch my fries!!*

I start up my car when I see Wheeler make his way out of the Circle D liquor store. I followed him here. Great to know that the beloved principal hits the fucking liquor store after school.

He comes out with a white sack, and I can eye two bottles of vodka through the translucent plastic. He gets into his car and drives off, and I'm right behind him.

The drive to his house is short, and I spend it in silence. What I'm about to do is something I've never done—but the way I know it's the right choice is how calm I feel. How relaxed I am.

He gets out of his car with the garage door open. After he gets his liquor store bag from the back seat, he penguin-steps his way up the cement stairs leading to his back door. With several quick strides and one simple roll, I'm in his garage before the door closes, but Wheeler is already inside.

I'm grateful that people are idiots, unaware of their safety and their cushy lives. If they were aware, then this would get a lot more complex.

And maybe that's another reason why I'm not freaking out or worried because tonight is a simple choice.

I could linger in the garage to kill time; allow Wheeler to change his clothes or maybe even pop a freezer meal into the microwave. But the truth is, the less time this takes, the better. Violet is waiting for me. So is dinner.

When I step inside the house, Wheeler doesn't even hear me, despite a very annoying house alarm that robotically says "BACK GARAGE DOOR." His nose is buried in a snifter of vodka, and his throat is working quickly to fill his gut.

I have an opportunity to not be seen. I could step behind him, his own gluttonous glug-glug-glugging masking my quiet steps. But I don't. Because we're in a private residence, and I don't have to hide.

"Hi."

The snifter skitters across the kitchen counter, and his arms flail before sausage fingers go to his chest. "Fucking Christ," he exclaims. And then I see it. It's just a split fucking second, but I see it.

The realization of who I am; the immediate sag of relief in his shoulders when he realizes I'm not an intruder. And then, the moment following that, when he realizes he's wrong. He may know me, but I *am* an intruder. I *am* a man to be scared of.

Wheeler's arms go up in self-defense because I don't think you can have a man like me coming at you without reacting that way. I don't think he believes he can stop me or even protect himself; he just can't fight the instinct to try.

But I put him out of his misery, connecting with his

temple on my first and only punch. He goes down hard, clipping the edge of the counter as he does.

He doesn't lose consciousness, though, I can see he's struggling with confusion from the hit and the fall. It takes him entirely too long to get to his feet, and in that time, I swipe a dishtowel from his counter and shove it into my back pocket.

"Jesus, get up already," I grit out, slamming my foot into his ribs. He grabs at the cabinet like he's a fighter on the ropes, except he hasn't fought me at all. Finally, he stands, and his hand finds the lump sprouting on his face, panic flooding his eyes.

"You think just because you're a cop you can fucking assault me? I've got friends on the force, pal. You're gonna lose your badge for this."

I honestly don't know where this fucking guy gets the balls. What is it with these assholes and their fucking audacity? Removing any distance between us, I hover over him, my breath surely hot against his face. "You think just because you're a male in charge that you can fucking assault women?"

I let that question hang in the air between us as I reach behind me and pull my gun from the waist of my jeans. I tap the barrel of the gun against my forehead. "*I've* got friends on the force, *pal*. You're gonna lose a lot more than your job for this."

He stares at the gun with horror, yet when he brings his eyes back to me, I smirk when I see his gaze tighten. "You really gonna try and act like a tough guy?" I ask with levity in my tone. There's nothing he can do–short of having a bank-style emergency call button in his kitchen that he can hit–that would stop me from my plans. Not now.

"She's not worth whatever you're going to do, you know," he says finally.

I tap the gun on his skull, right on top, using the butt. It sends a shudder through his spine. "Wrong thing to say, my man. Now, put your phone on the counter and get your keys."

He snorts. "You're not gonna fucking kill me over her." It's not quite a statement and not quite a question but a little of both. I give him nothing but the butt of the gun on his head, one more time–harder. Because what is it with old, piece of shit men standing up to the man with the gun?

"I can shoot you in the hand if you want. Would that motivate you to fucking listen?" I nudge him with my gun. "Walk. Go back into the garage and get in your car. Now motherfucker."

Wheeler is like everyone else. Fucking stupid. He gets in his car, making no attempts to lock me out or even struggle. If it were me and I were caught being a sexual fucking predator and general piece of shit, I would definitely fight.

Lucky for me, he's stupid. After putting a few easily accessible (and important) items in the backseat of his car– while he watches me do it, I get into the passenger seat and control the garage with the clicker clipped to the sun visor above Wheeler. Once the door is closed, I tell him to drive.

"Where are you making me go?" he asks, and still, there isn't any panic or fear in his voice. I have a gun. Evening is upon us. We are alone. I've already assaulted him. How the fuck is he so calm? Then I remember the snifter.

"Are you a drunk, Wheeler?" I ask him as he follows the coordinates I've input into the car's computer. I know a perfect spot for him.

He doesn't answer. So I poke him again, because why not.

"Are you a drunk and a predator? Shit, your parents must've done a number on you. Or wait, was it a woman? Did you fall for some woman who didn't like micro dicks and bald heads and just say, fuck it?" I press the barrel of the gun into his side, which causes him to jerk away from me, slightly taking the car across the lane.

"Don't you dare. You drive normally, or I'll do worse than kill you." I turn the navigation off so he can hear me. Besides, it was sending us to the liquor store. If someone checks his car, I want it to look like he was on one.

"There's nothing worse than being dead, you fuckin' moron."

See, this guy. I don't understand him. Even on the way to his fucking death, he's an idiot.

"Well, how about I tie you up and shove a snake up your ass and we find out." I smile, my sweetest smile of course. And fuck snakes. But if this fucker were to call my bluff, I'd have to do it.

He doesn't though because even though he's an idiot, no one wants a snake up their ass.

"You aren't gonna kill me," he says it with this fucking irritating smirk on his face, and I don't like it. It's insane to let this guy still get under my skin but still, I can't help it. An image of his ruddy pink fingers on Violet's shoulder flies through my mind and I have to roll my neck and crack my knuckles to diffuse the anger.

"There," I point ahead to a large grove of trees, so green they remind me of Violet's eyes. Listen to me. A fucking lovesick fool, and I wouldn't have it any other way. "By the cross."

There's a worn cross sunk into the Earth, a rosary and string of flowers draped around it.

I don't replace it as much as I should, but twice a year seems to be how often I can get out here. I have the time to come out here more, but visiting the site where my parents burned in their car isn't easy. Even all these years later.

But it has meaning. This is the spot where my life changed forever. So this is the spot where Violet's life is going to change forever, too.

Once he pulls off, I remove the things I grabbed from his garage out of the back seat and pull him out of the driver's seat by the arm.

I'm pretty sure he believes me now.

"Don't make me shoot your hand or foot to get you going. Seriously. Just fucking walk asshole. Because I'm gonna make you dig your own grave even if you've got a broken hand."

He stops, face paling, and then he doubles over and empties all that precious vodka into the energetic grass, which glows beautifully against the setting sunlight.

When he rises, that's when he realizes he can bolt. I see it in his eyes, the way they bounce around our surroundings, his body suddenly full of hard-to-contain energy. My knee connects with his groin with all the energy a man with the nickname *The Bodfather* can serve up, and it sends Wheeler back a few paces, howling.

"You aren't runnin' Wheeler," I tell him, pushing my glasses up. I shove a hand through my hair, and grab the shovel I'd dropped. "Now walk."

After a few minutes of Wheeler walking and whining, we come to a small opening amongst the trees, and it's the spot. The earth is soft and pliable, offering itself to us easily as I hold the gun to his head, forcing him to dig.

We don't talk. I don't ask Wheeler if he has any last

words. He doesn't beg for his life. There isn't a big moment. He just digs and digs, and he just keeps digging like he can dig himself out of this situation (spoiler alert: he can't).

I don't tell him he's done and I don't let him know that he can stop. Hell, I don't even step closer.

I just raise my arm and curl my finger.

A smoke serpent slithers into the sky, only to disappear amongst the burgeoning darkness of sunset. From my back pocket, I take the gloves I sniped from his garage. I wear them as I backfill over his lumpy body, his shirt soaked crimson.

I drive his car back, still wearing the gloves. And when it's back in his garage and I replace the shovel, I slip out the side gate. Taking the street quickly, I get to my SUV and pop the back door. After stripping out my clothes, I take an extra pair from my duffel bag and put them on. Part of this outfit? My Willowdale PD baseball hat.

Twelve minutes later, I'm dipping my fries into Violet's leftover ketchup and tasting chocolate milkshake off her lips.

A fucking good night.

Chapter Forty

VIOLET

The only problem is, now she has my brain going.

"He's bringing me lunch at school today. We're going to eat on the benches out under the Red Oak and have a little picnic."

Sasha rolls her eyes but grins. "Gah, too adorable for me. Seriously."

I can't help but grin, too. Because we are adorable, and I really don't freaking care how sickening it is to witness.

"I don't even care," I admit to Sasha as I try to comb my hair in a tiny compact mirror over my desk. "Sash, I'm like freaking vibrating when I think about him."

She slips into a child's desk next to mine, and props her head up on a closed fist. A dark curl slides over her eye. She pushes it back with a sigh. "I can tell. I'm happy for you."

I snap the compact closed, and smooth my hands down my pencil skirt, willing the wrinkles away. "Yeah?" I say, tipping my head to analyze her body language. Slouched, eyes unfocused. "Then what's going on?"

She swallows, glancing to the door behind her. She knows it's just Van on his way, so why is she worried about him walking in on us?

I sit down because it feels like a moment I want to be seated for, I don't know why but it does. "What's the matter, Sash?" I ask, my heart rate increasing as the silence stretches.

"Did you know Mr. Wheeler has been out all week?"

I wrinkle my nose because, no, I didn't know that. "Really?" I think back to the Friday assembly this morning, and yeah, now that she says it, the assembly was pretty carefree and enjoyable. "Shit, yeah, you're right huh."

She twists a curl around her finger, and it makes me think of the way Van loves to tangle his fingers in my hair. My body warms at the thought of him handling me, even just my hair.

"Violet, I want to ask you something... or... say something but I don't want you to be offended or upset."

Well that's definitely not how any *good* sentences have started. "Okay."

She releases her curl and it bounds back to the masses. "Do you think Donovan... knows maybe what happened?"

I swallow, and she looks back, checking the door again, and that makes my stomach spike with unease. "You think Van told Mr. Wheeler to take the week off?" I ask, confusion peaking in my words.

She bites the corner of her mouth, studying me. "Maybe. Or like, I don't know."

"I don't know?" I repeat because clearly, she *does* know. "What are you saying, Sasha?"

Our gazes hold on one another for what feels like forever,

but eventually, she smiles, sending a crack through the tension between us. "I don't know. I guess maybe he'd have the inside scoop. You know, since he's a cop."

I drape my hand over my collarbone, sighing out in relief. "Oh, well, I can ask."

Then our eyes idle—she knows what she meant and she knows I know it. And when she gives Van a massive, warming hug when he comes into the classroom with my lunch, I know we're good. I know that I've heard the very last of her speculations.

The only problem is, now she has my brain going.

Another week has passed and Mr. Wheeler has still not been to school. The first week—the one where I was completely freaking oblivious—didn't seem to alert anyone. I'm not even sure anyone reported him missing until after that first week. Seriously.

As it turns out, when you're a despicable human, people aren't so worried about your whereabouts.

But the police had been down here this week. Not Van or Mally, but some detectives. They talked to our Vice Principal, but really didn't seem to poke around too much. I didn't know if I should be grateful for that or if I should have any reaction at all.

"Ready?" Van pops his head into the bathroom, where I'm just finishing blow drying my hair.

"Yes, sir," I smile wide, because tonight we're going out to celebrate, and I am freaking excited.

When I got home from school today, Van was waiting for me with a surprise. A white envelope.

He'd already gotten me a contact on the school board to send my letter of interest to directly, and I had done it. I hadn't expected to hear back so soon, knowing how many applicants there were. Even though I had a direct pipeline to someone on the board, I didn't let my hopes get too high.

As it turns out, the woman he'd connected me with was impressed by such a young teacher wanting to drive so much change from the top-down. I'd attached some lesson plan criteria per grade level, in addition, plans to overhaul the library system in order to make books more accessible through tablets and other devices. Any plan I'd written, I'd attached it to show them how serious I was. And I'm glad I did.

"Here's a piece of mail for you... school board member Violet Carlisle," he'd said, passing me the envelope. I couldn't believe it. I couldn't believe they'd actually read everything I'd included and wanted me.

They wanted me.

"No way!" I squealed before leaping into Van's arms, which easily held me. He kissed my neck and stroked my hair, telling me how proud he is of me the entire time.

Five minutes later, I had him on his back, his cock splitting my lips apart, my throat flooded with his hot come. Good news makes us horny, apparently.

Now, we're going out with Bran, Mally, and Sasha to celebrate.

"What's the guest of honor want to eat tonight?" he asks, looping his arms around my waist as he kisses the nape of my neck from behind.

"You know what I've been craving?" I spin so our lips meet, and his kiss makes me wish we were staying home. "Burgers," I finally say when his teeth release my bottom lip.

"Yeah?" he asks, moving the tip of his finger slowly down

the bridge of my nose. He likes touching my face, and though I didn't know subtle facial touches could be hot, yep, they are.

"Yeah, that one last week was so good. I've been thinking about it basically ever since."

He lifts me by the ass, setting me on top of the bathroom counter. We share a slow kiss, and like a slap across the face, it hits me that *this* is a perfect moment to ask.

We're alone.

We're both in good moods.

The space is safe.

I could just say, *do you know anything about Mr. Wheeler?* Or I could even ask... *have you heard about Mr. Wheeler?*

But as his tongue sweeps the roof of my mouth, I just don't want to. I want to enjoy this evening, my friends, my boyfriend, and the fact that the school board people want me.

"You gonna drink tonight? You want me to drive?" he asks, smoothing my freshly dried hair back off my shoulders. His fingers play at the ends behind my back as he kisses my nose, then my lips again.

"Yeah," I moan my response as I tilt my head toward my shoulder, letting Van's beard chafe my throat, instantly making me hot. "Oh, am I getting dessert first?" I tease, fishing my fingers up the back of his soft dark hair. The heat of his hard body looming before me makes me want that burger less and less.

He growls into my collarbone before pulling away, the tip of his nose pink, his lips swollen from kissing. Sexy as hell. "Nope. Off to celebrate. We can do this when we get back." He slides me off the counter, and turns the light off as we walk out. "We *will* do this when we get back." He swats my ass, and then we're in his car, me sending out text messages for our plans while he drives us there.

Bran holds the salt shaker to my mouth, like a microphone, waiting for my response.

"The first thing I'll do is install quarter machines full of temporary tattoos and sticky hands so the kids love me," I hiccup into the condiment shaker as Sasha grabs my arm laughing. Mally takes the pepper and holds it up to me.

"And how will you respond to the haters?"

Another hiccup, but fortunately, I caught it with the back of my wrist. "I'll say, lady, the only time in life that's cool is when you're a kid. Let them have fun." The words sound clearer in my head because as I hear them tumble out of my mouth, they're pretty smooshed.

Mally snaps up, his lopsided grin going straight. "That's so true. Everything is someone else's worry when you're a kid."

"Totally," Bran says, staring off into the distance, his hand playing with his eye patch.

"Jesus Christ, you two. You both have fucking great lives," Van says, shaking his head as he takes the last bite of french fry off his plate. I finished off mine tonight. Because I am drunk.

Sasha is, too. Actually, we all are except Van since he's driving.

"Hey," I gripe, leaning away from him with horrid offense. "What about me?" I puppy dog pout, and he reaches for me, worry etched into his forehead, his glasses lifting with his brows.

"You're solid now baby," he says, his voice both rough and

smooth, like someone pulling a silk tie through my folds. Even drunk I can feel myself getting wet. His lips brush mine as he grips me by the back of the neck. "I'm sorry."

I kiss him, closing my eyes to delight in the warm buzz and soft spinning in my brain. He feels good. This feels so good. "I love you," I tell him, as if he doesn't know. That's how I feel at this moment, like I want him to know exactly how vital he is to my existence. That I can't function without him. "Seriously, I love you Van. Like, so fucking much."

"Get a room," Mally says through cupped hands and a wild hiccup. We drank craft beer. I never drink, but I don't know why Mally is so drunk. I laugh at him, but grab onto Van's shirt, his chest grazing my knuckles, spreading warmth up my arms.

"I love you," I say again, though this time it's much harder to focus.

He kisses my temple but presses a glass of water to my hand, wrapping his fingers around mine. "Drink."

"I should probably drink, too," Sasha slurs, and Van produces another glass of water, handing it to Sasha.

We drink, the guys do, too, finishing their food as well. The night has been fun, light-hearted, and Sasha hit it off with the guys. Bran said things are going well with his girl, but didn't want to elaborate. We decide to call it after Mally and Bran eat three molten lava cakes and have a serious debate about an oreo milkshake.

Van buckles me in his car, and his lips brush mine as he ducks out, going to help everyone else in. After various drop offs, we find ourselves headed back to... *our house*. Van rubs my thigh, his other hand perched on the top of the steering wheel like he doesn't have a care in the world. God, it's sexy.

I hiccup, the alcohol fuzzies now starting to slowly clear.

Then I just say it. I don't know why. It doesn't seem to be at the forefront of my brain; it must be the alcohol.

"Do you know anything about Mr. Wheeler? He's been missing for two weeks."

Silence drops between us, even though we were quiet before. His eyes find mine through the dark cab, moonlight dropping intermittent moments of clarity over us in short bursts. He faces the road again, swallowing loudly.

"I want to show you something, okay?"

And I just stare at his tantalizingly beautiful profile. How he pulls off a crotch-grabbing male and passionate lover all at once, I don't know. But I'm glad he's *my* hybrid.

"Okay." My heart is starting to beat too fast, making my skin grow slick from nerves. I don't feel scared though, and as sobriety and I reacquaint ourselves, I remember the conversation I'd had with Sasha.

"You look beautiful tonight, Violet," he says, his fingers spreading out over my thigh. My head tips back, and I get lost in the way it feels to be loved by Van. The timbre of his voice evokes hard nipples and goosebumps every time. His fierce protection of me, then how he both powerfully and tenderly loves me between the sheets. It's... freaking a, it's good.

A few minutes pass and then the SUV is off, and we're pulled over on a stretch of highway only vaguely familiar to me. I've definitely driven it before... it takes me a moment to place it. But it's the East side of Willowdale.

His headlights illuminate a white cross stuck into the ground, some sort of makeshift roadside shrine. An accident must've happened here. Pinching my gaze down, I look for names, dates, photos, but it's just the cross and some rosaries.

"This is where my parents were killed," he says, the lights

from the dashboard reflecting on his glasses. "I replace that cross twice a year."

My heart freefalls. "This is where your life changed."

He turns to me, nodding, his eyes wide, brimming with emotion. "That's right, Violet. That's *exactly* right."

My chest expands, so much love and affection filling it that it gets hard to breathe for a second. I clutch my chest, and his hand grips my thigh tightly now. "Thank you for showing me this place," I reply because it feels like maybe this is the deepest thing he could show me. And it's bonding.

"I have something else I want to show you," he says, nodding his head towards the grove adjacent to the highway shoulder. "I have a flashlight in the back."

At the back of his vehicle, the door lifts, and there sits a duffle bag. When he unzips it, I don't know what to expect to see, but I exhale when it's just the flashlight.

We weave our fingers together, and he leads us, our huffed breaths fading into the quiet whoosh of cars and the gentle stirring of trees.

We stop, and Van squeezes my hand, so I look up at him. The moonlight blankets his dark eyes. I want to reach up and shove my fingers into his beard, find his lips, and have a moment in this beautiful, dusky evening.

But he looks at me, and I meet his gaze. With his eyes on me, he clicks the flashlight on, spraying light across the stretch of flowering grass in front of us.

Slowly, I catch up to the light and blink a few times, my brain in shock at the sight.

I never see them.

I mean, they aren't rare or uncommon, but still, I never see them. Especially not in the lush, overgrown hillside.

"Violets," I say in awe, my eyes pouring over the hundreds

of velvet-petaled flowers, their variance spanning from mulberry to lilac in shade. But all so beautiful. The only time I really like my name is when I'm face to face with real violets. They're so incredibly beautiful.

"Oh my god, Van, it's beautiful." My eyes warm but I force myself to look away from the gorgeous sight, because I feel his eyes pinning me.

"I planted them," he says, his brows heavy.

"Yeah?" My head is dizzy, but I feel sober now.

"Two weeks ago."

My words from the car come rushing back. *He's been missing for two weeks.* My knees start to give, even though I want to stay standing by his side.

His arms are around my waist before I falter, and he hauls me up next to him. The flashlight pours light on the flowers in front of us from its spot at our feet now. He strokes my hair as his beard brushes my temple and cheek.

"I planted them the next day," he says, voice dripping into my ear. "He was bad," he explains, "and now he's beautiful flowers for the world to enjoy. He's part of the earth, so you can bloom."

Burning tears through my chest, but not pain or fear. I'm overwhelmed with how far he's gone for me. I'm overwhelmed at the lengths he'd go to keep me safe. Risking his life for me.

I slide my hand down between us and cup his straining cock. He braces his thumb and forefinger around my jaw, yanking my face up to meet his.

My fingers pull down on the silver tab of the zipper. His grip on my jaw tightens, and my chest flares with that same inextinguishable heat.

On my knees, soil wetting my bare skin, violets tickling

my calves, I press the head of him to my lips and kiss. Then I suck him, letting my tongue horseshoe around the slick underside of his cock. He groans, both of his hands on either side of my head, his hips jutting forward toward my face. God, it's hot when Van wants more of me. I don't think I'll ever get used to it.

Keeping my lips sealed tightly around him, I suck and bob. He groans, sending bursts of salty precome down my throat, making my cheeks tingle. After rolling his balls in my palm, I drag a finger up and down the seam of his ass.

I keep my hand between his legs, kneading the sensitive skin behind his balls, when his grip on me tightens.

"Fuuuuuck," he warns. His dick throbs on my tongue, stiffening in its last attempt to hold back. I trace the crown of his swollen cock with the tip of my tongue before taking him deep to the back of my throat.

He groans, he curses, he hold my cheeks, and watches me like I'm solving world hunger. It floors me, and I suck him harder one last time. His pubic hair tickles my upper lip as he jerks and pulses on my tongue, flooding my throat with thick, salty come. I cough a little, my body's reflex, but swallow it down.

"Good girl," he praises, stroking his thumb across my cheekbone as I take down the final shot of his orgasm. "*Good girl.*"

Then he has me on my feet, our lips fused.

"I'd do anything for you; you know that, right Violet?"

I nod. "I know that."

"I love you," he says. Then from his pocket, he produces a pen. Twisting it beneath the burgeoning moonlight, I can see my name across it in cursive. My pen. The one Mr. Wheeler took. Holy crap.

My bottom lip trembles like an idiot but not because of the pen. That he got it back for me. "I love you, too," I respond, taking the pen from him.

We turn together and head back to the car.

Chapter Forty-One

DONOVAN

AFTER A BLOW JOB, I shouldn't be confused, but... I am.

Because Violet was quiet the entire drive home, she smiled at me, and she didn't glue herself to the opposite side of the cab in a passive-aggressive attempt to let me know she's not quite right. And it's not even that something isn't quite right but... I'm worried.

To calm myself, I try to make sense of what just happened.

I'd come clean to her about something pretty fucking heavy. Anything that puts you in prison if you're caught... It's not good. I didn't know how she'd react... and then she dropped to her knees.

She blew me.

But was it the heat of the moment? The intensity of what I shared with her... maybe she was overwhelmed, but now that the moment has passed, maybe she's rethinking things? I drum my thumb nervously on the smooth leather steering wheel. Probably the only fucking time you don't want a silent car.

My mind races loudly. I killed that man. I fucking killed him, and now she knows it.

Once we're home, I know I need to make sure things are okay. I need to feel okay with this. Or else... I don't know.

The garage door opens—*does it always fucking go this slowly?*—and then I'm closing it behind us. Our seatbelts unclick in unison, and we make our way up the back steps almost in identical stride.

"Talk with me in the kitchen?" I ask as we toe off our shoes in unison, lining them up against the back door.

"Sure," she says, her voice giving nothing away. And I know her well. Still, this version of Violet is foreign to me.

After all of this, I can't beat around the fucking bush. My thoughts are shooting off like poorly packed fireworks, and I can't handle much more.

"How are you feeling about everything?" The work it takes to maintain a steady voice is... surprising. Worry is worming its way into my brain.

"I-" She's cut off by a panicked thudding at the front door. Someone's beating it with their fist; I know the sound. I do it on calls all the time. It's a cop. And I hope it's my partner.

"Van!" Mally's muffled voice calls, tone a little strangled. I swallow thickly. He's on-call tonight, right? Fuck. My mind goes blank as my pulse picks up. Why am I getting fucking dizzy right now?

Then I'm answering the door.

"Let me in," he bustles past me, out of breath, stopping short in the entryway. "Violet, hi."

He looks between us, and the subtext is powerful. *Is it safe to say this in front of her?* I notice right then he's in uniform. His chest cam is off.

I nod. "It's okay."

He swallows, then focuses on me, his eyes stormy, brow furrowed. "Wheeler's neighbor has a security camera. Faces the East side of his house. Toward the street." Silence moves through the room like an atomic blast. "Two weeks ago. The 13th. It was a Friday."

"There's a hooded figure. That's all. I've seen the footage." He finally takes a desperate breath, his chest heaving as he peers over at Violet.

"Now that you two are together, and if it comes out what kind of guy he was–you'll be a suspect. You could be, at least." He swallows and rests his hand across his body cam, fingers tracing the edge of the radio. "If it's cool, then it's cool. Just–"

Violet's voice is powerful like she's been standing above this flood of awful information and remains unaffected.

"He was with me."

Chapter Forty-Two

DONOVAN

MALLY'S VOICE IS DEEP, serious. "Would you testify to that... if it came to it?"

Her answer is immediate. "Yes."

And my chest fucking explodes. Seriously. Fireworks detonate beneath my ribs, traces of color and heat tear through my every fucking molecule.

We bonded already, in a ton of ways. But this. This is her ultimate gift to me. Showing me her commitment, that she really fucking loves me.

I'm struck with the masculine urge to fuck her feral like an animal, and I suddenly need Mally out of this fucking house.

"He was here. We had burgers. I picked it up. I have the receipt." She folds her arms across her chest. "Though I hope it doesn't come to that. I'd hope you all have more faith in this man. A good man."

Mally's head slowly dips down. "So you were here?" he confirms, looking at the tips of his shined black work boots.

"Yes, I was here. It's not me in the footage." I parked my car far enough down, and under a broken street light, so even the best camera can't penetrate black.

"Okay then." He keeps his hand over his chest, turning to Violet. "I'm sorry to bug you guys. Have a good night."

He sticks his hand out towards me, and I shake it. "Paradise in the morning?"

I tip my head toward Violet. "Once we're up, yeah." He nods, then he leaves.

When I turn to face Violet the charge between us is thick, fucking electrifying.

"You can change your mind. It's just Mally, okay? If you want to change your mind, you can." It is my responsibility to make sure she knows her choices. "I want you to take a second. Take a breath," I steady my hands out in front of me, between us.

"I don't need a second, Van. I don't need a minute. I don't need to take a breath. I know what I'm doing." Bringing our hands together, her expression of certainty is overwhelming. "I love you, and I have the chance to protect you. I'm not missing any more chances."

How a woman so full of hurt and defeat ends up so completely fucking unflappable in the face of true danger, I don't know. But that woman is *my woman,* and I'm fucking proud to say that.

Bringing our linked hands behind me, pressing on my tailbone, we kiss. Her chest presses to me. Her hardened nipples are no match for two layers of clothes between us, and I feel them against my skin as our lips fuse.

"Thank you." My most is at her ear when I let her know how much I appreciate her. How much I love her. "Thank you for everything, Violet."

She pushes back, putting what feels like distance between us, making it harder to breathe. I want her fucking close. She rests her hands on my chest, and the contact revives me.

"We saved each other."

"Is that right?" I know I should be the one filling her with affirmations, telling her she's the reason why I live, but after fighting so hard for her, that praise is addicting.

"You said that to me, you know. The afternoon you snatched me."

I think back to the day in the parking lot at school. Violet's hair glowing under the bright sun, her long legs taking wide strides, eating up the walk. So fucking sexy. Then I saw her fucking eye socket and, well, that's a different story.

But she's right.

The day I took her rolls through my consciousness, and the moment comes back clear as day. *I would've gone crazy, so taking you saved me from that.* Once I'd seen her eye, I took her. And if I hadn't... I shiver at the thought.

"You did save me," I say finally, surprised at just how fucking true that statement really is.

"Now, let me say thank you."

I can't think anymore. I'm shaking. Literally, my hands are fucking shaking to hold her. This woman who I watched from the shadows for a year, wants me. She doesn't just want my dick, and she isn't creaming over the badge.

She just dedicated herself to me in a way that no one else could possibly understand. And it makes me want to fucking marry her.

But right now, I need to make her come.

We're stripped to nothing in a minute, and my cock flag-poles between us. "Get on the counter, on your back."

Like a good girl, she does, leaving the plump end of her ass just barely hanging off the edge. Legs open like she knows what she's there for, hair strewn across the granite, hands cupping those big tits of hers–fuck me.

This is my life now.

And she's fucking devoted to *me*.

I take off my glasses, sweat already thick on my forehead. Tossing them to the side, I swipe the back of my wrist across my hairline. "Fuck, baby, you're so hot. You're so fucking hot; I'm sweatin' here."

She smiles shyly at me, but when I really focus on her eyes, they're hazy. They're also willing; my agreeable girl will do anything for me tonight.

And that goes both ways.

"You're so loyal to me, Violet," I start in, my voice low and raspy the way that drives her crazy.

My fingers crawl over the damp, taut skin of her belly. Her nipples tighten, areolas puckering. I align my glistening crown to her silky wet folds, and fuck she's drenched for me. Hips roving forward, I slide into her with ease, her tight little pussy swallowing me, drawing me in deeper.

"You're such a good girl." I pet her hair tenderly with one hand, the other resting on her mound, thumb stroking her swollen clit.

She turns her head, sucking my thumb into her hot mouth. Fuck, her tongue twisting around me while my balls are pressed to her ass–it's too good.

Pulling out of her, I squeeze my cock at the base. She reaches between her legs and begins slowly stroking her clit while her eyes roam over my ink.

"Good girls get to come," I tell her as I slide my cockhead into her silky pussy again. Groaning at our connection, I take my thumb from her greedy mouth, and pinch her nipple hard. "Do you want to be my good girl, Violet?" My voice is so raw, it nearly breaks.

"Yes," she pants, wiggling her ass against me, trying to find more friction. Her pussy tightens around me as heat swirls in my balls. My engorged dick throbs, and that's not a good sign if you're trying not to come.

"This good girl pussy makes me want to fuckin' come. Goddamnit, Violet, I wanna empty my sac into your good little cunt until I'm dripping down your thighs." My hips jolt forward, and this is not sex you see in a movie. There's no slow caresses and deep eye contact.

I need to fill up my good girl, or I'll fucking die.

And she needs me to give her everything I have, and right the fuck now.

"Oh Van, *ohmygod*," she presses her hands to her lower belly, head tossing back. "Yes, yes, yes," she chants to me, and I pay her homage, too.

"Oh yes, *oh yes, fuuuuck*," I groan, filthy words spilling out of my lips as my orgasm sears down my spine. "That's a good girl, making that tight, hot pussy come all over my cock."

She starts spasming, those velvety lips clamping around me, forcing me to drain myself into her. I have no choice, and God, emptying myself into my girl feels so good.

Her body goes concave, her words slow. Her pussy drinks me down as her lower half dances rhythmically to the pulsing of her orgasm.

"Good," I soothe, feeling my groin tighten. "Good girl," I continue, and she moans so deliciously that I can't hold back. Not a fucking stupid second longer.

I grab her hips and slam her down on my cock one final

time, hard and fast. I hold myself as deep as I can get, and once I feel snug, I let go.

When the first stream of come tears out of me, her eyes jerk open, and her lips fall apart. "Oh," she moans in response to the liquid heat flooding her insides. Me filling her in the most private way possible. Then I come again, my mouth open in a silent stupor as my cock flexes and thrums, over and over.

I'd come inside of her before, as we talked about Violet's birth control early on. But this time, this feels like we'd cut our fingers and made a blood pact. This feels like our names carved in bark. Rings on our fingers.

This feels fucking huge.

It feels pretty fucking amazing, too.

I keep myself tight inside of her for a few minutes, just massaging her tits, and stroking my hands down her tight little belly.

But as I grow soft, we have to separate.

After cleaning her up, I climb into bed next to her. And I swear to God, when my eyes open the next morning, I smile realizing we are still in the same position.

Chapter Forty-Three

VIOLET

Seriously. Goodbye.

Van and I are sitting at the kitchen table, one of his hands spreading a paperback while the other casually strokes up my calf. I'm eating a bowl of Frosted Flakes. Why Frosted Flakes? Because I never got them growing up.

No, I wasn't starved as a kid or anything crazy. But if I actively wanted something? Yeah, no way was it happening. My dad would get a whiff of my dreams and immediately put his foot down. Pop-Tarts, yellow hand towels, peach-scented hand soap, hydrangeas, a Honda Pilot–if I liked it, he loathed it.

When I'd mentioned some things that my dad always said no to, Van went out and got as much of the food and drink items as he could. This morning's trial? Frosted Flakes. And for lunch, he's making taco salad, and I'm using French dressing.

Growing up I'd had taco salad at my friend's house and her mother used French dressing. I'd never had it until then but holy orange creamy heaven. I wanted so badly to have it again that I'd asked my mother to buy the dressing. I'd planned to make it myself; we usually had those ingredients on hand.

But when my dad saw the bottle and asked my mom why she'd purchased it, she said I was wanting it for something specific. And I never saw the bottle again. What he did with it, I don't know, but at this point, it's all just laughable.

He is a deplorable human being, and that's all there is to say about that.

The doorbell rings, and I swear I think the notification chimes on his phone a sliver of a second before the actual doorbell itself.

"Hmmph," Van groans, wrapping his vast palm around my calf, giving it a firm squeeze. I don't want him to have to let go of me for the stupid door either. My lip pops out in a pout. His gaze tapers on me. "Do we have to?"

I grin, biting into my bottom lip. "What if it's Mally?"

His head volleys for a moment as he decides. Reluctantly he lowers my foot to the floor, and makes his way to the intrusion. My breath catches when I hear who it is, because I was expecting Mally. Maybe even Bran. Possibly Sasha.

Never Rose.

But there it is, the inept but still pointed voice of my younger sister, Rose.

"Can I please come in?"

Van steps away from the door, leaning back to find my gaze. I shrug, because if I were to say no to her now–no matter what she wants–I would be as bad as them.

And Van and I are not like them. We never will be.

"Come in." He nods her inside, and the way she practically crawls around the corner with her tail between her legs makes me feel better than it probably should.

"Hi," she says, nervously shifting on her feet. I hate that it makes me a little speechless, but it does because Rose hasn't been served a slice of humble pie before. Not once in her life.

I can't believe she's having it now, but she is.

She drifts closer, helping herself to a chair at our table. Van stands behind her, large arms folded over his chest, looking like a superhero. His fingers stroke his beard, and my pussy clenches in tribute because *damn*.

"What's up, Rose?" I manage, forcing my eyes down to my sister. Well, half-sister, I guess now.

"I heard what mom told you. About dad not being your real dad."

"Yep." I don't know what she wants but I have nothing to give. "Is that it?"

"I didn't know that," she rushes out, inching her palms towards me on the table. I just stare at them.

"I didn't expect you to."

She rubs her lips together, kind of nodding, kind of just floating. Finally, she says, "is this guy your boyfriend?"

She swallows, just barely tipping her head back to the direction of Van. I let myself look at him, and he tosses me a wink.

Not just any wink.

The kind that makes me remember naughty praises and filthy promises, and the kind that makes it hard to do anything but want. And I *want* him.

"Fiancé." I lie, but it hits differently to say fiancé.

Boyfriend is fine, yeah, but that dose of *"screw you"* is really punctuated with fiancé. And I know Van—he'll roll with it.

His smooth pink lips curl into the sexiest grin, and my fingertips tingle at the idea of feeling my way through his rough beard.

God, I want to feel that beard between my thighs. Feel the tickle of his mustache against my swollen, bare lips. Yes, *yes, I want that. Right now.*

"Rose, you should go."

"Why?" she blurts out, but doesn't follow up with anything, like she wasn't prepared to be rejected. And that in itself is part of the freaking problem.

"Why what?"

"Why don't you report him?" She looks truly puzzled, and I don't want to be mad because I want to kick her out and jump on Van. Seriously, he engages every trip wire inside me, and I am not ashamed.

"We kind of tied you guys up, we're not exactly innocent." My eyes flit to Van's, and he gives me another smoldering wink. My belly flutters like a butterfly on cocaine. Rose needs to go already.

"If you want to report him, mom and I remember what happened. We know he attacked you. And it was just the four of us. There was no one else." She swallows, her gaze flitting to Van for a second. I hear her saying she'll lie for me, but I don't want them to do a single thing. I used to want so much from them, and now I want nothing.

"We weren't tied up. He just came and got you after Dad... after he hit you." She winces as she says the words.

"You can barely say the words." I lean over the table, and she inches away. "Imagine actually being hit," I hiss, clicking my top and bottom teeth on the t.

She sinks away from me. I lean back to my side.

"I don't need your support now. I needed it then. When it mattered."

She jumps around in her seat like the words are ice sliding down her spine. "Violet, I–" she can't finish, and I wouldn't want her to.

"Goodbye, Rose. Seriously. Goodbye."

Van pulls her chair out from the table with her in it, and it makes me smile. She leaps up and throws me a final pity glance over her shoulder before stalking out the front door, worse off than when she came in.

"She thought it would be okay," I laugh at Van as he returns to me. He refills our coffees, and he slides me into his lap once he sits down. Stroking my hair, wrapping it around his fingers, he brings our mouths together.

"She's fucking stupid that's why."

Then we laugh, because in his low, thoughtful tone, he knew I was expecting something a bit more complex and sensitive than that.

Yet, it was just what I freaking needed.

"Thank you for making me laugh right now," I say, fingering his beard with both hands, my laugh dying against his lips. "I love you."

"I love you, too, baby." Stroking his tongue across my bottom lip, Van tugs me into a kiss, one dominant hand gripping the back of my neck.

It feels so good. It always feels so good with Van.

Then he splays me across the kitchen table and immerses himself in my body, namely that heavenly place (his words) between my thighs. He lathes and licks, his fingers pressed into my flesh so hard I moan. Propped up on my elbows, drunkenly tipping forward, I come on his tongue, drunk off the look of his handsome face spreading me at the seam.

He praises me as he smooths the wide pad of his tongue slowly over my clit, wringing all of my orgasm out of me. "Good girl."

My favorite two words.

Chapter Forty-Four

DONOVAN

Hiking is really fucking lame.

"It's not as bad as I thought it would be," Violet says, her bottom lip rippling as she blows hair off her face.

"It works muscles you don't work in the gym," I reply, smoothing my hands along her hamstrings as she stands, drinking water.

We're hiking. Trying something new together.

I also get to massage her muscles every time we take a water break, so, yeah, my hands all over Violet when she's all warm and damp from the sun? Uh, *fuck yes.*

She reaches behind her to hand me the bottle, and I take it gladly. Watching that sweet little ass in those tiny khaki shorts for a mile going uphill has my mouth completely fucking dry. I think I caught some bugs on the way up.

I finish the bottle and return it to the side of her backpack. She stretches her spine, giving a little moan of satisfaction. My dick perks up. This is not a secluded trail by any means, so I diffuse the situation internally by focusing on something serious.

Like... proposing.

I have my mom's ring.

I really didn't think I'd ever want it to go to anyone. I couldn't understand loving someone more because I'd never been in love before.

Now the idea of my mom's ring on Violet's finger makes my chest tight. My mom would have fucking loved her. And it kills me that they won't meet. But for Violet to have my mom's ring makes my parents part of us, and it's as close to perfection as possible. I have to go for it.

I had her name engraved on the inside of the band to make it really hers.

I fucking hope she likes it.

I know Violet loves me. We've talked about our future, too. And yet here I am, one sketchy fart away from crapping my pants because I'm so fucking nervous that this beautiful person may not want to marry me.

Maybe she won't feel the need to legally marry since we'd already bonded so much over other things? Maybe she'd realized how dangerous of a person I could be, and she'd changed her mind.

She could say no as easily as she could say yes.

No matter what, I was going for it. I tapped my hand over the pocket that homed the ring. I could feel it. My pulse quickened. *Here we fucking go.*

"Baby," I said, then I cleared my throat like a complete nervous fool. She turned around, eyes on her tricep where she was slathering on sunscreen with her other hand.

She glanced at me for a moment before a sudden double-take. She gaped at the blue velvet box, which was currently split open in two, mom's ring sitting inside.

"Be my wife." I couldn't ask. Because I couldn't let her say no. No fucking way could she say no.

And she didn't.

"Absolutely."

Suddenly, I was very glad I'd only waited until a few miles into this hike to do this. The further we went, the more we'd have to go back down before I could get my mouth on my... fiancée. Fuck, just the word had my blood abandon ship and sail to my cock.

I pulled her into a deep kiss, and someone in the near distance gave us a thrilling little whoop. I smiled against her lips as I finally pulled away, loving her hiccuped breaths so close to my face.

"You didn't do this because of what I said the other day, did you?" she asks, chewing the corner of her mouth.

I roll my eyes. She hates when I roll my eyes but it's warranted. "You think you gotta drop a fucking hint for me to want to marry you?" I shake my head in disapproval. "Baby, I've wanted to marry you since before you knew I existed. So there."

She melts a little, I can see it the way her shoulders droop and her cheeks soften. Her energy is pliable and delicate, and I love her for it.

"Good," she agrees with a gentle smile. "I didn't think so." She bites her lip playfully, then adds, "I said that because it felt bigger than *my boyfriend*. I mean, it is bigger than *my boyfriend*. I just, I don't know."

Embarrassed, she presses a palm to her forehead, shaking it. "It packed more of a punch."

I trace the slope of her nose until my finger rests against her lips. "Well, now it's true."

She smiles, and that one smile under the sun with willows whipping our calves, the chatter of fellow hikers in the distance–I see our entire lives. I hear her laughter in our house, smell her skin on the sheets, feel her body writhing beneath me–forever. My mind builds the future where she's round with our child–not even our first; lesson plans scattered across a messy kitchen table, happiness, and a home-cooked meal filling the air.

"We're gonna be so fucking happy, baby," I tell her, sealing my promise with a kiss.

But it's not even a promise. It's a fucking vow. I am devoted to her, forever. "I'm yours, Violet. And you're mine." I tip my head back, gulping in sunshine and reality– "Fucking finally."

She giggles, and we kiss again, and it's at that moment we both decide that hiking is really fucking lame.

"Let's go home."

She smiles coyly, still smoothing white cream into her skin. I think of the day in the closet, Violet with the lotion, me with my dick. "What's at home?"

"You straddling my face."

We hike straight down to the car.

Chapter Forty-Five

VIOLET

A wise yet fictitious paper company manager once said, "how the turntables" and I couldn't agree more.

The gun vibrates loudly. "Ready?"

My head practically vibrates it nods so quickly. "Ready."

My nails go white as I claw my leg, the gun dipping into my flesh fast, leaving a blaze of color in its wake. "It's gonna look so good," Sasha smiles, peering over my leg to watch.

"How bad does it hurt?" Mally asks from his spot next to Sasha.

I snort, but try not to move. "You have tattoos. You know what it feels like."

His blue eyes roam over my calf, where Van's tattoo artist Paul, is working on me. "Yeah, but I don't have any on my legs."

Sasha leans back from Mally, her gaze narrowing with inspection. "Seriously?"

A slow grin turns up his lips, and I can see he's looking at her mouth. "I can get naked and prove it if you'd like, CQ."

CQ. That would be the nickname Mally has given to my best friend Sasha.

In the five weeks since we'd gotten engaged, Van and I had worked hard to align our friends. When in between work trips, Cadence had even been joining us, and it made me so freaking happy. Because it meant that my friend circle was growing, and family can be anyone you want—not just blood. My family grew, too.

Sasha and Mally had hit it off right away, and even though there wasn't anything seriously romantic there, watching two professional flirts was like watching a playful rom-com that never quite makes it through the second act.

And I'd learned that nicknames were a very serious deal in this group. The Bodfather, Malibu, Bran, and Batman would not accept three new women into their social circle as Violet, Sasha and Cadence.

"Way too fucking dorky. Sorry, ladies." Mally had said after a round of spirits the first night we'd all hung out. He tapped his chin, whispered to Bran who nodded as if they'd solved world hunger, then spat out with a pronounced point towards Sasha, "CQ."

Sasha cocked an eyebrow. "CQ?"

Mally's lips quirked, but Bran and Batman looked smarter than to grin. "Curly Q," he said to her. A beat passed, and she rose to her feet. "I'm only agreeing to that because it makes me sound good." She winked and damn it, how do they not catch feelings for each other with that level of flirtatiousness?

Though Van wouldn't allow them to give me a nickname without his approval, they'd begun calling Cadence "Tiara" because of her prim and proper manners—which were really sharp because of how "on" she was while working.

But nicknames.

Nicknames meant comfort. Comfort to me is always love. And it trips me out to know that this is my life, these people watching me get a tattoo on my leg the day of my wedding are *my people.*

I have *people.*

I almost have a *husband,* too.

Holy crap.

A wise yet fictitious paper company manager once said, *"how the turntables"* and I couldn't agree more.

"No," Sasha replies to Mally as Paul begins work on the most important part of the piece. "And quit lookin' for reasons to show me your penis, Christian."

"Ohhh," Mally retorts, wiggling his finger at her. "First-naming me." He studies her though she refuses to give him any more attention, her eyes focused on my ink. "I think you wanna know, CQ. I think you want to know and it kills you that you don't."

I don't say that I think he's right.

"Get over yourself, Boo," she says, waving him off but using the even more personal version of his nickname, Malibu. "Don't you have an eighteen-year-old to go show it to?" She blinks, her thick dark lashes intoxicating. Sasha is gorgeous, and Mally knows it.

"Oh yeah," I add through gritted teeth because holy crap, tattoos are needles going into your skin over and over, and yeah, it *feels* like that. "Aren't you still seeing Donna's grand-daughter?"

He shoots me a death stare but I honestly have no clue as to why because Sasha already knows all this. "What?" I wince, and Paul lifts the gun momentarily while I hiss out a curse word or two.

He pulls at the ends of his hair, turning away from us dramatically because Mally is many things. And drama queen is definitely one of those things.

"Ahhh," he groans out, letting his poor hair go only to turn his hands onto the back of his neck, wringing it. "She's a fuckin' clinger. She won't stop text messaging me, she says she'll show Donna a picture of my dick to prove we're sleeping together if I don't keep seeing her!"

Paul's gun stops. He lifts from his studious crouch. "You let an eighteen-year-old take a picture of your dick?" The gun sounds, and he tips his head forward again. "Duuude."

"Nooo," Mally groans defiantly. "I did not let her take a picture of my dick. She hasn't even seen my dick because we only hung out like, three times."

Sasha snorts. "Hung out. Did you guys eat popcorn and watch all the best after-school cartoons?"

Mally steps toward her, hands still safely on his neck, elbows out. "Jealous?"

She rolls her eyes, but I don't miss the second glance she gives him as he drops his arms and slinks into a free chair in the small room. "But she's got some poor dude's dick on her phone, and how the hell am I supposed to prove to Donna it's not me? Take my dick out in dispatch and have her compare?" He shakes his head. "She's got me by the short hairs."

"Sounds like it," Paul adds as he shades his work. I glance down, seeing it's almost done, and get excited. Yeah, it will be in plastic and vaseline for the wedding, but it's his wedding gift. I had to have it done for today.

"So what, you're going to date her, marry her, have kids

with her all so Donna doesn't think you're the dirty dog.... that you are?" Sasha folds her arms over her chest. "That's disappointing."

Mally opens his mouth to fight back, to banter, anything to not let conversation with Sasha die down but his phone rings. "Van," he says, reading the name on the screen after lifting his ass on one side to retrieve the phone.

He hops up and takes the call in the hall, which gives me time to prod Sasha. "Close your ears, Paul."

He mimes zipping then locking his lips before tossing away an invisible key.

"Weddings are the place where two people come together, you know." I wiggle my eyebrows at her and grin broadly, which earns me the eyeroll of all eyerolls.

"I'm not," she pauses to use dramatic air quotes, "coming together," she rolls her eyes, "with Malibu. Okay?"

I stare at her. Paul works silently. Finally, her gaze flicks back to mine. "Stop, Violet, seriously."

I wrinkle my nose as the gun makes a pass over sensitive, burning flesh again. "Well," I grimace through pain. "Don't close any doors. At least do that for me, as my wedding gift, okay?"

She wags a finger at me. "You're abusing that. You already used the wedding to get breakfast and a pedicure out of me."

I grin as reality rushes in around me. "I'm getting married today."

She does a wiggle-squeal of approval and rubs my shoulder since we can't hug. "I'm so happy." She pauses, watching Paul put his last strokes in. "You at all sad your mom won't be there?"

She knows not to ask about my dad or Rose, especially after Rose's pathetic attempt at closure... or whatever that was. I shake my head, happy to be honest. "No way. I'm the happiest I've ever been, and that's not all Van."

"Just nine inches of it?" Mally asks, sauntering back into the private room with a cheesy grin on his face.

I roll my eyes, but can't help that my cheeks flare with color. "I was saying," I say pointedly, "part of my happiness is the fact that they're *not* in my life anymore."

She nods sagely. "Fuck, yes. I just, I know you kind of feel bad for your mom."

I shake my head. "I used to. But she's choosing her existence, every moment of the day. To be different, you have to *be* different. It's pretty simple."

When I look at Malibu, I find him with a ropy arm draped over his chest, head shaking. "Fuck, that was deep. That hit me. I needed to hear that."

"What did Van say?" Sasha asks while studying her nails, not giving him any attention.

"We need to go grab the tuxes and the dresses from the dry cleaners because the guy just called Van and said they're all pressed." He nods to Sasha. "You wanna drive us, or leave your car for Violet?"

Sasha digs in her purse until she finds her keys, then sets them on my bag. "See you in a little bit?"

I nod and grin, excited that the next time I see her I will be getting in a white dress so I can promise forever to the man who saved my life.

My leg will be sore for a few days, Paul said, but for tonight, I know I'll be okay. I'm running on adrenaline and champagne, and once I see Van, I'll be so high that pain will be impossible.

I have it taped up, but easy to retape so that I can show Van. He got the Violet on his neck—the one inside the eye socket of a skull–touched up this morning. So it would be vibrant for our big day. I didn't tell him that Paul was going to be doing a custom piece on me today.

It's a surprise.

SASHA DRAWS the zipper up and smooths her hands down the back of my dress. Turning to her, I haven't seen a mirror but her face tells me what I need to know. Not that I look beautiful or how perfect my hair is, but... I'm making the right choice. Because her eyes are full of tears of happiness, her smile is wide with peace, and her arms that wrap around me give me comfort.

"I'm so happy for you," she whispers as she smooths her hand down the back of my head tenderly, the way a mother would do.

"Thank you," I squeak, not wanting to cry and smear my makeup this soon.

"I want to tell you a lot of things, Sash, because I love you and owe you so much. But I don't want to cry yet. So can we have champagne and ugly cry together later?" I hold her hands tightly, and she giggles, only one tear slipping free.

"That sounds good. I don't want to ugly cry either."

The music starts.

A white sheet pinned to two trees for my makeshift dressing space, Sasha peers around it. "Ready?"

I don't have a traditional aisle. We don't have a pastor or preacher. We're out in a grassy valley at the base of the hill where Van proposed. Sasha is here wearing a scarlet-colored slip dress. Her locks are up, tied into an easy ponytail with a black satin ribbon. Batman is our ordained minister, though because it is my freaking wedding day, I'm calling him Henry Burke, his actual name.

Mally and Bran are here, and Cadence, too. Batman's wife and Bran's new girlfriend are here, too, and I can't wait to get close to them.

Even though it's just eight of us here in the weeds next to a mountain, it's perfect.

My dress isn't technically even a wedding dress. It's just a formal dress that happens to be some shade of white. Pearl is what I think the saleslady called it. With a high neck and a low back, and a slit to the high heavens, it's much sexier than anything I would have ever imagined for myself.

But when I saw it, it felt like me. The me that doesn't do what she should, the me that does whatever the hell she wants.

So I wore the dress and nearly burned alive from feeling Van's rough hands against my skin all night as we danced. We didn't even hire a DJ. We just made a playlist on Spotify and connected it to a bluetooth speaker. We passed around bottles of champagne and danced, danced, and danced.

Henry and Robin–because for the life of me I will not call them Batman and Robin–went and got taco truck for everyone once the champagne was really setting in. After spreading a quilt out, we all kicked off our shoes and lazily ate tacos under the setting sun.

The perfect wedding.

The best part of the evening was showing him the tattoo. After our first dance–a slow one–fast music came on. House music. Van instructed me to hoist my thigh to his hip to bring our pelvises closer together.

It seemed like the perfect time to swivel the slit in my dress to the opposite leg and show him my calf.

"I want to give you your gift before we really start dancing, okay?" I asked, stepping back from him. His dark eyes went confused behind his dark frames, but he nodded his agreement.

"Hold my foot?" I asked, and he grinned, realizing part of his gift would include touching me.

"Please." His smile was dark and naughty, and then I swung my foot into his hand, and hiked up the thin dress, exposing my leg.

His eyes went to the plastic covering the ink, then up to me, wide. "What is this?" he asked, voice dropped to a private tone. His thumb smoothed over the bottom piece of tape holding the plastic to my skin.

"Peel it back and find out."

He swallowed hard and my heart thumped. Slowly and carefully, he untaped the plastic barrier and peeled it back. I watched his dark eyes study the art on my skin. His chest lifted and lowered heavily as he studied me.

"Oh my god, you don't like it," I said finally after what felt like way too much silence. "Oh my god, I should not have–"

When he looked up, his expression shut me up. His eyes were full of warmth and tears. One slipped down his cheek, getting lost in his beard. "I can't believe you did this."

My eyes magnetized to the art on my leg.

In an oval, traditional vignette style, is a picture from my mind that Paul had brought to life. Over-saturated shades of green composed a grove of trees with one particular tree in focus on the forefront. On the trunk, chiseled into the bark, is a heart with the initials DD + VC inside. Littering the ground around the grove are a field of wild violets. The backdrop is a melting sun.

I guess it means us, together forever, with our journey at

our feet, the best ahead. I mean, that's what it means to me. It's definitely special. But seeing Van's reaction to it made me realize it is so much more. I stepped toward him, letting my leg fall down. Moving my thumb over the violet inked on his throat, I kissed my husband.

"I love you."

I wiped his tears.

"I love you, too," he responded tenderly.

We partied, then we went home, and we made love like the world was ending.

The truth was, our world was just beginning.

Epilogue

DONOVAN

One fist full of sweaty little bike shorts, the other full of my aching dick, and yep, I'm all set.

"Is this the first one you're missing?" Mally asks, shifting the cruiser into drive. We drift from the curb, blending into traffic. I roll my window down for fresh air. For a breath.

"Yes," I grit, barely opening my jaw.

"Sorry, man," he shakes his head, knowing how much I hate missing the school board meetings.

Ever since Violet has been on the school board, I've gone to every single meeting. I went at times where it was probably a bit strange that I went—seeing as some of the actual board members didn't even show up. But they'd gotten to know me. Officer Drake, the school teacher's devout husband, keeping his finger on the pulse of the schools.

The truth?

I was more fucking obsessed with Violet than ever before.

And it got me rock-hard listening to her plans. Hearing her recite tons of ideas, with more up her sleeve. Seeing her eyes light up excitedly as she spoke. God, her *spirit* fucking made me hard.

Tonight, a call ran long, and I had to text my wife and tell her that I couldn't be there for her meeting. She sent a text back assuring me that it was okay, but still, I was pouting. Full on.

I know part of the thrill is listening to the keeper of the minutes call out, "*Violet Drake.*" A year later and hearing her bear my name still did shit to me. Shit that men don't talk about out loud.

"There will be a shitload more though, man," Mally offers as he drives us toward the station.

"I don't like missing them," I repeat, still not done sulking.

He reaches over and pinches my shoulder. "I know, buddy, I know."

I yank my shoulder back. "I'm not four, Mally."

And yet, when the cruiser pulls up in front of our favorite ice creamery, my pulse picks up like I'm four. "I know you're not four, but if this would help your shitty mood, I'd pay."

I pop the door open, "I'm getting toppings."

He rolls his eyes. "I assumed you would."

It doesn't cure my mood, but I definitely feel at least $7.43 worth of ice cream and toppings-worth better than before.

Violet texts me as I'm closing the garage door on my SUV, freshly showered from the station and wearing joggers and a t-shirt–her favorite thing on me she says.

Violet: *Freaking A. Mr. Mathews just ran in here with a last minute pitch. Won't be home til after 9. Love you.*

I text her back, hiding my disappointment.

Van: *taking Mathews off Christmas card list* *Hang in there, baby. I love you. See you soonish.*

It's already eight, so I can handle one more hour. Taking lasagna that we'd made together last week out of the freezer, I preheat the oven, and wander the house. Guess I could start some laundry.

Violet and I aren't the kind of couple who asks the other person to do something. We just take care of shit, both of us. No bickering necessary. I toss in the load sitting in a basket labeled dirty, a few loose items missing the machine.

Scooping the items from the floor, I realize it's a pair of Violet's bike shorts and a sports bra. Probably from her run this morning.

I toss the bra in the washer, hesitating with the shorts in my grip. My jaw burns and spit floods my mouth. My cock pulses and my heart rate zips. This is how I felt when I saw her in the park two years ago.

Like I'd fucking die without more of her.

And now that I have her, I'm so fucking hopelessly addicted that I can't even handle her coming home late from work one night.

I lick my lips, debating whether or not I should actually do what I *want* to do.

I shouldn't.

But when has that ever stopped me?

"Fuck it," I growl, opening my belt with an eager clank. The tie on my joggers gives way easily, then I shove them down. Clothes don't stand a chance when my palm is greedy and my urges are unstoppable.

One fist full of sweaty little bike shorts, the other full of my aching dick, and yep, I'm all set.

The fabric is salty and tangy, the way she tastes when I

eat her out after we leave Paradise. I suck the fabric deeper onto my tongue and swallow the dampness. My dick leaks in my palm, so I stroke it harder. Fuck she tastes so good, even sweaty. My eyes fall shut as I imagine making deep, slow strides into her, filling her with cock and flooding her with praise.

"Good girl," I murmur to myself at the fantasy, pumping myself quicker now.

I could just see her peeling these fucking tiny shorts down those silky, sexy legs. Her cunt puckered from the exercise, back glistening with sweat. Fuck, I'm sweating now, my hairline dripping. The heat in my palm pulses and I jerk myself faster, a slave to my release.

I shove her sweaty shorts in my mouth as I shoot hard, hot come dribbling over my knuckles, dripping down my forearm. Fuck. Just tasting her and thinking about her and I blew in a matter of a minute. Glad I got that out of my system.

"What's in your mouth, Van?" Her sultry voice sends a shock up my spine, and I straighten. Come drips onto the tiled floor below, off my hand. Removing her shorts from my mouth, I turn around, completely controlled. She fucking knows I'm crazy for her; why hide it?

Her emerald eyes turn dark as she takes in the sticky scene. She swallows, and I can't wait to dip my fingers through her hair and shove my dick between those perky little lips. *Goddamn.* "I missed you," I rasp, not embarrassed, just honest.

"I can see that," she says, her foreboding gaze taking its time ascending my body. "Are those panties?"

"Your workout shorts."

Her lids droop and her tongue darts across her lip.

Nipples scrape silk as she steps towards me, tossing her hair behind her shoulder. "Those are *dirty.*"

I kiss her, and she licks her flavor from my lips. "I like my wife's pussy, dirty or clean."

She lets out a soft sigh. "I missed you today, too."

She reaches out and strokes me, getting sticky remainders on her hand. "Make me come so we can go take a shower and then eat lasagna in bed."

Fuck, see that? She gets me. My wife is my other half.

My Violet with the emerald eyes.

THE END.

Acknowledgments

To my core readers—thank you for taking the journey to a slightly darker side with me on this book. I know this is a small step outside my norm, so thank you for following me and giving me your time by reading— I want you to know how much I appreciate it.

To my husband who supports my early mornings, my late nights, my thousand-yard stares as I plot in my head—you put up with it all while endless support. Enjoy your Easter eggs. 143.

Thank you to everyone who reads. You're making my dreams come true.

XO Daisy

If You Liked This Story...

Leave your review on Amazon! I'd love to hear your feedback.

Thoughtful, comprehensive reviews are the best way to help Indie authors grow, both their skill and their business. Next to reading our books, reviews are the next best gift!

If you have time, I'd love to hear your opinion.

And thank you again for reading!

Sign up for my newsletter to keep up-to-date with my projects, deals on books, sneak peaks, and much more.

About the Author

Daisy Jane is an Indie author of forbidden love and taboo romance. This is Daisy's fifteenth full-length forbidden novel.

When not writing romance, Daisy enjoys reading, finding new ways to eat peanut butter, black coffee, funk music and cool cover bands, Yosemite, browsing Reddit, true crime, trying to keep up with BookTok, and so much more.

She lives in California with her husband of fourteen years, their two daughters and three cats.

She is always looking for new friends and readers!

facebook.com/DaisyJaneAuthor
twitter.com/authordaisyjane
instagram.com/authordaisyjane

Patreon

I write erotic novellas over on my Patreon. So if you like my writing style but want something shorter in length, I release a chapter every week.

Also, you'll get access to commissioned NSFW art featuring your favorite heroes and heroines from my books, Men of Paradise and Wrench Kings included!

You'll get access to everything in my one and only tier. Quarterly merch coming soon!

Come on, hold my hand.

Patreon.com/DaisyJane

(Content ages 18+)

Also by Daisy Jane

Series:

Wrench Kings (3 Books)

The Wild One / a reverse age gap romance / MF / Book 1

The Brazen One / a grumpy/sunshine romance / MF / Book 2

The Only One / a femdom romance / MF / Book 3

Men of Paradise (3 Books)

Where Violets Bloom / a stalker romance / MF / Book 1

Stray / a femdom romance / MF / Book 2

With Force / a CNC romance / MF / Book 3

Oakcreek (2 Books So Far)

I'll Do Anything / a bully femdom romance / MF / Book1

After the Storm / an alpha MM romance / MM / Book 2

The Millionaire and His Maid (3 Books)

His Young Maid / an age gap boss/employee romance / MF / Book 1

Maid for Marriage / an age gap romance / MF / Book 2

Maid a Mama / a surprise pregnancy romance / MF / Book 3

The Taboo Duet

Unexpected/ an age gap Daddy figure romance / Book 1

Consumed / a Daddy kink romance / Book 2

Standalones:

The Other Brother / dual POV / MF

The Corner House / single POV / MFMM, MFM, MFM with an HEA

My Best Friend's Dad / age gap instalove novel / MF

Waiting for Coach / age gap novel /student teacher / MF

Hot Girl Summer / a taboo step sibling romance / MF

Pleasing the Pastor / an age gap virgin romance / MF

Release / a taboo MMF, MM, MF romance

Raleigh Two / a taboo MFM romance / MFM

The Man I Know / a married couple romance / MF

Novellas:

Cherry Pie / very taboo why choose / MFMM

Made in the USA
Las Vegas, NV
24 November 2024

12581979R00249